A Touch of Confidence
By Jess Dee

He kissed the girl and he liked it. Now to convince her it could be love...

When a coveted retail space opens up in Rose Bay, Claire Jones and her sisters waste no time grabbing the perfect spot to relocate their expanding children's bookshop. But when Claire arrives to sign on the dotted line, she discovers someone else got there first.

Worse, the new tenant is shaking hands with a man who is definitely *not* the elderly Jack Wilson with whom she made a verbal agreement three days ago. This Jack Wilson is a tall, hunky giant—and no amount of righteous indignation can mask her body's bone-deep sexual response.

Jack never planned to take over the family company; he's a teacher, not a businessman. But with his grandfather in the hospital, he's taken up the reins—and steered straight into trouble. Now he's faced with a serious mistake, and a beautiful, Amazon warrior of a woman who's demanding satisfaction.

He'd love to give it to her, but his idea of *satisfaction* has nothing to do with business, and everything to do with getting the curvy goddess naked. The sooner the better...

Warning: If you've never made love to a man who quotes Shakespeare during sex...be warned. You're gonna want to after reading this book.

Ballroom Blitz
By Lorelei James

She's got the rhythm, but he's got all the right moves.

After years on the road, rock drummer Jon White Feather is home from tour to reassess his music career. When his shy niece begs him to take a ballroom dancing class, Jon agrees, aware he's not Fred Astaire material. Still, it stings when his sexy-hot instructor—who makes his heart do the cha-cha—deals his ego a low blow: he has no rhythm.

Maggie Buchanan is doing everything to make ends meet since her IT career fizzled, including teaching couples dancing at the community center. She's prepared for anything—except her immediate attraction to the bad boy rocker who doesn't know his right foot from his left.

As Jon sets out to prove he can rock his body—and hers—their sexual chemistry burns a path across the dance floor, straight to the bedroom. And Maggie wasn't expecting a man with limited dance skills would know exactly how to sweep her off her feet.

Warning: Sweet and hot...this couple knows how to bump and grind.

Where There's Smoke
By Jayne Rylon

When old flames unite, the heat is on!

Kyana Brady never intended to return to small-town life in upstate New York, but reality doesn't give a damn about plans. She dropped everything to care for her dying aunt. Now that Rose is gone, Kyana realizes something else has changed—her priorities. Her high-paid, higher-stress law career no longer holds any appeal.

While debating her future, an insomnia-driven stroll turns into a desperate dash to save Rose's elderly friend, Benjamin, from his burning house. And he's always believed one good turn deserves another. So the old man rewards Kyana's bravery with a little meddling in her love life.

After Ben's great-nephew Logan witnesses his childhood friend's bravery on the news, he rushes home to help his uncle rebuild. But before his hammer hits the first nail, sparks are flying. The heat between him and Kyana melts old affection into a completely new—and combustible—relationship.

Before they have a chance to discover how hot their love will burn, another disaster threatens to separate them forever. After all, they say bad luck comes in threes...

Warning: A love affair that's been ten years in the making is sure to be hot enough to scorch. And everyone knows, where there's smoke there's fire.

Two to Tango

SAMHAIN
PUBLISHING

Samhain Publishing, Ltd.
11821 Mason Montgomery Road, 4B
Cincinnati, OH 45249
www.samhainpublishing.com

Two to Tango
Print ISBN: 978-1-61921-421-7
A Touch of Confidence Copyright © 2013 by Jess Dee
Ballroom Blitz Copyright © 2013 by Lorelei James
Where There's Smoke Copyright © 2013 by Jayne Rylon

Editing by Lindsey Faber
Cover by Kanaxa

A Touch of Confidence, ISBN 978-1-61921-148-3
First Samhain Publishing, Ltd. electronic publication: October 2012
Ballroom Blitz, ISBN 978-1-61921-149-0
First Samhain Publishing, Ltd. electronic publication: October 2012
Where There's Smoke ISBN 978-1-61921-150-6
First Samhain Publishing, Ltd. electronic publication: October 2012
First Samhain Publishing, Ltd. print publication: September 2013

Contents

A Touch of Confidence

Jess Dee

Dedication

Jayne and Lorelei...anytime you wanna try another number, call me.

With special thanks to Dawn, Fedora and Kelly (yes, again).

Chapter One

Claire Jones pressed her face close to the shop window and peered inside. Someone had washed the glass, and with the Sydney sunshine streaming in behind her she could easily make out the large, empty expanse.

Perfect.

Location, size, shape... Everything they needed.

This place suited her and her two sisters to a T. *Li'L Books and Bits* would do brilliantly here. With a children's shoe store next door, an art and craft shop down the road and a baby store around the corner, a specialist shop selling children's clothes, books and toys was just what the neighborhood needed.

Claire flexed her fingers, stretching them to make sure they were in adequate working order to sign the lease. If her watch was right, Jack Wilson—the property manager—was due here in the next two minutes. Three days ago, they'd agreed to meet at the store to fill in the papers.

Soon the shop would belong to them. Well, for the next three years anyway. They could move in and start fixing the place up, add the necessary shelving and clothes racks, put in wooden floors, paint murals on the walls and get the place to look like a child's—and mother's—paradise.

Movement inside the shop startled her. Someone was there. A man. Although "man" would be an understatement. Giant was more like it.

He must surely tower above Claire, which at her five foot nine was no mean feat. His shoulders were massive, almost hiding the door from which he'd just stepped through, the one leading to the back rooms of the store.

What on earth was he doing there?

Just when Claire thought she couldn't be more surprised, a second man followed him out. The giant turned to face him, the two men shook hands, and the smaller one took his leave, opening the front door and walking through it.

"Nice doing business with you, Jack," he said. "Wilson Property Management has impressed me once again."

The giant saluted, touching his finger to his forehead, and the smaller man walked away.

Claire's heart lurched. Jack? Wilson Property Management? What on earth was going on?

She glanced around, looking up and down the road behind her, but there was no sign of Jack Wilson. The only Jack anywhere in sight was the man who stood inside the shop, slipping a file into his briefcase.

Claire took a deep breath and knocked on the door.

He looked up. "Can I help you?"

"Yes. I'm looking for Jack Wilson. I have an appointment with him."

"I'm Jack." He stepped closer, a question in his eyes.

Claire had to blink, startled by the stunning green shade of those eyes. This man might have the same name, but he was not the Jack Wilson she'd expected.

Her Mr. Wilson was not a day under eighty, had a stern but likeable way about him and a savvy business sense that made Claire trust him instinctively.

This Mr. Wilson could not be a day over thirty-five. His long, muscular legs seemed to go on forever, and his face... *Mm, mm, mm.* What a face. Chiseled chin, high cheek bones, a strong nose and those striking green eyes were all framed by thick and wavy light brown hair.

If she'd been forced to describe him, she'd have to invent a hot Avenger concoction. Like a mixture of Captain America, Thor, Bruce Banner and Tony Stark all rolled into one heart-stopping, sexy guy.

He was gorgeous. A giant who looked like he'd be more comfortable on an Aussie Rules football field, tossing a footy to other giants, than managing various property rentals.

She shook her head. "I'm looking for an older man." Much older, much less potent. The eighty-year-old had never made Claire's heart skip a beat, or made her think of long, hot nights and tangled sheets. "Grey hair, neat beard and moustache, glasses."

"Right, yeah. That would be my grandfather. I'm sorry. He's not here."

Okay. That explained the names and the age difference. "I had a meeting with him scheduled for now."

"Look, I'm sorry, Miss...?"

Much as she wanted to look into his exquisite eyes, her gaze seemed pinned to his mouth. To a pair of delicious-looking lips that just begged to be kissed. By her. "Jones. Claire Jones." She stuck out her hand.

He shook it.

"I'm sorry, Miss Jones. My grandfather couldn't make his appointments today. I'm taking his place. But..." He shrugged apologetically. "I have no record of any meeting with you."

It took a good few seconds for Claire's brain to process his words. It had kind of gotten stuck on his hand shake. On his warm skin that seemed to burn straight through hers.

"We made the appointment a few days ago," she supplied. "Agreed to meet here at eleven. I guess if he can't make it, I should be speaking to you?"

The G.G.—gorgeous giant—nodded with a smile. A very nice smile at that, sexy, with a dimple creasing his right cheek. The kind of dimple she'd like to spend time exploring...with her tongue. "I guess so. How can I help you?"

"I've come to sign the lease for the shop." She gestured at the room around them. Her palm tingled now that he'd released it, and she feared she might be tempted to grab his hand again. "Your grandfather said he'd have the papers all ready to—" She broke off mid-sentence. "Uh, are you okay?"

He stared at her, slack jawed, not looking so okay.

Maybe he'd need mouth-to-mouth resuscitation?

"You've come to sign the lease for the shop?" He pointed to the floor. "*This* shop?"

She nodded, distracted by the idea of mouth-to-mouth with Jack Wilson Jr.

"And you set up the appointment when?"

"Three days ago. My sister and I viewed it last week, made an offer, and your grandfather accepted. Signing is the last step in the process, and the shop is ours for the next three years." She grinned, getting excited and nervous all over again. Expanding their business was a big step. An expensive step, but a necessary one, if they hoped to make money from *Li'l Books and Bits.*

"Oh, um..." The G.G.'s face paled just a bit. "You've discussed the contract with my grandfather?"

"In depth. A three-year agreement, paying eight fifty a week for the first year, with an annual increase of ten percent thereafter."

Jack Wilson squeezed the bridge of his nose between his thumb and forefinger, placed his briefcase on the floor and grimaced. "Perhaps you'd better come inside," he invited. "We need to talk."

Claire's stomach twisted as he stepped aside to let her in. His discomfort gave her a bad feeling.

"There seems to have been a misunderstanding, Miss Jones. I had no idea you'd made an appointment with my grandfather, no idea you'd agreed to take the shop." He crossed the floor to stand before her. "I've just rented it out. The lease was signed not five minutes ago."

"Pardon me?" She did not just hear what she thought she heard.

"I've just leased the shop. The new tenant walked out of here a moment before you knocked."

It was her turn to blanch. The blood drained from her cheeks. "Wait a minute. He signed the lease? You have his signature on the papers?"

Mr. Wilson Jr. leaned down and removed a file from his briefcase. He held it up. "Signed and sealed, I'm afraid." His expression was troubled, as though he regretted causing her pain. But he didn't offer to run after the other man and break the contract.

"That's nice." She pasted a saccharine-sweet smile on her face, trying to contain her emotions. Just beneath the surface, anger and disappointment boiled in equal measure. She, Maddie and Julia had searched for months before they'd found this shop. They'd researched their client database, carried out extensive market research and quite conclusively found that Rose Bay would be one of the best areas to open their new store. Finding an unoccupied shop in this market had proven almost impossible, until Maddie had stumbled across Wilson's advert.

They'd offered to rent the property the same day.

Claire had no idea what she'd do if they lost it now. Cry? Rant and rave? Hit someone? Or give up on their dream of expansion because the idea of finding another shop was too overwhelming and too time consuming to contemplate?

Uh-uh. No way. She wasn't going to lose this store. Not when the Jones sisters' plans were nearing fruition. Didn't matter how gorgeous this giant may be, how damn sexy and distracting—or how regretful he looked, he wasn't going to rob her of the property. "Nice for *him*, I mean." She pursed her lips. "Unfortunately for you, it means Wilson Property is in breach of contract."

He froze, with the folder held in mid-air. "Breach of contract?"

"Your grandfather and I had an oral agreement. We settled on the terms and he promised the shop to me. That's a legally binding contract. The question now is, how should we proceed?"

He didn't answer, just looked from her to the contract and back again.

"You have to understand, Mr. Wilson, I'm not willing to give up on this shop. It took us too long to find, and we have neither the time nor the resources to find something else. This property was a done deal for us."

"I understand that. Unfortunately, my hands are tied. I had no idea my grandfather had promised you the property. I proceeded as I saw fit, renting the shop to a different tenant. I'm sorry to disappoint you. Truly, I am, but there's nothing I can do to change it at this point."

"Nothing you can do?" Oh, no. She wasn't giving up. Claire was too stubborn for that—too stubborn for her own good, as her sisters pointed out all too often. But damned if she wasn't going to dig her heels in right now.

"Nothing. I'm sorry."

She shook her head. "I see the matter differently. I'm thinking this can go one of two alternative ways."

Interest flared in his eyes. "And those two ways are?"

"You could let the new tenant know what's happened and convince him to break the lease."

He frowned. "Or?"

She hesitated with the second option. If she brought up this alternative, things could turn sour fast. Much as she wanted the property, she didn't believe he'd rented it out to someone else with malicious intent. He simply hadn't known about her and her sisters. Still, the shop was now in someone else's hands, which left the Jones women nowhere. "Or we could let our lawyers handle it from here."

Jack stared at the Amazonian warrior standing before him. With her hazel eyes flashing, her mouth set in a serious expression and her honey-blond hair tumbling over her shoulders, he thought he'd never seen a more fascinating woman.

Not an appropriate factor to fixate on while she threatened legal action, but there you had it.

She was...enchanting, with a voluptuousness Mother Earth herself would envy. Her tall frame lent her the height that put her closer to eye level with him than he was used to with women.

"You don't have anything to say in response?" she prompted.

Her voice hummed through his stomach. Low and a little raspy, it made her sound like she'd just woken up. Or just had great sex. It rumbled through his stomach and tugged on his balls, sending a jolt of awareness racing through his blood.

Concentrate.

He shook his head, clearing it of the sexual fog that threatened to swamp him. Wilson Property Management was apparently in breach of contract, and Miss Jones had just mentioned taking legal action.

Shit. Three hours on the job, and already he'd made a monumental fuck up. His background had not prepared him for running this business, but he'd refused to let his pop down. Especially after last night. His grandfather, Big Jack, simply hadn't needed any extra stress.

Still, he'd never met the woman, and he couldn't be sure she had in fact been in contact with Big Jack. He'd found no evidence of it anywhere in his pop's office—and Jack had searched the office.

"Look, before I respond, I'm going to need to verify the validity of your contract."

Her jaw dropped. "Pardon me?"

"I'd like you to see this from my perspective. I don't know you, and I have no record of any of your dealings with my grandfather. It would be foolish to chase after a client with a signed lease and demand he break it based on your say-so. I need proof before I can proceed with this."

"I'm standing here, ready to sign the lease. What more proof do you need?"

"Evidence of the contract perhaps?"

She glared at him as if he were mad. "It was an oral contract. There is no 'evidence'."

"Then there is very little reason for me chase up the current tenant."

"There is every reason." Her cheeks turned scarlet. "Our agreement included the three elements that make a contract legally binding." She stepped forward and pointed a finger at his chest. "One, our contract included an offer. I offered to pay to rent this property."

He took an instinctive step backwards. Not because he found her threatening. On the contrary, when she stood this close, her scent wafted around his nose, tantalizing him with its alluring fragrance. She smelled like...a spring breeze, fresh and perfumed with a hint of flowers. Roses maybe?

No, the reason he stepped back was that her nail was long, and if she prodded his chest, it would dig into his skin.

Now if she dug her nails into his back as she clutched him while he drove into her naked, alluring body, he'd have no problem with the scratches she'd leave behind. Truth be told, he'd relish them, drive into her a little harder, a little faster, encouraging her to scratch deeper. A little pain always made pleasure that much better. But fully clothed like this, he doubted he'd appreciate the sting without the complementary pleasure.

She took another step forward and whipped out a second finger.

"Two, your grandfather accepted my offer. We shook hands on it, as a witness—my sister—can attest to. And three..." A third finger appeared, this one grazing his chest as she moved her hand.

Lust exploded behind his ribs, a sudden, unexpected desire to haul the woman closer and kiss the living shit out of her.

"...The consideration. Your grandfather told me a figure, eight hundred and fifty dollars, and I agreed to the value he'd put on the property." She waved all three fingers at him. "And that, Mr. Wilson, is your proof. That is what makes the contract binding. In the eyes of the law, it is a legal agreement, one that cannot be broken."

Her voice was stern, her shoulders stiff and her eyes so focused on his he couldn't look away. The only thing out of whack with the professional yet irate picture she painted was her uneven breath. She inhaled as though she couldn't fill her lungs. Quick, shallow pants that ensured every time she exhaled, her breath puffed over his neck in short, warm bursts.

And damned if it didn't make him crazy. His body, already alerted to her magnetism, tightened with a base physical attraction. What was it about the woman that inspired this reaction in him?

Damn it, desire had no place here. He needed to use his head and sort out the problem he'd inadvertently caused. Jack had no doubt that Miss Jones told the truth, that he owed her an apology and that he needed to fix up his mess. He did not need to imagine stripping her naked and exposing her voluptuous breasts to his hungry gaze or mouth.

Think, Jack.

What would Big Jack do? How would he sort everything out, leaving Miss Jones satisfied?

Offer her another property, of course. A better one, but at a discounted price. That would neutralize her anger, give the Jones sisters another option and provide a solution to all of their problems.

The question was: Did his pop have another property on his books?

Christ, he hated not having the foggiest idea how he was supposed to run this business. But he'd received an urgent phone call last night, and he could hardly refuse to help Big Jack out in a crisis.

Not for the first time, he wondered if he'd made the wrong decision all those years ago. If he'd studied something other than teaching—a business degree maybe, or economics—he'd have no problem now looking after Wilson Property Management for a few days. He'd also have no problem fulfilling a dream he'd had for a few years now—buying a property for himself. A house he could live in comfortably.

On his current salary, that was a dream he could never hope to realize.

"Look, Miss Jones, I apologize. I had no idea about the oral contract between you and my grandfather. He said nothing about it and left no notes about your meeting. The fact remains that this shop is now leased, the contract signed and I doubt I can break it."

Her face darkened with ire.

"But I would be more than happy to check the files back at the office and see what else we have available." More than happy—so long as he worked out how to use the damn software. "I'm sure if we take a minute to calm down and look at our options, we'll find something that would suit your needs just as well, if not better, than this shop."

She shook her head with a disbelieving smile. "Do you think it's that simple? You'll check your books, come up with something else, and we'll all be happy?"

"I don't see why it can't be."

"Because there aren't a whole lot of properties in this area." The smile vanished. "When one becomes available, it's snapped up like that." She clicked her fingers. "I would expect you to know this."

He should know it. But other than being all too aware of the rising price of residential housing in Sydney, Jack knew nothing about the property market—especially not the commercial market. He wasn't a property manager. While he knew the ins and outs of the high school English and History syllabi, shop rentals remained a mystery to him. The only reason he had time now to help Big Jack was because school was closed for the spring holiday.

Maybe, just maybe, it was time to leave teaching. Time to get into a profession that would at least allow him to earn enough to buy his own home. A home he could raise a family in if he ever settled down. He could join his pop at Wilson Property Management and slowly learn the business until he was confident enough to take over the reins when Big Jack retired.

It was an idea he hated all the way through to his bones. The thought of leaving teaching, leaving his students, made his stomach twist.

"I can't pretend to remember every property on our books, Miss Jones. There are just too many of them. As I said, I would be more than happy to check our files—"

"Don't patronize me. I don't want another property. I want this lease signed so I can open my new store, right here."

"I'm trying to find a way to get you a new store."

"By urging me to take another shop? I don't think so. Why not start by getting your grandfather on the phone and sorting out this mess with him? Perhaps your other tenant would be happy to settle on another property. This one is already spoken for."

Jack shook his head. "Much as I'd like to get my grandfather involved in this, I cannot contact him now."

She arched a brow. "Oh? And why is that?" She gave him a scathing look.

"Because my grandfather had a heart attack yesterday. No matter how pressing your need to rent the shop may be, I assume you'll allow him the time to recover before dropping this bomb on him?"

Chapter Two

Claire stepped back with a gasp. "Oh, my God." Her shoulders drooped and her hand covered her mouth. "Is he okay?"

"No, Miss Jones." For some reason, Jack couldn't contain his sarcasm. "He had a heart attack. Of course he's not okay."

"I-I'm so sorry. I had no idea." The look in her eyes changed from furious to distressed, and it was that distress that ripped through Jack.

He'd been running on autopilot since his father had phoned him yesterday.

Big Jack had suffered chest pain and gone to the hospital—on his father's insistence. The old man had tried to argue that a little chest pain wasn't going to kill him, but his father had refused to listen. Thank God, because the tightness in his chest had in fact been a full-on myocardial infarction, and had his pop not been seen in emergency, it might have killed him.

As it was, his grandfather had been scheduled for a triple bypass in eight weeks' time.

Jack's own heart stuttered then. He hadn't reacted last night. Hadn't had the time. He'd been too busy sorting through folders and files at the office, trying to work out what the hell needed to be done.

If he'd had the choice, he'd have spent the night at his pop's bedside. But Big Jack's distress doubled when he thought about his business. So out of fear that the man might suffer another heart attack, Jack soothed him in the best possible way. He'd taken the reins and hadn't had a minute to think since.

But now he did. Suddenly he couldn't not think about what had happened to Big Jack. Couldn't think about anything else.

Christ. He'd nearly lost his pop.

Nearly lost the man he'd looked up to his whole life. The same man who'd taught him to play rugby when his father had been too busy. The man who'd encouraged him to follow his heart and become a teacher when his parents had urged him to study law or accounting or business management.

His grandfather. The man he'd spent weekends with when he was young, fishing and hiking. Learning a respect for the great outdoors his parents would never have instilled in him. A man he loved more than he did his own parents, a man who'd been more nurturing to him and his brother, Anthony, than their parents ever had.

Shit. Pop had almost died.

Someone called his name. He heard it, but his mind was focused totally and utterly on his grandfather, who'd lain in that massive hospital bed, his usually ruddy cheeks and sharp eyes pale and dull against the stark white sheets.

His stomach lurched. His grandfather wasn't just sick. He was critically ill. If he didn't have the bypass surgery, his heart could give in at any time, could surrender permanently to a blocked artery.

Hands touched his arm, shook his shoulder, but still he didn't respond. Couldn't.

A scene played in his head like a movie. He and his pop on his grandfather's fishing boat, rods in hand and something mighty tugging at the end of his line. Big Jack had helped him reel in the massive snapper. Far too big for a nine-year-old to conquer alone, Pop had aided him every step of the way without ever taking away his glory. And when the fish had been snared and the boat returned to the dock, Big Jack had shown him how to gut it, and together they'd barbequed the massive fish for the whole family.

Jack's gut clenched. Would he and his pop have another chance to fish? Would they go out on his boat again? Lately Jack had been the one helping Pop reel in the fish, but neither of them had complained. It wasn't about the fishing. It was about spending time together. It always had been.

"Mr. Wilson?" The hand was on his arm again. A sturdy touch. Gentle but firm. "Jack?"

He blinked and found himself face to face with Claire Jones. Her hazel eyes were filled with concern, her gaze searching his.

"Are you okay?"

He didn't answer, just stared into her beautiful eyes and wondered what he'd do if he lost his grandfather.

"I think you're in shock." Her hand slid over his face, soft, warm and comforting. "You're cold as ice."

He almost laughed at her. Puh-lease. Grown men didn't go into shock. They took life's little blows with straight shoulders and a proud stance.

But then losing his grandfather wouldn't just be a little blow.

"You need to warm up somehow." Her hand disappeared, leaving Jack oddly bereft by its absence. Then his shoulders were cloaked with a light weight and her exquisite fragrance surrounded him, intoxicating him.

He stared at her, noticed her bare neck for the first time, and wondered how she'd respond if he pressed the smallest of kisses to the exposed flesh.

Then he wondered how he could think about kissing her at a time like this.

He blinked. Minutes ago she'd worn a scarf. A long one that she'd wrapped around that neck and let the ends hang down over her breasts. Now it was gone. Which explained the feather-light wrap on his shoulders.

"It's not helping." She sounded worried. "Stay here. I'll be right back."

And then the statuesque Miss Jones was gone, leaving Jack alone with his thoughts and his fears.

He lowered himself to the floor and scrubbed an exhausted hand over his face.

Damn it. He didn't want to be alone. Didn't want to face what he'd so stoically avoided since his phone had rung. It would be so much easier to forget real life. To deny his grandfather had a problem. Perhaps if he lost himself to the subtle scent of roses and the not-so-subtle rise of full breasts and creamy white skin, he could forget the trauma of the night before.

Long moments passed and there was Claire again, crouching in front of him, pressing a paper cup into his hand. He took it, and almost smiled at her attempts to look after him when she held her hand around the cup too, looping her fingers over his, making sure he didn't drop it. Then she guided their hands towards his mouth, as if he were incapable.

"Drink," she insisted. "It's tea, with lots of sugar. It'll get you warm and help with the shock."

He frowned in disdain. "I'm not in shock. Men don't go into shock."

Her replying nod showed exactly how much she believed him. "Yeah, okay. Drink the tea anyway." She tilted her hand.

Hot, milky liquid spilled into his mouth. Hot and very sweet. For someone who took his drinks without sugar, the taste almost made him retch. But to give the woman credit, the tea slid down his throat and landed in a warm puddle in his belly, and when Claire tilted the cup for a second time, he took another sip, and then a third without arguing.

Three swallows were as much as he could handle. The next time she attempted to feed him, he shook his head and lowered both the cup and her hand. "Thank you. That's enough."

She looked at him in disbelief.

"Honestly, I don't need more. I'm fine." Again he became aware of the scarf around his shoulders filling his head with her beguiling scent.

He set the cup on the floor, removing her fingers from it so it could balance.

Claire shook her head. "You're white as a sheet and icy cold. You did not respond once when I called your name and barely even noticed when I shook you."

"Delayed reaction is all," he assured. "I'm fine." And he felt it. Felt...calm again. Maybe the tea had helped. Although he suspected it was Miss Jones who had soothed his worries, not the hot drink.

"You, my friend, are not fine. You're in shock." She shot him a look that dared him to disagree, and the patience and kindness in her eyes took his breath.

He had a sudden, desperate urge to kiss her.

He almost snorted aloud. Yeah, right. This was no time for a kiss. His grandfather was in hospital, he'd just fucked up a lease agreement, and she was madder than hell and threatening legal action.

His thoughts sobered him. Maybe the woman was right. Maybe he had just experienced a delayed shock reaction.

"Would you like to talk about it?" Her voice was gentle, nothing like the irate firecracker who'd stood before him threatening to contact her lawyer.

He shrugged, pulling himself together. Yes, his grandfather was unwell. But he could cope with it. He didn't have a choice. "There's nothing to talk about. He had a heart attack. He's in the hospital. They're looking after him. End of story." It wouldn't do him any good to get caught up in the severity of the situation again. No way could he think clearly if he focused on the trauma.

"That's a short story. Especially for a man being hospitalized with a heart attack. I'd expected something...a little longer. A little more serious."

"I'm not sure my grandfather would appreciate my talking about him to you."

She pulled back and held up her hands, palms facing him. "You're right. It's none of my business."

He mentally slapped himself, feeling like a jerk for cutting her off when she'd done nothing but try to help.

Claire stood, straightening from her knees to her full, impressive height. "I suspect you need some time out, so I'll leave you alone. The tea's beside you if you change your mind about wanting more, which I hope you do."

Jack searched for something to say and came up with nothing.

She reached into her handbag and pulled out a business card, handing it to him. "I'll come past your offices tomorrow morning. Eleven okay? We can continue our discussion then." She hesitated, probably giving him a chance to nix the meeting or maybe reschedule.

He didn't—because he had no idea what was scheduled for tomorrow. Hard as he'd searched, he had yet to find Big Jack's diary. Perhaps if he'd found it last night he'd have known about the appointment with Miss Jones.

"My number's on the card if you need to get hold of me before then. But that should give you some recovery time—and some damage-control time." She nodded at the floor. "Drink your tea. Whether you want it or not, it'll make you feel better."

"Wait!" It wasn't shock that had him calling out. His mind had cleared. He was focused now.

Claire turned to look at him.

He just didn't want her to walk away from him. Not without thanking her for her kindness. Or apologizing again for fucking up the lease agreement. He extended his arm to her. "Can you give me a hand up?"

Confusion fluttered through her eyes, but she blinked and it was gone. "Of course." She reached over and grabbed his hand with hers.

The second their hands touched, a shock of energy smacked him in the stomach, and Jack knew his every good intention was about to go to hell. He knew he should use his common sense, knew he needed to keep things professional. But damn it, her touch burned a hole through his skin, her perfume played havoc with his balls, and she stared at their hands with huge eyes, as though she'd also experienced the electric charge.

Using his weight and position as leverage, he tugged hard on her arm, and instead of pulling himself up, he yanked her down.

She toppled with a startled cry.

He caught her, breaking her fall with his body. He should have taken her size into account before acting so impulsively. But he hadn't, and her weight knocked him over.

Jack landed on his back, clasping her in his arms, ensuring she came to no harm.

He hadn't meant to land like this—so close. He'd only hoped to...what? Fill his arms with Miss Jones like he'd felt compelled to do since she'd walked into the shop?

But now that she lay above him, her curves pressing against his body, common sense eluded him. Logic left the shop.

Her face turned crimson and an expression of horror—or maybe embarrassment—creased her features. Before she had a minute to catch her breath, he pressed his hand to the back of her neck, pushed her head down and kissed her.

Shock rendered Claire immobile. She'd fallen on Jack Wilson, had the breath knocked out of her, humiliated herself so badly her cheeks burned like the devil, and now the very man she'd almost crippled with her considerable weight was kissing her.

Molding his lips to hers, plunging his moist tongue into her mouth, tasting her, feasting on her.

Dear God, he wasn't just kissing her, he was making love to her mouth. Seducing her with his expertise, ravaging her lips and wreaking havoc on her senses.

He surrounded her. With his arms wrapped around her back, his lips pressed to her mouth and his massive, solid body cushioning hers, she was eclipsed by him. Never before had a man made her feel...small. Or fragile. But in his embrace she felt petite. And feminine. And clumsy as all hell.

Oh, God, instead of pulling him up and giving him a supportive hand, she'd fallen on him. Instead of offering him comfort about his grandfather, she'd almost knocked him unconscious.

She attempted to hold on to that mortification, reminded herself that the man was in shock, but it proved impossible. How could she focus on the negative when his very taste overwhelmed her and his scent did funny things to her belly?

He smelled like a man should smell. Woodsy, like the great outdoors, but also... She inhaled, pulling in his aroma. *Sexy.* She couldn't put into words what made her want to tear his shirt from his body and allow her hands to roam free over his huge chest, she just knew he smelled intoxicating.

Although that inebriated sensation could be a result of his kiss. Of the way his mouth plundered hers, taking whatever he could and giving back a hundred-fold.

There was nothing calm or gentle about the kiss. He sought to pillage, own and devour. She could do nothing but allow him free access. And maybe kiss him back. Just a little.

Okay, a lot. Maybe she kissed him back as ravenously as he kissed her.

Damn it. She kissed the man who'd leased her shop to someone else. The very man she should be mad as hell with. Where were her priorities? She needed to get up and walk away. At least until Jack had time to come to terms with his grandfather's illness and work out a solution to the lease issue.

But she couldn't motivate her body to leave. Couldn't force herself up and off him. Couldn't even stop her hands as they crept up his sides, molding to the shape of his muscles, imbibing his warmth.

Had she thought him cold just a few short minutes ago? Now he burned beneath her hands. Heat radiated from his body, singeing her palms. That was a good thing, right? It must mean he was getting over his shock.

Claire yanked at his shirt, pulling the tails from his pants, letting her hands creep beneath the cotton.

Holy shit. Hot male flesh pulled taut over rippling muscle.

He felt so damn good, a moan of appreciation escaped her throat. Jack kissed her harder, more thoroughly, and Claire couldn't get enough of the wet heat of his mouth.

The arm around her back tightened, pulling her closer. He shifted, straightening out his legs so Claire lay on top of him. Her hips pressed to his, her breasts squashed against that substantial chest.

A low groan vibrated through his lips as he ground against her, revealing an impressive erection.

Claire's head spun.

The man was hard. Aroused.

Wow.

No man had ever acted with such erotic abandon around her. No man had ever kissed her as though his very life depended on it. As though the taste of her lips was enough to send his temperature soaring, or the feel of her body against his made him groan in ecstatic agony.

Claire was under no false illusion. She would never be one of those gorgeous, model-type women who had men falling at her feet. She was the big, clumsy, overweight girl next door who...well, who fell at men's feet apparently. While trying to help them up.

Perhaps the shock had muddled his brain? Perhaps his grief had left him shaken and vulnerable, and his instinct was to reach out to whomever was close at the time?

Her.

That would explain the way he held her so tight, the way his mouth seemed reluctant to release hers. It would also explain the feverish groan that rumbled through his chest, vibrating against her breasts and making her pussy clench with excitement.

It didn't explain the erection. Didn't explain why he rocked his hips, rubbing his cock over a spot so sweet that had Claire not been wearing pants, she'd have been thrown into a spiraling orgasm.

Oh, God.

It didn't seem to matter whether or not she was dressed. Didn't matter that she and he were fully clothed. The pressure against her clit, so unexpected, so intense, was enough to build sensation that could send her over the edge in no time.

Her wild rocking in return helped matters not at all. Without being conscious of her body's actions, she found herself grinding down on his erection, her knees on either side of his legs, meeting every seductive thrust of his hips with a twist of her own.

She no longer focused on her inhibitions. Couldn't even think about them. As the pressure and sensation built, and his tongue stroked over hers, she dug her fingers into his sides, seeking purchase on his hard flesh.

Claire was going to come. Going to orgasm, atop Mr. Wilson in the very shop he'd leased to someone else.

With a last reserve of energy, Claire ripped her head away, breaking the kiss that held her captive in his arms. She tried to throw herself off him, twisting over to the side, but he held her tight, even as he stared at her with passion-fogged eyes.

"Easy, Miss Jones. You lurch over to that side, and you're likely to crash into a cup of tea."

His calm, practical words were at such odds with his dark, sexy gaze, Claire stilled mid-twist. And then had to swallow a moan, as the position pressed her clit firmly against his erection, almost making her see stars.

"P-please. Let me go." She'd dismount on the other side.

The breathless quality to her voice ashamed her. Although which part of her behavior caused the most shame she was unsure. Was it the fact that the last thing she wanted to do was climb off him? She was close, so damn close to coming, that even shuddering might send her over the edge.

Or was it the fact that she'd fallen on him, like a giant hippopotamus, with no rhythm or grace or even a slight attempt to right herself?

Or was it the fact that she'd so blatantly and wantonly fallen into his kiss, she'd let go of her inhibitions without even remembering she had any?

Or maybe, just maybe, she'd horrified herself, plunging head first into a kiss and a grope with a man overwhelmed by stress and worry. Perhaps she was horrified at herself for taking advantage of a man so obviously shaken by a family member's ill health.

A combination of all of the above. Without a doubt. And that didn't even begin to focus on her reasons for being here in the first place. The professional woman seeking to lease a shop from the property manager.

Still, a part of her—a very big part—wanted to dip back down and kiss him all over again.

His arms loosened around her, giving her the chance to climb off him, like she wanted. So why did she hesitate?

As though he sensed she might be in two minds, he rocked his hips one time. Claire leaped off him with a gasp she could not suppress. She landed on her knees beside him, with all her usual lack of grace and finesse, a heaving mass of crazy-assed female hormones.

Was there any way she could humiliate herself more with this man?

Pushing up to a standing position, and knowing her face was stained red—probably permanently—she did her best to apologize, patting down her shirt at the same time.

"I-I am so sorry. Falling on you like that. I have no idea what happened, other than I'm clumsier than a baby elephant, and probably shouldn't have offered you my hand in the first place. D-did I hurt you?"

He propped his lower arms on the floor and rested his weight on them, looking up at her, bemused. "Hurt me?"

Shit, this was excruciating. "Uh, yeah. You know, when I landed on you." Yes, he was big. Huge. Still, she was no lightweight. She could have caused him serious harm.

"Do I look hurt?"

She scanned his body. He looked positively scrumptious, although his shirt was a crumpled mess and his pants did nothing to hide the glorious erection he'd pressed against her so enticingly. Her gaze kind of got stuck on it and wouldn't move on.

"I pulled you over, Miss Jones. You didn't fall on me."

Flushing even more than before, she darted her gaze back to his. He just said that to make her feel better.

"And for the record? You're welcome to land on me any time." He squeezed his eyes shut and shifted to a sitting position, then groaned and immediately shifted again. "But maybe next time, you won't be in such a hurry to get up?"

Speechless, embarrassed and more than a little aroused, Claire fumbled for an appropriate response and found none. She just knew she had to get out of there. Get some space, some air and pull herself together. No way could she conduct herself in any way befitting a professional now. If she wasn't careful, she'd throw caution to the wind and launch herself at the man now seated on the floor.

She might break his neck in the process, but at least she'd be back in his arms—an idea she found she craved a great deal. Okay, so she practically drooled at the thought of being held by him again. Touched by him. Kissed. "I er, have to go," she muttered.

No, she didn't. She'd set the morning aside to complete this meeting. Neither Maddie nor Julia were expecting her back at *Li'l Books and Bits* any time soon. But she couldn't stand here a second longer. Not if she wanted to preserve her last ounce of pride.

"Go?" he asked.

"Back to my shop. Do some work. And, er, you should probably go too. Go visit your grandfather. I suspect you need to see him, for your sake as well as his."

"What about your lease?"

She nodded. Good question What about it? "As I said, I'll come by your offices tomorrow morning. We can sort it all out then. It'll give you a chance to cancel the agreement with the man who just signed it."

Much easier to talk about the lease than the outrageous kiss they'd just shared. Funny how she could obsess about it internally, reliving every second of it while looking at the G.G., yet not allow a single word to cross her lips that may give him the impression she'd given it another thought. She kind of reckoned she'd be giving it endless thought all the way back to the shop and well into lunch. And dinner. And breakfast the next morning.

He shook his head with a small, mystified smile. "You're just going to ignore that kiss? Pretend it didn't happen?"

She stared at him, speechless.

"You're going to pretend I'm not sitting here, on my ass, with a massive hard-on?"

She bit her lip, not wanting to answer at all. "That's exactly what I'm going to do. I'm going to pretend the last five minutes didn't take place. You're in shock about your grandfather, I'm furious about the lease, and should our lawyers need to get involved in the situation, a kiss and an uh, erection, are not going to hold either of us in good stead."

"Ah, so we keep it professional." He narrowed his eyes. "Ignore the fact that we both almost climaxed, fully clothed on the floor here. Ignore the chemistry that's telling me to haul you into my arms once again—despite the fact you're acting as though it doesn't exist?"

She wiped her hands on her pants, aware her palms were damp from nerves. Or from arousal. "We should have kept it professional all along. We didn't. This is the only way I know to rectify the situation. Pretend it didn't take place."

One half of his mouth creased into a frown. The half that showed off his dimple, and again Claire felt the need to explore it—with her tongue. "I guess I should be grateful you're not denying the chemistry."

How could she possibly deny it? Whatever hummed between them wasn't just chemical, it was highly explosive. "I'll see you tomorrow, Mr. Wilson. At your grandfather's offices."

He contemplated her in silence for a long moment before giving a humorless laugh. "You know where the offices are?"

"Yes. Your grandfather gave me the address."

"Then I guess I'll see you tomorrow."

She nodded. "Eleven o'clock."

"You should know something, Miss Jones."

She raised her brow in question.

"This isn't over between us. You might deny what just happened. I can't."

Chapter Three

Overwhelming relief was Jack's first experience as he walked into his grandfather's hospital room.

The man's pallor had improved. His cheeks were rosy, and he sat up in bed, resting against three or four pillows. Even the drip attached to Big Jack's left arm couldn't detract from his grandson's relief. He was no doctor, but the change was obvious. The man was better.

A thousand kilograms lifted from Jack's shoulders. Seeing his pop like this did more for him than a cup—or even a pot—of tea ever could.

He couldn't explain how it all happened, or why, but Claire had eased his worries. Something about her presence had taken away the horror of the previous night, of realizing his grandfather might die. Her calm had soothed his shock.

And her kiss had blown his mind, but that was another story altogether.

The second she'd left the shop, however, he'd jumped into his car and headed straight to the hospital, needing to see Big Jack.

Now, as he stood admiring his grandfather's color, he couldn't help but think that it might not be too long before they took the boat out again.

Pop welcomed him with a smile, and Jack hugged him hello, kissing him on the cheek, aware of the papery texture of his skin. While the old man might be better, he was still old, and more fragile than Jack had realized. Jack had just kind of assumed he'd live forever. Stupid really, but when a boy idolized someone the way Jack had always idolized Big Jack, thoughts of death and mortality just never came up.

"Your father just left. You missed him by a couple of minutes."

"That's okay. I didn't come to see him. I came for you. How are you feeling?"

Big Jack looked down at his chest as though assessing it. "I don't think I'll be running any marathons in the near future, but otherwise okay." His voice was soft and wispy.

"I brought you some magazines to read." He laid the pile on the hospital cabinet beside the bed.

His pop looked disappointed. "No food?"

"I have no idea what you're allowed, or if you're even allowed to eat, so no. No food."

Big Jack huffed. "I could use a Big Mac and chips."

Jack snorted. "Pop, you've just had a heart attack from clogged arteries. Your burger days are over."

"Might as well kill me now if I can't have another Big Mac," the old man grumbled. "I'm holding out for chips as well."

"Tell you what. Get through the surgery okay, and I'll treat you to a Big Mac meal *and* a McFlurry afterwards." Anyone who craved Macca's had to be feeling better.

"You have a deal, my boy. Now tell me what's happening at my office."

Jack frowned.

"That bad, huh?"

"Worse."

"Jacky, come on, you're a teacher. You guide teenagers every day of your life. How hard can it be to run a one-man property management business? Compared to school, it's a party."

"I get kids, Pop. I understand them. I like them." All of them—even the princesses, the troublemakers, the geeky nerds and the arrogant jocks.

He didn't just like them, he loved them. Loved his work. Came home at the end of every day with a sense of accomplishment, a knowledge that he'd found his life's purpose.

Unfortunately, it was the getting home that always knocked the wind out of his sails. Because how could one enjoy one's life's purpose when one's salary didn't even allow one to own a home? Or a new car, maybe with leather upholstery?

God help him if he ever settled down and started a family. The expense would be financially crippling.

Working with his pop, however, and earning decent money could open up his life to all possibilities. And what better opportunity to join his grandfather than right now? But even with this opportunity, he hesitated, hating the thought of leaving a job that made him happy.

"Your business? I swear, I can't fathom it. I'll take History and English lessons over business any day. Anthony is way better suited to run your business while you're away."

"Anthony is in Perth. He can't run my business."

Jack wished his brother weren't away. Anthony would've understood how worried Jack had been about Big Jack, and although they'd spoken last night, more than once, a phone just wasn't an adequate means of communication at a time like this. Anthony would also have been able to run the business effectively. He'd studied Business Management.

"I stuffed up, Pop."

"What did you do?

"I rented out the property on New South Head Road."

"How's that a mistake? I asked you to rent it out. Got a good feel about those Jones girls. Thought they'd be good tenants. Who signed the lease? Claire or Maddie?"

Jack cringed. "Neither."

"Neither?"

"Greg Parker did."

Big Jack stared at him. "Parker?"

Jack nodded.

"Now why on earth would Parker sign on that shop? I never showed it to him."

"Yeah, um, I did. This morning."

"Why?" The old man looked baffled.

"Because you told me to rent out the shop today. I think your words were, 'Get the lease signed, my boy. That property *must* be rented out tomorrow.'"

"Yes. So?"

"So you never mentioned *who* should sign the lease. I had no idea who you had in mind. When I searched your desk, the only name I found was Parker's. His number was there, alongside a handwritten note to 'show him the shop ASAP, with a view to leasing'."

"Yes. That was for a property in Surry Hills, not Rose Bay."

"I had no idea."

"Did you look in my diary?"

"I couldn't find your diary."

"On my computer. Or my phone."

Damn it. He hadn't thought to look there. Hadn't imagined his pop was that technologically savvy.

"Do me a favor?"

Jack nodded. "Anything."

"Next time you visit, bring my iPad along. I'll go through everything with you."

"You have an iPad?"

"Of course I have an iPad. It's in the third drawer of my desk. How can anyone work without one these days?"

Jack hid a grin. He didn't know a single other person over the age of sixty with an iPad. Big Jack was a remarkable man indeed. "So what do I do about the shop now? What do I say to Miss Jones?"

"Miss Jones?"

"Claire." Just saying her name sent a sharp longing through his gut for another taste of her sweet mouth. No, things were definitely not over between them. Not by a long shot. "She came past the shop while I was there with Parker."

"To sign the lease."

"Apparently."

"Ah, Little Jacky, you messed that one up."

"Yeah, I know. But thanks for reinforcing it. How do I fix it?"

Big Jack shook his head. "Parker signed?"

"He did."

"Then you're in trouble. He's a good client, a steadfast one. He's not going to give up the shop now."

That pretty much mirrored what Parker had told him over the phone on the way to the hospital. "I thought I might show Miss Jones another of your properties."

"Which one?"

"I have no idea. Which one would you recommend?"

"The New South Head shop is the only one I have in Rose Bay. The next closest property is office space in Bondi Junction."

Jack pinched the bridge of his nose with his thumbs and swore under his breath. This was so not going the way he'd hoped. Parker had refused to break the contract. He may not have known about the shop in the first place, but once he'd seen it, he'd refused to let it go.

Miss Jones was going to be hopping mad.

While Jack regretted screwing her around—no matter that he'd done it inadvertently—he kind of looked forward to seeing her hopping mad. The striking Amazonian warrior would have a few choice threats to throw his way. And Jack looked forward to hearing each and every one of them.

"Are you kidding me?" Claire stared at the man before her, dumbfounded. "You want me to do what?" She hoped to God he could not see any sign of her erratic heart, which slammed into her chest as she struggled to keep her wits and her hormones about her.

"Come for a drive with me. I promise you won't regret it."

She took a deep breath, drew herself up to her tallest height and spoke very patiently. "Mr. Wilson, I am here to sort out the lease to the shop in New South Head Road. I'm not interested in gallivanting around Sydney with you."

Funny her voice could come out so patient, because her lungs weren't working well and her palms had grown clammy. Reliving Jack's kiss over and over had not prepared her for the reality of standing in front of the G.G. again. His physical presence hit her like a blow to the solar plexus, making breathing almost impossible.

He was even more striking than she remembered. Large, solid and so jam-packed full of muscle she suspected he'd be about as easy to move as a house.

Her crazy-ass female hormones were doing a crazy-ass happy dance at the sight of him, and her stomach dipped madly up and down. Much as she tried to convince herself it was just a case of worry and anxiety that he may not have sorted the details out with the other tenant, she couldn't quite believe it.

Her physical reaction to him had nothing to do with the shop and everything to do with the man. Even her pussy clenched, reminding her how close she'd come to orgasming on top of him yesterday.

"Look, I buggered things up yesterday, signing over a lease for a property that had already been promised to you, and I apologize for that. How about we start again, Miss Jones? From the beginning. Let's do it right this time."

She didn't need to start again. She just needed to know he'd made things right with the lease.

He stuck out his hand. "Hello. I'm Jack Wilson, grandson of Big Jack Wilson. While he's in hospital I'll be looking after his business. And you are?"

Really? They were really doing this? Standing on the footpath outside Wilson Property Management offices, where Mr. Wilson had headed her off before she could even enter the building.

She raised an eyebrow. "Big Jack?"

Jack grinned. "My childhood name for my pop. Now, c'mon," he coaxed. "Humor me. I screwed up. I only want to make things right. In whatever way I can."

So long as it meant he was giving her the store, Claire was willing to go along with anything. "It's good to meet you. I'm Claire Jones. I had an appointment with your grandfather yesterday, but he couldn't make it." She hesitated then, getting sidetracked. "How is your grandfather?"

He nodded. "He's much better today. A different person from the man who was rushed to emergency." His smile was big, and she sensed immense relief in his answer.

"I'm glad to hear that. And I hope he continues to recover. Please pass along my regards to him, Mr. Wilson."

"Jack."

"Jack?"

"Call me Jack. I'm Mr. Wilson ten months of the year. For now, I'd really just like the freedom of being Jack."

Cryptic response. Still Claire hesitated, not sure she felt comfortable addressing him by his first name. At least if she addressed him as "Mr." she could keep him at some kind of emotional distance.

"You could always call me Little Jacky, like my pop does."

Claire repressed a snort. "Little?"

His eyes twinkled. "Hey, I was young when he gave me the name."

"I think I'll stick with Jack." There was no way she could call him "Mr." after that. "Please call me Claire."

"Claire it is. Nice name, by the way. It suits you."

She considered responding...for all of two seconds. Jack was way too appealing to her senses. If she responded to his personal comments, she'd never get any work done. She'd be too focused on the man and not the business at hand. And knowing her, she'd trip and fall on him all over again—although this time it would be quite deliberate. And if she fell on him deliberately and broke his leg or arm as a result, she'd *never* live it down.

"So, Jack. Instead of taking a trip in your car, why don't we head into your office and see about signing that lease?"

"Nope, a trip in my car is a way better idea. And far more productive. I swear it."

"Is the lease in your car?"

Jack nodded. "There is a lease in my car. And as soon as we arrive at our destination, I will give it to you."

"Your office—"

He cut her off. "No can do. The office is being fumigated. We can't go in there."

Uh, why did she not believe him? "Fine, then let's head over to the coffee shop across the road. That'll do just fine."

He shook his head. "Again, I have to nix the idea. Look, there's a property I need to see over in Mosman today, and I figured I could kill two birds with one stone. I could view the place while you and I talk about the New South Head shop."

Claire had no idea what made her agree—probably a desire to spend more time with Jack—but she finally nodded and allowed him to place his hand on her elbow and guide her to his car.

The hand on her elbow was not close to enough. She wanted his hand on her—

Good God, no, she didn't. She didn't want his hand anywhere near her. Regardless of the speed her heart raced or the clamminess of her palms or the recurrent flashbacks to the kiss they'd shared, she didn't want to even think about Jack Wilson in that way.

What happened between them had been an...anomaly. Yes. Perfect description. She'd fallen on him—or been pulled, she still wasn't sure—and he, in his grief and shock had responded on instinct, reaching out to the closest person he could to find comfort. That must have been all he'd been seeking. Comfort during a difficult time. Everyone needed consolation when a loved one took ill. Everyone needed a way to work through one's grief. His kissing her was just that. Nothing more. And if she did make anything more of it, she'd only mess up an already messy property negotiation.

Once he'd ensured she was comfortably seated in his Ford Territory, he set off in the direction of the Harbour Tunnel, with the car radio playing soft rock in the background.

"Thanks for coming with me. I'm excited to see this shop. The lease is just coming up for renewal, and the current renters aren't interested in re-signing. Since it's in the heart of Mosman, on Military Road, it's a sought-after address. There's going to be a lot of interest generated as soon as we put up a notice about it."

Claire wasn't interested in the Mosman shop, but she could hardly be rude. Besides, if she made small talk and got to know Jack a little better, the lease negotiations might be more amenable. "Who's renting it now?"

"Two women who sell handmade jackets. Very expensive, very exclusive."

"Nice gear?"

He shrugged. "Never seen it. As I said, this is Big Jack's business. I'm just watching it while he recuperates."

"What do you do when your grandfather is well enough to look after his own business?" She'd be willing to lay money on his answer being something sports related. A professional footy player, or something similar.

"I'm a teacher."

"You are?" She tried to temper her surprise. Sports coach maybe?

"Yep. Teach high school English and History."

She gaped at him. "I had you pegged as a professional sportsman."

"Nah, not me. I play rugby with my mates on the weekend and coach a Uni team on Tuesday evenings, but my kids are my true passion." His face lit up with genuine affection. "They give me a tough time sometimes, but they're worth the effort I put into them. And they seem to like me too, so it's a win-win situation."

Claire put two and two together. "It's school holidays now, so you have time off?"

"A little. Enough that I can help my pop out for a couple of weeks. No one else could. My parents couldn't get time off from their law practice, and my brother is in Perth. I'd like to do all the drudge work while he's recovering. Visit properties, sort out rent issues, leave him the easy bits he can do from home, or at least without leaving the office."

Claire went all squishy inside. Jack sure knew how to look out for his grandfather. Taking care of his business while the old man was in hospital, doing all the physical stuff so Jack Sr. didn't have to. That kind of caring appealed to a woman in a big way. Well, okay, it appealed to Claire in a big way.

"When does he get out of hospital?" Judging from Jack's shock earlier, his grandfather was a very sick man.

"I'm guessing within the week. But then he goes back in two months for surgery."

"He's having surgery?"

He nodded. "A triple bypass."

"Shit," Claire muttered. "That's a huge deal."

"'Specially for an eighty-two-year-old. The doc said it'll be about six weeks before he's back to normal."

Claire frowned. "I'm sorry, Jack. That can't be easy for anyone. A man of his age is going to find it even harder."

"I know. I'm trying not to worry about him, but it's difficult. We're close, my pop and me. I hate the idea of him being unwell."

Much as she wanted to reassure him, she couldn't. She really had no idea whether his grandfather would be okay or not. If it were anyone else, she'd give their hand a supportive squeeze and offer to help in any way she could. But with Jack, both of those gestures would be inappropriate. She settled for saying the only thing she could. "It's a shitty situation. For you and your grandfather."

"That it is," he agreed. "That it is." He lapsed into silence.

Claire didn't push him further. She sat quietly as he lost himself in his thoughts. But sitting in silence made her all too aware of where she sat—beside him, in his car.

Jack took up a lot of space. His SUV, no small car by anyone's standards, seemed to have halved in size when he got in. His seat was pushed back as far as it could go, giving him room to stretch his legs to the pedals. Whenever he braked or accelerated—which yes, was all the time—Claire had to force herself not to look at the flexing of his muscle in his thigh. Or at the long, slim fingers handling the wheel.

Though she pretended she was not affected by his proximity, it was hard to deny his presence. Hard to ignore that woodsy, sexy scent of his. Hard to forget that just one day ago he'd kissed her senseless in the empty shop.

"I haven't forgotten, you know," he said softly.

"Forgotten what?"

"The kiss. Yesterday." He touched a finger to his lip, as though remembering what he'd done with that lip the day before.

Holy shit. Had he read her mind? She snapped her mouth shut and refused to answer him. *Not going there. Not stepping into that minefield.*

"Just because we haven't discussed it, doesn't mean it never happened. We kissed, on the floor of the Rose Bay shop, and it damn near blew my mind."

Shop. She hooked on the word. "Talking about the shop, are we going to go back there after this? It's not necessary. We can sign the contract anywhere."

"You're changing the subject."

"No. I'm focusing on the very reason I'm in the car with you now. Did you speak to the man who signed the lease yesterday? Tell him about the mistake?"

"You're a coward, Claire Jones."

"I'm a woman intent on getting the property I was promised. Did you speak to him?"

He smiled that same mystified smile he'd smiled yesterday. "We did speak. I spoke to Big Jack as well, who corroborated your story about coming to the shop to fill in the contract." Before Claire could say anything, he asked, "Mind if I ask what you're planning for the shop?"

Now look who changed the subject. Jack hadn't even told her what the other leaser had said. "Not at all. I own a small, specialized children's store. We sell kids' books, toys and clothes."

"I? Or we?"

"We. My two sisters and I. We have a shop in Clovelly, called *Li'l Bits and Books*, and now we're looking to expand. The shop's too busy. Business has grown since we added the clothing and toys to our inventory. We need more space and wider customer sales."

"Since you added clothing and toys?"

Claire nodded. "We started out as a children's bookshop, but with the explosion of eBooks and the collapse of the bigger book chains, stocking only print books just wasn't keeping us in business. We either had to expand our product range or close our doors. We chose to expand."

"Successfully, I take it?"

"More successfully than any of us expected." Claire, Maddie and Julia were all blown away by the shop's sales.

"So now you're opening up a second branch, also in the Eastern suburbs?"

Claire shrugged. "Most of our customers are from Vaucluse, Rose Bay, Double Bay and Bellevue Hill. It makes sense to open up closer to them."

"Even if they're willing to travel to Clovelly?"

Claire nodded. "Even so."

Jack guided the car through the tunnel. "Wouldn't it make more sense to open up farther away? A fifteen or twenty minute drive isn't going to deter customers from coming to your shop if they really want something from you. But half an hour or more might."

"Our products are expensive. We're targeting the market that could best afford it. A shop in New South Head Road is the perfect location."

Jack cocked his head to the side. "What about a shop a little farther out. Say, for example...across the bridge in Mosman. You'll have a similar clientele, and driving out to Clovelly from there is just a little too far for the average shopper."

Claire almost laughed. "Our shop is doing well. But we're not at a place where we can afford rentals in an area like Mosman. The cost would cut too deeply into our profits. Now, what happened when you spoke to—"

Jack suddenly leaned forward. "Damn, I love this song." He turned the car radio volume up, making further conversation difficult, then proceeded to sing along with Coldplay at the top of his lungs.

Damn it, he'd done it again. Changed the subject when she tried to ask about the lease. And what a way to change the subject this time.

Claire couldn't help her graceless snort as Jack's voice filled the car. The G.G. might be built, gorgeous and supremely fuckable, but he was no vocalist. His flat, toneless singing was so off-key Claire could barely recognize the song.

She slapped a hand over her mouth to prevent any further inappropriate responses, but couldn't help snickering as he hit the chorus, out of tune and off beat.

Jack stopped singing and looked at her. "Are you laughing at me?"

Claire didn't dare answer, nor did she dare move her hand away from her mouth. Instead she shook her head and stared straight ahead, refusing to make eye contact. She couldn't risk letting the laughter that bubbled inside her out.

"You are," he accused. "You're laughing at me."

Another graceless snort erupted from her nose as she shook her head again.

He lowered the volume as he picked his way along Military Road. "Honestly? That's how you respond to all the property managers you try to lease shops from? You laugh at them?"

"Only the ones who sing at the top of their voices while they have potential renters in the car."

"There's nothing wrong with my voice, I'll have you know."

Claire nodded primly. "So, what did you do with the money?"

His brow creased. "What money?"

"The money your mother gave you for singing lessons."

His jaw dropped. "You did not just go there."

Laughter peeled out of her. She couldn't hold it back anymore. "Apparently I did."

"My students used to ask each other that." He rolled his eyes. "When they were in primary school."

"I bet your students sing better than you do."

"They sing as well as I do, since I'm their music teacher too."

Claire gaped at him. "You are not."

"Oh, nice. Not only do you mock my voice, now you trash my teaching abilities as well?"

"Tell me you don't teach your kids music."

His lips twitched. "I don't teach my kids music. But as punishment for your blatant disbelief in my vocal ability, I'll sing the rest of the way to the shop."

And with that, he turned the radio back up and belted out his own inspired rendition of "Paradise".

By the time he swung his car into a parking space, Claire had given up all pretense of holding back her mirth and was laughing out loud in his passenger seat.

Jack switched off the car, removed his seat belt, turned to her while still singing out of tune, and before she had a chance to paste a serious expression on her face, he swooped in and crushed his lip to hers.

Chapter Four

Jesus, he had no idea what it was about Claire that had his balls all tangled up in knots, but spending twenty minutes in a car with her sent his libido sky rocketing.

The second he'd closed the driver's door, her perfume had overwhelmed him, and he'd known he was going to have to kiss her again. So kiss her he did. With her body trapped between his and her seat, he took ownership of her mouth and refused to release it.

Her laughter died on her lips, and her breath hitched. For a good few seconds she froze, her jaw slackening with surprise.

Good enough for Jack. It offered his tongue free entry into her tempting mouth. He dipped it inside and ran it along her tongue, then withdrew, driven by a consuming need to nibble on her lower lip.

Dragging his teeth over that pouty flesh, he sucked it into his mouth and nibbled to his heart's content. Only his heart demanded a whole lot more than her lower lip. It demanded full ownership of her mouth and body, and he had to force himself to go slow, to focus only on the nubile flesh between his teeth, sucking, nibbling and releasing it in slow succession.

A throaty groan erupted from Claire, and then her hands were on his head, pulling his face closer. Her fingers tunneled through his hair, tickling his scalp, massaging it, holding him there.

She was responding, kissing him back, nipping at his lips, seeking his tongue. Their mouths melded together and the kiss turned hot so fast, the windows steamed up.

Fuck, he'd damn near come in his pants from kissing her yesterday, and he feared he might face the same dilemma today. Still, it didn't stop him, didn't inspire him to pull his mouth away even one inch.

Claire emitted soft, hungry moans that played havoc with his already knotted balls. She kissed him as though she fed off his mouth, gaining sustenance from him. And damned if it didn't give him an erection from hell. Damned if her enthusiasm and her taste didn't have his hand on her breast and his fingers gently squeezing the abundant flesh.

She more than filled his palm, making him greedy to touch all of her, greedy to have both breasts in his hands—unencumbered by shirts and bras.

All his life he'd favored small women. Short, thin and small-chested, everything Claire was not. Yet here, with her tantalizing tongue tempting his, and the nipple of her ample breast tightening beneath his touch, he had no idea how he could ever have found skinny women more appealing than this beauty.

Jack lost himself to her kiss, to her feel, to her touch. Their mouths worked in perfect accord, as if they each instinctively knew what the other sought or needed.

Or perhaps Jack just knew what he instinctively needed and sought to give her the same. One thing he did know was that kissing Claire Jones was an experience he wished to relive over and over again. Or maybe he'd just ensure this kiss never ended.

But a kiss would never suffice. His cock pointed out that fact as it swelled against his zip, demanding attention, demanding satisfaction, demanding access to Claire's body.

He pulled away with reluctance, then almost sealed their lips together again when Claire groaned in protest.

He forced his eyes open, forced himself to look at her, and had to bite his cheek hard at the sight that greeted him. Claire's head was tipped back, her eyes closed and her lips swollen and parted. It took every iota of willpower he possessed not to clamp his mouth back over hers.

"Unless you want me to strip you naked and fuck you in this car, right here, in the middle of Mosman," he rasped, "I suggest you climb out very quickly."

Her eyes popped open, their hazel rims almost invisible around huge black pupils.

"I seem to have very little control when you're around, Miss Jones." He grit his teeth, pain and frustration radiating from his pelvic area, making speech almost impossible. Jack pushed through it, aware that his hand was still on her breast, his thumb brushing over the distended nipple. "Go now, before I rip off your shirt and suck on your nipples." He yanked his hand away, knowing if he moved any slower, he'd never release her.

They sat in his car on Military Road in broad daylight. Anyone could look inside. And while the idea of being watched bothered him not at all, he couldn't bear Claire facing that indignity. She'd blushed just discussing their kiss yesterday, done her best to deny it. If strangers saw her getting naked with him, he suspected she'd never get over the humiliation.

She stared at him with dazed eyes, blinking rapidly. It took a while, but her gaze began to clear. Her pupils contracted and the hazel rims grew bigger. As her gaze sobered, so did her expression. She snapped her mouth shut and color flooded her cheeks.

"Go now," he half whispered, half threatened and pushed back, freeing her. He used the hand that had been on her breast to unclip her seatbelt, lest he slip and replace it on her soft, round globe and tease her nipple with his thumb once more.

Claire scrambled from the car, clonking him on the shoulder in her haste. Her color grew deeper as she called out an apology, but at least she was no longer beside him, beneath him, tempting him with her presence.

Fuck, if his pop could see him now, he'd smack him one on the back side of his head. It was bad enough he'd messed up with the contract. But to mess around with one of his clients would never suffice. Big Jack would not stand for it.

Except this didn't feel like messing around. This felt more like compulsion, an undeniable need to get closer to Claire, to touch her, kiss her, and yes, to fuck her. It was an undeniable need to get to know everything about her.

He took several deep breaths, willing his erection down. Climbing out the car with a raging hard-on was not a good idea. But watching Claire smooth her hair and pull her blouse down helped not a bit.

He turned his thoughts to two nights ago, to the shock of receiving the phone call about his pop's heart attack, to his deathly fear his pop might not make it.

A long moment later, his cock half the size, Jack climbed out the car. He walked to stand beside Claire, placing his hand on her elbow and steering her towards the shop.

"You gonna pretend that kiss didn't happen either, beautiful?" he breathed into her ear.

Claire's shoulders stiffened, and heat radiated from her cheeks. "Shut up, Jack."

"I told you the chemistry between us wasn't going anywhere.

"If you stop kissing me all the time, it would."

He laughed out loud. "I'm not going to stop. Believe me, the next time I kiss you, I don't think I'll be able to pull back. I intend to strip you naked and fuck you six ways to Sunday. And don't even try to deny you want it just as much as I do."

Jack straightened, pushed open the store door, and invited a startled Claire to look around as he walked over to the front desk. While he took care of business, checking the state of the property and finalizing details with the current lease-holders, Claire studiously examined as many jackets as she could. But every now and again he caught her glaring at him, staring daggers in his direction. He also noticed a yearning in her expression. One that mirrored his own hunger.

Several times Jack had to force his concentration back to the tenants. No matter how much he might want to toss caution to the wind and act on his impulses, throwing Claire to the floor of this up-market boutique and fucking her senseless was not going to score him brownie points...with anybody.

Jack scrubbed a hand over his face. He'd never reacted to a woman like this before. Never wanted anyone so immediately or so feverishly.

Her reaction to his kisses served only to inflame him further. Jack was permanently horny, on the verge of getting hard every time he thought about Claire. Funny he should have such a strong physical reaction to this woman.

Funny and frustrating.

"So, what did you think?" he asked when they were once again seated in his car, and he was maneuvering the SUV through traffic.

Her cheeks turned pink. "Of you stripping me and fucking me six ways to Sunday?"

His mouth split into a smile, even as her question punched a hole in his gut. "Actually, I was asking about the shop. But now I'd much rather know your thoughts about my fucking you."

Claire stuck her nose in the air. "You've already fucked me, Mr. Wilson. Or have you forgotten about your blunder with my lease?"

Ouch. "Avoiding the subject, Miss Jones?"

"Coming back to the subject. One *you* seem to be studiously avoiding."

"It's hard to think about lease agreements when all I've wanted to do since you left the Rose Bay property is get you naked."

"Well, perhaps that would explain why I still haven't signed my lease. You haven't had a chance to think about it."

"Have you had a chance to think about fucking me?"

"You're quite determined to get an answer out of me about this one, aren't you?"

"Hey, you brought it up. I simply asked what you thought about the Mosman shop." He grinned at her little growl of frustration.

"It's a nice shop. Beautiful jackets, but way out of my price range."

Jack let her off the hook. For now. "I mean what did you think about the shop as the new location for *Li'l Books and Bits?*"

She turned to look at him, her mouth pursed. "I didn't think anything about it. The idea never crossed my mind."

Hopefully because she'd been thinking about him fucking her. "I think it would be great. In the heart of Mosman. Foot traffic all around, and just your kind of customer living in the area."

Her gaze could have frozen water in the tropics. "That's why you brought me here? To check out the property?"

He didn't bother denying it. What surprised him was that it had taken so long for her to realize as much. "It's the best shop on my grandfather's books. The most sought-after area, newly renovated and almost the same size as the shop in New South Head Road."

"I'm confused." She pushed her hair off her face. "Do I have *idiot* tattooed on my forehead?"

Oh, he liked her feistiness. Altogether too much. "I don't for one minute think you're an idiot. I'm just asking you to explore all your options before settling on a location."

Fury ignited in her eyes. "We explored our options in depth before choosing Rose Bay. We didn't settle for it on a whim. We took our customers' statistics and data into account and made the best choice for our business. What do you think? That three women running a retail outlet are incapable of making logical decisions? That we chose to rent in Rose Bay on an emotional whim?"

"My actions have nothing to do with you not knowing your business and everything to do with me broadening your horizons. I'm simply showing you that you have choices outside the limits of the Eastern Suburbs."

"Thank you, Mr. School Teacher, for your concern and willingness to help us explore different horizons. We could never have done that without your innovation."

Ouch, again. She'd just hit him where it hurt. In his inexperience with the property market. "I fucked up, Claire. I leased the shop you'd been promised. I'm trying to make reparations. I'm doing this as much for me as for you. Hoping to find something else that'll suit you."

She shook her head in distaste. "So tell me, how much are you asking for the Mosman shop."

"Eighty thousand per annum."

Claire's outraged laugh almost silenced him. Almost. "But we'll offer you a discount. A big discount, to make up for my earlier mistake."

"Unless your big discount is somewhere in the ballpark of fifty percent then you are out of your mind."

He cleared his throat. "I was thinking closer to ten percent."

Again she gave a derisive bark of laughter. "You're talking about a rental of more than six hundred dollars a week over and above what we'd agreed to pay in Rose Bay, and what, you expect me to be grateful?"

"It's a good deal. One Big Jack agreed to because of my mess up." Okay, so it wasn't such a good deal for the Jones sisters. Too expensive, as he'd known all along. But there was method to his madness. If he showed her something out of her price range now, maybe when he showed her something cheaper later, she'd be more interested.

And he had a property he suspected she would be *very* interested in.

She regarded him in silence for a long moment, her eyes narrowed, her head shaking from side to side. "You don't even have my lease for the Rose Bay shop, do you?"

No, he didn't. Though fuck knew he'd tried to convince Parker.

It was Jack's turn to purse his lips and once again avoid the question. He kinda wished he could put up the volume and sing again, but she wouldn't fall for the same trick twice.

"You never explained the situation to the other tenant, did you? Instead you chose to broaden my horizons, and hope you could net two leases in the process. Mine and his. How gallant of you, Mr. Wilson. I can only *assume* you're doing it with your grandfather's best interests at heart. Saving him the trouble of finding something else for my competition when he gets out of hospital."

He shook his head. "This has nothing to do with my grandfather. I'm simply trying to show you areas I'd thought you may not have explored before."

"Get me the lease, Jack. Let me sign it and take me back to my car. Soon as we have everything squared away, I promise not to bother you again." The air around her was charged with static electricity and a whole heap of suppressed lust. Just inhaling that air seemed to light Jack's blood on fire. "I'll happily wait until your grandfather is well enough before I have any further interaction with Wilson Property Management." Claire's voice was icy and her arms were folded across her chest—in a defiant, stuff-you gesture—yet sparks of awareness flew all around the car.

"And I'll understand if you don't want to deal with me professionally once Big Jack is back on his feet. But don't try and kid yourself that there's nothing else going on between us. Whatever happens with the lease, I suspect you and I are going to be seeing a lot more of each other." He smiled, letting the innuendo in his words seep into her mind. "A lot more."

"Don't try and use the attraction between us as a means of avoiding the problem."

There was something about arguing with Claire that set his blood on fire. And from the way her nipples poked at her shirt—how could he not notice, with her arms pushing those bountiful breasts up?—Jack suspected Claire felt exactly the same. "So you're not denying there's an attraction?"

"We've kissed twice. It'd be both difficult and hypocritical to deny there's an attraction."

Satisfaction roared through him. "Have dinner with me tonight. We won't talk about properties and leases. We won't even think about them. We'll just concentrate on you and me, and where we can take this mutual attraction."

"In other words, have dinner with you so you can strip me and fuck me six ways to Sunday."

His cock jumped to attention. "Would that be so bad?"

She didn't answer, just glared at him.

Dumb answer, especially because he hadn't actually had sex on his mind when he'd asked her. "I invited you to dinner, Claire. Not to bed. I thought we could get to know each other a little better, without having the pressure of a business agreement sitting between us."

Claire shook her head. "I can't."

"Can't, or won't?"

"This shop is too important to me. I can't let my personal feelings interfere with my business judgment. Regardless of what you have on your books now, my heart is set on the Rose Bay property, and I will do whatever is necessary to get it. Which means nurturing a personal relationship of any kind with you is not only going to be a bad idea, it's going to be pretty impossible."

He sighed. She wasn't going to change her mind anytime soon. "You were right."

"About what?"

"My not having the lease."

"So get it."

"It's not that simple."

She glared at him, invisible daggers hitting him in the chest with deadly precision.

"Parker, the other tenant, won't budge. Far as he's concerned he's signed, and the property is his."

Claire let out a low, sexy growl and swung her furious gaze away from him, staring out the window instead. She counted slowly to ten, but before she reached seven she gave a howl of indignation. "Where are we?"

"In the car."

Another dagger hit him square in the chest. "Where are we going? This is not the way back to your office."

It was the darnedest thing, but every dagger that hit him only increased his hunger for her. He liked watching Claire getting all fired up and doing her best to temper her anger. There was something extraordinarily sexy about her control, and he'd be willing to bet that getting her to lose that control would be a million times sexier.

"Didn't I mention I needed to check out a couple of properties? We're going to see another one."

Her little yelp of disbelief hit him right in the belly.

"*Uh-uh.* No, *we* are not going anywhere. You are going to take me back, and you're going to sort out the Rose Bay lease, at which point you are more than welcome to visit as many properties as you like. On your time, not mine."

Jack shook his head. "Sorry. No can do. I've already taken the off-ramp. Getting back to the East now is going to be hell. We'd have to go through the city. And with traffic, it'll take forever. Quicker just to come with me and see the next place."

Claire remained silent for a minute or two. Her fingers tapped on the door in a rhythmic beat. One tap, two taps, three taps and one again. Oh, he could imagine her tapping out that beat on his ass—with her feet—as he threw her onto his bed and took full possession of her strong body.

She reached into her bag, pulled out her iPhone and hit a few buttons. "Maddie?... Yeah... No, I didn't... Long story." She chewed on her lower lip. "Do I *sound* happy?... Yes. My point exactly... I have no idea. Driving into the inner city I think... Again, I have no idea."

Jack didn't attempt to interrupt. He listened to her side of the conversation, content to hear Claire's just-woken-up voice ringing through the car. He couldn't make out what Maddie said in response, he just heard a faint rumble through the phone.

He did not for a minute think Claire had accepted his decision to drive her to another shop. It was clear she was way too stubborn to let him convince her of anything, including agreeing with him to let the lease remain with Parker. A minute later she proved him correct.

"Here's what I need you to do, Mad. Can you phone Epstein please? Fill him in on what's been going on with the lease, find out exactly where we stand, and tell him we're willing to take whatever action is necessary to either get that property or... Uh-huh. I think we should... Look, if legal action is our only option, then that's what we'll do... Yeah. Of course you should talk to Julia first."

Her conversation continued on, and Jack knew most of what she said out loud was voiced for his benefit.

Still, Jack wasn't panicked. Yet. Probably had a lot to do with his next destination, and the fact that Miss Jones's smoky voice was tying his balls in knots again.

Ten minutes later Jack pulled into another parking spot, this time in a trendy area, not quite so up-market as Mosman.

"Glebe?" Claire looked not the least bit impressed.

"Glebe," he confirmed. "There's an empty shop I want you to see."

Sandwiched between two universities, Glebe was like a little village, crammed full of coffee shops, restaurants, vintage clothes stores and funky bookshops.

"I'm sure there is." She nodded at his door. "So why don't you go look at it, and I'll wait here in your car. When you're done, you can take me back."

"Nope."

"No?"

"I'm not going in there without you."

"Then it seems we'll both sit in the car. And if we're both just sitting here doing nothing, you might as well drive me back to my car."

"No, again."

"No?"

"See, if I'm forced to sit here beside you, I won't be doing nothing."

"What will you be doing? Trying to convince me of the delights of Glebe?"

"No, much more simple than that."

"What then?"

"You have two choices. Either I can sing out loud, to the radio or to a song of your choice..."

She pulled a sour face, telling him without words exactly what she thought about that option. "Or?"

"Or, regardless of your thoughts about getting to know me personally, I'm going to lean over and kiss you again. And this time I won't stop because we're parked on a public road."

With a vicious growl, Claire turned up the volume.

Fortunately, Jack recognized the song playing, a Katy Perry tune, and he sang in time to it. Or tried to, anyway.

"You know you have got to stop that God-awful racket?"

He shook his head. "No can do. Until you walk into the shop with me, I'll just sit singing my heart out." And with that he threw said heart and soul into the song. Pity for Claire he had no idea what the words were and had to make up his own as he went along, but the originality just added more soul.

Claire turned off the radio with a *harrumph.*

He grinned at her, and continued singing, projecting his voice as far as he could when he reached the high notes.

For the second time that day, Claire scrambled out of the car. "How old are you anyway?" she grouched as he followed suit. "Fifteen?"

"Close. Thirty-five."

"You act like a child."

Jack fell into step beside her with a triumphant wink. "Then I figure I'll be perfectly happy in your shop."

"You're welcome there anytime—just so long as you don't sing. You'll scare off my other customers."

"You'll love this place."

"I'm not interested in this place."

"I kissed a girl and I liked it."

Claire clamped her hands over her ears.

He nudged her arm out of the way. "I did like it. Heaps."

"The song?"

"The kiss. Both kisses."

"You really are fifteen."

"You really need to give this place a chance."

And in a move he didn't see coming, one he'd never have expected from the lovely Miss Jones, she placed her hands on her hips, glared in his direction and...pulled a tongue at him.

Jack snorted. And she'd had the gall to question his age? He chuckled out loud as he unlocked the door, liking Claire more with every moment that passed.

Chapter Five

Much as Claire hated to admit it, Jack was right. She did love the shop. Heaps. From outside she couldn't see much. Someone had pulled the blinds down and it was locked up tight. But Jack opened the door, revealing beautiful, polished wooden floors, bright color-washed walls and ample space to set up all their goods. There were even shelves made of beech wood lining one wall, which would serve as perfect display cases for their books.

It didn't take a lot of imagination to picture the store set up as *Li'l Books and Bits*. Without lifting a finger to renovate, they could move straight in. And the fact that it stood open only acted as an added benefit. They could take occupation immediately.

The only two problems? It was in the wrong freaking area, and it wasn't the shop Claire had set her heart on.

"Go on," Jack nudged her arm with his elbow. "Admit it. You like the place."

Claire refused to give an inch. "Yes. I do. It's a lovely shop. And whoever rents it will be lucky. But it has no bearing on me or *Li'l Books and Bits*."

He pushed the door closed. "Have you seen the back area? It's huge." He led her through, and although Claire didn't want to get excited, she couldn't help the little flare that sparked in her belly. Again, he was right. The back room was huge. More than double the size of the Rose Bay shop. And right behind it was another room, perfect for storage, which the Rose Bay shop did not have any of.

"Eight-fifty a week," Jack said. "You can have it for eight. At a nine-percent increase every year for three years."

Okay, that was an undeniable bargain. She whirled around to glare at him, then had to swallow because he looked so...damn appealing. Like a gorgeous giant. "You don't give up, do you?"

"You like the place, and if you're honest with yourself, you'll acknowledge it's a great area to set up a second store."

"Trying to avoid a lawsuit, Mr. Wilson?" Darn it. Did he have to be so big and so beautiful? It was difficult to hold on to her cool when all she wanted to do was wrap her arms around him and pull his face down to hers. Or maybe fall on top of him again so they could land in a big, tangled pile on the floor.

Refusing his dinner invitation had taken every last ounce of her willpower.

He smiled, his delicious, full lips curving at the sides, showing off his sexy dimple. Her stomach flip-flopped at the sight of it. "The only thing I'm trying to avoid is throwing you to the ground and fucking you mercilessly for the rest of the afternoon. I'll tell you something, Miss Jones, that is a battle I find myself losing quite hopelessly."

His outlandish comment whipped the breath from her lungs. Claire wanted nothing more than to be thrown to the ground by her G.G. and fucked until she could hardly stand. At this second in time, she wanted it more than the Rose Bay shop. "You're incorrigible."

He shook his head. "Nope. What I am is aroused and horny and half-blind from wanting you."

"Then you'll have a good idea how I feel about the property on New South Head Road." Yeah, it was a wimpy comment. She should have been more honest with herself and him. Should have confessed she felt the same. That all she wanted was to strip off her clothes and his and get very naked with him on this very floor at this very time.

But too many factors played against her wishes. First and foremost, the lease. Secondly, if she gave into the temptation that was Jack even once, she suspected she'd be putty in his hands forever. And third, but not least of all, Jack had switched on all the lights, and although the blinds were down, the shop couldn't have been brighter.

Which to anyone else may not have been a problem, but to Claire it was. Nudity was a big issue for her. Having been cut down by previous lovers because of her size, she'd developed an inhibition when it came to getting naked around men she desired. Experience had taught her that most men were not attracted to large women. And Claire was not small.

It was one thing arguing with Jack with her clothes on, kissing him with the cover of her shirt and skirt.

But the thought of him stripping them away terrified her. In essence it would be akin to stripping her defenses away. Clothed she could be the confident, self-possessed woman she knew herself to be. Stripped bare she could focus only on her flaws and insecurities.

Much as Claire wanted to be free of her clothes, the thought of Jack seeing every blemish in her very flawed body ensured she stayed good and truly covered up.

He looked surprised. "You lust over the Rose Bay shop?"

"I want that shop. Badly." Not quite as much as she wanted him at this moment, but badly nevertheless.

He lowered his voice. "Does it make you horny...like you make me?"

Claire cleared her throat, finding it difficult to talk. "I have no idea what I do to you so I can't answer that."

"Okay, lemme ask you more specific questions. Does the Rose Bay store make your blood race?"

She stared at him, not gracing his question with an answer. Her blood was racing all right, taking one-hundred-meter sprints whenever he spoke, but that had nothing to do with the shop.

"Does your chest get tight every time you look at it? As if taking another breath is a task too monumental to manage?"

"I'm not answering you."

"Does it start your skin tingling? Or send goose bumps racing over your flesh?" As he asked, he ran his finger over her bare arm, and a million tiny goose bumps flared to life.

Jack noticed them and smiled a sinful smile. "Same thing happens to me every time I think about you, look at you, imagine your touch on my skin, or better yet—your tongue." A shudder shook his body. "I break out in goosies." His eyes were glued to the telltale bumps on her arm. "If you ran your fingers over my back now, you'd feel them."

Claire raised her hand, intent on doing just that, on helping herself to handfuls of his firm, muscled flesh, then dropped it when she realized what she'd been about to do.

"Touch me, Claire." Jack's voice had dropped to a deep, slumberous baritone. "Run your hands over my back."

He met her gaze, and Claire couldn't look away, didn't want to. "I-I can't."

"Yes, you can."

"I shouldn't."

"So you've said. But you should. You most definitely should. Stop pretending there's nothing between us. There's more to you and me than just properties and rentals. We've moved beyond professional. We hit personal the first time your lips touched mine."

Again her hand fluttered in mid-air, then dropped back down to her side. No, she really shouldn't. It didn't matter how badly she wanted to. It wasn't just about keeping things professional between them. For Claire there was so much more at stake.

Sharing kisses with Jack might be a huge boost to her ego, and it might make her pussy weep with need and excitement, but she wasn't ready to face the disenchantment she was sure to see on his face when he got a look at her dimpled thighs and soft belly.

Claire preferred to let them both hold on to the fantasy that Jack found her attractive. Soon as he got a peek at her naked body, that fantasy would burst like a popped soap bubble.

"Claire," he demanded. "Touch my back. Please."

The huskiness in his tone could not be ignored.

Reaching up, she ran her hand over his shoulder, forcing herself not to squeeze, not to hold on and never let go. He was huge. Solid. Touching him made her insides all squishy and needy.

"No goose bumps." Her throat was almost too dry to speak.

"That's not my back."

Her hand moved by its own volition, sweeping up to his neck, brushing her fingers over the hot skin there. Ah. Yeah. Definitely goosies.

It was her turn to shiver.

He stared down at her, his green gaze compelling, trapping her. "Still not my back."

With no other choice, Claire stepped closer. She was too far away to reach his back from where she stood. As soon as she stepped forward, so did he.

"Now..." his voice was hoarse as a whisper, "touch my back."

The second she curved her hand over his shoulder and onto the swell of muscle beside his spine, he moaned. "This is personal, Claire. Very personal."

Jack ducked his head and fused their lips together.

Goose bumps were forgotten in the heat of the kiss, as were property leases and shops for rent. All Claire knew was the giant taking possession of her mouth and her will. The giant who hauled her against his body, molding his hips to hers, pressing his hands on her ass so she had no choice but to cradle his solid erection with her pelvis.

Pelvis shmelvis. That was her pussy rubbing up against his cock. Her very aroused, very alert and very wet pussy. And it was her clit that swelled in response. Her clit that sent shock waves of desire through her with every twist of his hips.

His erection caressed her tender nub, and his hand moved her ass and hips rhythmically, pushing her against him every time he thrust into her, then releasing her as he pulled back.

They rocked together in a simulation of sex. The only reason she was not stuffed full of his cock right now was the layers of clothing that separated them.

He tore his mouth from hers, panting hard, but didn't stop their erotic dance. His eyes brimmed over with lust, with a hunger so raw it sent a hot chill up her spine.

"I swear, Claire, I may only have known you a day, but it feels as though I've been waiting for you my whole life."

As she reeled from the sensuality of his words and honesty in his voice, he tripped her. Stuck his foot behind her ankle, kicked her heel off the ground and took her down.

For the second time in two days she toppled like a hippopotamus.

But she hadn't counted on his strength or his size. Where any other time she'd have landed hard, now he caught her before she hit the floor.

His arms were her safety net, and rather than dropping like a stone, she was lowered gently to her back. Even as she strove to catch her breath, he was all over her. His mouth was on hers again, nibbling greedily on her tongue and lips. His chest pinned her back to the floor, and his knees urged her legs apart. Her skirt fluttered around her thighs as Jack settled between them, and once again his cock was pressed against her pussy. He stretched out those long legs of his, placed his hands on her hips and rocked against her.

Claire was right there with him, kissing him back, giving him her tongue, her lips and her mouth. Her arms had circled his shoulders, and her hands were buried in his hair. She needed no encouragement to raise and drop her hips in time with his.

Jack may have no ear for music, but his body danced to a magical beat.

Claire began to climb again, reaching for that orgasm she'd ruthlessly suppressed yesterday. She'd have moaned in pleasure, but her mouth was occupied, otherwise entertained, enticed by his.

He must have sensed her growing excitement because he ground down harder and with more precision, zoning in on her clit, making Claire want to yell from the stimulation.

Just as she neared her peak, as her muscles tightened in anticipation and her thighs clasped tight around his legs, Jack stilled and broke their kiss again.

"Uh-uh, Miss Jones." His throaty denial almost made her cry out in frustration. "You're not coming like this. Not with me dry humping you like an animal." He arched his back and bent his knees, lifting off her.

Claire couldn't contain her shock. "No!" Damn it. Where was he going?

"Hush, beautiful," he murmured and pressed the softest kiss to her neck. "I'm not going anywhere." His hands found her shirt and swiftly undid the buttons. As he nudged her blouse open, he pressed those soft kisses over each millimeter of exposed flesh.

If Claire thought she'd had goose bumps earlier, now millions of them scuttled across her skin. Her breasts pushed against the confines of her bra and her nipples hardened into beads.

Jack raised his head to stare down at his handiwork, and instinctively Claire tried to cover herself. There was no need for Jack to see how her stomach spilled over the top of her skirt.

He shoved her hands away. "No hiding from me. Not ever. You..." His voice trailed off as her blouse opened all the way, revealing her belly.

Claire's heart dropped. That time had come. His disappointment was imminent.

She turned her head to the side and closed her eyes, not wanting to face the visual proof of his distaste.

"You..." he tried again, but seemed to have no luck voicing his displeasure.

Claire's muscles tensed, preparing for rejection. Regret swept through her. It was her own fault for letting things get this far. Her own fault for losing herself to his taste and his raw sensuality. She should just have left well enough alone, left the fantasy intact.

Tears sprang to her eyes, and she squeezed her lids shut, forcing them back. Now every time she'd have to face Jack again, she'd know she hadn't lived up to his expectations. That was if she could ever face him again. Maybe from now on Maddie could see to the lease agreement?

"Christ, Claire," Jack managed at last, his voice so hoarse she had no idea how he spoke at all. "You are beautiful."

She froze.

"So...real, so fucking sexy."

What?

His fingers grazed over her belly. "You're every man's fantasy."

She turned to look at him, opening only one eye in case he was messing with her head, but he didn't even notice. His gaze was pinned to her breasts, and his expression was one of reverence.

There was no hint of disappointment on his face. If anything, Jack seemed spellbound, entranced—by her. By her flawed body.

He raised his hand and covered her breast with it, his breath hissing out. "You're all woman, Claire. A thousand wet dreams in one perfect package." He squeezed her breast. Not hard, just enough to leave her desperate for more. "W-wanna touch you so bad." He shook his head. "But need to taste you more."

He tugged at the cup of her bra until her breast popped out, and then his head replaced his hand, and his mouth was on her breast, his lips tugging at her nipple.

Heat exploded in her belly.

His wet, warm tongue laved the sensitive bud, and his teeth nibbled around it. Claire arched her back, offering more of herself to his searching mouth, stunned to not only hear his admiration, but to feel it in his sensual suckling.

He freed her other breast, caressing it with his hand, stroking the nipple, teasing it into a sharp point before directing his mouth to the taut peak and cupping her other breast with his hand.

"Jack..." She couldn't hide the astonishment in her voice, the question in her tone. Could he really desire her so?

"Mmm?" The contentment in his mumbled response was all the answer she needed.

"N-nothing."

He released her nipple with a soft pop. "I think I'm in heaven." He smiled up at her, his eyes cloudy with desire.

"Y-you are?"

"Mmm. Oh yeah." He took both breasts in his hands, squeezed them together and ran his tongue from one nipple to the other. "You sound surprised."

She didn't answer, too shy to confess the truth.

His gaze was on her face again, clearer than it had been a few seconds ago. "Claire?" Now he was the one with a question in his tone.

She blinked and tried to twist her head away so as not to meet his prying gaze.

His question stopped her. "You have doubts that I could find you this exquisite?" He searched her eyes as though seeking the truth in their depths.

She didn't want to admit it, didn't want him to see her insecurities, but from his troubled expression, she suspected he'd already guessed the truth. All she could manage was a slight nod.

"Christ." He stared at her in disbelief. "I have an erection from hell, I can't keep my hands or mouth off you, and I'm two seconds away from tearing your skirt off and burying my cock in your incredible body, and you...you're doubting the effect you have on me?"

She closed her eyes, unable to keep looking into his altogether too perceptive ones. "I-I'm a big woman, Jack," she said, as if that would explain everything.

"I'm a big man, Claire. A lot bigger than you."

"But...you're perfect." Ah, God. This was excruciating. "A gorgeous giant."

"And you're a statuesque beauty. What's your point?"

"You don't mind my size?"

"Mind?" His laugh was one of pure incredulity. "I fucking love it." As if to prove his point, he buried his head between her breasts again and sucked lovingly on her nipples. "I love that I don't have to treat you like a porcelain doll, don't have to worry you'll break if I kiss you too hard. And I love how damn good you taste. And feel."

There was no point denying his actions. No one could invest himself in worshipping her like this if he didn't feel at least some attraction.

In seconds Claire was squirming, gasping, begging for more.

Jack gave it, releasing her breasts to leave a trail of kisses down her sternum, over her belly, to the waist of her skirt. He swirled his tongue just above her navel.

His hand found the hem of her skirt and pushed it over her thighs until cool air brushed the juncture of her legs.

"Shall I compare thee to a summer's day?"

Claire forced her fears and inhibitions aside. Forced herself to simply relish the pleasure of being touched by this man, adored by him. "You're quoting Shakespeare?" she asked on a breathless laugh.

"I am. For two reasons." He skimmed his hand over her left thigh. "One, so you never forget how truly stunning you are." His finger touched her panties, and Claire almost stopped breathing. "And two, to remind you that I'm not the ruthless property manager you think I am. There's more to me than leases and shop viewings." He raised his head to stare down at her exposed legs, and again the breath hissed from his lips, feathering over her skin, making her shiver.

"You're a teacher too. I haven't forgotten." She hadn't forgotten a single thing about him. Doubted she ever would.

"Good. Then know this is not about getting you to take a shop you don't want. It's not about distracting you from the other shop either. It's about you and me. Claire and Jack, and the attraction that neither of us seems able to deny."

"I...I can't deny anything when you look at me like that."

"Like what?"

"Like I'm breakfast."

He shook his head. "Not breakfast. Not even a summer's day. *Thou art more lovely and more temperate.*"

"Than breakfast or a summer's day?"

"Than anything I've ever seen on earth." This time when he lowered his head, it wasn't to suck on her nipples. His mouth landed firmly on her panties, exactly where her clit pulsed against the silk.

Jack pressed a soft kiss there, and Claire jerked with pleasure.

He buried his nose against her clit and inhaled, then groaned, a sound mixed with pain and exhilaration. "Fuck, you smell good."

Liquid heat pooled between Claire's legs, and she pushed her thighs open, giving up any thought of denying him access. How could she push him away when he made her body weep and her heart stutter?

How could she push anyone away when he looked at her like Jack did? When the hunger in his gaze was almost as arousing as the temptation of his lips?

"Rough winds do shake the darling buds of May,

And summer's lease hath all too short a date."

He opened his mouth and sucked her clit over her panties.

Claire gave up thinking at all. Between Shakespeare and Jack, she was a trembling sack of aroused female hormones. She dropped her head to the floor, closed her eyes and relished his sinful attack.

Big? Okay, yes. Claire was not small and fragile. Didn't mean she wasn't the sexiest woman Jack had ever met—ever had the pleasure of kissing. She deserved to have the beauty of the old bard's words showered down on her.

"Sometime too hot the eye of heaven shines,

And oft' is his gold complexion dimmed;"

Settling on his knees between her legs, he slipped his finger beneath the silk of her panties and tugged them aside, exposing her sweet pussy to his mouth.

He loved her size. Loved that he didn't have to wrap her in cotton wool for fear of hurting her. In his haste to get close to her, he'd tackled her to the floor, for God's sake. Twice.

It wasn't just a pleasant change to have a woman who could cope with his size. It was a huge fucking turn on.

Jack feasted on her clit, licking it, sucking it, kissing it and licking all over again. He did the same with her slit, spreading her pussy lips with his thumbs and licking at her juices.

"And every fair from fair sometime declines,

By chance, or nature's changing course untrimmed;"

It was hard not to notice how incredibly Claire responded to his words. Every time he quoted Shakespeare, she got a little wetter. This time she let out a choked sob and squeezed him with her thighs, the satiny soft flesh pressing against his ears. Yes, Claire was a substantial woman, but that just gave him more of her to appreciate.

"But thy eternal summer shall not fade,

Nor lose possession of that fair thou owest,"

Fuck, he struggled to talk, struggled to move his mouth far enough away from her to let the words out. He loved her taste, loved her response. Loved how she'd forgotten her shyness and inhibitions and just given herself over to his touch.

His own arousal inched up another notch—if that was possible. He was so turned on, so hot, his cock ached like the devil. If he could, he'd unzip his pants, free his cock and palm himself, just to get some relief. But this wasn't about him. This was about Claire. About making her feel as beautiful as he thought she was.

"Nor shall death brag thou wanderest in his shade,

When in eternal lines to Time thou growest."

He dragged his tongue from her clit, over her pussy and down, almost reaching her hidden rosette.

She froze. Her soft moans quieted. Even her breath was silenced. But she didn't object.

Jack grinned to himself, and wrapped that observation safely away for another time. Then he repeated the action, over and over and over, waiting for her breath to catch again and for her cries of pleasure to fill the room.

He didn't have to wait long. Her body stiffened beneath his hands. Her hips jerked against his face and she was coming. All around his tongue.

Her body convulsed in small sharp jolts and her thighs pinned his head to her pussy.

Jack licked her through her climax, tasting her pleasure, his cock throbbing in time to her release, desperate for release of his own. Long seconds passed as Claire's orgasm rippled through her. Long satisfying, frustrating seconds for Jack.

He wished he could see her face, her expression, look into her eyes. Wished he could show her his own satisfaction, his triumph in her release. But most of all he simply enjoyed her climax.

And when finally her hips dropped to the ground, her thighs slackened and she tugged on his hair, pulling him away from her pulsing pussy, he raised his shoulders, stared into her dazed eyes as he'd wanted to and said,

"So long as men can breathe, or eyes can see,

So long lives this, and this gives life to thee."

Claire's body shuddered again in what Jack suspected might be another tiny orgasm.

Still trembling, and with the exquisite vibrations of ecstasy rippling through her, Claire looked at the man who'd just taken her to new heights, and thought she might faint from bliss.

His lips were wet with her juices, and as her gaze settled on them, he wiped his mouth with a long finger, then sucked the finger clean. "Mmmm."

Claire couldn't talk. Didn't have the breath. Instead she tugged on his hair, pulling him closer. Soon as she could reach his arms, she tugged on those and then grabbed his hips and pulled him forward to exactly where she wanted him. Straddling her chest.

His eyes darkened as he looked down at her face, and his lower lip dropped open, emitting another hiss of air—a sound she was fast growing addicted to.

She would have smiled up at him, but forgot to when she got lost in his expression. As her fingers worked feverishly on his belt, tugging it open, struggling with his button and then yanking down his zip, her mind read a hundred emotions in his eyes.

Satisfaction, hunger, lust, happiness, frustration, contentment, delight, greed, need...

She stopped evaluating when her hands found his cock and freed it from the confines of his cotton boxers. Jack helped with this, pushing down his pants so she had easy access to both his impressive erection and tight balls.

He swore softly as she tentatively wrapped one hand around his thick shaft and caressed his scrotum with the other.

"Tighter," he demanded, and she closed her fist around him. "Yeah, beautiful. Like that."

His approval increased her confidence, and she held him a little more firmly still, pumping him with her fist.

Drops of pre-come beaded on his slit.

Claire raised her head and laved them away, the tang of his desire coating her tongue. God, he tasted good. Felt good too. Silky soft skin stretched taut over iron hardness.

She parted her lips, taking his cockhead into her mouth, testing its girth, running her tongue around and around, until he groaned and hitched his hips, guiding a little more of his length into her mouth.

She dropped her head back to the floor, tugging at his thighs, and he leaned over her, taking the strain off her neck.

It was all Claire needed. She gorged on him, taking as much of his length as she could manage, sucking him in deep, enveloping him with her cheeks and tongue, and releasing him in a slow, steady rhythm.

"Christ, Claire," he groaned. "What you do to me..." He dropped forward, stretching over her, taking his weight on his arms, as though doing pushups, and Claire half wished she could see his upper body, watch the muscles in his arms and shoulders flex and bulge. Only half wished, because nothing on God's earth was getting her mouth off his cock. Nothing was stopping her from giving him as much pleasure as he'd given her.

She let her finger slide past his balls to the fragile skin behind, to draw tiny, erotic circles there, and was rewarded by his thrusting into her mouth.

For a second she thought she might choke on his ample size. As it was, her jaw was stretched to the max. But she forced herself to breathe through her nose and relax her throat muscles, allowing him to slide a little deeper inside.

Still, he was a large man, and there was no way she could fit all of him in. So she once again wrapped her fist tight around his cock—this time at the base—and pumped him in time with his thrusts.

Between her fist, her mouth and her finger, she figured she had all bases covered.

Jack must have figured it as well, judging from the groans that he emitted.

"Jesus, Claire, fuck..."

His thighs turned to rock above her chest. Every muscle in his body tensed.

"Don't stop. Please, God, don't ever stop."

She didn't. Didn't drop her pace, not for a second. Not until he stiffened above her, for just the shortest of seconds. And then she took as much of him into her mouth as possible, held his cock in her tightest grip, and continued to tickle him behind his balls.

Jack came with a fierce growl. Spurt after spurt of come pulsed from his cock, filling her mouth and sliding down her throat. She waited as long as she could, until the pulses slowed and dried, and then swallowed it all.

He groaned long and loud above her. A last shudder trembled through him, before his muscles relaxed and she let him slide from her mouth. He shifted to his side, collapsing beside her on the floor.

For long moments, the only sound that filled the room was their uneven breathing.

Then he shuffled down until his head was in line with hers, leaned in, and sealed his mouth over hers. It wasn't a long kiss. Not like their previous ones. But it was fierce, it was hot, and it tasted like sex.

And when it ended, Claire knew, beyond a shadow of a doubt, that a blow job would never, ever be enough for her.

She wasn't sure how it had happened, or when, since she'd only known him two days and most of that time had been spent arguing. But when it came to Jack, she wanted a whole lot more than a magnificent orgasm on a shop floor.

Chapter Six

"I don't know," Julia said, her face thoughtful. "It might not be a bad option."

She, Claire and Maddie sat eating breakfast in a trendy coffee shop in Glebe—meters away from the property Jack had shown her yesterday.

"It's not *too* far away," Maddie offered.

"It's the other side of the city." Claire looked at them as though they were both nuts. "There's no short cut from Clovelly to Glebe."

"It's the other side of the city centre," Julia said calmly. "Not the other side of Sydney. It's not as if we'd have to travel to Parramatta. Besides, I like Glebe. It has some of my favorite restaurants. And a real funky vibe. There's something incredibly appealing about it."

Claire gestured towards the people sitting around them. "It's full of students. No wonder you like it."

Julia pulled a tongue at her. "Yeah, yeah, mock my age. Just because I finished Uni two years ago, doesn't mean I'm too young to make decisions."

"I'm not mocking your age—for once. I'm just pointing out a basic demographic of Glebe. It's full of Uni students. And Uni students are not our target market. New parents are. Different stage of life. Glebe is the wrong area."

Maddie looked up from her iPad. "I'm not convinced about that, Clairey. There's a primary school right around the corner for starters, and I've just Googled daycare centers in Glebe. There are at least a dozen in this area alone—and that figure doesn't take into account the neighboring suburbs."

"Besides, a shop here opens up business to the Inner West," Jules said. "Maybe Jack Wilson has a point."

"We spoke about the Inner West. And the Inner City and decided against both of them," Claire reminded her.

"Because we preferred the idea of Rose Bay. Glebe was still on the list of top ten suburbs that would suit our needs," Maddie reminded her. "Look, had we gotten the shop without a problem, we would have taken it. But we didn't, and I don't know about you, but I don't feel like going to court over this. Yes, I'm pissed off. But, I don't feel like spending the money on a lawsuit. Not if we have a decent alternative. I'd rather pump the money into the two shops or into buying new stock."

"And if we're talking money, you can't ignore the rental price. It's good. Too good to ignore," Julia added.

Maddie nodded. "Agreed. You said the shop was nice, Clairey?"

"The shop is perfect," she grudgingly admitted. "If we could pick it up and plop it down in Rose Bay, we'd be set for life."

"But we can't, so let's not think about that." Maddie took a sip of coffee. "I think we should take the shop if for no other reason than this is the best damn cappuccino in Sydney. I could get used to working next door to this café."

"Oh, great reason," Claire muttered, surprised her sisters were giving the shop such serious consideration. They continued debating the pros and cons of Glebe until their breakfast was done and it was time to meet Jack.

Yesterday, she'd agreed to keep an open mind and bring her sisters through to see the property before work today. Just bringing them here was a massive step for Claire, who still stubbornly held on to her beliefs they should have the Rose Bay shop. But frankly? She would have agreed to anything Jack had suggested. Her head had been so full of the delights he'd rained down on her, she'd found she couldn't refuse him a damn thing.

Feeling suddenly shy about seeing him again, Claire took care of the bill while Julia and Maddie went ahead to the shop. Yesterday they'd been caught up in the heat of passion. What if today Jack showed no interest? What if he'd woken up this morning to find the chemistry had fizzled away on his side?

It hadn't on her side. She'd fallen asleep thinking about him and woken up the same way. Save the distractions her sisters provided, he'd pretty much been on her mind since she left him at his offices yesterday.

She had another problem. What if in her excitement to see him today, she jumped him—in broad daylight, while her sisters watched? Claire almost laughed at their imagined shock. She hadn't told them anything about the personal aspect of her and Jack's relationship. Hadn't been ready to share the delicious details.

She dragged her heels paying, then took a slow stroll to the store. The door was open, and her G.G. stood inside, talking to her sisters.

Claire's heart slammed into her ribs, and her knees turned to jelly.

Her little sister, the smallest out of the three Jones girls, flirted with Jack as Maddie walked around the front room, checking out the shelving and paint work.

A wave of jealousy surged through Claire, shocking her.

Jealous? Of her own sister? Or of her sister's ability to flirt so easily, while Claire just got all inhibited around the men she desired? She cleared her throat. "Mr. Wilson."

He looked up, and a broad smile split his cheeks, showing his beautiful dimple. "Miss Jones."

His gaze swept over her body, from her face, down to her feet and back up again. Desire shone from his eyes, telling her his reaction to her yesterday hadn't been a crazy fluke. Nor had the chemistry ebbed.

"You've met my sisters, I see."

"They introduced themselves a few minutes ago."

"I love the shop, Jack," Julia announced. "Love it."

Maddie was more restrained. "I'd like to see the other rooms before making a decision."

Jack held out his hand towards the inter-leading door. "Please, go ahead. Take a look, and make sure you check out the storage section as well."

Maddie and Julia disappeared into the back room as Jack walked over to Claire. "Good morning, beautiful." His potent gaze made her breath catch.

She meant to be polite. Honestly. But the second she caught a whiff of his aftershave, of that gorgeous, woodsy scent, her manners scattered, her words vanished and instinct took over. She grabbed his tie, yanked him forward, and stole his lips in a blistering kiss.

Fortunately, Jack was quicker to respond to her advances than she'd been to his. He kissed her back with as much enthusiasm as she kissed him. The instant their lips touched, the chemistry between them sparked and heat tore through her, a scorching reminder of the passion they'd shared in the very room her sisters now explored.

Also fortunate for her, was Jack's excellent hearing, because Claire lost herself to their smoldering passion. She'd have kissed him for the rest of the day had he not pulled away with a harsh moan—an instant before Maddie walked back into the front of the shop.

"Clairey," she said, raising an eyebrow when her gaze landed on Claire. "Can you come through to the back room for a minute?"

"Sure." Claire smiled, but knew why Maddie gave her that searching look. Her cheeks burned and her lips felt swollen and thoroughly kissed. "Excuse us?" she asked Jack.

"Go ahead." He stepped out of her way.

Fortunately Maddie asked no questions, even though she flashed Claire an I-know-what-you-just-did grin.

It took less than a minute to gauge what her sisters wanted, and Claire knew it wouldn't matter how stubborn she was, this particular fight was one she was going to have to give in to.

"We have to take the shop," Julia insisted.

"It's perfect," Maddie agreed. "Absolutely perfect. We could open for business next week. All we need to do is move in, set up shop and put up a sign."

"Sign the lease," Julia urged. "Ask if we can add a clause based on profitability. If, as you feared, the store does not break even after the first year, then we can have an option of terminating the lease. Just so we don't tie ourselves into a contract we may not want in twelve months, but I don't think that will happen. Just sign the damn papers."

"And give up the Rose Bay shop?" This for Claire was the crux. Admitting there was an alternative scenario she hadn't considered. A viable alternative.

"The Rose Bay shop has nothing on this," Maddie said. "Apart from location, this store is better in every way."

Claire looked from one sister to the other and didn't bother arguing. They were right. About everything. She'd just been so inflamed by the other shop being signed out from under her nose, she hadn't been prepared to let it go.

Jack had done the impossible. He'd convinced her—and her sisters—that they didn't have to have the Rose Bay store. Glebe *was* a good area to open their shop. Maybe not the best, but she suspected they'd do well here.

Which was fantastic for business, but it opened up a whole new problem for her.

If she signed the lease, she'd have no reason to meet with Jack again after he handed over the keys. His grandfather would return to work, and Claire would deal with the old man from then on.

That meant either she and Jack went their separate ways—an idea she hated—or they tried to get to know each other on a personal level, independently of leases and property viewings—an idea that scared the bejeepers out of her.

Great choice.

At Maddie's insistence, Claire drove with Jack back to his offices. Because there was an amendment to the lease—an option to break the agreement after a year, which he'd agreed to even though he suspected it wasn't standard practice—the papers needed to be reprinted, and everyone decided it would be best to get it done and signed as soon as possible.

Maddie and Julia shot off to open *Li'l Books and Bits,* with Jack's promise that he'd deliver Claire there as soon as business was taken care of.

If he was going to keep his promise, he'd have to deal with the personal stuff first. And he did. The second they walked into the office, Jack closed the door behind him, thanking the powers that be that Big Jack worked alone.

Without giving her a chance to look around, he tossed his briefcase to the floor, backed Claire up against the wall and kissed her like he'd wanted to kiss her since they'd said goodbye the previous day. He fucked her mouth with his tongue, in a hungry, almost savage kiss that had blood gushing to his cock and Claire gasping erotically.

The small talk in the car hadn't dampened his passion one jot. If anything, listening to her speak in her just-woke-up voice while trapped in a confined space only fed his desire.

Her sincere thank you had warmed his heart, and her confession that he'd been right about the Glebe shop had done wonders for his confidence.

Perhaps he could make it successfully in this business. Perhaps, if he did consider it a long-term option, he could help the business thrive and grow. Knowing he'd found a good property for the Jones sisters felt fantastic. One day, Jack might even be able to get used to this kind of work.

He'd never love it as much as he loved teaching, never feel a passion for it. But he'd be able to afford a whole lot more. Like settling down and starting a family...an idea that curiously held endless appeal now that he'd met Claire.

His hands worked on her shirt, yanking it from her pants and tugging it up her waist and over her breasts. For a split second he regretted having to release her lips, but the benefits of hauling the shirt over her shoulders far outweighed the temporary absence of her mouth.

"I guess this means we're doing the personal thing after all," Claire said as she helped him, shimmying out of the offensive material.

"I've been doing the personal thing with you since you walked into the Rose Bay shop." He sealed their lips back together again.

Jack didn't leave it at that. Not when his hands itched to hold the full weight of her breasts. Yesterday his access had been limited by her bra. Today, he reached behind her, unclipped the hooks and tossed the bra to the other side of the room.

When his hands found her ample breasts and cupped them, he again had to break the kiss. This time because a ragged moan tore from his throat.

Heavy, soft, round, womanly.

Christ, he never wanted to let them go. He'd be content to caress them for eternity. He pulled away from her to admire her semi-nudity. Admire Claire with nothing obstructing his view from the waist up.

Immediately her arms covered her chest.

Her actions had shocked him yesterday and they shocked him again today. That she was shy and uncomfortable with her magnificent body was a crime. A sin. No woman who looked like she did should be inhibited or hide behind her clothes or her arms.

"No." His voice was harsh. "Don't cover up. Not from me. Not ever."

She looked up at him, uncertainty clear in her eyes.

"Claire," he whispered. "You're beautiful. Perfect. You have to believe that."

Her smile was shy. "You make me feel beautiful."

"Hold on to that feeling. Remember it always. Because whether I'm around or not—and I plan to be around a lot—you should always feel beautiful."

Her expression changed. From shy to...naughty? Damn, was that mischief he spied in her eyes?

Her next actions confirmed that it was indeed mischief. Instead of covering herself, she cupped her breasts, holding them together, so when Jack dropped his gaze to her chest once more, he was greeted with two plump, glorious globes thrusting up to meet him and two distended nipples peeking back at him.

He buried his head in their fullness, rubbing first one cheek against a breast and then the other against her second breast. When he could restrain himself no longer, he took her nipple in his mouth and sucked, making Claire whimper.

She did not remain idle. No, Claire's hands were busy.

"It's not fair that you're the only one who gets to play," she told him.

Her fingers were on his button, his fly, and his pants were being pushed over his hips and down his legs. Not just his pants, his boxers as well. He kicked off his shoes and the pants and boxers fell to the floor. He didn't give them another thought.

How could he, when Claire's hot fist had closed over his engorged cock? When her thumb dabbed at the slit on his cockhead, rubbing pre-come over it?

"I want to have some fun as well."

Jesus, skilled as her hand might be, tempting as it was, he wanted more. Not her hand. Not her mouth. He wanted to bury himself in her pussy. In the same sweet, wet, swollen pussy he'd feasted on yesterday.

Without releasing the nipple he currently laved, he imitated Claire's actions, undoing her pants and shoving them down her legs.

Soon as her knickers reached her knees, he swirled his finger over her pussy lips, and nearly fell to his knees when warm liquid spilled onto his hand.

She laughed hoarsely. "What? No Shakespeare today?"

Jack shook his head, distracted. He could hardly remember who Shakespeare was at this point, let alone identify appropriate quotes. "My head's so full of you right now, Miss Jones, I can't think of anything else."

He buried his finger deep, deep inside her channel, making Claire shudder.

"Jack..." Her voice was a breathless whisper, and he could only assume his finger made her forget Shakespeare too.

He buried a second finger inside her, loving the smooth slide, glorying in the spasm that ripped through her inner walls, trapping his fingers for just a second.

"Oh, dear God. That feels good."

Fuck, she was wet. So wet. So tempting. He rubbed his thumb over her clit, and his name tore from her throat.

Her fist pumped his dick, clasping him tight in its warm grasp, making him see stars.

He slipped his wet fingers from her pussy, and remembering her response to his teasing yesterday, slid his hand backward, between the full globes of her buttocks, and found her hidden hole, caressing it.

She stopped breathing. Her fist stilled around his erection.

Jack dipped his finger inside her, knuckle deep, and Claire yelped.

The sound resonated through him, sending a fresh surge of blood to his cock.

"Jack," she moaned, his name a desperate plea. "Please, God. Fuck me now."

For a split second, Jack blanked. The world went black. Claire's begging did something to him. Made molten lava rise in his balls. Turned him on in ways he never knew a man could be turned on. The woman who had threatened him with legal action, who had refused to get involved with him in case she had to involve a lawyer in their relationship, now begged.

The statuesque and beautiful Miss Jones wanted him to fuck her? Who was he to refuse? How could he refuse when images of spending the rest of his life giving her pleasure danced through his imagination?

Easing his finger from her hole, he dropped to his knees, scrambled for his pants, found his wallet, and thanked God he had the common sense to keep a condom in there at all times.

In a heartbeat, his dick was covered, and he was back on his feet, his mouth pressed to Claire's, his hand on her ass, urging her closer.

She spread her thighs, wrapped a leg around one of his, opening herself up to his searching cock. Her hand was on his erection, holding it, rubbing it, steering it towards her.

And then he was there. Poised on the brink, his cockhead brushing her pussy lips, his heart pounding in his ears.

Jesus, he wanted this. Wanted it more than he wanted air. Wanted Claire more than he wanted his next breath. He couldn't believe he'd known her just three days. Couldn't seem to remember a time he'd not lusted after her.

"Do it," she insisted, no hint of the shy, inhibited woman he'd undressed moments ago. This was a confident Claire, a lover who knew what she wanted. Demanded it. "Fuck me."

She tilted her hips towards him, and Jack was lost. He did the only thing he could have done, the only thing he wanted to do. He thrust upwards and drove inside her, thunderstruck by the ecstasy that surged through him as he seated himself balls deep in her hot channel.

Jesus, fuck. Even through the condom, her heat assaulted his senses. She was tight. So fucking tight, her pussy squeezing his cock. Clutching it in a loving grasp that blew his mind and made him want to come there and then.

Claire showed him no mercy, gave him no time to recover. She rocked her hips back, sliding right off his cock, leaving just the tip inside her, then lunged back down, enveloping him once more.

"Not gonna last, beautiful," he gasped. "Not even gonna make a minute if you keep on like that."

"Don't need...stamina, my gorgeous...giant." Her voice was as breathless as his. "Just need you to fuck me."

There was no holding back after that. No going slow. Jack grasped her hips, loving their curves and feeling undying gratitude for their size and sturdiness. He could hold on for dear life as he drove into her.

And drive into her he did, propelling his cock inside her, plunging in deep and pulling back with uncontrolled momentum—a new experience for him, a freedom he'd never had with other women.

She met him stroke for stroke, matching his eagerness and his strength, crying out as he filled her to the max and complaining as he withdrew. She used his body to balance her own, hanging on to him so her leg didn't slip as she rocked against him.

Just like he'd imagined her doing that first morning they'd met, she dug her nails into his back, scratching at his flesh. He relished the sting, loved the burn. The pain only increased his pleasure, and he drove into her harder, faster.

Jack did not restrain himself. Did not temper his strokes for fear of causing her injury with his size. She was more than his equal, more than capable of taking whatever he gave, and giving it back in equal measure. He slammed into her repeatedly, his cock surging as deep inside her as he could get.

It didn't last long. Couldn't last long. Impossible to sustain this kind of pressure.

Jack's balls constricted. Come bubbled within. His cock was stiff as a fucking pole, and he was surrounded by heaven.

"Gonna come, Claire," he warned, wishing he could hold out until she reached her peak, but realizing he was incapable of staving off the inevitable. "Can't hold back."

"Come," she moaned. "Do it. Come."

That was all it took. Jack plunged into her twice more and lost control. He climaxed, just like she insisted, his orgasm tearing through his shaft, semen spurting from his cock.

And as he exploded inside her, she came apart around him. Her inner muscles clamped down on his pulsing shaft, a tight glove holding him, milking him, making him come even harder.

He'd never experienced such a powerful orgasm. Never felt dizzy after sex.

But by the time his breathing began to normalize, his heart slowed to a sprint and his cock shrunk down to half its size, Jack was giddy. High. Intoxicated by his Amazonian beauty.

And if truth be told, already more than a little in love with her.

Chapter Seven

As they'd arranged after signing the lease, Claire made her way across the pier, seeking a small white fishing boat with a black canopy and the name *Big Mac* painted on its side.

She wondered briefly why it wasn't called *Big Jack*.

Jack had invited her to go fishing with him. Since it was a Saturday during school holidays, and Julia's turn to mind the shop, Claire was free. Which meant she and Jack could spend the entire day together.

She inhaled nervously. It was one thing arguing about property agreements and leases or poking fun at his terrible voice. She'd had nothing invested in Jack at the time.

But all that had changed now. Jack had put himself out for her. Displayed an amazing amount of confidence in his ability to make things right after messing up the Rose Bay lease agreement. He'd found her a shop he knew she'd love, and saved her and her sisters from filing a lawsuit and spending time and money on searching for another shop. Yes, he'd done it as much for himself as for her, but she suspected he'd honestly wanted to correct his mistake, and she appreciated that about him.

Jack had also seen her naked. One hundred percent nude, with not a stitch of clothing in sight. And he'd loved what he'd seen. Made her feel like a million dollars—a billion dollars. He'd instilled a sense of confidence in her. For the first time in forever, instead of hiding her body, she'd been proud to display it. And she couldn't wait to display it again. Maybe tonight?

The man had crept into her heart. She didn't know how he'd done it, or when, she just knew a little piece of her heart now belonged to him. Apart from the sensational sex, she genuinely liked him— everything about him. And that didn't just mean his size. She liked his humor and his caring, liked his sensitivity and his strength, liked that he could poke fun at himself and collapse at her feet when emotion overwhelmed him. She just liked Jack. Very much.

And in liking him, she'd invested in him. Invested her emotions in him. She wanted to spend time with him. Wanted to know him in all ways—not just sexually and professionally. She just hoped he wanted it as much as she did.

She found the *Big Mac* a couple of minutes later, identifying it by the massive man on board. Her knees turned weak at the sight of him. Up until now, he'd only worn formal pants and ties around her. Today he was dressed in jeans and a T-shirt that hugged his muscles and made her legs grow weak.

Oh, yeah. She had it bad.

As soon as he saw her, he took the cooler bag from her hands— the one she'd stuffed full with yummy food and treats for them to share as they spent the day on the water—set it on the deck, and helped her on board.

"Hey, beautiful." His voice sounded rough. A little off, as though he hadn't slept last night, but she didn't have time to analyze it or his expression. She had only a few seconds to notice the grey smudges around his eyes before he pulled her into his arms and held her there.

Held her tight. Held her close. Didn't release her for a very long time. Which would have been perfectly fine with her—she relished the feel of his hard body pushed against hers, loved how beautifully they fitted together—if she didn't sense something was wrong. Very wrong.

There was an unmistakable tension in his shoulders, and his breath was uneven, maybe too slow.

Even so, he held her as though he'd never let go, inhaled as though inhaling a little part of her.

"Jack?" She ran her hand up his back and down again, instinct telling her to keep her touch soothing. "Are you okay?"

He nodded against her hair. "Just want to hold you for a while. *Need* to hold you."

Though he pulled her even closer, so her breasts were squashed against his chest and they stood thigh to thigh, there was nothing sexual about his embrace. She got the impression he sought...comfort. Maybe even strength.

"Hold away," she whispered. "I'm not going anywhere."

Long moments later a sigh rippled through her hair. "God knows you calm me, Miss Jones." He gave her one more tight squeeze then released her slowly, placing a gentle kiss on her lips.

He didn't say anything more. Didn't explain why she'd felt knots in his muscles. Didn't elaborate on how or why her touch calmed him. He simply busied himself preparing for their departure, not giving her an opportunity to ask questions.

She didn't push him on the issue. If Jack wasn't ready to talk, then Claire was okay to just let him be—so long as her presence comforted him.

A minute before he steered the small boat out of the Rose Bay Marina, he held his arm open to her. "Come stand with me."

She made her way over to him and let him position her in front of him, her back against his chest, his arms stretching around her to direct the wheel.

Neither of them spoke as he expertly guided them past the hundreds of other boats and into open water. It was a beautiful, sunny day. Not too hot and not a breath of wind, save the air that rushed past them as the boat slipped through the water. A perfect day to spend on Sydney Harbour.

Claire still sensed the quietness in Jack, a need to just be. Whatever worried him still showed itself in his silence and his stance. And in the soft sigh that echoed through her ear. Even the air whistling around them could not conceal its melancholy.

Her chest constricted, and she turned to place a soft kiss on his neck.

He just tightened his hold on her and focused on the water ahead.

An hour later, when Jack had anchored the boat in a quiet cove, baited two rods and given her a quick lesson in fishing, they sat side by side, on two fold-up chairs. Seagulls squawked above them, looking on in hopeful anticipation of a big catch.

But her mind wasn't on the fishing or the seagulls. It was on the man beside her.

His color was off. It wasn't just the grey smudges around his eyes. He was paler than usual. And his mouth, usually so quick to twitch into a smile and show off that gorgeous dimple, had been set in a straight line the whole boat ride.

Jess Dee

As though sensing her gaze on him, he turned to look at her. It was then that she saw it. Then that he *allowed* her to see it. The ocean of grief in his beautiful green eyes.

Pain stabbed at her chest. She would have reached out and taken his hand, but his were wrapped firmly around his rod. So firmly, his knuckles had turned white.

"Jack—"

"He died."

"Pardon?"

"My pop. He died last night."

"Oh...my God."

"As I was leaving the hospital. I'd said goodbye. Promised to visit again this morning. I was in my car, and my phone rang."

"But...but I thought he was improving. Thought he was getting better every day?"

"It was another heart attack. A massive one. He never stood a chance. They tried to revive him, but it was already too late. By the time I got back to his room, the crash cart was just sitting there, useless." He laughed, a hollow, empty sound. "You know those paddles you see on TV? On *ER* or *Grey's Anatomy*? They used them on my pop. But they didn't help."

It was the expression on his face that got Claire out of her seat. His eyes were bleak, desolate. He looked lost. As though his anchor had been ripped out from under him, and he now bobbed on a directionless tide.

She rested her rod on the floor, crouched beside his seat, and placed her hands on his thigh. "I'm so sorry," she whispered. "So very, very sorry."

"He's my favorite person in the world," Jack said. "W-was my favorite person." His voice broke, and it took a while before he could speak again. "He raised me. While my parents worked, while they were too busy, my pop brought me up. Me and my brother."

He had a brother?

"He taught me to fish. Took me out every weekend. We spent hours together on this boat. Hours." His shoulders shook. "I'd hoped we'd go out again after his surgery. When he was stronger. When I didn't have to fear hooking a large fish would cause another heart attack." His breath turned raspy. "Jesus, Claire. I thought he was better. Thought I'd be fishing with him for years to come. But...but I won't." A shudder wracked his body. "He's dead. Big Jack is dead. Now my favorite person's gone."

With precise, but jerky motions, Jack reeled in his line, clipped his hook safely over his string—leaving the bait dangling from it—and finally laid the rod on the floor. In one stilted motion he stood, turning to face Claire.

She stood too, instinctively holding open her arms.

Jack took one look at them and his face crumpled.

Claire didn't hesitate, didn't stop to think. She just grabbed him, pulling him close, clasping him to her heart. "I've got you. You're safe now. You're okay. Let it out. Let it all go."

He shook his head, holding himself rigid.

"Grieve for your pop, Jack. Let the tears come. Don't hold them back anymore."

Still he refused.

She stroked his hair. "I'll hold you, my giant. We'll do this together. Your grandfather's gone, but you don't have to mourn alone. I'm here for you."

As though every last bit of his self-control disintegrated, he dropped his head to her shoulder, let out an agonized cry and began to weep.

And true to her promise, she held him through his grief. Held him as sobs wracked his body and his tears soaked her shirt. Held him as tremors shook through him, supporting him when he was incapable of supporting himself and giving him her strength when he had none of his own.

She held him forever, until his tears finally ran dry and only dry sobs wracked his shoulders, and then she held him some more, until his body stilled and a hesitant peace seemed to creep into him.

His muscles relaxed beneath her arms, and his breath no longer came in shallow, shaky spurts. After an eternity, he turned his face to hers, a world of sadness shimmering in his gaze. But at least the worst of the storm was over.

She brushed his hair from his face. "You doing okay?"

He nodded. "Getting there. Slowly."

"There's no hurry, you know? Take as long as you need."

"I'm okay for now. Thanks to you."

"I didn't do anything."

"You were here for me."

"You needed me."

"I did. It's like I said earlier. You calm me, Miss Jones. When you're near, I... *I feel within me a peace above all earthly dignities, a still and quiet conscience.*"

"Shakespeare?"

"Shakespeare."

"Do you have any Shakespeare quotes for your grandfather?"

Jack's eyes slid shut, and for a long time he didn't answer. "Just one," he said at last.

Claire waited in silence.

"*Good night, sweet prince, and flights of angels sing thee to thy rest.*"

"Would you like to go back to shore? Spend some time with your family?"

Jack was still pale, and Claire ached for him. They sat cross-legged on the deck, the food she'd brought along spread between them. She doubted he had much appetite. He'd picked up a bread roll, but instead of eating it, Jack methodically tore off small pieces and one by one, dropped them on his plate, probably unaware he even held the roll.

He shook his head. "No. I spent the whole night with my parents, first at the hospital and then at their house. This is where I want to be now. On the water, where I feel closest to him."

The whole night? "Did you get any sleep?"

"Tried, but every time I closed my eyes I saw him, lying in his bed. His eyes closed, his face blank." He tore off another strip of the roll. "I held his hand, you know. After he... Afterwards. He was still warm. Still...still looked like my pop, just older. Years and years older."

Claire imagined Jack would see that picture of his grandfather in his mind for years to come. "Did you speak to him?"

"I did. A bit. Said goodbye. Thanked him. Told him I'd miss him." His eyes filled again, but he blinked back the tears. "He didn't hear me."

Claire's own eyes filled. "At least you got to say goodbye. That's a big thing."

"It is, I guess."

"Is there anything you would have said or done differently last night? Anything that would have given you comfort today?"

Jack thought about her question. Then smiled, a quirky, sad smile. "I'd have stopped in at Maccas on the way to the hospital. Bought him a Big Mac."

She blinked in surprise. "McDonalds?"

"The old man loved their burgers. Asked for one in the hospital. If I'd known last night it would have been his last meal, I'd have moved heaven and earth to get it." He grinned then. "I swear my pop would have put off death by a few minutes just to take that last bite."

"Tell me he didn't name this boat after a hamburger?"

"He did." Jack chuckled. "Had the name painted on the side before he even told me he'd bought a new boat." Jack stared at her in wonder. "Look at me. My grandfather's dead, and I'm sitting here laughing."

She squeezed his hand. "Don't stop. You're laughing from the joy your grandfather gave you. It's all part of grieving for him. Remembering the good while experiencing the bad."

He sobered. "Sounds like you understand death all too well."

"I do." Her heart heaved. "My mother died of cancer about eighteen months ago. Hard as that time was, and believe me, it was terrible, we also laughed a fortune. Me and my dad and my sisters. Remembering the good times and the fun parts and Mum's quirks... I swear, we laughed 'til we cried." She smiled at him. It was her turn to quote a classic. "*When you are sorrowful, look again in your heart, and you shall see that in truth you are weeping for that which has been your delight.*"

Jack looked up in surprise. "That's not Shakespeare."

"Kahlil Gibran, *The Prophet.*"

He gazed into her eyes for a long time. "Thank you, Miss Jones."

"For what?"

"Helping me find a reason to smile today. Because it's true. My grandfather was a delight."

"It's my pleasure."

"He liked you."

"Your grandfather?"

"Yep. Told me he got a good feeling about you."

Claire smiled. "That's nice to hear."

"I told him the same thing. I have a good feeling about you too."

"That's very nice to hear."

They spent the rest of the day on the boat, fishing and talking. Jack told Claire about Anthony, who, just as devastated about Big Jack's death as he was, was flying into Sydney tomorrow in time for the funeral. He voiced his concerns about his grandfather's business, and what would come of it now.

Jack discussed the pros and cons of running his grandfather's business on a fulltime basis. With his grandfather's death, the decision could not be put off any longer. It wasn't a matter of slowly learning the work. It was a matter of diving in headfirst, and running the one-man show.

Also, Wilson Property Management was his pop's company, his dream. If Jack didn't head it up from now on, what would happen to it? What would happen to the dream? Big Jack had given him a dream childhood, encouraged him to follow his dreams and teach. How could Jack let him down by destroying his pop's dreams?

Still, as much of a motivating factor as the money was, and as much as Jack hated the idea of his pop's dream dying with the old man, the thought of giving up teaching—his own dream—still made his stomach cramp.

Claire had no answers for him, but talking to her helped him voice everything he'd kept inside for so long, and it felt good just to express it finally.

At some point during their conversation, Claire got a bite on her hook, but was so horrified at the thought of injuring and killing the black bream, she begged Jack to free it and throw it back.

And when the setting sun forced them back to the marina, Claire insisted Jack come home with her. She cooked him dinner, and to his surprise, he ate every last morsel, finding himself suddenly starving. Then she ran him a bath and made him soak in it for ages, even topping it up with hot water twice.

There were many moments during the day that Jack thought he may have found a new favorite person in his life. No, Claire could never replace his grandfather. But she sure did help fill the emptiness his pop's death had left in his heart.

It was when they climbed into bed that night, sleeping together for the first time, that Jack knew he was right. She wrapped herself around his back, once again offering him her comfort and security, and he closed his eyes, expecting to see Big Jack's lifeless face. Instead he felt only calm.

Moments before he slipped into dreamless oblivion, lines from a D. H. Lawrence novel danced through his head.

"All hopes of eternity and all gain from the past he would have given to have her there, to be wrapped warm with him in one blanket, and sleep, only sleep. It seemed the sleep with the woman in his arms was the only necessity."

Indeed, sleep with Claire was all he needed right now.

Chapter Eight

Four weeks made a huge difference to Jack's mood and life. He no longer felt quite so raw or so torn apart. He'd begun to come to terms with his grandfather's death, although he doubted he'd ever grow accustomed to missing him.

What hurt the most was the permanence of death. Sure, he'd missed Anthony while he'd been in Perth. But he'd known his brother would come back. He'd also known he could pick up the phone and talk to him whenever the urge struck.

His grandfather was gone forever. And wherever he was now, there were no phone lines. There was no way of contacting him. None at all.

Thank God for Claire over these past few weeks. A mere month ago he hadn't even known her, and now she'd become his rock. His voice of reason. His calm. Even while she and her sisters had worked their hands to the bone to prepare their new store for the grand opening, she'd had all the time in the world for him.

They'd spent hours together discussing his future. She'd helped him put his work in perspective, decide what path to take and determine what was most important in his life.

"So I was over at Wilson Property Management offices today," he told her now.

Claire looked up in surprise. She held the knife she'd been chopping carrots with. "You were?"

"Anthony asked me to drop by. Said he needed to discuss some things with me."

"How did it feel, going back there?"

Since he'd been back at school for the last few weeks, he hadn't had time to pop into the office. "Okay. I guess I'd gotten used to being in the office without the old man while he was in the hospital, so his absence today didn't hit me as hard as I thought it would."

"That's good. Progress even." She chopped another carrot before lifting a board full of diced veggies and tossing them in a pot.

Jack enjoyed spending his evenings at Claire's place. Loved her cooking. She'd made him several meals now, each one more delicious than the last. He'd tried to repay her in kind, but one look at her face after she'd tasted his spaghetti bolognaise, and they'd come to a mutual decision that she'd do the cooking thereafter.

"So what did Anthony want?"

"To tell me what he'd found while going through all the books and files."

Claire added chicken pieces to the pot, covered it, checked the temperature, then gave Jack her full attention. "And what was that?"

"That my grandfather had a total of seventy-one properties on file. Each and every one of which he owned."

Claire's jaw dropped. "He what?"

"He owned them. All of them."

"Seventy-one properties in Sydney?"

"Yep."

"Their combined value must be staggering."

"To say the least."

"Are they all leased?"

"Most of them. About ten are still standing open."

"Holy shit," Claire said, pretty much mimicking his response earlier.

"Know what's even more staggering?"

"I can't think *anything* could be more staggering than that."

"Just one thing. He left all of those properties to Anthony and me."

Claire opened her mouth, then closed it again, as if at a loss for words. "Holy shit," she uttered once more. "You're rich."

He laughed. "Very." The irony of the situation was not lost to him. For so long he'd debated the idea of giving up teaching so he could finally earn enough money to buy his own property.

Now, when he'd finally decided that he needed job satisfaction more than he needed to buy his own place, he discovered he didn't just own one property, he co-owned seventy-one of them.

"Is this going to affect your decision? About working in the business, I mean?"

Jack shook his head. "No. I considered it again today, but property management is not my dream. It doesn't turn me on. I'm a teacher, Claire. It's what I was always meant to do. What I love. I can't give that up to follow my grandfather's dream, and I think he'd be furious with me if I did." It had taken heaps of soul searching before he'd come to a final decision about working in the business.

Heaps of soul searching, heaps of Claire-Jack time and heaps of in-depth discussions with Anthony.

They'd concluded that Anthony would take over the company—an idea that excited his brother no end. The first order of business had been hiring a secretary and an assistant property manager. Someone to take care of the paperwork and someone to help go through each property on the books and determine what needed to be done with it, if anything.

Claire's smile shone from her eyes. "So I can count on you to keep citing the great playwrights to me?"

"At least until I run out of quotes."

"Good. I've grown kind of fond of your soliloquies." She walked over to him, took his cheeks in her hand and pressed a kiss to his lips. "I'm glad you didn't give up on your dream, Jack. Your students would have missed you."

"Not as much as I'd have missed them." He caught her mouth in another kiss, one that lasted a lot longer. "Ah, I almost forgot. I found something while I was at the offices. Something I think you'll be happy to see."

"What is it?"

"Close your eyes. I'll surprise you."

Her lids fluttered closed.

"Now put your hands together in front of you."

Immediately she cupped her hands, waiting for him to put something in them.

He grinned and pulled it from his pocket. But instead of placing it in Claire's hands, he wrapped one end around her wrists, tying them together.

"What the...?" Her eyes flicked open in surprise. "My scarf?"

"Yep. You left it in the Rose Bay shop that first day, after you'd wrapped it around my shoulders to keep me warm."

She laughed. "Didn't do a very good job, now did it? It's too insubstantial to provide any warmth."

"It did a great job, believe me. Surrounding me with your scent didn't just get me warm, it got me hot and horny."

"Can you untie it now?" She held her arms up to him.

He shook his head. "Nope."

"No?"

"Nope. See, that scarf is still getting me all hot and horny. And wrapped around your wrists like that, leaving you bound and helpless, it's giving me all sorts of ideas." He tugged on the other end of the scarf, walked to the opposite side of the table and tied the wisp of material to a chair.

"Really?" Claire gave him the evil eye. "You're really doing this?" The scarf was long, but not long enough that Claire could stand upright. She was forced to lean over the table.

Jack walked back around to her, admiring the luscious curve of her ass in this position. He grew hard just contemplating everything he had in mind. "Oh, yeah, beautiful. We are really doing this."

Claire snorted. "I've heard of barefoot, pregnant and in the kitchen, but tied to the kitchen table is a new concept for me."

He leaned over her to nuzzle her cheek, making sure he caressed her ass with his erection in the process. He also pressed his weight down on her back, flattening her chest on the table. "I'm not just *tying* you to the kitchen table, Miss Jones." His hands were on her sides, molding to the hourglass curves of her waist. "I plan to fuck you on top of it too."

"Y-you do?" It wasn't nerves or inhibitions that made Claire's voice tremble. She'd lost all sense of shyness around him over the last few weeks. Every time they made love, and they made love a lot, Claire seemed to relax more and more about her body. In fact, last night she'd had no trouble flaunting it in front of him, dancing naked to his tuneless singing, making him half crazy with lust.

She'd given him a whole new view of the tango. A dirty—filthy actually—view that he couldn't wait to grab another glimpse of.

No, the tremor in her voice was excitement. Pure and simple. The wash of goose bumps over her neck told him as much. As did her sudden sharp inhalation of breath. "I most certainly do."

He slipped his hands beneath her belly, undoing the zip and button of her pants. Then ever so slowly, he tugged her pants over her hips, and down her legs, making good and sure to take her knickers too. He paused after exposing each inch of skin, stopping to admire her shape, her womanliness. Stopping to press tiny kisses to her bare skin and nip provocatively at her buttocks.

She moaned and clutched the far edge of the table with her bound hands, shimmying her hips, trying to get her pants off.

"Uh-uh." He smacked her butt. Not hard, just enough to leave the slightest sting, and she gasped in response. "We do this on my time."

He nuzzled the pink skin he'd just slapped before dropping to his knees, moving down her legs and paying attention to her thighs and the back of her knees. He took his sweet time, enjoying every inch of her, loving her response, her taste, her moans. Loving the way she trembled beneath his hands and lips, and begged him for more.

When at last the lower half of her torso was nude, free of pants and shoes and socks, he smacked her other buttock. Again, not too hard, just enough to leave a sting. A little pain always increased the pleasure.

"Spread 'em," he demanded in a guttural voice, sounding not at all like himself.

She showed him the slightest hint of her wet, puffy pussy and her puckered, pink hole.

"Wider."

Her breath hissed from her, and she obeyed, letting him see exactly how aroused she was. Her pussy lips glinted beneath the kitchen light, wet from her juices.

He rubbed her buttock, easing the sting. "Much better," he praised. Christ, she looked good enough to eat.

Jack grabbed handfuls of her buttocks, spread them as wide as he could, knelt behind her and helped himself to a taste of her sweet cream.

No, a taste would never do. He helped himself to as much of her as he could, licking her juices away, gorging himself on her ripe lips, pushing his tongue into her channel, seeking more of her nectar.

Claire shivered around him, begging him for more. And he gave it, dipping his finger inside her, wetting it and then gliding it back, from her pussy to her ass, until he found that puckered hole, and let his finger play to its heart content.

Tonight he would make Claire his—in every possible way. Starting with her pussy, then claiming her ass, and after, demanding her heart. She had his. Absolutely and completely. It was only fair she give him hers.

"Jack..." Her legs began to shake, and she pushed against his finger, twisting her hips. He gave her an inch, slipping it inside just past the first knuckle, and continuing to lick her pussy.

The tension rose in her. Her muscles flexed, relaxed then flexed again. Her knees locked together and her torso began to quiver.

Jack placed one last, chaste kiss on her delicious lips, and withdrew from her altogether, almost laughing when she swore viciously at him.

Almost laughing. But his cock ached like the devil and blood boiled in his veins and humor was the last thing on his mind.

"Damn it, Jack," Claire groaned. "Don't you dare stop. Not now." She couldn't believe he'd pulled away. Seriously, the man seemed to have orgasm radar. Soon as he sensed hers approaching, he backed off, leaving her stranded, so close to coming she wanted to scream, yet unable to reach her peak without him.

"Giving me orders, Miss Jones?" He must have taken a step back, because now she couldn't feel any part of him.

"You bet I am," she huffed. "Get back here right now."

He smacked her on the ass, harder than before. It hurt like the devil, and reverberated all the way through her pussy and clit, like a red-hot wave of pain and pleasure. A fresh gush of liquid seeped from her channel.

"You should know by now, I don't take orders too well."

Claire considered swearing at him, but didn't. He'd probably smack her again, and as tantalizing as the smacks were, it wasn't his hand she wanted on her ass.

She tried a different tactic. "Please, Jack. I'm begging you. Don't leave me hanging." With any other man, she'd have been too proud to beg. Or too inhibited. But Claire had learned that Jack loved it. It inflamed his passion to greater heights. And when he was inflamed, he ensured she was too.

He rubbed her buttocks. "I won't leave you hanging, Clairey. I swear it." As though sealing his promise, he swiped his finger over her pussy, slipping it just between her lips as he did, and then dragging it back over her anus. "I love you too much to do that."

A tremor shook her body, and her heart smashed into her chest. What did he say?

"But I need to get something. So I'm going to leave you here, with your hands tied to the chair, while I find it. When I come back, I want to see your pussy wet and ready for me."

What the...? He'd just told her he loved her, and was following the confession up with orders? Really? "You can't just say something like that and then walk away."

He laughed. "That's where you're wrong. With you in this position, I can do or say almost anything." He slapped her again, and she jerked at the pulse of pain and pleasure.

Claire squirmed, pressing her thighs together, trying to exert some pressure on her clit. God, she needed to come. Jack was acting bossier than usual, more dominant, and his behavior and comment sent an almost perverted thrill through her, escalating her need and hunger for him.

He placed his hands on her legs, stilling her desperate squirming. "Keep your thighs open the entire time. Stay right where you are and don't try and make yourself come. When you orgasm, it will be because *I've* brought you to that point. Not you."

"Hurry up," she growled.

"Pardon?"

She closed her eyes and grit her teeth. "Please, Jack. Hurry up, please."

He swiped his finger through her wet folds one last time and was gone, leaving Claire exposed and aroused and draped over her kitchen table.

She didn't question that he'd be back, didn't doubt that when he returned he'd take her to new heights, let her soar across the sky. She trusted him. If Jack said he'd be back soon, he would. And she couldn't wait. Not just because her pussy thrummed, hummed, clenched and needed to be touched. But because when Jack was around, Claire was happy. Filled with a pleasure no man had inspired in her before. He filled her heart and obliterated a loneliness she'd never realized was there.

When he was around she...lived. Whether they argued or laughed or grieved or watched telly together, she felt alive. And the part that stunned her the most? Jack seemed to feel exactly the way she did. When she was around he was...calm. Happy. He seemed content.

The seconds dragged by. Cool air wafted over Claire, hitting the juncture of her legs. She moaned at the conflicting sensations of hot desire and cold air pooling in her pussy and prayed Jack wouldn't be long.

She needed him. Wanted him. Loved him.

Claire froze.

Loved him?

Yes, loved him. Of course she did. How could she not? He was everything she looked for in a man. Strong, sensitive, kind, loving...bossy.

She closed her eyes, laid her cheek on the table and let the knowledge fill her. She loved Jack Wilson. She was wholly and entirely in love with him. And that love made her heart swell. A smile played on her lips. She loved Jack, and if his words were anything to go by, he loved her too.

"Fuck, you don't look half sexy." His voice broke through her musings.

She opened her eyes to find him standing in the doorway, leaning against the frame, naked as the day he was born, his gaze pinned on her.

He held something in his one hand which she couldn't see, and his dick in his other hand. Correction. He didn't just hold his dick, he pumped it slowly, starting right down at the base and sliding his hand over his length, all the way to the tip, enclosing his tip in his palm, and then sliding his hand back down to the base.

Claire noticed he wore a condom, whimpered at the sight and its meaning, and flicked her gaze to his eyes, knowing everything she'd just realized must be on display in her expression.

His breath caught. His gaze darkened. And his hand pumped a little faster.

"We've had fun up until now." His voice danced across the kitchen to a slow, sexy beat. "But tonight I make you mine."

She smiled at him. A slow, siren's smile, borne of her confidence. "I dare you to try, Mr. Wilson."

He stalked over to her. "Grab the edges of the table, Miss Jones. You're going to need to hold on to something."

There was almost no time to follow his instructions. Not with her wrists bound like they were. But she managed to grasp the edge with her fingertips, and then there he was.

His hands on her hips, his thighs between hers, and his cock at her entrance, pushing, plunging, driving inside her.

One thrust, and he filled her. His shaft, thick and long, stretched her inner muscles and teased her nerve endings, dragging along the walls of her pussy.

But one thrust was not enough. Not for her, and evidently, not for Jack either. He withdrew and thrust in again, not tempering his actions with soothing words. No, Jack was fucking her, hard. Slamming into her, filling her, then withdrawing only to slam into her again.

His hands were on her hips, holding her in place, pulling her back on his cock as he thrust in, then slackening their hold as he withdrew.

Claire loved it, loved every second, loved him. Loved the force with which he took her. And take her he did, claimed her as his, and she gave herself to him fully, gave her body over to him, to do as he pleased with. Knowing whatever he did would be as pleasing to her.

Then his hand was gone, only one arm pinned her down, and his thrusts slowed. He still filled her, utterly, but the pace was different. Not as demanding.

He slid his hand between her ass cheeks, and something cold and wet touched her hole.

She shrieked, the cold stilling her body.

It didn't stay cold. Not for long. Jack rubbed it into her, rubbed it around, teased her hole, all the while fucking her pussy.

A sob escaped her throat. She wanted...more. Jack had hauled her past a place where emotion and logic reigned. What he did to her, the sensations he inspired within went way past pure physical need. With the knowledge he loved her all wrapped up in the knowledge she loved him too, Claire threw caution to the wind, and lost herself to his demanding seduction.

The teasing was exquisite. But not enough. The next time he thrust inside her, she lunged back, lifting her ass up, silently begging for more.

And bless him, he gave it to her. Slid that finger right inside. And not just to the knuckle this time. He slid it in all the way.

The breath exploded from her lungs as sensation burst through her pussy.

Jack didn't miss a beat. He drove his cock inside her, fucking her ass simultaneously with his finger.

Oh, God. She was wild. Wanton. A carnal shrew desperate for more. So she begged for it, and he gave it to her. Gave her more. Slid another finger in her ass.

This time the sensation bordered on pain, and Claire missed a beat, allowing herself time to stretch, to accommodate his fingers. Just as she adapted, just as she felt her ass give, he added a third finger.

The pain wasn't borderline. It was instant. Burning. She had to breathe through it. But he must have added more of the cold, wet stuff as he'd slid that third finger in, because his fingers glided inside her. Just like his cock glided in her pussy. And though she was full, stuffed to capacity, that fullness somehow completed her. Made the pain worthwhile.

As he increased the speed of his thrusts again, his fingers working in time with his hips, so her orgasm began to build.

"Claire, you slay me." His voice was a hoarse tribute to her. She heard more than just sexual desire in it, more than just lust. She heard an emotion she couldn't identify. She just knew that emotion filled her heart just like his cock and fingers filled her below. "You're mine, you know? You have been since that first kiss."

His words flowed over her, and her muscles tensed, preparing for an orgasm.

And once again, he withdrew, pulling away from her, retreating completely, leaving her teetering on the edge.

She screamed. Literally screamed, frustration almost blinding her.

He moved, shuffled behind her, and then his mouth was on her pussy, eating hungrily at her, and his finger was on her clit, rubbing, arousing, demanding.

She couldn't stop it. Couldn't hold back the release. It wasn't what she'd expected. Not at all, but the pressure on her clit was undeniable.

Her orgasm slammed through her, sending her spiraling over the edge, tumbling and falling deeper and deeper into pleasure. His finger was merciless, playing, touching, caressing, drawing out her climax as his mouth licked her swollen folds.

Pleasure like nothing she'd ever experienced slammed through her as she convulsed and shuddered and cried out.

But even as her orgasm peaked and then ebbed, even as she collapsed, exhausted on the table, she knew it wasn't enough, knew she wanted—needed—more.

Jack was standing again, behind her, touching her. She couldn't see, couldn't open her eyes to look, didn't have the energy.

But he gave her what she needed. Gave her that something more. This time, when he breached her ass, it wasn't with his fingers. No, this time, when he slid in, past her tight ring of muscle, it was with his cock.

And this time he was relentless. Moving slowly, giving her time to adapt to his massive size, he drove his full length into her ass.

As the remnants of her orgasm shuddered through her pussy, she instinctively clamped her ass muscles, trapping him inside, holding him, growing accustomed to his girth and to the shock of having him there. It hurt. But in a good way. In a shocking way. A carnal way. A filthy way.

A way that had her pussy fluttering again in excitement, had her juices stirring.

He withdrew, and pressed in once more, faster this time.

She cried out, in pleasure and in pain, and he fucked her again. And again.

"Mine, Claire Jones. You are mine. You have been since day one, and you will be 'til the end."

Oh, she was his alright. And she suspected he was correct. She had been since day one.

His thighs were slippery with sweat. Hers were too, and as he drove into her, his rough, hair-covered skin slid against her smoother one.

Full, so full, and still shivering from her orgasm. But this was it. This was that something more she'd needed. A compulsion to move with him, to rock her hips as he plunged inside her could not be ignored.

Jack ran his hand around her hip, and his finger found her clit, stroking it. There it was again, the climb to orgasm, the impulse to lose herself in the extreme passion of his fucking. To come with Jack Wilson. To become one with Jack Wilson.

Claire's pussy fluttered, clenched and exploded once more into orgasm.

She screamed as she came, this climax more complete than the last, more whole. She didn't need anything more than he gave her. Especially not when Jack cried out behind her, when he thrust one last time, deep and hard, and then came as well.

Even through her own convulsions she could feel the way he pumped inside her, his movements still, but his shaft thumping within as he spurted. And spurted. Until he had nothing left. And then, as the last quivers of ecstasy rolled through her, he collapsed on top of her, squashing her into the table, and Claire knew their relationship had just changed irrevocably.

It was time to voice the words that had been screaming inside her head since he walked out the kitchen.

She feared she might not have the strength or energy to project her voice, but she gave it her best shot. "I love you, Jack."

Jack heard. She knew because he jerked above her, as if hit by an electric shock. "Wh-what did you say?"

"I said I love you too."

He was silent. Too silent. And for a heartbeat Claire feared she may have misheard him earlier. Perhaps he hadn't professed to loving her after all.

She dismissed the notion immediately. Whether he'd professed his love or not, Claire felt it with his every action, his every tender word, his every sensual kiss. And she'd felt it in his body as he'd made love to her tonight, claiming her completely, made her his.

"You have nothing to say in response?" she asked.

"*Love sought is good...*" She heard the smile in his voice. "*But given unsought is better.*"

"That's it?" she huffed. "I tell you I love you, and in return you...you quote Shakespeare?"

He nuzzled her neck. "You forget Shakespeare has a quote for every occasion."

"Then could you maybe quote something that makes me feel loved in return?"

"Ah, Miss Jones, maybe I could."

She waited expectantly, but no quote was forthcoming. Not only was a quote not forthcoming, but Jack withdrew from her. He climbed off her back and slipped off the table, disposing of the condom.

Before Claire had a chance to object, he stood in front of her, his hands on the scarf he'd knotted to the chair. He untied it, freeing her. Claire shook her hands, letting the blood flow through to her arms.

Jack kicked the chair out the way and knelt before her, so his eyes were level with hers. Then he smiled, and his dimple danced in his cheek.

"You sure you're ready to hear this?"

She nodded. "I'm pretty sure."

"Can you promise not to threaten me with a lawsuit once I've said it?"

Claire pretended to give it some thought. "I guess I can promise as much."

"And you swear not to change your mind, even if I break out in song after?"

She grimaced. "Can you maybe save the song for another time, just so you don't ruin the moment completely?"

It was Jack's turn to give her request some thought. "Okay then. But just this once, you understand?"

She sighed dramatically. "Okay then. Just this once."

His eyes lit up. "Well then Miss Jones, *I know no ways to mince it in love, but directly to say...I love you.*"

About the Author

Apart from her family and friends, Jess Dee loves two things: romance and food. Is it any wonder she specializes in dee-liciously sexy romance? Jess loves hearing from readers. You can email her at jess@jessdee.com or find her at www.jessdee.com.

Look for these titles by
Jess Dee

Now Available:

Office Affair

The Tanner Siblings
Ask Adam
Photo Opportunity

A Question of...
A Question of Trust
A Question of Love

Circle of Friends
Only Tyler
Steve's Story

Three Of A Kind
Going All In
Raising the Stakes
Full House

Bandicoot Cove
Exotic Indulgence
Island Idyll
Afternoon Rhapsody

Speed
See You in My Dreams
Colors of Love

Fire
Winter Fire
Hidden Fire

Print Anthologies
Three's Company
Risking It All
Red-Hot Winter
Three of a Kind
Tropical Desires
Red Hot Weekend
Tropical Haze

Ballroom Blitz

Lorelei James

Dedication

To my antho buddies, Jayne and Jess, it's always great fun working with you fab ladies!

Thanks also to Barb Hill-Kidd for sharing her insider knowledge about the world of competitive ballroom dancing with me. You got rhythm, darlin'.

Chapter One

"You cut your hair."

Jon White Feather pocketed the keys to his Land Cruiser and followed the sound of his niece's voice. She was sprawled on a concrete bench in an alcove between the driveway and the flower garden. He kissed the top of her head. "Raven, Raven, you been misbehavin'?"

"That is so lame, Uncle Jon. I'm not four anymore."

"True." He sat beside her. The last time he'd hung out with his niece, he realized she'd morphed into the too-cool-for-anything teen. As the fourth kid in a family of eight, she sometimes faded into the background.

It didn't help that Raven had entered that awkward stage, sporting acne, wearing braces on her teeth, glasses on her face and carrying baby fat. In the last year the normally outgoing kid had retreated into the world of books and video games. His brother and sister-in-law were concerned. Jon remembered Raven's older sisters had both gone through this gawky phase and now were pretty, confident young women. But Raven believed this *was* her final transformation and she'd always be the ugly duckling in a family of swans. And that broke his heart.

"So why did you cut your hair?" Raven persisted.

He shrugged. "I needed a change. Got tired of the braid. Needed something hipper." He exaggerated, tossing his mane like a supermodel. "So? Whatcha think? Is it rad?"

"No one says rad anymore, dork face." Raven brushed his hair back and inspected the ends that now touched his shoulders. "Actually, it looks good. Makes you look younger. Cooler."

Jon cocked an eyebrow at her. "Okay. What do you want? 'Cause you never give your old Uncle Jon compliments."

When she didn't answer, he patted her leg. "I was kidding." She finally raised her head and her soft brown eyes held such guilt Jon's heart sank. "Hey, little bird. What's really goin' on?"

"Don't get mad, but you're right. I do want something from you. But I didn't say that stuff about your hair to butter you up, because you really do look more like a rock star than you did with that old-man braid."

He didn't point out that her father wore a braid. Then again, his brother Jim *was* old. That made him smile. "What do you need? If it's money, I'll have to ask your folks first—"

"It's not money. It's..." Her finger swirled around the hole in her sweatpants. "I signed up for a dance class at the community center."

"Raven, that's great!" Her parents would be thrilled their daughter had taken an interest in something besides video games.

"But it's a couples' dance class."

"You want me there when you tell your parents about the boyfriend you're taking a dance class with?"

Raven rolled her eyes. "Do I *look* like the type of girl who'd have a boyfriend?"

"Not with that scowl." Jon kissed her nose. "Tell me how I can help you."

"I need you to take the class with me," she said in a rush.

He went still. Not what he'd been expecting. At all.

Before he could say no, she rattled off, "It's a three-week class, two hours a night, four nights a week. It's the really cool kind of dancing you see couples on TV doing, in those fancy dresses, all classy and romantic. I want to do it so bad, more than anything I've ever wanted in my entire life. I signed up before the class filled up, hoping I'd find someone to go with me before it started. And I haven't. I didn't tell anyone in my family because I thought they'd laugh at me." Her eyes were glossy with unshed tears. "You never laugh at me, Uncle Jon. You always tell me I can do anything I put my mind to. So please. I need you to be my partner."

Like he could deny her now. "Fine. Twist my arm. Make me say *uncle*."

Raven sighed. "You're such a dork."

"That's dancing dork to you, little bird. But I gotta warn you, kiddo. I am a shitty dancer. Like a scarily shitty dancer." When Raven opened her mouth to protest, he held up his hand. "I promise you, it's true. So I'll be your partner as long as you know it's at your own risk of broken toes."

"Same goes. Although I have been practicing some moves."

Jon watched as she popped off the bench and did some gyrating thing with her hips that he'd seen in strip clubs. Did all girls aspire to dance like that these days?

She held out her hands. "Come on. Let's go tell Mom and Dad."

"When does the class start?"

"Ah. Tonight. In an hour."

Shit. "Raven—"

"I would've asked you sooner, but you haven't come over. And we're not allowed to call you in case you're recording." She folded her arms over her chest, giving him an imperious look. "How long *have* you been home from your last tour?"

Two weeks. Two blissful weeks where he hadn't seen anyone. No one asking him questions. He'd slept in his own bed. Cooked in his own kitchen. Messed around in his studio until the wee hours. He'd needed to decompress after living on a tour bus for the last three months. So yeah, he'd avoided his brother and his large brood. Not because he didn't adore them, but he hadn't been the laidback, fun uncle they expected. He'd been a grumpy dick, so he'd stayed away for their own good.

"I know you're trying to come up with a plausible lie," Raven said with a sniff.

Jon grinned at his precocious niece. "I haven't been in hiding as long as you've been hiding your secret dance lessons from your parents."

Raven grinned back. "Busted. Now we hafta keep each other's secrets."

He draped his arm over her shoulder and they walked toward the house. "Please tell me I don't have to wear a damn leotard to this class."

She giggled. "A leopard-printed leotard. Like Tarzan. But you won't be able to pull it off with your short hair now. Maybe you can borrow a long-haired wig."

"Smart aleck. Seriously, what's the dress code?"

"The sheet said comfortable and casual. What you're wearing is fine. I'm gonna change."

Part of him wanted her to ditch the baggy clothes; part of him was glad for them because if she followed in her sisters' footsteps for the next teenage girl phase? She'd be wearing cleavage-baring shirts.

Once they were inside the house, a little person shouted, "Uncle Jon!"

Kids raced out of every corner, jumping like eager puppies. Six-year-old twins Jace and Hannah, ten-year-old Stephie and twelve-year-old Garth all talked a mile a minute.

The house was chaos central and the oldest three kids weren't home. "Where are Micah, Bebe and Cecily?"

"Micah is supervising at the youth forestry camp all summer. Cecily is lifeguarding at the community center pool." Garth peeled Jace off his back. "You'd know all this family stuff, Uncle Jon, if you ever called any of us."

"Ouch. You know that making me feel guilty ain't the way to change that, right?"

Garth snorted and threw a squealing Jace on the loveseat.

"What about Bebe? Doesn't she have her driver's license? I thought the two of you would be ripping it up, looking for trouble," he said to Raven.

"Bebe's working at Dairy Queen part-time and she's got a full-time boyfriend, so I never see her. Been a boring summer since I've been stuck babysitting."

"You babysitting for anyone besides the White Feather brat pack?"

"No." Raven stood off to the side, arms crossed, watching her siblings with the look of a put-upon older sister. "Dealing with them is enough."

"I smell food," Jon said.

When they reached the kitchen, Jon's sister-in-law, Cindy, exclaimed, "Jon White Feather. You chopped off all your hair!" She hugged him before she removed her oven mitts. "It looks great. Maybe you can convince your brother to do the same."

"I heard that." Jim rose from the table and hugged Jon. "Happy to see you, little bro." He held him at arm's length and studied him. "The hair does look good. But I ain't cutting off my war braids." He gave Jon a sly grin. "We've already got one good-lookin' rock star in the family. I'd hate to get a cool new hairdo and steal your thunder, eh?"

Jon laughed. "I missed you, old man."

"How long you back for?"

"Awhile. I'm burned out and need a serious break."

Jim's eyes went comically wide. "Wow. Never heard you say that before."

He shrugged. "Guess I'm finally ready to make some changes."

"I, for one, am happy about that. So can you stay for supper?" Cindy asked.

"That'd be great. But first Raven and I have something we want to talk about with both of you."

Jim and Cindy exchanged a look. "That sounds ominous."

"It is. Because I don't know any other way to break it to you."

"What?"

Jon hung his head. "Raven and I have been infected with boogie fever. And the only cure is to put on our dancin' shoes and head on down to funky town."

Chapter Two

Maggie Buchanan looked around the community center gym. No barre or mirrors, but the large wooden floor was excellent for movement and would accommodate all the couples that had signed up for class. By the time she'd finished warming up, her mentor, friend and official dance partner, Seth Fordham, wandered in, looking fantastic, as usual. Seth was a handsome, well-built man and his charm was evident, especially on the dance floor.

Seth grinned. "You ready for this?"

"I guess."

"What's the plan?"

It was weird for her instructor to ask her for direction. "I figured we'd stick to the basics. Jitterbug. The waltzes. Tango. Foxtrot. Two-step. Polka. Schottische. Line dancing."

"Sounds good. With the exception of spending too much time on the schottische. No one ever gets that. We should touch on it, as far as form and technique, but move on to something else."

"What do you suggest?"

"Extend the jitterbug class another night since it's so popular. And..." Seth wore an amused expression. "Add a hip-hop class."

Maggie shook her head. "No hip-hop."

"Why not?"

Because I'll look like an idiot hopping around, trying to be hip. "Because I'm not comfortable teaching a dance style I'm not familiar with."

"Which is exactly why you should do it. Dance is dance, Maggie." Seth bumped her with his hip. "Come on. It'll be good for you."

"Can you really see me popping and locking?"

"We'll see, won't we?" Seth scrolled through his MP3 player and plugged it into the sound system. Then he faced her. "Assume the position."

"You're serious."

"Completely. I know you're a fast learner." He performed some side-to-side movement with his upper body that looked like a funky robot while his bottom half slid the opposite direction.

"Where did you learn that?"

"Gay dance clubs."

Maggie groaned. "Unfair advantage."

"When we compete in a big city, I'll let you be my fag hag and we can hit the clubs. The way we dance together will blow their minds."

"Show off."

"So we'll work on some hip-hop moves to loosen you up at rehearsal tonight."

Part of the reason Seth had agreed to help her teach this class was to rehearse afterward. Their first competition was coming up in a little over a month. "All right. I'll set up the registration table."

As Maggie tracked down pens and nametags, she thought about how much her life had changed in the last six months.

She hated the term *corporate downsizing*, but it'd happened to her. After college graduation, she'd spent five years traveling the U.S. as a troubleshooter at a top Midwest computer security company. When the company was parted out, she was transferred to a smaller division at an Air Force base in South Dakota, where she'd spent the last four years.

Then six months ago...poof. Unemployed. At age thirty-two.

The economy sucked and full-time jobs were scarce in her field. Maggie probably could've found something if she'd been willing to relocate, but her grandmother had died suddenly and her brother and sister-in-law were having their first baby. Since Grandma Ingrid had left Maggie the small family cabin outside Spearfish, she'd sold her condo in Rapid City and moseyed up the road fifty miles to be closer to her family.

She'd found a part-time position at a doctor's office, computerizing decades' worth of medical records. She was overqualified, but the position offered health benefits and she didn't mind being jammed in a small cubicle. She'd also picked up a part-time gig teaching computer literacy in the afternoons at the library, both community centers and the senior center.

Without the grind of a fifty-hour workweek and very low living expenses, Maggie had time to reflect on her life. What she'd accomplished. What she was missing. What would make her life better.

And that answer had been a no-brainer.

Dancing.

She'd missed dancing. The physical exertion; the stretch and pull of her muscles. The pure exhilaration of performing; the rush when she and her partner were in perfect synch.

Until she'd lost her job, Maggie hadn't realized how much of herself she'd left behind when she'd given up competitive ballroom dancing in college to focus on finishing her degree.

She'd understood her brother Billy's logic—career first, hobby second. But what he'd never understood; dancing hadn't ever been "just" a hobby to her during her formative years. She'd lived it, breathed it, dreamed it. While other girls had posters of teen heartthrob stars on their walls growing up, Maggie had pictures of Baryshnikov. Martha Graham. Fred Astaire and Ginger Rogers.

During the summer before her senior year of high school, her father had died, leaving Maggie with her crazy, grief-stricken mother. Dance became her refuge. She'd been proficient enough to earn a dance scholarship to a small private college in New York City. But after a year of living with her sister Lacy and seeing firsthand all the dancers waiting tables while awaiting their big break, she fled the big city and the cynicism.

So Maggie had returned to her home state, enrolled in a technology program at the local university. But a funny thing happened sophomore year on the way to her statistics class—she accidentally wandered into the fine arts building and a competitive ballroom dancing class.

Over the years Maggie had watched the major competitions on TV, sighing over the beautiful costumes, the glamor and grace of the couples. So it'd shocked her when the instructor chewed her out for being late, demanding she get in line for a partner.

Rather than calling more attention to herself, she'd obeyed.

In retrospect, wandering into the wrong building had been the best mistake she'd ever made. Turned out, the years she'd spent learning ballet, tap, jazz and modern gave her a great foundation for ballroom dancing. The teacher had been so impressed that he'd introduced her to Booker White, the owner of the biggest dance studio in the area.

Maggie hadn't told her family about her newfound passion. While she and her partner Miles racked up wins and were the top couple at the Booker White Dance Studio, her grades suffered. Although the studio paid for costumes, training, entry fees and hotels, she was responsible for paying her other travel expenses. And in those two years, she spent part of her funds allocated for extra college expenses on dance competitions.

That's when Billy had intervened. He'd convinced her that an activity she had to keep from her family wasn't healthy; she'd dropped out of dance, focused on school and hadn't looked back.

Until now.

Her grin was pure joy as members of the class started to trickle in, their excitement warring with nervousness—exactly the same way she felt.

Seth greeted them at the door before directing them to Maggie. The class signup sheet had been filled weeks ago and the mix of couples was more eclectic than she'd imagined.

After checking in newlyweds and married couples of all ages, Maggie looked up to the next couple in line.

Holy cow.

The Native American man standing before her was breathtaking on a purely physical level. Shoulder-length black hair. Sharply defined facial features. His brilliant white smile set off his golden coloring to perfection. And his eyes. A stunning shade of blue. He wore a sleeveless T-shirt that revealed ripped biceps, triceps and forearms. When she met his gaze, he seemed amused by her blatant once-over and she blushed deeply.

The young girl with him, however, wasn't amused. "I'm Raven White Feather."

Maggie's gaze winged between them. Father and daughter? Although this beautiful man looked a little young to have a teenager. Feeling unnerved by her immediate and unexpected attraction to the man, she was happy to refocus on the girl. "Welcome, Raven." She checked her name off the list, but noticed her companion's name had been left blank. "And who will you be partnered with?"

"This is my uncle."

The man offered his hand and a smile. "Jon White Feather."

"I'm Maggie Buchanan."

"Buchanan?" he repeated, retaining hold of her hand longer than polite. "Any relation to Eden?"

"Yes. She's married to my brother, Billy. How do you know Eden?"

"Eden and I palled around for a few years. I forget Spearfish is such a small town. I'm surprised we haven't crossed paths before now since your brother Billy and my brother Jim are partners in Feather Light. This is Jim's daughter."

She smiled at Raven, touched by the way she leaned back when her uncle squeezed her shoulders. "You guys go ahead and fill out your nametags."

A rancher and his wife from Sundance were the last couple to arrive.

Seth looked up from fiddling with the sound system. "You spent extra time with those two students. Any problems?"

"No. They know my brother and sister-in-law. Everyone on the list is here."

"Let's get started."

She stepped in front of the group. "Good evening, everyone. Welcome to Couples Dancing 101. My name is Maggie Buchanan and I'll be one of your instructors for this three-week session.

"Why am I qualified to teach dance classes? Not only did I dance ballet, tap, jazz and modern during my formative years, I danced competitively in college in the American style of ballroom dancing. What does that mean?" She paused. "Lots of blisters and calluses from hours upon hours of practice."

Muted laughter encouraged her to continue.

"That's not what we're expecting out of you, but we will be teaching several different dances."

Jon raised his hand before she could ask for questions.

It figured. "Yes?"

"Can you explain what you mean by competitive ballroom dancing?"

"To be a competitor in the American rhythm style, a professional dancer is paired with an amateur and that couple is judged on five different dances. The professional, such as Seth here, must be employed full-time as a dance instructor. Someone like me, while having a dance background, is considered the amateur because dancing or teaching dance isn't my main source of income. But it is a source of joy." Maybe that'd been too corny. Her cheeks heated and she broke eye contact with the captivating Jon White Feather.

Seth took the floor. "I'm Seth Fordham and like Maggie said, I'm a professional dancer. I moved home to South Dakota last year and I run a dance studio in Rapid City. My background is in theatrical dance. I've performed with traveling musical productions in the U.S. and abroad, as well as living every dancer's dream of performing on Broadway. My career was cut short by a freak accident and after two years of rehab, I decided to share my love of dance by teaching." Seth hip-checked Maggie. "And I've finally convinced my lovely Maggie here to jump back into the world of competitive dance as my partner."

Again, Maggie felt Jon's eyes on her. In fact, he'd kept his focus on her the entire time Seth had been speaking, but she hadn't dared look his way—difficult as that'd been—because the man defined distraction of the best kind.

"Any more questions?" Seth asked.

No one spoke up.

"Good. Then let's get started," Maggie said. "Tonight we'll begin with the basic jitterbug. Seth and I will first demonstrate the dance at a normal speed. Then we'll slow it down and break it down, step by step. So gather in a circle. This first part is easy because all you have to do is watch."

Seth turned on the music. He took Maggie's hand and they automatically walked together as if they'd stepped onto the competition floor. Seth had chosen "In the Mood" and they stuck to basic steps, adding in a few turns, but no double hops, double cuts or double twists.

When the song and dance ended, applause rang out.

Seth spun her into a curtsey and he took a bow.

"Now we'll break it down. First thing you'll notice is how we hold our hands."

After the demonstration, the female newlywed asked, "Does it matter who's leading in how you hold hands?"

"For the sake of simplicity," Seth said, "let's assume the men are in the lead. So guys, hold your hands like this."

Grumbling from the women.

"Ladies," Maggie interjected, "I'm an equal rights supporter, but in this case, Seth is in charge of showing the male steps, and I'm tasked with teaching the female partner steps because it'll be easier. And remember, just because a man has the lead on the dance floor, doesn't grant him the right to retain control off the dance floor."

Several women laughed and nudged their partners.

Maggie's gaze snagged Jon's. Everything about him said *man in charge, all the time.* Normally men like that didn't appeal to her, but seeing him so sweet and funny with his niece intrigued her—beyond the fact he was such a gorgeous male specimen.

She and Seth went through the steps slowly, then had the students perform the steps with them and finally on their own. They wandered through the group. If a couple was struggling, Maggie would dance with the man while the woman watched, then Seth would dance with the woman while the man watched. Usually when the couple was put back together, their technique had improved.

When they reached Raven and Jon, she heard them arguing in low tones. "You two do not look like you're having fun. Anything we can help with?"

Raven pointed at her uncle. "Yes. He keeps doing it wrong. He steps too close and then too far back."

"Someone wasn't paying attention when the instructors said the men were supposed to lead," Jon said tersely.

Seth intervened. "Show us the problem."

Jon held out his hands and Raven snatched them. The first few movements were decent, but then Jon completely lost the rhythm.

"Hold on a second. Watch us." Seth took Maggie's hands. "See what we're doing with our arms and our feet?" She and Seth demonstrated. "Keep it smooth and tight."

Jon had crossed his arms over his chest. He didn't look belligerent, just frustrated. "Isn't that what I was doing?"

Maggie, Raven and Seth all said, "No."

When Seth danced with Raven, she followed his lead without issue.

Jon sighed and lightly nudged his niece. "Looks like I'm the one with two left feet, eh? You sure you want me for your dance partner, Raven?"

His amused resignation had Maggie stepping forward to reassure him. "Let's see if I can help." She took Jon's hands and they were face to face. And what a face it was.

Jon stared at her, as if he liked what he saw, and tightened his grip when she attempted to retreat. "Is this too close?" he murmured.

"For dancing? Yes."

He flashed an unrepentant grin. "Guess I wasn't thinking about dancing."

Me either. "So, Mr. White Feather—"

"Jon. If I'm gonna be stomping on your feet, call me Jon."

Such a charmer. "Okay, Jon. Start with your right foot. Step. Together. Good. Now, step back. No. Stop. You don't have to alternate feet."

He froze. "I don't?"

"No." When their eyes met, her belly dipped. "Now, try it with Raven."

She turned and addressed the class, grateful for a diversion from the engaging man. "Let's add faster music."

She and Seth wandered through the couples separately. Most had mastered the basic steps. When Maggie glanced over to see Jon and Raven's progress, she half expected that once the music began their rhythm issues would work out. But music had made it worse.

Raven looked ready to cry. Jon looked defeated. Not good.

Seth caught her eye and they headed back to help.

"Heya, teach, back so soon?" Jon said nonchalantly. "I thought I had the hang of it until that pesky music screwed me up."

"Have you tried counting to keep the beat? One, two, three, four?" Seth asked.

"Of course."

"Let's see how you're keeping time." Maggie clasped Jon's hands, feeling that magnetic pull again. "Bring your partner toward you on every other beat. Like this."

Jon tried it, but he kept coming in a beat late, on the third beat, instead of the second. Every time.

She bit back a groan. He might be a fascinating combination of self-deprecating and charming, but the man could not keep time.

Raven threw up her hands. "See? I told you. It's not me, Uncle Jon. It's you."

"I'll remind you, darlin' niece, you roped me into this class. And I warned you I was sadly lacking in dancing skills," he said tightly.

"But dancing is about rhythm. That should be easy for you. Don't you count when you're playing?"

"Yeah, but it's not the same. I don't think about it. I just do it."

"Excuse me," Seth said. "Playing what?"

"The drums."

Maggie's jaw dropped. "*You* play the drums?"

"Yep." Jon's eyes narrowed. "Why are you so shocked?"

"Because you have absolutely no sense of rhythm."

Jon threw back his head and laughed. "Doll face, you are the first woman who's ever said that to me."

Chapter Three

Maggie blushed.

Raven said, "Eww, Uncle Jon!"

Seth smirked. But he rallied to Jon's defense. "Regardless, Mr. White Feather, it's obvious you don't have rhythm when it comes to *dancing*. So for now, it's best if I work with Raven."

Bonus. That'd pair him with the very sexy Maggie Buchanan for the remainder of class and Jon was all over that.

"...and you will watch us and learn."

Jon's gaze snapped to Seth. "Excuse me? That sounded like I've been benched."

"Only briefly. For tonight."

He looked at Maggie, but she'd floated off to help another couple.

So Jon had to stand there, propped against the wall like some second stringer. Studying another guy's feet, arms, hips and ass moving was fucked up on several levels. He'd never get this formal dancing shit, which was why he'd always limited his dancing to the slow type or the mattress type.

His focus strayed to Maggie, performing some cha-cha move that shook her ass enticingly. Way too enticingly; his brain conjured images of them doing a little mattress dancing, her perfect butt in his hands, his pelvis doing a slow bump and grind into hers as he tasted that pretty pink mouth.

A throat clearing caught his attention and Seth looked at him pointedly.

Jon shot him a sheepish grin. But he did manage to pay attention for the remainder of class. Raven was getting a lot out of the one-on-one instruction, including heaps of praise from Seth. And his niece's beaming face reminded Jon why he was here in the first place.

Raven was so anxious to leave after class finished that he couldn't shake the niggling feeling he'd somehow embarrassed her. He hoped the second night would go better than the first.

But the second night was more of the same torture. Jon was hapless and Raven tried not to act annoyed or mortified about the extra attention they received from the instructors because of his screw ups.

However, Jon certainly didn't mind having Maggie's soft curves pressed against him as she walked him through the dance steps. The woman was an enigma; confidently giving instructions to the entire class and yet blushing so prettily when they were pressed body to body. He was actually sorry when class ended.

After the rest of the students took off, Jon noticed Raven wasn't racing out the door, but in deep conversation with Seth. He wandered over to where Maggie sat on the bench, changing shoes.

"So it is true," he said, sitting sideways on the bleachers beside her.

Maggie glanced up. "What is true?"

"There is such a thing as putting on your dancing shoes." *Lame, Jon.*

"Different types of dancing shoes for different dances. Probably like you use different drums for different parts of a song?"

"You'd be correct." He angled forward. "So while I've got you alone...give it to me straight. Am I failing class?"

The corners of her lips curled into a smile even as she remained focused on buckling her shoe. "This isn't a pass-fail situation. I'm giving you an A for extra effort." Maggie's eyes met his briefly before her attention drifted to his arms. Her gaze started at his wrist and moved up to his bicep. "I'll admit I've been admiring your cool tattoos during class."

"Do you have any tats?"

"No. Never had much chance to see artwork designs up close to see what my options are."

He held his arms out. "Go ahead and take a closer look if you want. See if there's anything you like." *Feel free to touch as much as you want.*

Her eyes clearly broadcast *I want*, even if her alluring mouth stayed closed.

The first tentative touch on his forearm was potent as an electric charge. He held himself still, willing that charge not to travel straight to his dick.

Her cheeks were flushed. Her blue eyes bright. Tendrils of reddish-blond hair had escaped from her tight bun, tempting Jon to loosen it completely and crush the soft stands in his hands. Or smooth the strands back into place just to touch that creamy-looking skin. Maggie unsettled him. She was wholesome looking and a little shy—not his usual type. So his immediate attraction to her was baffling. Not unwelcome, just confusing. Question was, did she feel the same pull?

Yes, if he went by the way her hand trembled when she touched him.

When her soft fingertip drifted over the crease of his arm, he bit back a growl. Oblivious to his response, she continued the northerly progression, one hand clamped around his wrist, the other hand driving him out of his mind with a mix of innocent curiosity and overt sensuality.

"Are these marks tribal symbols?" she asked, continually caressing the same section of black swirls and scrolls.

"I told a buddy of mine who's an artist I wanted markings with a tribal feel, but more artistic. So they don't mean anything specific."

"So it's wearable art that's unique to you." Her thumb swept across the stylized barbed wire motif on his bicep. "Even if the design was used on another person it wouldn't look the same. Your skin coloring gives it a different dimension. As does your musculature." She ran a fingernail on the underside of his arm. "Your biceps and triceps are amazing."

"I can't take credit for that."

"I'm pretty sure you weren't born with all these muscles." Maggie looked at him, as if startled by what she'd said.

When she attempted to remove her hand, Jon placed his palm over hers. "Thank you. Most of the time I get grief for the tats. I'm happy to hear a beautiful woman appreciates them."

"I do." She wet her lips and her gaze dropped to his mouth.

Sweet Jesus. She was killing him. Everything about her embodied soft and sweet—her hands, her mouth, her eyes, her tender touch. Which ironically enough, made him hard as a fucking drumstick.

"Maggie?" Seth called out.

They both jerked back.

"Yes, Seth?" she said a little breathlessly.

"Can you show Raven a couple of steps?"

Maggie said, "Sure," and stood. She faced him. "Truly magnificent, Jon."

"Glad you like them."

"I wasn't talking about the tattoos." Then she spun, leaving him staring after her.

Whoa. That comment had dripped with sexual sizzle.

Hmm. Maybe Maggie Buchanan wasn't as soft and sweet as he first believed.

Jon sucked at dancing. Like epically sucked.

The third night of class Seth and Maggie taught a waltz. Part of him feared they'd switched to an easier dance because he'd mangled the jitterbug the first two nights. Not that he could ask either instructor to give it to him straight, since Raven had hot-footed it out of class as soon as it ended. Then in the car the surly teen refused to talk to him and bailed out as soon as he'd pulled up to the curb in front of her house.

The fourth night was devoted to the rhumba. Jon wasn't the only one having troubles. Two other guys in his class—the quiet cowboy and the newlywed—suffered from the same feet, eye and hand coordination issues.

During the break, Jon saw the cowboy leaning against the wall by the drinking fountain. He struck up a conversation. "You look ready to bolt for the door, man."

He nodded his black-hatted head. "Takin' a class together was my wife's idea, not mine."

"I hear ya. My niece roped me into this."

"At least you ain't gonna end up in divorce court if *you* quit," he grumbled.

Jon thrust out his hand. "Jon White Feather."

"Quinn McKay."

"Is your wife having a good time?"

"I guess."

Jon waited for the cowboy to complain more, but he wasn't much of a talker. He gulped down another mouthful of water and started to walk back, but the guy's voice stopped him.

"Know what I hate the worst?" Quinn said out of the blue.

"What's that?"

"I think I'm embarrassin' her."

"Right there with you."

Quinn lifted one dark eyebrow. "You gonna quit?"

Jon shook his head. "My niece is a teenager. I'd never hear the end of it. Besides, I'm too stubborn."

"Me too. I figure I'll get better. I sure as hell can't get any worse."

Jon laughed.

"If I wasn't so busy on the ranch I'd find a way to take private lessons. Then maybe my wife wouldn't look at me like I've got the grace of a damn bear."

Seth motioned everyone back to class.

Jon managed not to tromp all over Raven's feet for the rest of class. But on the ride back to her parents' house after his disastrous attempt at the rhumba, Raven mentioned she was considering dropping the class and Jon knew he had to swallow what little pride he had left and ask for help.

"Maggie?"

Startled, she whirled around so fast she almost dropped her car keys. "Jon. You scared me. I thought you left."

"Sorry. I did. But I came back."

"Did you forget something?

"No." He jammed his hands in his pockets. As if he was nervous.

Right. She should be nervous after she'd cyber-stalked him and discovered he wasn't just some hot guy in a local band, but an internationally known and respected musician in a critically acclaimed band that incorporated traditional Lakota music with hard rock. "What's up?"

"I need your help. I'm a hopeless dancer. And while I find the humor in that, Raven doesn't. She's ready to quit because of me and I don't want to embarrass the poor kid any more than I already have. So I thought I'd see if you have time to give me a few private lessons."

Maggie hadn't been expecting that. Jon White Feather didn't seem like the type of guy who'd ask for help. She found it incredibly...sweet that he was more worried about his niece's feelings than projecting a macho reputation to the class. The problem was, she didn't have much free time. She'd gone from worried about having no job to being too busy to take on any extra projects.

But look at that project—you'd get to put your hands all over every tall, dark and handsome inch of that ripped, sexy body.

Jon stepped back. "Since you haven't said anything, I guess that's no."

She put her hand on his arm to stay his retreat. "It's not that. I'm just mentally dissecting my schedule to find a place where I might be able to squeeze you in."

"Any time you can give me would be great. I'm flexible."

"Any time? Even five o'clock in the morning?"

He grimaced. "Yep. Although I'll need plenty of bathroom breaks since it'll take at least a pot of coffee to wake me up at that god-awful time of the day."

"I was kidding." Maggie realized she was still touching him and dropped her hand. "You don't want Raven to know?"

"That I need remedial dance instruction? No. Only because she'd feel guilty for asking me to take her to these classes in the first place." Those intense blue eyes studied her. "I definitely don't want to put you on the spot with Seth, either."

Maggie frowned. Why would what Seth thought matter...? Oh. Jon assumed—like many people did—that dance partners were together. "Jon. Seth and I aren't a couple anywhere besides on the dance floor."

Was that relief in his eyes? "That's good to know. So what do you say? Will you help me fix at least one of my two left feet?"

"When you put it that way..." She smiled. "Seth and I practice for two to three hours after we're done teaching class. It'd be best if we scheduled it for directly after that."

"Two to three more hours? Damn. You sure you won't be tired?"

Probably. "Nah. I'll be fine."

"Okay. That'll work great. Thanks, Maggie."

"Don't thank me until I tell you how much I charge an hour."

"Worth every penny, I'm sure."

"I know we don't have class tomorrow night, but be here after eight and we'll get started."

"So you're giving Johnny-hottie private lessons?" Seth asked.

"Yes. Why?"

He fussed with the beaded sleeves on her dress. "Because I think he's faking it."

"Faking what? Stop tugging so hard."

"Sorry." Seth studied her hair critically. "With this dress you'll need an elegant hairdo. Not something cutesy with curls, but sleek and sophisticated."

It drove Maggie bat-shit crazy, how Seth expected her to follow three or four different conversations with him simultaneously. She snatched his hand. "Seth. What is Jon faking?"

"That he's a bad dancer. 'Cause, honey, ain't no one that bad. Especially not a drummer. And the man is always eating you up with those magnificent eyes of his, which leads me to believe he's faking it so he can be alone with you. He set the scene the first night. Now he's begging you to teach him on the sly? It's a classic ploy."

"Why doesn't he just ask me out?" Maggie countered. "We're both adults. Jon doesn't seem the type to play games."

Seth shrugged. "Maybe he's worried his niece will accuse him only of taking classes with her so he could pick up chicks. Maybe he's afraid a smoking-hot white girl like you won't date an Indian guy like him. Maybe he's so used to groupies throwing themselves at him he doesn't have a clue how to ask a normal woman out on a date."

Her partner's comments made perfect sense and yet...her logical brain hadn't considered any of those reasons. "I guess we'll see, won't we?"

"No matter what his motives, I approve."

"You do?"

"Yes. Because if you happen to get naked with that man? Girlfriend, I expect explicit details." Seth reached into his magic bag of accessories and pulled out a hair clip. "Use this for now. I want to see how it looks with the costume."

Maggie bit back a groan as Seth cued up the music.

Taskmaster Seth didn't relent on rehearsal until Maggie literally cried "uncle" and broke away to get a drink.

Her lungs burned. Her feet hurt. She was sweating like crazy. Luckily she'd changed out of the costumes after the first full run-through. She glanced at the clock. Seth had been cracking the whip for two and a half hours.

"Are you throwing in the towel tonight, Maggie?" Seth asked.

"The towel that is soaked in sweat? Why, yes I am."

Footsteps echoed across the gym floor and they both turned.

Her heart, already beating madly, sped up at the sight of Jon, looking every inch the bad boy rocker, with his tousled dark hair, skintight black T-shirt, and faded, ripped jeans. And that smile. Good lord that fabulous smile was beyond sexy.

She drained half the bottle of water before she spoke. "You made it."

"I've been here for a half hour watching you guys."

Seth bowed. "So what did you think?"

Jon's focus was entirely on Maggie. "Beautiful. Amazing. Graceful. Sexy." Then Jon looked at Seth. "And you weren't too bad either."

Maggie got the *I told you so* look from Seth.

"As much as I'd love to stay and chat, I still have to drive back to Rapid City tonight." Seth scooped up the costumes. "You'll deal with the audio stuff before you leave, Maggie?"

"Of course."

Seth bussed her cheek and whispered, "I slipped condoms in your dance bag." Then he faced Jon. "Ta, Johnny Feather. Get the moves right tonight for a change, okay?"

Her face flamed, but Jon just laughed. "Will do."

After the door slammed behind Seth, they looked at each other. She fought the urge to run. But she wasn't sure if it would be toward him, or away from him.

Jon invaded her space. "You look ready to bolt, Maggie. Have you changed your mind?"

"No."

He handed her a check. "For two lessons. I'll let you decide if I need more. Truthfully, I'm glad to hand you the reins and let you take the lead in this."

Her eyes searched his. "In this?"

"I'm used to being in charge of everything. Professionally and personally. Intimately." He flashed his teeth. "So take the lead while you can get it, teach. Because it ain't gonna last long."

There was a glimpse of his cocky side. "Prove it, little drummer boy."

Jon laughed—a sultry rumble that sent a delicious curl of heat through her. "How?"

"Rhumba. No music."

"So you *do* intend to torture me."

"Completely."

His first five moves were good enough that Maggie wondered if Jon had been exaggerating his bad dancing skills. But then everything fell apart. His body became board stiff. He high-stepped as if he was auditioning for a marching band. When he stomped on her foot for the third time, she retreated and bit back a wince. "Okay. We can't blame your rhythm issues on the music distracting you, since there is none."

"Well that's reassuring," he said tersely.

Maggie had an idea. "All right, let's see how you do dancing with a wall." She towed him to the back of the gym.

"Whoa. Hang on, doll face. You're joking, right?"

"Nope. Palms on the wall, about where you'd be holding my hands. Stand straight. Keep your feet shoulder-width apart. Stay just like that."

"I'm damn glad no one can see me because I feel ridiculous," he grumbled.

She ducked under his arms, pressing her back into the concrete blocks. "Do you trust me?"

Indecision flickered in his eyes.

Maggie set her hands on shoulders. "Jon. Do you think I'm purposely trying to make you feel ridiculous?"

He bit off, "No."

"Good. I *am* trying to help you."

"I know."

"Do you?" She set her hands on his chest. His rock-hard chest. His body was so warm. And ripped. She wondered if she could feel the cut of his abs through his thin T-shirt. Her fingers inched down...

"Maggie?"

What was wrong with her? She'd practically been feeling him up. "I can't help you if you won't let me."

Jon glanced down at her fingers digging into his pectorals. When his gaze met hers, his eyes held sexual heat. "I like this hands-on approach."

Lord, he could stoke the embers inside her to a five-alarm fire in three seconds flat. "Is this helping you?"

He offered her that slow, sexy smile. "It sure as hell ain't hurting me."

"Don't move. I'll start the music." She slipped away and inhaled several deep breaths, trying to get a hold of her raging libido.

Jon hadn't budged an inch.

She couldn't help but sneak a look at Jon White Feather's backside. Yowza. Every bit as good as his front side. Damn, the man was fine. With a capital F. *Ogling his ass is not helping you control these urges, Maggie.* She stood behind him. "Now, I want to see those feet moving. Just like we've been working on. Ah ah ah, but I don't want you looking at your feet. Look straight ahead. As if you were gazing into your partner's eyes."

He nodded and shuffled his feet.

"That's awesome. Don't change anything."

But he did falter after another minute.

When Maggie curled her hands around his hips, tucking her body close behind his, he jumped forward. "Jesus, Maggie. What are you doing?"

"Teaching you. You said you liked the hands-on approach. I was trying to get you to use your hips."

Jon shot her a smug look over his shoulder. "Trust me, dancing queen, I *know* how to use my hips."

She imagined her hands gripping his biceps as he was propped above her naked, giving her firsthand knowledge of just how well he could move that pelvis.

"What's put that look on your face?" he asked softly.

Fighting a blush, she said, "Exhaustion," and stepped in front of him. "Now count out the beat with me."

Strong fingers dug into her hips and he snuggled his torso against hers—way too close. But she couldn't seem to tell him to back off.

"Feel how I move." Palms flat against the wall, she danced forward and back. "One, two. Three, four. One, two. Three, four. I don't hear you counting."

When his deep voice rumbled in her ear, she almost lost track of which damn number she was on.

"I'll face you and we'll do this for real. Don't change anything. Just keep counting." Maggie turned and his fingers drifted across her lower belly, sending her whole body on high alert.

Jon's eyes remained on hers as he slipped her hands into his. His husky voice repeated the numbers in a melodic cadence and the music faded into the background.

Forward. Back. His steps weren't perfect but his gait was much smoother.

She wondered how long they'd danced after the music ended. Something had shifted between them tonight. She attempted to pull away but Jon was having none of that.

"Thank you. I actually feel like I might not suck at this."

Maggie smiled. "You just need to be patient with yourself."

During the next half of the lesson, Jon even learned how to spin his partner and reverse steps. She was pleased with his progress and told him so.

Time passed quickly. But she had to get off her feet.

It took her longer than usual to pack up her stuff, but Jon wasn't inclined to leave. As much as she liked just talking to him, she suspected he'd stuck around out of obligation. "Jon. You don't have to stay. I don't want to keep you from your Friday night plans."

"I don't have any plans."

Tell him you don't either. Ask him to come over.

As good as that sounded...this week had drained her. Physically. Mentally. She wouldn't be good company. Heck, she'd probably fall asleep.

Jon asked, "What about your plans?"

"I plan on crawling into bed and not getting out until morning."

"What a coincidence. That's my favorite way to spend a Friday night too."

His meaning sent a dangerous shiver of longing through her. "You looking for an invite for a sleepover?"

He shrugged. "Never hurts to ask."

She stared at him, expecting he'd back off. Or at least take off.

But he didn't. He kept that penetrating gaze locked to hers. "I'll stick around until you're done. It's too late to be wandering around in a dark parking lot by yourself."

Jon did stick close as she checked both exits and entrances. Since the gym was a separate structure, the community center was already locked up.

He insisted on carrying her bag. He let his hand rest in the small of her back and she found her footsteps dragging on the jaunt to her car.

"I oughta pick you up and carry you," he grumbled. "You are dead on your feet."

What would it be like to have a big, strong guy whisk her into his arms?

Heavenly.

She sighed.

Then his warm mouth was on her ear. "You'd like that."

Yes. Yes she would. Too much. She stopped at her car and fiddled with her keys instead of meeting his gaze.

Thud. Her bag hit the ground. "Maggie." Jon inserted himself between her and the door, forcing her to look at him. "Come here."

"Jon. I'm okay."

"No you're not. Let me hold you up for a little while."

"But I shouldn't—"

"Just let go for a minute." He tugged her, gathering her in his arms. "I've got you."

Maggie melted into him, letting his warmth and strength flow through her. But her stomach made a loud gurgling noise and she reluctantly pulled away. "Obviously I skipped supper again."

"Then the least I can do is take you someplace to eat."

"That's sweet, but not necessary."

Then he was in her face. "You worked your ass off, you're hungry—so I *am* feeding you. Your choices are we go out, or I follow you home and cook for you there."

Maggie realized he wasn't taking no for an answer. She realized she really liked that about him. "All right. The Millstone is open. I'll meet you."

Chapter Four

Jon chose the booth at the back of the restaurant and ordered coffee. After ten full minutes passed and Maggie hadn't shown, he wondered if he'd been stood up.

But that didn't seem like Maggie's style. Then again, what did he really know about her?

He knew she'd felt the same zing between them whenever their eyes met and whenever their bodies touched.

Then she swept into the restaurant. Her reddish-blond hair was still contained in a hair clip that showed off her elegant neck and stunning profile. She had the haughty look of classic ballerina in her angular facial features, and she exuded the grace of a dancer in the way she carried herself.

Jon was completely taken with her.

She slid opposite him. "Sorry. My car was on fumes so I had to fill up with gas." She picked up the menu and flipped through it. "What are you having?"

"All-day breakfast special number three."

"That sounds good."

The waitress took their order and Maggie looked at him expectantly. "Tell me about yourself, Jon White Feather."

"What do you want to know?" He braced himself for the intrusive personal questions people felt entitled to ask because he had a public persona as a musician.

"Your family. Where you got those stunning blue eyes."

Not what he'd expected, which was a good thing. And was she flirting with him? "Threw you, didn't they? Most folks assume I wear contacts. I don't. This eye color is courtesy of my mother."

"Don't take this the wrong way, but I suspected you weren't full-blooded Lakota. Your genetic makeup resembles Eden's more than your brother's."

"True. That's why Eden and I got along so well—we're both half-breeds. Jim's my half-brother. His mother died when he was young. My mother came to the Eagle Butte Reservation right after she graduated from college in Minnesota. She met my dad..."

"And your mom helped heal a widower's heart?"

"Ain't quite that romantic. Living on the rez wasn't as noble as it'd sounded in her sociology classes. Anyway, Jim is twelve years older than me. My brother Jared is four years younger than me. He's still giving our parents fits over his daredevil acts as a smoke jumper."

Maggie's brow furrowed. "Smoke jumper?"

"He travels all over the U.S. fighting wild fires with an elite group of all-Indian firefighters based out of Eagle Butte." He smirked. "Jared is hard to contain."

"Ha-ha."

"What about your family?" he asked.

"You know my brother Billy. I have an older sister Lacy who lives in New York with her husband and three kids. My dad died when I was in high school and my mom passed on a few years after I graduated from college. That's about it." She sipped her coffee. "How old are you?"

"Thirty-six. How old are you?"

"Thirty-two."

Jon knew he looked shocked. "Really?"

She bristled. "Yes. Why?"

"I thought you were like...twenty-six."

"Disappointed that I'm not a young, hot thing, rock star?"

He didn't bother to bank the heat in his eyes. "Not at all. Because *winyan*, you *are* a young, hot thing."

Maggie blushed. "What does *winyan* mean?"

"Woman. And you're all that."

"Flatterer. So tell me how you became Johnny Feather, international music star."

He snorted. "More like inter-*nation* music star. Entertaining American Indian tribes from the Arapahoe to the Zuni."

"But your band has traveled abroad, right?"

"Several times. Sapa spent four long months overseas last year."

"Doesn't sound like you had a good time."

"The performances were great. But we were sick of each other halfway through the tour. At least when we're here, we can go home to get away from each other. We've been touring for months on end, year after year. Sapa isn't booked for any paying gigs for a while. We're taking a long break." Maybe a permanent break.

Maggie looked at him curiously. "Is Sapa breaking up?"

Was she really that intuitive? Or was he just that transparent? He hedged. "Technically Sapa could go on even if half of us quit. The band has ten members. We rotate gigs for the lead guitarists and the bass guitarists because they have families. It's always worked. But the married members of the band, who aren't interchangeable, are expecting their first baby and wanted to be home for the summer and fall. Another member lost his father this spring and he quit because he has to take care of his mom full-time. The other couple called it quits in their relationship, and they're not sure they can work together professionally anymore."

"And what about you?" she prompted. "Are you interchangeable?"

"No. I'm key. I write the majority of our music. I've always dealt with the business end. The booking agents, the accountants, the company putting on the tours and most of the media. If the band didn't like the venue, they blamed me. If we had to cancel or postpone a show, the booking agent blamed me. If we ran out of money mid-tour, the accountant blamed me. All I wanted to do was make music. My creativity has been totally tapped out because the last three years have been so stressful." Jon gave Maggie props for steering the conversation, but enough yammering on about himself. "What about you? Have you been overseas?"

"No. I always thought it'd be fun to go to the international dance competition world finals in London." She smiled. "I guess the regionals in Gillette in a few weeks will have to do."

"So that's why you're practicing all the time?"

"All the time is right. Evenings. Weekends. Hours of dancing. And that's after Seth has taught a full schedule at his dance studio and I've worked eight hours."

"Why do it?"

"Because I'm a sucker?"

Jon laughed softly. "No. Seriously. Do you love it that much?"

"Yes. I'd forgotten how much." She glanced out the window. "After I graduated from college I was lucky enough to land a job in my field. I took a break from dancing, which turned into a few years' break."

"What is your day job?"

"Computer technology."

"So you're smart, beautiful and graceful? Now I'm really feelin' inadequate."

"At least you're not unemployed in your field," she grumbled. "Up until six months ago I worked for a computer security company that contracted civilian jobs on various military bases. Then budget cuts and corporate downsizing happened. I've been scrambling to stay financially afloat."

"I've definitely been there, done that."

"Struggling with finances? Or your career?"

"Both." Jon drummed his fingers on the table. "Starving artist is a reality in all the arts. I lived that hand-to-mouth lifestyle for many years. I'm happy to be past it. But now I'm struggling with fulfilling the creative side."

"Do you do that a lot?"

"Do what?"

Maggie dropped her hand over his fingers, still tapping out a beat on the table. "Use everything within reach as a drum?"

"Yeah. I guess I don't notice it." Then he had a flash of embarrassment. "Why? Is it annoying?"

"No. It's cute."

Cute. Awesome. He hadn't ever remembered being called cute.

"Have you done anything fun since the band...disbanded?"

"Ha-ha, funny girl." Jon twisted his hand and threaded his fingers through hers. "I'm learning new moves from this sexy dance instructor I just met."

She blushed. But she didn't jerk her hand back.

Emboldened, he leaned forward. "Would you go out with me?"

Her pretty blue eyes searched his. "You'd want to go out with me? Seriously?"

"Yeah. Why not?"

"Because you're famous. You have gorgeous women all over the world falling at your feet. I did a little online stalking and I saw that picture of you and Desiree at some big music producer's house before your breakup."

Desiree—one name—was the up and coming darling of the indie rock world with ambition on becoming the "Indian Beyoncé". No doubt Desiree had talent; her voice was suited to a smoky blues style, pop or hard rock. She was a beautiful woman who proudly wore her Choctaw heritage. But Desiree had no intention of living her life out of the spotlight. She'd never settle down in South Dakota and he couldn't imagine settling anywhere else.

"The tabloids get a lot of shit wrong. I'm not nursing a broken heart over her. And here's where I point out that you're a gorgeous woman and I've fallen at your feet, more than once, in public, if I recall correctly."

She laughed. "My God. You are so smooth."

Jon brought her hand to his mouth and kissed her knuckles. "And sincere. And really happy you're here with me."

Their food arrived.

After Maggie devoured every morsel, she shoved her plate aside. "So about this date. When are you thinking?"

"You busy tomorrow night?"

"I'm free after rehearsal."

"Good. I'll pick you up..." Wait a second. He wasn't free. "I just remembered Saturday night won't work for me. Here I'm telling you Sapa is on break, but we're doing one set at the Heritage Bar. It's a benefit we agreed to months ago. But if you don't mind a late date, we can go out after I'm done." It'd be good for her to see him in action. Doing what he did best. Which wasn't dancing.

When Maggie hesitated, he cranked up the charm. "Come on. I deserve a chance to show you that I can keep a steady beat in some capacity."

"All right. It's a date."

"Excellent." Jon caught her trying to mask a yawn and he dropped cash on the table to cover the check. "Now that your belly is full, I don't feel guilty sending you home."

"I am fading fast."

Jon offered his hand to help her from the booth. He didn't release his hold on her until they reached her car. "Thanks for the lesson tonight, dancing queen."

"My pleasure. What time should I be at your show?"

"We go on at eight. There might be a crowd—" an understatement, "—so maybe get there a little early."

"Where will I find you once you're done playing?"

Security would be tight around the stage, by the back door and the tour bus. "I'll meet you by the east side door. It might be as long as thirty minutes after the encore before you see me, so don't think I'm not coming. I will be there."

As much as Jon wanted to curl his hands around her face and take the kiss he craved, he settled for brushing his lips on her cheek. "Drive safe."

Chapter Five

Maggie's feet were killing her. Her body ached from holding dance pose after dance pose. Seth had run rehearsal today as a sadistic drill sergeant. Six hours with one fifteen-minute break.

She'd been so tempted to hobble home, soak her feet in Epsom salt and crawl in bed.

But when she'd turned on the radio in her car, the station was promoting the benefit concert. Then they played a couple of Sapa songs. And holy shit, it wasn't at all what she'd expected. She figured Sapa's musical style would be a cross between folk and instrumental, like those pan-flute playing South American Indians who annoyed the piss out of everyone at local fairs and festivals, with a few drums thrown in to call it hard rock.

Not so. Sapa rocked it hard, musically a mix of Godsmack, Evanescence and Alice in Chains. A primal tribal drum line alongside a chunky bass, and screaming electric guitars. The vocals alternated between male and female leads. Melodic one song, discordant the next, and punctuated with screamo sections any heavy metal fan could dig.

So there was no way she was missing it.

At her small cabin, she let the hot water soothe her sore muscles. After eating, she downed four aspirin and searched her closet for something edgy to wear.

Her job working for a civilian contractor on a rural Air Force base, sitting in front of a computer in a roomful of men, hadn't unleashed her inner fashionista. Pathetic to realize she didn't own anything funky or hip. Which made her feel...decidedly uncool.

At least the years dealing with hair and makeup in dance competitions allowed her to add a more dramatic look to her face. She shimmied on her favorite pair of jeans and a red camisole that'd shrunk in the washer; the shorter length did show some skin and her belly ring. After slipping on her red cowgirl boots, Maggie headed to the Heritage.

She'd given herself enough time, planning to arrive an hour early. The line to get in was unbelievably long. By the time she was inside, the place was wall-to-wall people and she couldn't get near the stage. But from what she could see, it'd be impossible to get past the multitude of security guards anyway.

It took fifteen minutes to flag down a cocktail waitress. Maggie checked her phone and saw she'd missed a call from Billy. Strange that he was calling her on a Friday night—hopefully everything was all right. But it was too loud to hear his voice message now. She'd call him in the morning.

Finally the lights flickered off and on. The crowd's anticipation electrified the whole place. She found a spot against the far back wall where she had a view of the entire stage.

Chants of, "Sapa, Sapa," ended abruptly when the area in front of the stage went dark.

A man's high-pitched voice sliced through the air in traditional Native American chanting, singing without recognizable words. Another male voice joined in. And another. Then the steady *thump thump thump* of a drum. Deep tones that blended perfectly with the high notes. The sounds built and built...and then everything stopped.

The crowd collectively held its breath.

Then guitars and drums blasted from the stage, along with an explosion of light.

Maggie was absolutely blown away. One song segued into the next. A different style that showcased each musician's strength. She was a little shocked to see the person shredding guitar was a woman. When it came time to showcase the drummer, she was surprised when the stage hands rolled out another, completely different set of drums than the ones Jon had been using for the previous songs.

Jon jumped behind the new drum set and twirled his drumsticks above his head. The crowd roared when he began to play. The main beat was slow and steady. Very primal. The kind of deep thud that passed through her muscles and tissues and settled in to vibrate her bones. Her body tensed in anticipation for the next pulse. Then the next. And the next.

He layered a variety of drum jams—fast, syncopated, off-tempo, but no matter how quickly his drumsticks moved between drums, that first low, seductive beat never faltered.

No rhythm my ass.

Even when the guitars and voices joined in, turning the primitive beat into a song, Maggie felt the reverberation of the drum inside her body. Her pulse mimicked it. Her blood throbbed with it. She'd never had music affect her on such a visceral level.

She closed her eyes and imagined touching Jon, this primal rhythm in the background. Stroking him with her hands. With her mouth. Feeling the heat of his body as he rose above her. Feeling that hot, sweet throb of need as his flesh teased hers. Over and over. Until she was begging. Until they were joined and moving as one to the same rhythm.

That's when she realized her panties were slick. Lust burned through her so thoroughly that when she opened her eyes, she saw couples sating that same overpowering sexual need. Locked in a passionate kiss. Grinding and rubbing their bodies in sensual motion.

That jungle beat, hypnotic and strangely melodic, called to her. She couldn't see Jon behind the wall of drums, but she felt his presence every time his drumstick connected with the drum skin.

The song ended and the band exited the stage. But the crowd wasn't ready to let them go. Maggie stomped her feet, ignoring the sting of pain, clapped her hands and whistled right along with them.

Several minutes later Sapa returned to the kind of deafening applause she was used to hearing in a stadium. The first encore song was a hard rock cover tune and Sapa knocked it out of the park. The second song was a stripped-down bluesy number, which morphed into an oddly compelling dissonant lullaby. The lead singer introduced the band members, the lights went up and the show was over.

Maggie wandered up to the bar, ordering a Coke and letting the crowd thin before she ventured outside. Security was still tight by the stage. As they moved the drum sets, Maggie wondered if Jon stayed backstage to supervise, or if his crew had done it so many times he didn't have to worry, and he was basking in fan adoration.

After finishing her drink, she wended her way through the people gathering for the next act, exiting out the side door. The night air cooled her cheeks, but did nothing to quell the heat burning inside her. Unused to the edginess, she paced. She spun and ran into a brick wall. A warm, flesh-and-blood brick wall.

She stepped back to apologize, but he spoke first.

"Maggie? Hey. I thought that was you. Sorry to keep you waiting."

She had to look away from his potent blue eyes. "You didn't. I just got out here." But her gaze dropped to his corded neck.

Do not imagine pressing your lips to the spot where his pulse is pounding as erratically as yours.

Jon didn't immediately speak. He didn't move either. Finally he asked, "Is everything all right?"

No. You practically gave me an orgasm just from hearing you play the drums.

"Maggie?"

Her hands had somehow landed on his chest and she squeezed his pecs.

"Why won't you look at me?"

"Because then you'll see," she said softly.

"See what?" His fingers were under her chin forcing her gaze to his. His focus moved from her eyes to her mouth, then back to her eyes.

"See that." She didn't have to put a name to it; the man recognized lust.

Curling his hand around the back of her neck, he brought their mouths together, only allowing a whisper-soft brush of his lips across hers. But each successive near-kiss silently urged her to part her lips. Then she could feel his breath in her mouth. A tease. A taste. She wanted more. Now.

When Maggie made a distressed sound, Jon consumed her mouth in a kiss that robbed her of reason. A kiss packed with passion as his tongue invaded her lips, licking into her mouth. Cranking her desire to fever pitch as he proved he was a man in complete command. He situated her head to deepen the kiss to his liking. The tips of his fingers—so adept at creating hard driving music—stroked her jawline in the perfect mix of rough and tender.

She pressed her body to his, wishing for a solid surface behind her so she could twine her arms and legs around him.

Almost as if he'd read her thoughts, he propelled her backward until her spine connected with the building. He gripped her ass and lifted her, his pelvis held her in place as his hands roamed. Every spot he touched made her purr. Made her arch. Made her dizzy and greedy.

Her hands dove into his hair, twining the silky damp strands around her fingers.

If a kiss was this mind-blowingly explosive, sex with this man would be off the charts.

Jon slowed the pace from frantic to flirty. Interspersing long, hot kisses with sweet, affectionate pecks. A tug of his teeth on her lower lip. Or her earlobe. A fleeting flick of his tongue on those same spots. Then that wicked mouth skated over her neck. Sucking. Licking. Biting.

She moaned when he placed his open mouth on the swell of her breast. "Don't stop."

He rested his forehead in the curve of her shoulder, his breathing ragged. "We have to stop. I'm not gonna maul you out here where anyone can see us."

Maggie dug her fingers into his scalp until he lifted his head and looked at her. "Then take me someplace private and I'll let you maul me all you want."

He released her. Once her feet were on the ground, he clasped her hand and led her by the tour buses.

At seeing the crowd, she panicked for a moment and hung back.

Jon spun around to face her. "Are you changing your mind?"

"No. But there are so many people. And I don't..." Want to be just another groupie you bang after a show on your tour bus.

He correctly read her anxious expression. "I'm not taking you to my bus. I'm taking the shortcut to my car."

"Oh."

When he kissed her again with a mix of authority and seduction she was lost to everything but how right his arms felt around her. How perfect his mouth fit against hers.

"Jon?"

The surprising sound of her sister-in-law's voice had her ripping her mouth from Jon's and turning around.

Eden and Billy stared at them in complete shock.

Then her hotheaded brother grabbed Jon's arm. "Jesus, Maggie. *You're* out here sucking face with White Feather?"

Jon didn't acknowledge Billy at all. Keeping his gaze locked to Maggie's, he said to Billy, "Get. Your. Hand. Off. Me."

"Billy," Eden said, "you're causing a scene. Let him go."

He listened to his wife, but kept his focus on Maggie. "I want to know what the hell you're doing with him."

Maggie raised her chin. "Hi, Billy. Nice to see you too. I see you know Jon."

"Yeah, I know Jon. But my question is do *you* know him?"

"What is your problem?"

"That." Billy gestured to the women gathered around the tour buses. "Because that's who he is. Johnny Feather. His fuck 'em and leave 'em reputation doesn't bother you?"

Jon swore and lunged at Billy, but Eden inserted herself between the men.

"Jon. Back off. And you—" Eden poked Billy in the chest, "—leave it alone. This is not our concern."

Maggie wondered why Billy had overreacted. He never pulled the *I'm your big brother* bullshit when it came to her relationships. There had to be more going on here, but this wasn't the time or place to find out.

Eden faced Jon. "So, the reason we tracked you down, Jon, was to tell you awesome show tonight." She stroked her hand over her rounded belly. "Even the papoose was rockin' out in here."

"How are you feelin'?" Jon asked, giving Eden a soft smile.

"Fat. Happy." She shot her husband a sideways glance. "Most of the time. But it is past our bedtime and we'll be goin' home."

A fuming Billy looked at Maggie. "Need a ride?"

"I'm good. But thanks."

The other band members exited the back door. A group of fans broke free from security on the opposite side and they were surrounded.

Jon let go of Maggie's hand, stepping in front of her, but people moved between them—and Maggie got pushed back by the doors.

It was total chaos. She jumped up and down, waving to try and get Jon's attention, but he had his back to her. When she finally caught a glimpse of his face, he was deep in conversation with someone.

He hadn't been looking for her at all.

Disappointment dogged her. She scoured the crowd to see if Billy and Eden had escaped, but mostly to make sure they hadn't seen that Jon had forgotten about her. She also didn't want her pain-in-the-ass brother to think he'd been right.

On the long walk back to her car, Maggie realized she hadn't given Jon her phone number. The fact he couldn't call her didn't bother her as much as the thought she would've slept with him without them exchanging basic information. That was so unlike her. She'd practically done a full background check on other guys she'd just considered dating.

By the time she'd reached her cabin, she'd almost convinced herself the interruption from her brother and the crowd had been for the best.

Almost.

Chapter Six

Jon wouldn't say he stormed into Billy Buchanan's office on Monday morning, but the new secretary working at Feather Light might argue that point. And she did.

"I tried to stop him, but he wouldn't listen," she huffed, following Jon into the room.

Billy looked up from the drafting table, his eyes decidedly frosty. "It's okay, Dani. This is Jim's brother. Evidently that entitles him to walk into whatever office he wants, whenever the hell he feels like it."

"Would you like me to tell Jim his brother is here?" she asked.

Jon and Billy said "no" simultaneously.

Dani slunk out and shut the door behind her.

Billy moved from behind the drafting table and pointed to the chairs in front of his desk. "Sit."

Jon preferred to stand. And pace. So he could take a swing at Billy if he got the chance.

Tough talk. He wouldn't do it. Not because this was his brother's partner, but he'd left his fighting days behind him.

He watched Billy, trying to find a family resemblance between him and Maggie. Same blue eyes. Same blond tones in their hair, although Maggie had more red in hers. Besides that, they looked nothing alike. Acted nothing alike either.

Billy seemed to be scrutinizing him too. "So, you're here because you're pissed off about what I said Saturday night?"

"Do ya think? Where do you get off—"

"She's my fucking sister! She deserves better than you."

"Because I'm Indian?" Jon had clenched his jaw so tightly he wasn't sure how the words had forced themselves out.

Billy shook his head. "Race has nothing to do with this. And fuck you for even bringing that up. I'm married to an Indian woman and our child will be mixed race. My partner is Indian. My sister Lacy's husband is part Indian. The goddamn color of your skin plays no part in it."

"Then what?"

"You really need me to spell it out for you? You use and discard women. A different city, a different girl every night. That's not hearsay, Jon. You yourself told me that. So I'm just supposed to smile and say nothing when I see you practically fucking my sister in public?"

Jon tapped his fingers on the armrest. "Number one, I wasn't 'practically fucking' Maggie; I was kissing her. Number two, you sure your feelings aren't misplaced out of guilt? You don't want me around your sister because you're afraid I'll tell her that we had a threesome...with your wife?"

Billy glared at him.

"I'm not off base, am I?" Jon prompted.

"Fuck. Maybe that is part of it." Billy ran his hand through his hair and muttered, "We can't change the past."

"But we sure as hell can hide it, right?"

"I'd hoped that would be a given."

Jon shrugged. "I haven't told anyone, because contrary to what you believe, I don't blab about my sex life." When Billy started to contradict him, Jon held up his hand. "And please don't pretend you think you know me, based on that one time we stayed together in the condo, for two days, over four years ago."

Billy snorted. "You saying you've changed?"

"I'm saying what we talked about, how much pussy I was getting back then was brought up by you—not me. I won't deny I've taken what was freely offered to me. Does that make me a man whore? No doubt. But I take offense to your statement that I use and discard women. I don't."

"Maybe that's the way you see it, or how you justify it. But I watched you Saturday night. Within minutes of being surrounded by adoring fans, Johnny Feather forgot about Maggie Buchanan entirely. She tried to get your attention but you didn't see her. Know what sucked about that? I had to witness the disappointment on her face. I tried to prevent my sister from getting hurt and it happened anyway."

152

Jon hated that Billy was right on that point. He hadn't realized Maggie hadn't hung around until the crowd had thinned and everyone had gotten a piece of him.

"Go ahead and call me a dick for saying this, but I'm glad Maggie saw that side of your life—of you—before you two get more involved."

And what really stung? Jon wished Billy was wrong, but he wasn't sure he was.

"Did you call her and apologize?" Billy asked.

"I don't have her phone number." He scowled. "And I wasn't about to call you or Eden to get it."

"Smart choice." Billy leaned back in his chair. "Make another smart choice, Jon. Walk away from her."

I don't know if I can. "I'll remind you that Raven and I are taking dance lessons from Maggie and Seth."

"I wish Eden wouldn't have suggested Maggie teach that dance class. It's just giving her false hope about returning to dancing when she needs to look for a real full-time job."

"Jesus, Billy. Have you actually said that bullshit to Maggie?"

"What's wrong with telling her the truth?"

"That's not the truth. That's crushing her dream and her spirit. Maggie loves dancing and she's damn good at it. Why shouldn't she have a chance to do something that she loves?"

Billy leaned forward. "Because it is a dream. Dreams don't pay the bills and provide for the future. I'm sure you're telling her something completely different, you creative types don't tend to be grounded in reality. But Maggie is. She had a great job and a great career. That dance partner has filled her head with pipe dreams. She'll just end up disappointed again."

"Again?"

"Like in college. She got to the point her dance schedule affected her academics. I sat her down and talked to her about her future, telling her the best she could've hoped for with a performance degree was to end up teaching. She buckled down in a field of study that would be financially rewarding and stabilizing, made decent grades and ended up with a better-than-average job right after graduation."

Jon kept his mouth shut. But his gut clenched, thinking of the joy on Maggie's face when she danced. And the wistful look when she'd told him how much she'd missed that part of herself. What would Jon have done if his brother had sat him down and told him not to pursue a music career? Because Jon respected Jim so much, he would've listened.

Luckily Jim had backed Jon one hundred percent. Neither his siblings nor his parents had projected their life goals and expectations on him and he was grateful for that. More grateful than ever, now that he understood how rare that was. Jon didn't doubt Billy had done it out of love and concern for Maggie. But it broke his heart a little that she'd just given up.

The intercom on Billy's phone buzzed. "Yes?"

"Jim said to tell his brother he wants to see him in his office when you're done with him."

"Will do, Dani. Thanks." Billy cocked his head. "So we done?"

"Yep." Jon got up and walked out. Straight to his car. Jim would be pissed he'd ignored him, but he'd deal with it later.

Right now he just needed to think.

Mid-afternoon, Jon's cell rang. The call wasn't from his brother, as he'd expected, but his agent. "Johnny-boy! How are ya, kid?"

Kid. Anyone under forty qualified as a kid in Marty Goldman's world. "I'm all right. What's up?"

"I'll cut right to the chase. Someone from *Indie Rock* magazine was at Sapa's show in Spearfish Saturday night."

"Yeah? Why's that matter?"

"Because she heard rumors that the band is going on hiatus indefinitely."

Jon paced to the big window in the living area. "Not a rumor, Goldman, as you know."

"That's what I told her yesterday. So is it a coincidence that today I get a call from Darkly Dreaming's management company? They're auditioning drummers. They want to talk to you."

"Whoa. Wait a damn second. I'm on hiatus too. Remember our conversation about me being tired of touring and having no life? That hasn't changed."

"Which I understand. But damn, kid, Darkly Dreaming is big time."

"I don't care. I'm burned out. I need this time off."

An exasperated sigh echoed in his ear. "It's almost been a month."

"That's the longest break I've had in years and it hasn't been near long enough." Jon rubbed his forehead against the impending headache. Did his agent understand him at all? Or did he just see dollar signs? "Tell them I appreciate their interest but no thanks."

"That mean you don't want to know who else is expressing interest in you?"

Fuck. Marty just had to dangle another carrot, didn't he? "Who?"

"Push and Radioactive Tar are also auditioning drummers."

Holy shit. He'd kill to work with Van Conner, who produced Push and had scored a Grammy on their last CD. Radioactive Tar was a group of studio musicians in Nashville that had a rotating roster of who's who in music. Just making contact with any one of those bands could give a big boost to his music career.

But you're taking a break, right?

"Kid? You still there?"

"Yeah. Just picking my jaw up off the floor."

"I thought you might say that," he said smugly. "But here's the catch. All of them want to set it up for this week."

Dammit. He had dance class with Raven in four hours. "Is there any way we can get it postponed for another week?"

"Nope. In fact, Push wants the meeting in Seattle tomorrow night."

As much as he still needed a break from his hectic lifestyle, meeting with these bands wouldn't be like touring and promoting. It would be about music. His music. No harm in hearing what they had to say, was there?

His artistic subconscious sneered at him for being fickle, accusing him of missing the rock-star life of fawning fans and fame. Throwing in a final jab about lying to himself and everyone else about settling down.

But his practical side warned him opportunities like this didn't come along every day and he'd be a fool to let it slip away.

The phone clunked. Paper rattled. Marty sighed. "I hate to pressure you, but my secretary says there's one seat left on the nine o'clock flight to Denver tonight leaving out of Rapid. And the flight from Denver to Seattle puts you in Seattle around midnight."

He'd figure out something to tell Raven—just as soon as he made sense of his decision himself. "That'll work. Have your secretary book me at the Cooper Hotel in downtown Seattle."

"Done. I'll have her book your flights to L.A. and Nashville to meet with the other bands. Call me in the morning and I'll give you all the details. But remember; keep a lid on this, kid." Marty hung up.

Jon showered, packed and closed up his house, although he wouldn't be gone more than a week. While getting ready, he'd come up with a possible solution to his dance class dilemma. Or at least, he had an idea who could help him. He paced while he was waiting for her assistant to ring him through.

The line clicked. "This is Eden Buchanan."

"Knock, knock, knocking on Eden's door..."

"Jon, you magnificent bastard. I miss you serenading me."

"Doubtful, or you would've picked me over old what's-his-face. Still... How is it you look more beautiful now that you're knocked up? It pains me to admit you'll always be the woman I let slip through my fingers. The gold standard that I hold all other women to."

She laughed. "That sweet talking means one thing... What do you want?"

"A really big—and we're taking huge—favor..."

Chapter Seven

The week had started out on a bad note and had gone downhill from there.

Maggie had ended up working extra time at the doctor's office when they had a security breach with their server. She'd fixed it, but it was a pointed reminder that she missed the challenge of working in her field and not just killing time doing data entry.

Seth had been in a lousy mood all week, which hadn't made rehearsing fun. When she called her BFF Sara, who was also Seth's sister, to ask what was going on, Maggie ended up confessing her problems and the perplexing situation with Jon. She and Sara dissected it ten different ways and neither could come up with a plan besides to let it ride.

Maybe Maggie was a fool to think there was something there besides a few sexy looks, hot touches and stolen kisses, but that didn't stop her from hoping she'd see him again, either in class or outside of it.

Right now, she had a bigger problem. She turned the key in the ignition one more time and heard nothing but clicks.

"Piece of shit car." Maggie banged her fists on the steering wheel.

Of course it had to be pouring rain. Not the warm, summertime showers, which were a welcome relief after a scorching day. No, the wind blew so hard it shook her little car. The inside of the windows were so fogged up she could barely see her headlights.

That was a good sign, wasn't it? That the headlights were working even if they were dim? When she reached forward to wipe off the condensation, she accidentally laid on the horn and spooked herself good.

Get a grip, Maggie.

She unplugged her cell phone from the car charger and groaned. Even her cell was dead. Looked like she had no choice but to go back into the gym and call a cab.

Just as she turned to open her car door, she noticed a hooded figure peering in her window. She screamed and scrambled into the passenger's seat, thoughts of psychotic killers disabling cars in deserted parking lots running through her brain.

The door opened and the hooded figure's head was inside the car. "Maggie? It's me."

"Jon? What are you—"

"I was driving by and I saw your car was still here. Is everything okay?"

"No. My car won't start and I don't know what's wrong with it."

"It's pouring out here too damn hard for me to take a look." He held out his hand. "Come on. I'll get you home."

Touching him released a pulse pounding rush of sexual awareness, and she knew by the dark look in his eyes he felt it too.

Maggie grabbed her stuff and made a mad dash for Jon's vehicle, but she was still soaked to the skin when she climbed inside.

Jon shoved her bag in the backseat. "It's a frog strangler out there, eh?"

She shivered. "I won't complain because we need the rain, but doesn't it just figure I'd have car trouble tonight."

He reached over, letting his thumb sweep over her jawbone.

Maggie shivered harder, but she didn't jerk away. "What?"

"You splashed mud on your face."

"Thanks." She stared at him. "You missed class this week."

"I had to deal with band stuff."

That was evasive.

"Raven didn't tell you?"

"No, she was pretty enamored with her substitute partner."

Jon frowned. "I would've called you directly to let you know but I didn't have your number."

Or you were avoiding me after that steamy kiss Saturday night and the run-in with my brother.

She waved him off. "Doesn't matter."

"It does to me. Look, Maggie—"

"Forget it. I'm tired, wet and I just want to go home. I do appreciate you rescuing me tonight, so thanks."

"No problem." Jon started the vehicle and paused at the parking lot exit. "Which way?"

"Left. I live out on Burner Road."

Rain fell in sheets, so heavy at times Jon slowed to a crawl on the city streets. "I don't know that I've ever seen it rain this hard."

Maggie peered out the side window. Water was running over the gutters and at least six inches of water covered the city streets. "Me either."

"My brother would make a crack about the tribe's rain dances finally working. I'll bet the creek is running high."

Creek. She hadn't even thought about that. "Dammit."

He shot her a glance. "What?"

"The only way to get to my place is over Burner Bridge and it crosses the creek."

Jon pulled into a parking lot. "That's a problem. Too dangerous to try and cross it now, either on foot or by car."

She knew he was right, but that further limited her options. It'd be rude to show up and Billy and Eden's place this late, without calling. Chances were high all the hotels were full since they were in the height of tourist season. Her friends lived in Rapid City.

"I know this puts you in a bind. So if you want, you can stay with me. I have an empty guest bedroom. Tomorrow morning I'll bring you back and maybe I can figure out what's wrong with your car."

Alone. With Jon White Feather. All night. This would definitely be a test of willpower.

"If you're worried I'm gonna tie you up with duct tape, call Eden and Billy so they know where you are."

That conversation wouldn't go well since Billy had already warned her off Jon. Plus, Maggie would be mortified to make the call—she was a thirty-two-year-old woman, not a sixteen-year-old girl reporting in that she was breaking curfew. "The phone call isn't necessary. If you do decide to tie me up, I hope you use something besides duct tape. That gummy residue is a bitch to scrub off skin."

He was shocked for a millisecond before he granted her that sexy smile. "Good to know."

They didn't speak for the rest of the drive, unless she counted him muttering about the lousy visibility and horrible road conditions.

He veered off to the right onto a gravel road outside of Spearfish Canyon. The Black Hills spruce trees formed a canopy above them, softening the deluge. When they reached a big iron gate, he pointed a remote control device at the box on the fence post and the gate swung open.

"Wow. Fancy."

"It discourages pesky relatives, door-to-door salespeople and bible thumpers who want to save my eternal soul."

Maggie suspected it also kept out fans, or groupies, or whatever they were called.

Water had pooled in spots in the road, turning it into a mud bog.

Jon dropped it into four-wheel drive and said, "Hang on," before he gunned it.

They bumped up a hill and when it leveled out she caught her first glimpse of the place he called home. Security lights illuminated a ranch-style log house with a small deck on the front and a two-car garage on the far left side. "This place is so well lit."

"The security system attached to the gate alerts me if someone enters through it. The sensors tell me if someone tries to get around it on foot."

"Got a stockpile of valuables you're protecting?"

"Nope. Just my privacy." He poked the garage door opener clipped to the visor.

"You sure I won't be intruding?"

He stopped the vehicle halfway through the garage door and turned to look at her. "I wouldn't have asked you to stay with me tonight if I wasn't sure."

That could be taken a couple of different ways.

Maggie whistled after they'd parked. "This is the cleanest garage I've ever been in. How long have you lived here?"

Jon grabbed her bag from the backseat. "Three years. It's clean because I haven't been here that much."

He kept his hand on the small of her back as they exited the garage into a mud room. He set her bag on the washer, unzipped his hoodie and tossed it in a big sink.

Oh man. Her mouth dried seeing the wet T-shirt clinging to every muscle of his upper arms and chest. This man had such a beautiful body. Well-defined arms, contoured pecs, flat stomach. He unlaced his hikers and peeled off his socks, dropping them in the sink. He glanced up at her. "I freakin' hate wet socks."

Don't you hate wet shorts too? Maybe you oughta strip off those camo shorts so I know firsthand whether you're a boxers or briefs guy.

When her gaze met his, his startling blue eyes danced with amusement. "Do you have dry clothes in your bag?"

"Nothing besides dance clothes."

"I'll lend you something. I'll show you to your room."

Maggie had the impression of bright colors and Native American artwork as he led her down a long hallway. He opened the second door and flipped on the lights. "The bathroom is through that pocket door. Hang tight for a sec and I'll grab some clothes."

She had time to wander the cozy room, with its terra-cotta-colored walls and vibrant turquoise accents. The queen-size bed faced a window, although it was too stormy to see the view.

Jon was back before she ventured into the bathroom. "My former tour manager left these on the bus and somehow they ended up at my place." He passed her a pair of neon yellow Capri sweatpants and a gray tank top with Sapa emblazoned across the front.

"Thanks." Maggie's bra and underwear were fairly dry so she didn't have to go commando beneath the borrowed clothes. She tracked Jon to the kitchen. Not an ostentatious space, but homey. A cooktop was in the center island, which was surrounded by a horseshoe-shaped eat-in counter and six leather barstools. Lightning flashed above her head. She glanced up at the reflection in four enormous skylights. "Those are great."

"Jim knows I like to look at the stars, so he designed this house with that in mind." He took a sip of bottled water. "Would you like something to drink? Water, soda, iced tea. I'm not much for alcoholic beverages, but there's probably a bottle of wine rolling around here someplace."

"Water is fine. Although it seems silly to be thirsty when I was just drenched to the skin." She was still shaking, but she was beginning to think it wasn't from the cold. The heated way Jon looked at her should be setting her blood on fire.

"I'll show you around the rest of the house while I still can. Electricity can be wonky out here during storms." He hit a switch, flooding the living area with light.

The furniture faced a brick fireplace that took up almost the entire back wall. A coffee table crafted from a gnarled tree root was centered on top of a vivid rug, patterned with Native American symbols. When Maggie ran her hand along the back of the couch, her fingers encountered baby soft leather. "I could just curl into this couch and doze off."

"Go ahead. I spend a good chunk of my time with my feet up, staring aimlessly upward."

After she'd stretched out, she noticed a glass ceiling that nearly spanned the length of the room. "Holy shit."

"That's what the insurance company said when I applied for a homeowner's policy," he said dryly. "I love it, but it does have drawbacks. Luckily there's a retractable metal covering, so if something happens while I'm out of town, my house wouldn't be open to the elements and the critters for months on end."

"I wish I could see the stars."

He moved behind her and dimmed the lights.

"Do you have a telescope?"

"Nope." He sat on the edge of the coffee table, his forearms resting on his thighs. "I prefer looking with the naked eye."

I'd prefer you looking at me naked with those sexy eyes of yours.

Another smirk curled the corners of his mouth, making her wonder if she'd said that last thought out aloud. "So you're an amateur astronomer?"

"Not really. It's not even a hobby. Just something I do for relaxation and fun. What about you?"

"Meaning...do I have hobbies?"

"Meaning...what do you do for relaxation and fun?"

"I haven't indulged in my favorite way to relax for a long time."

Pause. Then, "Now you've aroused my interest."

When she realized how suggestive that sounded, she blushed to the roots of her hair. Wait. Had he said aroused?

He chuckled. "The fact you're blushing gives me all sorts of ideas on how you like to relax. And if I can help you out with that, just let me know."

Yes, please.

Rain pattering on the glass made a soothing sound. After a bit she said, "I'm surprised you don't have a TV in here."

"I'm not a fan of how media has overtaken every part of day-to-day life. It's like no one can stand silence."

"Before I lost my job I was always too busy to pay attention to a pretty sunset or a wren warbling in a tree. But now even if Seth keeps me dancing until ten o'clock at night, I make time to empty my head. Just me and nature."

Jon reached for her hand and kissed the tips of her fingers. "You're not at all like I imagined you'd be the first day I saw you teaching dance class."

"Really?"

"Really. And I meant that in a good way." He rubbed his thumb over her knuckles. "You looked every inch the prima ballerina. Beautiful, graceful. I expected temperamental, which I haven't seen. An uppity white girl, which I haven't seen either. Passionate, which I've had just a little taste of."

She held her breath, waiting for him to say he wanted to see more of that side of her.

But Jon just kept his compelling blue eyes on hers. "You want a tour of the house?"

"Ah, sure."

Keeping hold of her hand, Jon skirted a large sculpture of an eagle soaring into the sky with a fish clutched in its talons.

They walked past her guest bedroom and he showed her another empty room, which held two sets of bunk beds. "My nephews and nieces stay here a lot when I'm home."

How sweet that he was so involved in their lives. The next door was set back about ten feet from the hallway. "That's the den. There's where you'll find the flatscreen, DVD player, gaming consoles, foosball table, dart board. Typical single-guy stuff."

"Do you spend much time in there?"

"Depends on how long I've been on the road. But I usually only hang out in there when someone comes over."

Maggie poked her head inside. Everything looked brand new. He must not do much entertaining.

Jon dropped her hand and faced her at the last door. "This is my bedroom."

"Do I get to see it?"

"Depends on if it makes you uncomfortable when I admit I've imagined you in my bed since we first met. That said, I didn't offer you a place to stay so I could sweet talk you into a tumble between my sheets."

Outwardly she stilled, but inside her heart galloped and her stomach did pirouettes. When he stepped aside to allow her into his room, she murmured, "Well, that's a shame."

Maggie took in the king-size bed, the dressers, more big windows, covered with draperies. She peered into the adjoining bath, done in black and chrome. Then she wandered out and perched on the edge of the bed. "Bet you're happy to come home to this place after being on the road."

Jon still leaned in the doorway, arms crossed over his chest. "Yep. And today is one of the rare days I've made my bed."

"You sound proud of that."

"I am."

"Is this where I finally get a glimmer of rock-star behavior?"

He smiled. "Maybe. I stay in hotels and the maids clean up after me. I stay in the tour bus and we have a service that cleans it or I sleep on an unmade bunk. I tend to forget I'm responsible for those mundane things when I come home."

Her fingers pleated the plush comforter fabric as she tried to figure out how to phrase her next question. "Your house is great but I expected—"

"It to be bigger? More ostentatious?"

"No. I expected you to have a music room."

Jon's posture relaxed. "I have an entire studio behind the house. You didn't see it when we drove up?"

She shook her head.

"I wanted to keep the spaces separate. One where I could work on music and write. And a home where I could just be."

He sauntered forward with that sex-on-legs walk and she couldn't look away from him.

Then he gently pushed her shoulders and she rolled down onto the mattress. He loomed over her. "So we staying in here and messing up the sheets? Or returning to the living room for polite conversation?"

His pupils were so dark she couldn't see any blue in his eyes. He radiated enough body heat any chill on her skin evaporated. This potent, sexy man wanted her. *Her.*

Maggie wreathed her arms around his neck. "Fuck polite. Let's get wild."

Chapter Eight

Jon lost his focus for a moment as he kissed her, cranking the heat simmering between them into an inferno.

Maggie's body arched, one hand twisted in his hair, the other gripping his hip. Her soft lips clung to his as her tongue stroked and teased, her mouth urgent in expressing her need.

He pushed up and looked down at her.

Seeing the flush on her cheeks and the passion darkening her eyes almost had him throwing caution to the wind, giving into the hard, fast fuck they both wanted now and slowing it down for a second round.

But Maggie wasn't taking the lead in this dance.

"I like seeing you in my bed," Jon said silkily, pressing a kiss below her ear. Then he let his lips follow her jawline to the other ear. "But I'd like it even more if you were naked."

"Have I mentioned how fast I am at getting in and out of my clothes? I can show you if you want."

He smiled against her cheek. "Nope. Because we're doing this my way."

"Meaning slow."

"Meaning...my way." Jon rubbed his mouth over hers, keeping their eyes locked, which increased the intimacy of the connection.

Maggie undulated beneath him, her impatience palpable.

"Got some place to be?" he asked.

"On top of you, riding you like a pony."

"That's something we'll have to try. Later." He captured her mouth with a kiss packed with such sexual greed, she whimpered when he broke free. Jon scooted forward on his knees, forcing her to straddle his legs. "Lift your arms."

She sat up and he removed the tank top.

Jon curled his hands over her shoulders, sweeping his thumbs across her clavicle. "So pretty."

"If I'd known I'd end up here tonight, I would've worn something sexier than my sports bra."

He tipped her chin up. "Ask me tomorrow what bra you wore and I won't remember. But I will remember the taste of your skin and how it felt when I touched you. Take it off."

Maggie pulled her bra off and flopped back on the bed. "Now it's easier for your hands to fulfill the promises that sweet-talkin' mouth of yours just made."

"And fulfill they will."

She gestured to his shirt. "You are lagging behind."

"Can't have that." Jon performed a slow striptease with his sleeveless T-shirt as he removed it.

Her eyes ate up his chest, arms and abdomen once he was completely bared to her. "God. I want to lick every one of your tattoos."

"In time." He hovered above her chest, his hot breath drifting over her damp skin. Then he dipped his head and his hair fell forward, brushing the upper swells of her breasts and the puckered tips of her nipples.

She hissed when his wet tongue lashed a tight point. "I'll give you about an hour to stop doing that."

Jon chuckled. "I'll promise I'll pay them the proper respect next time. I've got something else in mind for now."

His hair zigzagged across her belly as he scooted down her body. He teased and tormented her until she writhed. Finally he tapped her hip and when she lifted up, he peeled off her sweatpants.

She was gorgeous naked. Firm muscles beneath her ivory skin. A small strip of strawberry-blond curls striped her mound, leading to that sweet, pink pussy.

Jon reached for her hand. He nuzzled her wrist and his mouth moved upward, kissing the center of her palm before he sucked her middle finger completely into his mouth.

Maggie hissed. She'd propped herself up on both elbows and studied him from beneath lowered lashes, her body so restless he could feel sexual energy emanating from her.

He released her finger and placed the wet tip over her clit. "Show me how you touch yourself."

Her cheeks flushed with color. "Shouldn't you be doing that?"

"I'll do more than watch, trust me."

At first Maggie was self-conscious. But when Jon murmured encouragement and started trailing the backs of his fingers over her thighs, she gave herself over to self-pleasure. Swirling circles around that nub. Flicking it lightly. Watching his eyes, she slowly pushed her middle finger into her opening. She rocked her wrist back and forth, grinding the heel of her hand against her clit.

As soon as she removed her finger, Jon bent down and sucked it, releasing a tiny growl at his first taste of her. After he'd licked away all the sweet juice, he demanded, "Again."

Maggie glided her fingertip up and down her slit, adding more cream before vigorously rubbing her clit in a side-to-side motion. A moan escaped and she plunged her finger into her pussy, bumping her hips up to drive that digit in deeper.

Jon's erection dug into his stomach when he dropped to the mattress. But he ignored the pain and latched onto Maggie's butt cheeks, pulling her sex against his mouth. He thrust his tongue into her pussy alongside her finger.

"Oh God."

He scraped his teeth over her knuckle. "Move your hand." As soon as she complied, his thumbs spread open her swollen sex. He licked and sucked every inch of her intimate flesh, feasting on her.

Maggie had clamped her hands to his head as she thrashed beneath him. She jerked his scalp after he'd lightly grazed her clitoris with his teeth. "Sorry."

"Don't be," he growled. "It turns me on when you pull my hair." He used the very tip of his tongue to flick across that distended nub. She made sexy whimpering mewls and he fastened his lips to the pliant, throbbing skin and sucked.

"Keep doing—yes, just like that." Her body seized up and he felt the climactic pulses against his mouth.

After Maggie's legs quit twitching and the pressure on his scalp disappeared, he placed a soft kiss above her mound. He pushed off the mattress, ditched his shorts and rolled on a condom.

Their eyes met and then he was on her, in her. Thrusting into that tight, wet, hot cunt.

She locked her ankles on his ass, trying to pull him deeper with every stroke. "This feels so good."

Jon intended to push her a level or twenty above good. This first time would be spectacular. "Maggie," he murmured between thrusts. "Let me take care of you. Let me get us there."

"Yes. Anything you want."

He gradually slowed, groaning when her channel clamped down, trying to keep his cock inside. He rested the tip just inside the opening to her sex. Despite his thundering heart and the urgency pounding at him, he found that Zen spot and began.

One, two, three, four shallows thrusts, where he only went halfway into her pussy. On the fifth thrust, his cock stayed buried deep. He stayed that way, not moving, for five beats.

Then one, two, three, four shallow thrusts. On the fifth count he pulled out completely. After five breaths, he slowly stroked the tip of his cock up the contour of her mound, stopping at her clit. Then he dragged the wide, blunt head down, separating her pussy lips with his pulsing flesh until he reached the opening to her body.

He began again.

Maggie went wild. Arching against him. Her fingernails digging into his shoulders. Gouging his ass as she fought for a grip on his sweat-coated skin. Her mouth nipping at his neck. Her tongue tracing the edges of the tattoos on his biceps.

Jon kept up the primal pattern until he started to lose count. He said, "Hang on," and rolled upright, keeping their bodies connected as they faced each other. With his knees spread wide, he sat on his heels, holding onto her ass, raising and lowering her body to counter his upward thrusts.

"I'm gonna come again," she wailed.

The almost violent ripples of her orgasm unleashed his.

Hot pulses jettisoned out of his cock with every squeeze of her pussy muscles around his shaft. His mind blanked even as his body erupted and he gasped for breath.

Teeth scraping against his neck brought him out of his sexual stupor.

"I take it back," Maggie panted against his ear. "Everything I said about you not having rhythm."

For a brief second when Maggie woke up, she forgot where she was.

Then soft kisses peppered her shoulder. A rough hand on her belly caressed her bare skin. "Mornin', beautiful."

The deep, heavy rasp of Jon's voice was even sexier first thing in the morning. "Mmm. That it is."

"Did you sleep well?"

"When you finally let me sleep." She snuggled her naked body into the warmth of his.

"That didn't sound like a complaint."

"It wasn't."

"Good." Jon's hand slid up to cup her breast. "You want breakfast?"

The rhythmic stroking on her nipple had her arching into his touch and a moan slipped out.

His low-pitched growl drifted into her ear. "That purr is the sexiest thing I've ever heard, so maybe we oughta get out of bed now before we end up spending the whole damn day here."

"I'd like that, except I have to be in Rapid City this afternoon for dance rehearsal." She groaned. "Crap. And after a night like that, I completely forgot that my car is dead."

Jon rolled her over to face him. "I'll call up my mechanic buddy and send him over to look at it. He'll probably need to tow it."

"That's fine. Tell him there's a spare key in a rip in the upholstery underneath the passenger's seat."

"Handy. Now we won't have to leave." His lips glided over hers in a barely there kiss. "Eggs and toast all right?"

"Mmm-hmm." Maggie pressed a kiss to his Adam's apple. "Do you have an extra toothbrush?"

"Bottom right drawer in the guest bath." Jon got up and stretched beside the bed.

Talk about a nice visual first thing in the morning. Perfectly round buns, slim hips widening into a muscular back, defined biceps, triceps and forearms—all wrapped up in that gorgeous tawny skin. Such a shame that he tugged on a pair of long athletic shorts and covered up before he headed to the master bathroom.

Maggie snatched the tank top off the floor on her way to the guest bath. Maybe she snooped while searching for toothpaste. She didn't find anything that'd lead her to believe he regularly entertained overnight female guests.

Would it have made a difference if you'd found fruit-scented body wash?

No. But she'd be wary if she'd found tampons, makeup or a hair straightener. Those items suggested a permanent, recurring female presence.

After scrubbing her teeth, washing her face and attempting to de-snarl her hair, Maggie padded to the kitchen.

Jon's wide smile made her weak-kneed. "To hell with cookin'. You look good enough to eat."

"I believe you dined on me last night. Twice."

"True. But it didn't fill me up. Only increased my appetite for more." He grabbed a fistful of her hair, angling her head back to plunder her mouth with a thorough kiss.

There was the belly-churning sensation she experienced every time he touched her.

"You're too tempting," he murmured and released her. "You want tomatoes and cheese in your scrambled eggs?"

"Sure. Do you want me to do anything?"

"Just look pretty at my breakfast table while I serve you."

"How much honey did you pour in your coffee this morning, rock star?"

Jon laughed. "None. It's all the gospel truth. Sit."

Maggie sipped strong coffee and watched him multitask, cooking bacon, eggs and toast and slicing fruit. Then he slid a plate in front of her, heaping with food. "Do I look hungry?"

"We burned plenty of calories last night and you'll burn even more dancing today so eat up." He sat across from her with an equally mounded plate.

She shoveled in a bite and swallowed. "These eggs are amazing."

"Thanks. I got to thinking… I'll drive you to Rapid today since you won't have a car. There's stuff I need to do and I can hang around in town until you're done rehearsing. Maybe I'll convince you to have a late dinner with me and breakfast tomorrow morning."

Maggie drained her coffee and got up for a refill, absentmindedly refilling Jon's cup too.

He placed his hand on her wrist. "Did I say something wrong?"

"No. It's just…" Her eyes searched his. "Why are you with me?"

"I like being with you. I want to get to know you outside the dance studio. And outside the bedroom." His fingers skated up her arm in that seductive way that caused goose flesh to cover her arms. "Although you won't hear me complaining if you wanna get better acquainted there too."

She smooched his smirking mouth. "Fine. I'll accept your gracious offer, but you've gotta do one thing for me."

"Name it."

"Come out with us tonight. I usually hang out with Seth, his partner Stanis, and Seth's sister Sara after rehearsal."

"Sounds like fun." Jon left the kitchen to call the mechanic.

After Maggie finished loading the dishwasher, she turned to see Jon leaning against the wall. She still did a double take whenever she saw him. The man was stunning with his fiercely beautiful face and his badass posture. It seemed like a dream that she'd had her hands and mouth all over his incredible body last night; and that he'd had that sinful mouth and those talented hands all over her.

Jon was the most enthralling man she'd ever met, but he was difficult to read. There was almost a…"proper" aspect to his personality and mannerisms. Did that stem from him being Native American? Or had the record label's PR agency put all that polish on Johnny Feather over the years? The only glimpse she'd seen of the wild man rock star had been on stage, when he was lost to everything but the music. Although, she had gotten a hint of that intensity last night, when he'd been focused solely on her.

"You're staring at me," he said with amusement.

"You were staring at me first. Besides, you are very easy on the eyes, Jon White Feather."

He kept his arms folded over his chest and continued studying her.

"What? Do I have egg on my face or something?"

"No. Just thinking about how hot last night was. It's taking every damn bit of my willpower not to bend you over the counter and fuck you until you fall apart in my arms again."

There was that animalistic side.

"That thought will keep." Jon inclined his head toward the sliding glass door. "Come on. I've got something to show you."

Maggie looked at the tank top that barely skimmed her hips. "I'm not wearing pants."

"Nobody around besides me to see you. If I had my way? You'd be wearing just that creamy skin."

Oh man. He'd cranked the seduction meter on high today.

He opened the sliding glass door.

Maggie stepped onto a concrete patio and her gaze followed a stone pathway that ended at a large asymmetrical structure. Pine needles, leaves and broken pinecones were scattered across the walkway.

"The storm did some damage." He moved in front of her and bent at the waist. "Climb on."

"Seriously, Jon? A piggyback ride?"

"Yep. You wanted to ride me like a pony. This is kinda close."

How was she supposed to think about anything besides sex with her crotch pressing against his spine, her chest rubbing over the firm muscles of his upper back and her arms draped around his neck?

Maggie released a little whoop and jumped on.

He raced forward. Upon reaching the door, he turned his head. "This is handy. I can spin you around and have my wicked way with you up against the wall."

"Was that what you wanted to show me?"

"Nope."

"Dang. Dash a girl's hopes."

Jon set her on her feet, and all of a sudden seemed hesitant to open the door.

She remembered how much he valued his privacy and suspected he regretted the spontaneous invite into his private domain. "I'd understand if you've changed your mind and don't want me invading your sacred space."

"I want you here." He touched her face. "I once had a teacher who swore no space was truly sacred, except for sexual organs."

"Well, we've already breached each other's sacred spaces. Several times."

Jon laughed and opened the door.

The clean lines and neutral colors utilized feng shui to create a sense of peace and order. A lounging area with deep-cushioned couches was away from the creative heart of the space—the sound-proofed recording area. A window in that room faced out; everything else was closed off. The entire back wall was lined with percussion instruments. Along the outside walls were guitars and cases that held string instruments, woodwinds and brass. She squinted at a table in the corner with an auto-harp and a mandolin. Drums didn't have a place of honor, but were scattered everywhere in sizes and shapes she'd never seen.

"Jon. I'm blown away. What a perfect creative environment. Although I'd be tempted to goof around with all the...omigod, is that a xylophone?"

"Yes, ma'am."

"Do you play it?"

"Sometimes. I used to have to move it to sleep, since I built the studio before the house."

"Because your music matters more to you than anything," she murmured, running her hand over the top of a kettle drum.

His deep voice tickled her ear. "I don't want to say music is my life, but I guess it is because I cannot imagine my life without it."

"No wonder you wanted to stop touring. You have everything you need right here to make music and be happy."

She felt Jon tense behind her. Had she said something wrong? Before she could ask him, he sidestepped her and grabbed a mallet and pounded on the skins, not randomly, but in a rapid-fire pattern that sounded melodic. Who knew drums even had a melody?

Maggie faced him.

Immediately Jon stopped drumming. "What?"

"If it's not too much bother will you play something for me today?"

"Maggie. I'd be honored to play for you." His gaze moved over her as thoroughly as a caress. "Would you dance naked for me while I play?"

"No." She bit her lip. "Well. Maybe. I've never done that before, so it might be fun."

He picked up a maraca and rattled it. "Know what else might be fun? If I recorded you playing something in the background of my drum solo while you're dancing naked."

"No way. I don't play an instrument, not a real one anyway. I don't sing."

"Not even karaoke?"

"Especially not karaoke." She poked him in the chest. "But I'll warn you, I rock at *Rock Band*."

He lifted a brow. "Is that a challenge?"

"Absolutely. Seth, Stanis, Sara and I have a *Rock Band* play-off. I think he mentioned this Saturday night we were gonna shred it." She cocked her head. "But I'm sure you wouldn't be interested. Probably worried you'd get shown up by two gay guys, a nurse and a computer geek."

"You do know that I'm *in* an actual rock band, right?"

"I've heard that doesn't make a difference."

Jon laughed. "Wanna bet?"

Chapter Nine

Maggie shouldn't have bet against Jon. He ruled at *Rock Band*, destroying all of Seth's previous high scores.

Jon's victory demanded concessions from Maggie—including her spending Saturday night and all day Sunday with him.

She hadn't minded losing at all.

They'd stayed up late Saturday night and stargazed. Afterward they'd rolled around naked in his living room and in his bedroom. After a leisurely breakfast, where they'd lost track of time discussing everything from philosophy to books to movies, they adjourned to his studio.

She dinked around with his computerized sound system while he laid down drum tracks for a mysterious project. Jon was tightlipped when it came to his career—maybe because he feared it was stalled? She didn't sense restlessness in him, so maybe he was content living in one place for more than a night or two. The more they hung out, the more Maggie understood how important it was to him that she saw him as a regular guy, not just Johnny Feather, rocker.

Rather than take Jon's car, Maggie bummed a ride to work from her brother on Monday morning. It seemed odd that she and Billy saw less of each other since she'd relocated to Spearfish from Rapid City. Granted, he had a lot on his mind with a major project he was designing, and a baby on the way, so when he asked about her recent job interviews, she didn't mention the upcoming dance competition. Or Jon.

Maggie raced around town Monday afternoon after she retrieved her car and barely made it to the community center on time for the dance class. Jon was a no show and she checked her disappointment. She'd hoped he would finish out the last week for his niece's benefit, but his absence hadn't bothered Raven. She and her replacement partner, a cute charmer named Thomas Fast Wolf, were enthralled with each other. Enthralled to the point she'd heard Seth quietly threaten to spray the teens down with the fire hose if they didn't quit grinding on each other.

The day off from rehearsing had turned Seth into a taskmaster. After dance class ended, they performed each competitive rhythm dance fully—the entire thing, not just the focused snippets—three times. Maggie's muscles screamed. The insides of her thighs burned. Her hips were sore.

Maybe that ache wasn't only from dance. Spending the weekend in bed with Jon had been quite the workout—the man defined insatiable. It'd been an embarrassingly long stretch since Maggie last had a lover, but none of the men she'd been with had that much stamina or sexual creativity. She'd never look at drum tie-down straps the same way again.

The door to the gym banged open. She whirled around and saw Jon. Huh. Usually he was more stealthy than that and she hadn't been sure he'd show up.

His focus remained on her as he strolled across the wooden floor. The tickle in her belly morphed into a full-body tingle when he pulled her into his arms and kissed her.

And kept kissing her. A toe-curling, panty-dampening kiss.

Seth cleared his throat behind them.

Maggie broke the lip lock, but couldn't look away from his heated blue eyes.

Jon grinned. "Hi."

"I like the way you say hi, rock star."

"Thought you might." Jon looked at Seth. "Heya, teach. Is your ass still smarting from me handing it to you this weekend?"

Seth grinned. "I could totally take that the wrong way."

He laughed. "You heading back to Rapid City so I can steal Maggie away now?"

"Yes. I won't miss making that drive after this class ends." Seth mopped his face and tossed the towel into his duffel bag. "You'll lock up?" he asked Maggie.

"Sure."

"See you tomorrow night, sugar." He smirked at Jon. "Ta to you too, sugar."

Maggie jammed all her belongings into her bag. "I thought maybe you'd come to class tonight."

"I intended to. But this riff wouldn't leave me alone after I dropped you off last night, so I worked on it and didn't go to bed until the sun came up."

"Riff? Isn't that guitar?"

"I play guitar. Having a melody helps me find the right beat."

"Seth will freak out if you kick his ass on *Guitar Hero* too."

Jon gave her that cocky grin again. "He already challenged me and I accepted."

"What were you working on that kept you up all night?"

"I laid down some tracks after I finally got them to sound right. By the time I got up, worked out, and caught up on business stuff, it was too late to come to class."

"Were the tracks for any project in particular?"

He shrugged and snagged her bag, draping the strap over his shoulder. "Nothin' I can talk about."

"Or don't wanna talk about. Still, it's gotta be a relief to work without pressure. Not having to worry about wrapping up an idea too fast because you've gotta get back on the road or meet some record label deadline."

"If only it were that easy."

Sometimes the man was so damn cryptic.

As Maggie locked the door she couldn't help but yawn.

"It appears my timing is still off." Jon swept his thumb under her eye. "You're exhausted, dancing queen."

She bristled. "I know I look like shit, but I worked eight hours today and danced for five—"

Jon smothered her protest with his mouth, gifting her with a kiss that had her melting against him. He slid his lips down her chin and nibbled beneath her jawline, knowing it drove her crazy. "I only meant you're too tired for what I had in mind tonight."

"Which was what? Crazy wild monkey sex hanging from a tree?"

"No. A candlelight dinner and..."

"And...what? Because you seem awful disappointed I'm dragging ass."

"I hadn't gotten further than that, except hoping we'd get in wild-monkey-sex naked-time afterward, which ain't exactly romantic to admit before I've wined and dined you. But right now I'm leaning toward just tucking you straight in bed."

Maggie tipped her head back to gaze at him. When she wore flat shoes Jon was eight inches taller than her five foot five. "You're sending me to bed without supper? Was I bad or something?"

"No. You're good. Very, very good." Jon teased her lips with deceptively gentle kisses that packed an erotic punch. "That's the problem. I can't stop thinking about you, Maggie."

"I know. I thought we'd figured this out over the weekend when we both said we wanted to see where this goes...and it seems like we're going in opposite directions with opposite schedules."

"Well, then, we'll have to learn to compromise." Jon crowded her against the brick wall, bracing his hands beside her head. "You have to eat, right? Some days we can meet for lunch."

She twined her arms around his neck. "And some nights we'll have a late supper."

"Some mornings, we'll have breakfast in bed." He nuzzled her temple. "Selfish of me to hope that's most mornings?"

"Then that'd make me selfish too, because I have the same wish." Maggie had a moment of panic after the words tumbled out. She never put herself out there so fast. She always held part of herself back in a relationship, especially early on, not wanting to appear overeager or act desperate.

He peered into her eyes. "What just happened? You tensed up."

"Nothing."

"Bull. Talk to me."

"I've never known another man like you. Not personally. I've watched hot guys like you from afar, in class, or on stage, or on TV, but I haven't ever been the lucky one who gets to make time with the gorgeous man all the other women want."

"Make time?" he repeated. "You think that's all I'm doing? I lured you into my bed because I was bored? I'm killing time with you until someone better comes along?"

"Or until you get bored and leave town."

His mouth tightened.

"I know it's my insecurity, but I can't pretend I've been in this position before."

"What position is that?"

Maggie ran her fingers down his face. "Scared. Wanting those breakfasts in bed. Wanting to believe every sweet, raunchy word you say to me."

"Then take a leap of faith and believe it," he said softly.

"That's the thing about leaps of faith; I'm not so good at taking them because I tend to fall flat on my face."

"Then let's take it together, because I've never been in this position either."

She found that hard to believe. "Really?"

"Yes. I haven't stuck around here long enough to get to know a woman on any level besides sexual. And it wouldn't matter anyway because I've never been with a woman like you, Maggie. You're classy. And smart. And generous with your time. You're patient. And so damn sweet it makes me ache." His eyes took on a glint of pure male animal. "Then I watch you dance and I almost can't breathe. The way you move is the sexiest thing I've ever seen. It's passion and poetry."

She couldn't be more stunned. "Jon—"

"Let me finish. Being with you is starting to strip the barriers I've had up for years. Because even though you do see me as the guy who's a hit with the ladies, that's not all you see. You treat me as Jon, not Johnny. You make me laugh. You make me think. It's not all about sex with you. Yet, you make me so fucking hot that I want to slide up in you, right here, right now, just to see that dreamy look you get when I'm inside you." He rested his forehead to hers. "So yeah, this is beyond my realm of experience. But I'm not scared by it because it feels so damn right." He paused and murmured, "Am I wrong?"

"No." She kissed him then. Not with tenderness, but an openmouthed explosion of need, showing him his faith in her—in this, in what was building between them—wasn't misplaced.

By the time they broke apart, her panties were wet, her nipples hard, her head was buzzing and she seriously considered ripping his clothes off with her teeth.

"Come home with me," she panted against his throat. "And we'll get started on that breakfast thing."

Tuesday night after Maggie's dance rehearsal, Jon picked her up for a romantic moonlight stroll by the creek.

Wednesday they indulged in a long lunch, picnic style, in Jon's bed.

Thursday Jon snuck into the gym for the last night of dance class. Staying in the shadows, he watched his niece move with more confidence, shyly flirting with the too-charming Fast Wolf boy, who should've been named Fast Hands. Lurking gave him a feeling of disconnection and he left without letting anyone know he'd even been there.

His melancholy mood didn't go to waste; he channeled it into his music. He'd been inspired to write more than usual in the past week. So when his agent called, Jon mentioned his recent increased output and that he'd already passed the audio files to Push, Radioactive Tar and Darkly Dreaming. But Marty also wanted to know if Johnny intended to enter into serious negotiations with any of the three bands.

That was the crux of Jon's problem; although the music-career fairy had knocked, he wasn't sure which door to open—if any. When his Sapa bandmate Jeps had called a few hours later to discuss the future of the band, Jon hedged. He loved and respected his Sapa bandmates, yet, he'd experienced an unprecedented burst of creativity in the last month and he was damn proud of the work he'd finished.

He wondered how much of it was due to breaking away from Sapa. Maybe when he wasn't collaborating with other musicians he had a clearer vision of his own musical style. Maybe the possibility of working with the most respected producers in the business forced him to step up his game. Maybe being settled at home for an extended period of time allowed his creativity to flow more freely.

Or maybe he could attribute it all to being around Maggie and truly being happy.

Friday night he whisked her back to his place after her rehearsal with Seth. Filled with excess energy, Maggie jumped him, riding him to an orgasm so intense he had rug burns on his ass and he'd momentarily lost the ability to speak.

Since the dance competition was a mere week away, Seth had scheduled an all-weekend rehearsal. Jon knew if he began a new project he'd obsess until he finished it, so he opted to drop by Jim's house on Saturday instead of working. He riled up the kids, drank a beer and pretended he wasn't counting down the hours until he saw Maggie.

He loved surprising her so he'd rented a room at a secluded bed and breakfast and arranged the candlelight dinner he'd promised her. After returning to the room, Jon massaged her sore muscles and made love to her in the big Jacuzzi tub and the enormous four-poster bed. It was one of the best weekends of his life—the perfect mix of work and play, family, romance, passion, fun and relaxation.

So it was bittersweet when Marty called him and insisted he get to L.A. for meetings on Monday. He knew the meetings wouldn't be limited to California, and he resigned himself to being gone another week. But since all of this was preliminary, he couldn't discuss the particulars with Maggie or anyone else.

Normally Jon waited outside in the parking lot of the dance studio for Maggie to finish because Seth insisted on closed rehearsals. But he didn't have a lot of time so Seth could overlook the interruption just once since Jon was leaving town.

The entryway of the small studio was a dancer's ready room, comprised of lockers, wall pegs, bins and benches. The largest wall was also a window; observation glass on one side and a mirror on the other.

Even with the door to the studio closed, Jon could hear Seth and Maggie yelling at each other.

Whoa. He'd never seen Maggie so angry.

"I cannot do it like that, Seth. I've told you ten times. It won't work. I haven't done that technique in years and I'm not about to add it into the routine less than a week before competition!"

Seth got right in her face. "That's a load of crap, Maggie. You don't want to do it just because it's hard. You'd rather make the easy move and you know what? It'll make you look lazy. And make me look lazy, because not only am I your partner, I'm your dance coach."

"Lazy?" Maggie repeated. She shoved Seth back a step. "Fuck off. I've busted my ass and I haven't taken the easy way out on anything. You're just afraid no one will take you seriously as a choreographer if you don't put some stupid, worthless fancy-ass dance move in just to show you know how to do it."

"That was a bitchy thing to say."

"It's the truth. And you're being an asshole about it."

"Tough shit. You will do what I say. Period. End of discussion." Seth stomped off, grabbed the remote and turned the music back on.

Maggie didn't budge.

A door opened and Seth's partner, Stanis, exited the office. But he didn't offer his usual flirtatious smile.

"They still snapping at each other?" he asked Jon.

"Yeah. How long has it been going on?"

"An hour. And before you ask why I didn't put a stop to it, I'll remind you of my 'no interference' policy."

Jon lifted a brow. "So you're good with them verbally assaulting each other? Or do you step in only when it turns physical?"

Stanis smoothed his fingers down his silk tie. "It won't ever get to that point."

A loud crash sounded and Jon spun around to see Maggie sprawled on the floor with Seth yelling at her to quit being such a baby and get back up and do it again.

Jon stormed into the studio, stepping between Maggie and Seth. When he glanced down and saw Maggie's face wet with tears, it took every ounce of restraint not to knock Seth on his ass. Jon plucked her off the floor and set her on a bench.

Seth shouted, "What do you think you're doing? This is a closed rehearsal and you have no right to barge in here—"

He was looming over Seth in two seconds. "I have every right when I see Maggie on the floor! What the fuck is wrong with you, Seth? I know you're her coach, but I didn't think you were a bully. It's obvious she's had enough if she's crying."

That seemed to knock the fight right out of Seth.

Stanis wrapped his arm around Seth's shoulder. "Jon is right, sweetheart. Take a break. Come on." He led Seth out of the studio and the office door closed.

Jon forced deep breaths into his lungs before he faced Maggie.

She'd stopped crying, but she still looked miserable.

"You all right?"

She shook her head and tears spilled down her cheeks.

He scooped her onto his lap, running his hands down her spine as her body was racked with sobs. "Ssh. Baby. It's okay."

"I hate him," she said with a hiccup.

"No, you don't. You're both on edge and you've spent way too much time together."

"I want to quit."

Jon pressed his lips against her forehead. "No, you don't."

A few minutes passed before she said, "But I could. The company in Billings I sent my resume to after I was laid off has an opening. They want to interview me this week."

"Which is great. But Maggie, you shouldn't be making any career decisions before your first major dance competition."

"Maybe I should take it as a sign that I should quit."

"You'd be kicking yourself if you didn't follow through with competing in regionals after all the work you've put into it the last six months."

"You're probably right. Anyway. Why are you here?"

"To tell you I have to deal with some business out of town."

She lifted her head. "You're leaving again?"

He smoothed damp tendrils of hair from her face. "Yeah."

"I thought Sapa was on an extended break and you were taking time off?"

Jon hated sidestepping the issue, but Maggie had enough stress in her life this week. And he was scared she'd just walk away if he told her the truth. "It's just...I didn't want to leave without saying goodbye this time."

"Thanks for that." She sighed. "It's probably for the best that you'll be gone."

"Since I won't see you anyway because of your intensive rehearsal schedule?"

"Partially. But also because of this." Maggie angled her head so he could see the large hickey on her neck.

"Shit. Sorry about that."

"No, you're not. I'm not either, because last night was incredible." She pressed her lips to his. "But I will say Seth wasn't happy about the obvious suck marks on my neck and chest. He warned me that if you

184

continued to act like a horny teen then he wouldn't allow me to see you at all this week."

Jon whistled. "Is he grounding you from TV and your car too?"

"And he's taking away my allowance and my cell phone."

He couldn't help but grin that she'd retained her sense of humor even under duress.

"As you can probably guess, his threat didn't go over very well. The day started off on the wrong foot and went downhill from there."

"So you're doubly happy I bulled my way in and told him off?" he asked dryly.

"Yes. Because no one ever sticks up for me." Maggie rested her cheek against the curve of his neck. "But I am going to miss you."

"Same here." Jon adjusted her position so she faced him with her knees on either side of his thighs. He framed her face in his hands and devoured her with a drawn-out kiss that wasn't nearly enough. "Don't overdo it this week, dancing queen."

"I won't. Don't sweat it if you can't make it back for the competition on Saturday."

He locked his gaze to hers. "I'll be there."

"But—"

"No buts. I'll be there. I promise."

Chapter Ten

"Stop fidgeting."

Maggie gave Seth a cool look. "Gimme a break. I haven't competed in years. I'm entitled to fidgeting. And pacing. And pure panic."

Seth curled his hands around her shoulders. "Listen to me. We are on top of the world, baby. We make a fabulous team. Some dancers are already asking who we are. We're the sandbaggers, Maggie."

She blinked at him. "Isn't that a given? Since we're unknown?"

"It's a head game. I saw you eyeing the others' costumes. Yes, they are much better than ours." Seth dropped his voice. "Sweetie. That's intentional. I can get my hands on top-of-the-line costumes, but why overplay our hand? Better to underplay it and have our competitors dismiss us as country bumpkins trying to dance in the big leagues."

"I see your point."

"These dancers have sponsors. We don't. Luckily for us, that means when we win this competition, we'll be attractive to sponsors because no one has heard of us. And the sponsors will look smart for snapping up an up-and-coming dance team."

Sponsorship was almost too much to hope for. "Not to put the cart before the horse, but say we win. We score sponsors. Then what happens?"

Seth adjusted the seams on her sleeves. "Then we have the means to hit more competitions, notch more wins, which will get us invited to dance in exhibition showcases and we both know that's where the real money is. Plus, we build name recognition while we're doing it. And fingers crossed..." He paused a beat too long before he stepped back. "Never mind."

Her stomach lurched at his vague tone. "What?"

"I've been hesitant to tell you this before now, because I knew it'd freak you out. But if we win, Vladimir Konski has agreed to audition us for possible coaching for nationals."

"Seriously? He's huge. He coached... Well, obviously I don't have to tell you who he coached." Maggie narrowed her eyes. "Hey. How did you manage that?"

Seth winked. "I dated Vladimir's son Niko when we were in *The Will Rogers Follies* in New York. Niko and I've stayed on good terms and he might've mentioned to his father that I'm dipping my toe into the competitive dance waters."

Pumped up by the possibilities, she gave him a smacking kiss on the mouth. "Let's show them how it's done, partner."

Maggie's butterflies didn't settle as she checked her makeup. Her hair. Her costume. Her shoes. She glanced at Seth, performing the same rituals.

Then they were in the chute, waiting for their number to be called. They didn't speak to anyone, nor did they chat with each other. She mentally reviewed the steps for the first dance.

Finally they heard, "Dancers in position."

Seth smiled, snatched her hand and then it was game on.

Now they just had to get through the next ten minutes, dance their asses off and blow the other eleven couples out of the water.

At the start of the music, Maggie became someone else. She and Seth circled each other. Not as dance partners, not as friends, but as potential sexual conquests, turning up the heat as they set their bodies in motion.

The first dance was the cha-cha, flirty and fun as she made promises with her eyes and her hips. During the second dance, the rhumba, she morphed into the seductress, using sensual moves to entice her potential lover. The third dance was swing, a hopping, energetic show of stamina and athleticism. The fourth dance, the bolero, was filled with passion and longing as their bodies undulated in unison and opposition. And the fifth dance, the mambo, was back to a sexy tease.

She and Seth were in perfect synch throughout all five dances. They maintained the intensity even during the thirty-second pause between each ninety-second piece of music.

After they finished dancing, Maggie's body pulsed with sexual energy and adrenaline. Waiting for the results was excruciating, but at least they were expected to leave the dance floor while the judges made their decision.

Seth clasped her hand as they dodged other dancers, who were also pumped after their performances.

By the time they reached the corner they'd staked out in the dressing area, the *touch me, fuck me, take me now* vibe between them had cooled.

Or so she thought.

Seth handed her a bottle of grape-flavored Gatorade and took one for himself, staring at her with an expression she'd never seen directed at her.

Maggie wondered if there'd be awkward moments in the aftermath of suggestive dancing. She'd become sexually involved with her dance partner in college, so this situation wasn't uncharted territory for her, but Seth was gay.

Then Seth allowed her a wolfish grin. "My God, woman, if I was straight I'd be fucking you balls deep against that wall right now. Which tells me our performance was off the charts."

That had been the perfect thing to say. She grinned. "It just proves that having the steps drilled into my head works best because I could concentrate on the presentation, not the choreography."

Seth nodded. "I don't want to ruin this beautiful high by dissecting our performance. I want to bask in my foresight for choosing such an excellent dancing partner." He toasted her with his plastic bottle.

Maggie blushed from his praise. "I'm grateful you believed there was potential in me."

"There's better than potential, baby, there's heat between us on the floor. I'll bet Stanis is fit to be tied after our sexy presentation." Seth drained his Gatorade. "I imagine bad-boy rocker came to support you?"

"Of course he knows about it, but..."

"But what?"

She hadn't heard from Jon at all the last five days. "I'm not sure if he's back in town. And I don't want to pressure him to support me because we're keeping this casual."

"I've seen how that man looks at you, Maggie, and there's nothing casual about it. Johnny-hottie is completely smitten with you," Seth continued. "So don't assume he's only interested in playing a little grab-ass with you before he moves on."

"I wish I could believe that."

Seth gave her a thoughtful look. "Maybe this will convince you. Do you remember the last week of dance class when newlywed Ashley popped into the gym on Friday night, wearing tiny booty shorts and her tight sports bra that showed off her gigantic fake boobs?"

Confused, Maggie squinted at him. "I was there? I don't remember."

Seth pointed at her. "Exactly. You were engrossed in working with the scarves for perfecting movement flow. Johnny-hottie didn't pay attention to Ashley at all; he was absolutely mesmerized by you."

Her mouth dropped open. "Jon was at our rehearsal?"

"I'm pretty sure he'd been lifting weights, because his muscles were all bulgy and he was covered in a delicious sheen of sweat." Seth laughed when Maggie's eyes widened. "What? I can look. Not that he noticed me ogling him since he only had eyes for you."

"Ladies and gentleman, we have our winners," boomed over the loudspeakers.

"This is it." Seth took her hand and dragged her out of the dressing area and into the arena.

Her gut clenched. Her heart raced. But she plastered on a smile as they lined up on the dance floor.

The committee chair went on about each judge before announcing their decisions in the top three slots.

Third place was announced and it wasn't them.

Second place was announced and it wasn't them.

A drum roll sounded. "The winners of the American Dance Federation Rhythm Style competition, who will represent the Mountain States region at the National Finals in Orlando, are..."

And their names were announced.

Maggie was pretty sure her feet didn't touch the floor as she and Seth performed a sweeping bow and deep curtsey to the crowd before they floated to the judge's stand to accept the medals, the check and flowers.

Other dancers surrounded them to offer congratulations—a few remarks were even genuine.

After the floor cleared, Maggie spun around, her gaze searching the stands.

Then she saw Jon. The intense way he looked at her put her feet in motion and she tried really hard not to skip.

Jon dangled over the railing so far Maggie thought he might fall. And that grin. Boy howdy it made her all tingly.

"You came." Brilliant observation, Maggie.

"I told you I'd be here. That was the most amazing dance performance I've ever seen."

"Man, you guys totally rocked it!" Raven gushed. "You were so much better than everyone else. It was obvious after the first dance that you and Seth were gonna win."

Her focus on Jon had been so absolute she hadn't noticed Raven. She smiled at her. "I'm glad you came. It was nice of your uncle to bring you."

Then Seth bounded over. "If it isn't my two favorite students!"

Raven started chattering to Seth and Maggie glanced at Jon. He stepped sideways, motioning for a word in private. "You look beautiful."

"Thank you." She noticed he held a single white rose with pink-tipped petals. "Is that for me?"

"Yeah. Makes me look cheap, compared to those." Jon pointed to the bouquet of a dozen red roses in her arms.

"These weren't bought specifically for me, like your rose was. So gimme."

He laughed. "I was told this color is called minuet, so I thought you'd appreciate that." He bent down until they were eye to eye. "But the real reason I bought it is because the pink on cream tones reminded me of the color of your skin after you've come undone in my arms."

The rough rasp of his voice sent sexual heat surging through her.

"You're ramped up right now," he half growled. "I can feel it. Baby, it's pulsing off you."

She turned her head, letting her lips graze the corner of his mouth. "I'd like to drag you off and put this excess energy to good use."

"Let's go. Right now."

His warm breath teased her ear and she wanted to feel his whispers drifting over every inch of her skin.

"Maggie?"

Seth's voice pulled her out of the moment, forcing her to step back from the magnetic hold Jon had on her. "Ah. What?"

"A couple of potential sponsors want to talk to us and we shouldn't keep them waiting."

"Go on," Jon urged. "I'll catch up with you later."

Maggie gave him a promising smile and dashed away with Seth.

Four hours later, Maggie stood on the front porch of her cabin. The day had been a scorcher and the sudden rainstorm caused steam to rise from the pavement like ghostly fingers.

Leaning against the railing, she listened to the steady din on the tin roof as raindrops splashed her bare feet. The humid air smelled clean, heavy with the earthy scent of soil and vegetation.

What a whirlwind week. In addition to hours of rehearsal, she'd decided to meet with that rep from the consulting company based out of Billings. He hadn't offered her a job, but the interview had gone well enough she suspected an offer would be coming in the next few weeks.

Would she take it? In the last six months she'd enjoyed having a job and not the pressure of a career. As much as she loved dancing, she didn't want it to become another obligation she'd resent. But now with this win, she was in limbo for two more months.

The meetings with potential sponsors had gone better than expected. Evidently word had spread of their couples dance classes at the community center. The owners of a travel agency, big supporters of the arts, offered to sponsor all their airfare expenses for preparation for the national competition in Florida.

Seth had spent the drive back to Spearfish on the phone with Vladimir, setting up an audition in Salt Lake City next weekend and a backup audition with another teacher in Dallas. Maggie could swing the price of hotel and food costs, but those were a drop in the bucket compared to Vladimir's fees for private instruction. How would she pay for them?

She'd cross that bridge when she came to it.

Speaking of crossing the bridge...headlights bumped up the drive and Jon's Land Cruiser pulled into view.

Anticipation rolled through her. She'd missed him more than she thought possible in the last week, not just the sex but talking to him. Jon was a great listener—not a trait she expected from a man used to having people fawning over him. His stories about life on the road entertained her, but also indicated how hard he'd worked to grow his career and showed his joy at the connection he'd built with his fans. He had her laughing whenever he talked about his family and growing up on the reservation. Jon White Feather was a sweet, funny, thoughtful man who didn't let his onstage persona define him offstage.

And Maggie was falling for him so fast it scared her.

Jon climbed out and sauntered toward her. His hot, sensual gaze traveled from her eyes to her mouth, lingering on her chest and then meandering back up to her eyes.

Maggie felt that erotic caress as if his hands were already on her. No denying a large part of their attraction was purely physical. So while she appreciated all the other great traits Jon had, right now, she wanted to gorge herself on the sexual side of him.

She jumped the two stairs and raced toward him, her feet sinking into ankle-deep mud.

Jon met her halfway, catching her when she launched herself at him. Their lips connected, the openmouthed kiss a ravenous explosion of passion and need.

Maggie clutched his neck, then her hands moved down his muscled biceps, dragging him closer as his fingers twined in her hair.

He groaned and broke the kiss, his hot mouth following the arc of her neck. "Maggie. God." He nipped at the section of skin where her neck met her shoulder. "I couldn't take my eyes off you today. You had me under your spell. You owned me."

Maggie dropped her head back, allowing him access to the other side of her neck. She was so lost in the total seduction of his mouth on her skin that she barely noticed the raindrops on her face.

His hips rocked forward, driving her toward the steps.

Her toes were cooled by the spongy wet grass, but her body was on fire, craving his deft touch. "I want you," she whispered against his mouth. "Now. My way."

"Yes. You've got me."

Her fingertips raked his chest as her mouth continued its southerly progression. Palming his hips, Maggie dropped to her knees and dragged his athletic shorts to his ankles.

How lucky that Jon had gone commando.

"Maggie. Baby. You don't—"

"Shut up and lose the shirt."

When the soaking wet cotton fabric was gone, she had access to his gloriously hard, wonderfully long cock. Maggie's hands followed the outside of his lower half, from his ridged calves to his knees, and across those strong quads. She nuzzled his groin, breathing him in.

Jon tugged on the stretchy strap of her camisole. "Fair's fair, dancing queen. I wanna feel your skin against mine."

Maggie yanked off her top. Although the night was dark, the light from the window reflected off his face and body. Rain drizzled down his torso, highlighting the dips and valleys of his incredible musculature. He was magnificent naked, even more magnificent naked and wet.

She brushed a kiss over the sun tattoo below his left hip and the moon tat mirrored on the right side. His belly quivered beneath her lips. Tilting her head back, she locked her gaze to his as she sucked his shaft deeply into her mouth.

"Ah. Dammit. That's so..." He moaned. His legs were rigid and he maintained a firm grip on her head.

She reveled in the power of rendering him speechless. Her fingers formed a circle at the base of his shaft and she stroked up while her mouth and tongue worked him from the cockhead down.

Each bob of her head made her as wet on the inside as she was on the outside.

He'd never let her go this far before, always pulling out before he finished in her mouth. But this time she wanted to feel the pulses on her tongue as he spilled his seed. She wanted him to feel her throat working as she swallowed every spurt.

"You're killing me," he panted. "Stop."

She shook her head vehemently and clamped his tight butt cheek in her left hand, holding him in place.

"I..." was all he managed, along with a deep groan as he erupted, warm and wet, against her tongue.

Her mouth formed a seal around his dick as she sucked down every drop. His cock remained hard even after he'd been spent completely. She continued to suck and nuzzle him, aching for relief from the sticky heat that throbbed between her thighs.

Then Jon's fingers curled over her jawline to lift her chin. His thumbs traced her cheekbones. He didn't say a word—he didn't have to—everything he felt was right there in his eyes.

Rain still fell. Not in a torrential downpour, but soft drops.

Maggie might've been cold if not for the inferno burning inside her.

Jon recognized that fire—that primal need—and pounced, pushing her onto the grass. He followed her down, making short work of her shorts. His hands spread her thighs apart and he buried his face in her pussy.

She gasped at the shock of his cold cheeks and lips against her hot tissue. Then his warm tongue lapped the juices coating her sex. He licked her slit, a growl vibrating as he suckled her pussy lips.

"I fucking love how wet you are after you blow me." His hands slid beneath her buttocks and he raised her hips, burrowing his tongue more deeply inside her channel.

This time there was no finesse to his oral hunger. He took after her like a starving man. A long lick, a tongue thrust, a deliberate graze of his teeth. Not teasing her, but feasting on her slick, sensitive flesh until he'd had his fill.

So when his mouth settled over her clit, all it took was four hard sucks and she climaxed. Hard. Thrashing beneath him, throwing water everywhere, but he held her tightly through each intense wave.

A loud clap of thunder forced her from the deep well of pleasure. She opened her eyes and looked down her body to where Jon's beautiful face rested on her stomach.

He slowly raised his head. And holy shit, the primal look in his eyes stole her breath. He pushed back to his knees, his hand dropping to his groin. He rolled on a condom and stroked his erection. "Turn over."

That rough demand sent a fresh onslaught of heat through her. But something in his posture encouraged her to push him a little further, daring him to give in to that animalistic side completely. So she balanced on her hands and scooted backward, away from him.

"Maggie."

A warning—which she didn't heed. She tossed her wet hair over her shoulder and moved back. "What?"

"I said: Don't. Move."

The wet grass squished between her fingers and toes as she kept moving backward.

Then Jon was on all fours, inching toward her with a lethal sexiness that made her heart race and her sex clench. "You think I won't chase you?"

"I'm counting on you chasing me," she tossed back.

He growled and kicked up the pace.

She tried to crab crawl faster, but Jon was already on her. Water and mud splashed as he flipped her onto her hands and knees, caging her body beneath his.

Her body shook. Not from cold. Not from fear. From this explosion of feelings he forced to the surface. He wanted her. All of her. Without questions or limitations.

His hand was in her hair, pulling her head up and holding it in place. His breath was hot on her neck. "You want me to fuck you like this, Maggie? Down and dirty?" He sank his teeth into the curve of her shoulder, directly on the spot that made her unravel.

She whimpered and bucked against him, but he had her locked down tight.

"Yes or no?"

"Yes. Damn you. Yes. Do it. Do it now."

Jon plundered her mouth with a brutal kiss as he reached between them to drag the wet rim of his cockhead from her clit down to her opening. A brief, breathless pause and then he rammed that hard shaft all the way in.

She gasped at the edgy spike of need. She waited, desperate for another forceful thrust.

But he didn't move. His voice rumbled in her ear. "Can you hear those rhythms? The driving sound of the rain. The crashing thunder in the sky. The soft ping of tiny water droplets on the roof."

"Jon. Please."

"Hear it. Feel it. But focus only on this. My heartbeat. Yours. Our blood pumping fast and hard. Our bodies so connected that's all there is in this moment."

Maggie almost came right then.

Jon pulled out and slammed back in.

Each thrust was a tiny orgasm, sending chills up and down her spine. She was attuned to him on a deeper level than she'd ever thought possible. The rapid exhalations of his breath on her neck. The muscles in his biceps bunching against her arms. The upward roll of his hips. The sting of his skin slapping into hers. The ground digging into her palms and her knees as he fucked her into oblivion.

"Come for me, Maggie." He pounded into her flesh. "Scream for me."

His hot mouth connected with her rain-cooled skin. He used the rhythm of their bodies to drive her to that soaring crescendo—a peak that Jon held her to until his own cadence synched with hers. Then they rode that long, final pulsing beat together, tumbling end over end into the abyss.

After the white noise stopped roaring in her head, Maggie lifted her face, blinking away the rain to gasp for breath. The swirling mist made her wonder if she was dreaming.

But Jon's molten body moved off hers and his cock slid out in a rush of moisture.

Her arms gave out and she slid gracelessly to the ground. Into the mud. But she didn't care.

He rolled her over and kissed her. And kept kissing her with such fierceness and tenderness, she forgot they were naked outside on the lawn in a rainstorm. Until she started to shiver.

"I know, baby. I'll warm you up."

He lifted her into his arms and carried her inside.

Chapter Eleven

The next morning, Jon said, "There's this family thing I have to go to today."

"I'm sure the bridge is passable after last night's rainstorm if you need to leave."

Jon ran his fingertips across the indentations in her lower spine, teasing the fine blond hairs with every pass. "I wasn't trying to skip out on you. I want you to come with me."

She lifted her head and looked at him. "Really?"

"Uh-huh." He kissed her shoulder. "Unless you don't want to."

"It's not that. It's just..." Her eyes searched his. "You're taking me to your family thing?"

"Yes, because my family is important to me. And you're important to me. I would've asked you last night, but I didn't want you to think the afterglow of mind-blowing sex was the reason for the invite."

Maggie rolled flat on her back and smirked. "Speaking of mind-blowing sex...maybe you should use that sugar-coated mouth of yours to convince me."

"You know I live for a challenge, woman."

And because he'd risen to the challenge—twice—they were late to the party.

"Are you sure we aren't supposed to bring something?" Maggie asked as they headed up the driveway.

"Nah. My mom and Cindy have it planned down to coordinating plates and napkins."

When Maggie fidgeted with the straps on her sundress, he snagged her hand and kissed her knuckles. "Relax. You look gorgeous. They're gonna love you." *Like I'm starting to.*

Rather than traipsing through the house, Jon led her over the brick walkway to the backyard. Two white canopies had been set up. Food under one, tables under the other. Kids ran everywhere and for once he wasn't mauled the instant he walked in.

He headed toward where his father and brothers—Jim and Jared—were hanging out on the patio.

"Hey, Pops," Jon said, clapping him on the back.

"Good to see you, son." His father focused on Maggie. "You've brought a beautiful guest to our family gathering, eh?"

"Yep. Maggie Buchanan, this is my father, Lyle White Feather."

"Nice to meet you," Maggie said.

"How do you know our Jon?"

Raven butted in. "She's the dance instructor for the dance class Uncle Jon and I are taking." She lightly punched Jon's arm. "Or were taking. Since *some* of us skipped out and didn't finish the class."

"That means I'll have to take private lessons to catch up. Besides, I heard your new partner Thomas is great at slow dancing," he teased.

Raven blushed.

Jim said, "Great to see you again, Maggie. I keep hoping you'll stop into the office and give that brother of yours grief."

"I would, but Eden claims that's her job and she scares me with all those crazy pregnancy hormones."

Jared stepped forward. "Hey, big bro. Ain't you gonna introduce me to your pretty lady?"

"No."

Then Jared, that buff bastard, laughed and jerked Maggie into a tight hug. "Welcome to the powwow. I'm Jared. The rock star's younger, better-looking, more charming brother."

Jon placed his hands on Maggie's hips and pulled her back, flashing his teeth at Jared. "Find your own woman, she's mine."

Maggie went motionless. She turned her head and looked up at him.

He kissed her surprised mouth. "What?"

"Do you want me to move so you have room to beat on your chest too?"

Both his brothers and his dad laughed.

"What's so funny, boys?"

Jon faced his mother. "They're picking on me."

"Poor baby." She gave Jon a hug and bussed his cheek, but her focus was on the woman at his side. "You must be Maggie. I'm Jon's mother, MaryAnn. My son has said good things about you."

"I've said good things too, *Unci*," Raven inserted. "You should've seen her and her partner Seth dance at the competition yesterday. They were spectacular."

Maggie grinned. "I wouldn't go that far, Raven, but we were good enough to win."

"Jon, dear, why don't you get Maggie a glass of punch?"

Meaning, take off so I can grill this girl without you hovering.

No way would he subject Maggie to the green goo known as his mother's lime sherbet and pineapple juice punch. He opted to just leave, detouring to the driveway where his nephews were playing basketball.

Among the motley crew of players was Jared's fellow firefighter and best pal, Gabe. "I see my brother dragged you along again."

"Jared needs a keeper."

"No doubt. He suckers you in every time."

"I don't mind." Gabe was always quiet—the opposite of Jared—and Jon wasn't sure how the guys ended up staying roommates for so long.

"Uncle Jon is on our team," Garth crowed.

The score was tied when lunch was announced.

Jon tracked down Maggie, who had been cornered by the twins and looked a little frazzled. Heaven knew his large, loud family could overwhelm him sometimes.

After a gigantic meal, the guys were tasked with cleanup duties. When Jon came back from hauling out the trash, that sneaky bastard Jared had taken the seat next to Maggie and they already appeared to be in deep conversation.

Jon pulled up another chair on Maggie's other side.

"Do you think you would've scored sponsors even if you hadn't won yesterday?" Jared asked Maggie.

She shrugged. "I'm just glad local businesses want to support us." She went on to talk about fostering community involvement in the arts, the great response to dance classes and the request to teach more.

Jared said, "I don't know how you'll be able to teach any new classes if you'll be gone every weekend training until nationals."

That was a new development—and it didn't make Jon happy. "You didn't tell me that you'd be training out of town." Then again, they hadn't done much talking last night. Or this morning.

"Didn't make sense to mention it until it was a done deal. Seth is working out the details. Since there aren't qualified teachers around here, we'll have to go out of state to train."

"How long until nationals?"

"Two months. Which isn't much time to learn a new routine."

Jon frowned. "You'll be gone every weekend for two months? Can't you just use the routine you won with?"

Maggie shook her head. "Whole different playing field, so we have to step up our game. We won't know if we'll be training in Salt Lake or Dallas until mid-next week anyway. If we bomb the auditions this weekend, then we're back to square one finding an instructor on short notice."

"Wait. You're flying to Salt Lake *and* Dallas this weekend?"

"Yes. We leave early Friday morning."

Talk about being left in the dark. "Why didn't I know any of this?"

She fiddled with the hem on her sundress. "Because you were gone last week." *And I didn't hear from you* wasn't said but it sure as hell was implied. "I also had a job interview with the Billings firm on Wednesday." Maggie finally looked at him. "And it went well."

"But I thought you weren't going to add that stress to your week."

"I had to prepare for the possibility we might lose. Our rehearsal schedule will get more intensive. Winning a regional championship was the first leg of the race. Now we're training for a marathon."

Jared leaned over and patted Jon's leg. "Sorry, bro. How much does that suck?"

"What?" he practically snarled.

"You decide to settle down at home after years of nonstop touring and the first woman you hook up with will be on the road as much as you used to be. Is that karma? Or irony?"

Silence.

Maggie stood abruptly. "Excuse me." She took off before Jon could stop her.

"Jesus, Jared, way to be an ass," Gabe said.

Jon pushed to his feet and glared at his brother. "Hook up? Really Jared? Maggie isn't just a hook up for me and you damn well know it."

"That's not what I meant." Jared pleaded with Gabe. "You know what I meant, right?"

Gabe shook his head.

Jared tipped his head back and stared at the sky. "I'm sorry. It's just...you don't drag every woman you're seeing home to meet the family, so I know Maggie is different...Christ. I should keep my damn mouth shut."

"Good plan."

Jon hadn't seen which direction Maggie had gone. He ducked around the side of the house and caught his mother sneaking a cigarette behind the garage. "Hey, cheater. I thought you quit."

"Nope. I'm down to four a day, which is pretty good." She blew out a stream of smoke. "You like this Maggie."

That was a major understatement. "Yep."

"You've been dating what? A couple months? And you're already bringing her to meet us? That's fast for you."

"It happened pretty fast. Since the minute I walked into her dance class I haven't been able to stop thinking about her. Have you seen her?"

She pointed to the front of the house.

He tracked her to Raven's favorite hiding spot in the small rock garden. "You trying to ditch me? Or are you just getting ready to run, now that I've subjected you to the White Feather gang?"

"Don't be like that, Jon. Everyone in your family has been great. But as I've been sitting here, trying to put a lid on all the doubts, and focus on these lovely clematis vines, I realized Jared does have a point—several of them in fact."

"Maggie—"

"Please don't deny it. There's stuff going on in your life you haven't talked about, so you have no right to get pissy with me."

"I wasn't pissy. Just surprised, okay?"

"So why are we avoiding a discussion about what happens next?"

Jon straddled the bench and gently grabbed her chin, forcing her to look at him. "We aren't avoiding it. We're prioritizing how we spend the time we do have together."

"Naked and sweaty?" she said with an edge.

"Something wrong with that? 'Cause, doll face, you sure didn't seem to mind last night. Or this morning."

Her eyes narrowed. "There's the *I-gave-it-to-you-good, baby,* rock-star attitude."

"Don't do that. That's not me, Maggie, and you damn well know it."

"Then tell me why you went out of town last week."

Fuck. He couldn't.

Yes, you can. Trust her. Tell her you're working on a project and that's all she can know for now.

But that was a lie. He'd rather dodge the question than lie to her. And that sucked because he didn't have anyone besides his agent to talk to—and Marty wasn't unbiased when it came to a potential commission. Jon was adrift on so many levels and he just wanted to forget about all the decisions hanging in the balance when he was alone with her. "Can we talk about this later?"

Maggie frowned. "You aren't blowing this off, right? Because it is important."

"I know. But so is this." He cupped the back of her neck, bringing her sweet mouth closer to kiss the frown right off her luscious lips.

"Great. Like I didn't get enough of watching you swallow my sister's face last time I saw you two together," Billy said behind them. "Classy."

Maggie opened her eyes, locking her gaze to Jon's before she broke the kiss with a smile. "Here's a piece of advice: the next time you see Jon and me in a private moment? Walk away so you won't get your virginal sensibilities offended."

Jon heard Eden snicker.

Maggie didn't stand; she just crossed her arms over her chest. "What are you doing here anyway?"

"Jim invited us."

He should've kept his mouth shut, but Jon still hadn't come to terms with all the bullshit that'd gone down in Billy's office a few weeks back. "So you show up for a White Feather family gathering, but you couldn't be bothered to drive to the CAM-PLEX in Gillette to support your sister at the regional dance finals yesterday?"

Billy's gaze turned razor sharp. "What are you talking about?"

"Jon," Maggie warned, "let it go."

But he didn't. "I'm talking about the dance competition that Maggie and Seth have been training for, for months? Why weren't you there?"

Billy's mouth fell open. "The contest or dance-off or whatever it's called...was yesterday?"

Shit. Maggie hadn't told him?

Eden looked between Billy and Maggie. "Well, it appears *someone* forgot to tell us. So maybe you oughta tell us what gives, Maggie?"

Maggie's chin came up. "I didn't tell you because I was already on edge about competing after so many years away from it. Knowing how Billy feels about my dancing...can you really blame me?"

Jon disagreed. She should've at least given her brother the option of attending. And Billy wore such a look of sorrow Jon almost felt sorry for him.

Eden took a step forward. "I love you, Maggie, but that's a load of crap. I understand that it seemed like Billy didn't support your dance aspirations in the past, but that was years ago. Now you're the one making assumptions about what level of support he's willing to offer you? How about if the two of you boneheads leave the past in the past? Oh. And here's a novel idea. Talk to each other. Don't continue to fall back into those big-brother-little-sister roles." She whirled around and poked Billy in the chest. "That goes for you too, mister, when it comes to relationship stuff. Maggie and Jon are together. Find a better way to deal with it than sarcasm."

"Yes, ma'am."

"And because you're both here, we're gonna deal with the fallout from this right now. Billy, my beloved. Tell Maggie what you're feeling."

At first, Billy looked like he'd call bullshit on Eden's demand, but he kept his focus on Maggie. "I would've liked the chance to be in the audience cheering you on because I've never seen you dance like that."

"Maggie?" Eden said. "It's your turn."

"I don't hold a grudge about that. You always supported me in math and science and technology because those were things you understood. Tendu, tutus and relevé—not so much."

"I'm a worrier, Maggie. Add to the fact I'm an engineer, and your older brother and I'm an epic anal worrier." He smiled sadly. "I've always thought you were like me, but you're not, are you?"

"On some things. You had a career and life-altering revelation at age thirty-two. And here I am, dealing with the same thing."

Jon had a pang of guilt. There was a lot of stuff he and Maggie hadn't talked about and rather than taking the chance and opening up to her a few minutes ago, he'd distracted her. No wonder his relationships were short-lived and he suspected it wasn't entirely due to his on-the-road lifestyle.

"I'm not making the choices you would," Maggie continued. "That doesn't make either of us right or wrong, just different."

"So you don't want my support?" Billy asked tightly.

Maggie got to her feet and hugged him. "I absolutely want your support. But I want you to remember I'll either thrive or fail on my own. But neither of those outcomes is on your shoulders this time."

"Old habits are hard to break, little sis."

"I get that. But you can transfer all that bossiness and overprotectiveness to baby Buchanan." She smirked. "I'm off the hook for at least the next eighteen years."

Billy laughed. And he hugged her. "Fair enough."

Eden clapped her hands. "See how much better everything is when you talk it out and everyone gets along?" She nudged her husband. "Now you and Jon shake hands."

Billy said, "Don't push it."

Maggie and Eden laughed, but Jon knew Billy wasn't trying to be funny.

"You guys going back to the party?" Eden asked.

Jon stood and draped his arm over Maggie's shoulder. "No, we're leaving. But have fun."

"I'll call you this week," Maggie said to her brother.

It wasn't until they were in Jon's car that he realized what Maggie hadn't said. "You didn't tell him that you and Seth won."

She shrugged. "He won't be able to attend the finals anyway so there's no reason to make him feel guilty. Besides, I talked to my sister Lacy yesterday and she's already volunteered to fly to Florida and represent the Buchanan family. I know Billy will be good with that."

They didn't talk much on the way back to Maggie's place. He knew she was preoccupied so he didn't push.

She invited him inside. After she'd poured them both a glass of iced tea, she asked the question he'd been dreading.

"So Jon... How long were you and Eden together?"

It didn't escape Maggie's notice that Jon froze.

"What makes you think we were anything besides friends?"

Maggie rolled her eyes. "Look in the mirror, rock star. No woman would turn down a chance to get naked with you. Plus, my brother doesn't like you, which tells me you were more than friends with the woman he loves."

When Jon remained quiet, Maggie blurted, "Holy hell, Jon. Please tell me you aren't still in love with her."

"No. I never was in love with her. Sad commentary, but we used each other for sex and neither of us pretended it was anything else. Then Billy came along, and after one night where the three of us got wild together, I saw how much Billy loved her, so I stepped out of the picture completely."

Maggie's mouth dropped open. "You had sex with my brother?"

"No. Jesus. I don't swing that way. You've been in bed with me, doll face, and you know how much I love pussy, so why would you even ask me that?"

"Because you're accepting of Jared and Gabe's relationship."

Jon frowned. "Jared isn't gay. He and Gabe are just roommates."

Evidently Jon had blinders on when it came to his little brother's sexual orientation and it wasn't her place to remove them. "My mistake. So what happened the night you three got wild?"

"Billy and I both had sex with Eden. Separately and together."

Silence. Then Maggie laughed. "I never thought my uptight brother had it in him to be a sexual wild man, let alone participate in a kinky threesome. But it makes sense why he didn't want you and me to get involved. 'Cause I'm pretty sure that wasn't your first or your last ménage."

"Nope." Jon kept his gaze on hers. "Now that you've heard my dark sexual secrets, you gonna hold stuff against me that happened a long time ago?"

She shook her head.

That seemed to surprise him. "Any wild nights you wanna share with me?" he asked lightly.

"My life—sex and otherwise—has been very tame compared to yours."

He flashed her that pure bad-boy grin. "Lucky thing you have me here to further your raunchy education."

Maggie raised an eyebrow. "The student becoming the teacher? Bring it."

"Well, I have had this fantasy of smacking your ass with a ruler."

"Not a chance, little drummer boy. But if you do well on the oral exam I might let you bang my erasers."

Chapter Twelve

The next weekend was a blur of dancing, airports, trying to catch sleep, and discussion about routines and strategy. Maggie returned to Spearfish late Sunday night. Although exhausted, she called Jon and he insisted on coming over. Apparently he'd missed her as much as she'd missed him.

He'd be missing her a lot in the next eight weeks because Vladimir had agreed to coach them. She and Seth would be spending Friday, Saturday and half of Sunday in Salt Lake City.

While Maggie was pumped for the opportunity, she realized her life would not be her own for the next two months. They'd still need to rehearse the other four nights of the week, which meant driving back and forth every day. Although her hours at the doctor's office were somewhat flexible, she couldn't afford to take off every Friday from work and stay overnight in Rapid.

After scoring one of the best teachers in the business, there was no way Maggie could back out and take the job offer from the company in Billings. They required an immediate start date, not two months down the road after nationals, so she declined their offer.

Maggie heard a voice in the back of her head, calling her a fool for letting such a great job opportunity pass her by. At first she believed the voice belonged to her brother, but the louder it became, the more she realized it was her own.

Leaving the computer securities business hadn't been her choice. It'd been a blessing in disguise, giving her a break to evaluate her career and her life.

And now Jon was in her life. For how long?

Hopefully forever. If they could just get through the next few weeks with her hectic schedule they could sit down and figure out what to do for the long haul.

They'd just have to make it work.

This wasn't working.

Jon watched Maggie sleeping. They'd tumbled straight into bed after her late arrival from the airport. Even after three months together, sex between them continued to shake the rafters, but they rarely talked afterward anymore.

It'd been years since he'd forged a friends and lovers connection with a woman. Now that he had that, he missed that side of his relationship with Maggie. Just hanging out at his place or hers, doing their own things, but together. Indulging in normal couple stuff he'd neither had the time nor the interest in doing before.

So lately, when they had the rare chance to spend time together, Maggie was so tired or uptight all she wanted to do was sleep or fuck.

That would've suited Johnny Feather perfectly. But it didn't suit Jon White Feather at all.

It'd be hypocritical if he mentioned he was tired of only seeing her twice a week. Maggie was finally getting to live her dream—who was he to make any demands on her?

Besides, eight weeks of travel on weekends was a drop in the bucket, time wise, compared to how long he'd be gone if he took the tour spot with Push. Would she be all right with him being on the road for several months after he'd sworn he was taking a break from that lifestyle?

That's probably why he hadn't given them a solid answer—he wasn't sure if he was ready to go back to that untethered life when he might've finally found an anchor.

Jon was in limbo all the way around and he hated every second of it.

One good thing about losing her job: Maggie had the chance to teach, sharing both her love of dance and her love of technology. Teaching computer literacy to senior citizens in the afternoons twice a week took some of the sting out of her missing her spunky grandma, especially since a few of her students were from her grandmother's former nursing home.

Her teaching hour was up and she shelved the various laminated hint sheets in large type. She heard *squeak squeak* and saw her late grandmother's best friend wheeling toward her.

Hilda Helfenstein had the grandmother stereotype down cold: white hair, pleasantly plump, wearing a sweet smile, dowdy clothes and orthopedic shoes. However, behind her glasses were the shrewd eyes of a woman who'd seen a lot at age ninety-two. Her hearing might be spotty, and she had difficulty walking, but there wasn't anything wrong with her mind.

"Well, Maggie, you done good today. Even Ester followed along before she fell asleep."

"What about you? Did you find that link I told you about?"

Hilda sighed. "No. I accidentally forgot to type in the letter 'l' in *clock* and... Whoo-ee. Some of them pictures that popped up were..."

Maggie shuddered to think of the types of sites Hilda had stumbled across. "There should've been a security lock to block out those graphic images. I'll have the software fixed—"

"Don't you dare." Hilda gestured to the young woman from the rest home, who ran herd on the sometimes rowdy senior set. "Young Tiffany here was more embarrassed than me and kept trying to get me to leave the site, but I figured I was already there so I might as well look around." She shrugged. "I found out them young fellas ain't got nothin' on old Boris."

"Who is Boris?"

"The guy who lives in room one ten at the home. And he's got a solid ten inches, if you know what I mean."

How in the world had Hilda seen Boris's...? Maggie changed the subject. "What's on your agenda tonight?"

"Bingo, I think. What about you?" Hilda's birdlike gaze pinned her in place. "You need to get prettied up and go out and hook yourself a man."

"I already have a man."

"Is he good lookin'?" Hilda demanded.

"Very."

"Why haven't I met him?"

"Because I've been traveling a lot." That had become a point of contention between her and Jon and they'd exchanged a few harsh words about it two nights ago. So despite the fact she missed him, she'd suggested they needed time to cool off and he'd agreed.

"Bring him in sometime, dearie. So I can check him out. Your granny would expect nothing less of me." She sighed. "I miss that wise woman."

"Me too."

Hilda backed away from the table and tossed over her shoulder, "Oh, you might take a look at that computer's cup holder. It's broken."

Cup holder? Maggie glanced at Tiffany, still lingering by the desk. "What is she talking about?"

"Hilda thought the CD drive was a cup holder. She pushed the button and complained that her coffee cup kept falling through."

Good lord. "Thanks for the heads up. I'll put in a request for Phil in repair to check it out."

Maggie had time to kill before she had to drive to Rapid City. Since the library wasn't busy, she settled in a comfy loveseat in the corner, propping her feet on the ottoman to catch up on gossip in the world of entertainment.

She'd finished *US Weekly* and *OK*, when she heard, "You know those rags are full of half truths and cleverly disguised lies, right?"

That voice was as smooth and warm as a snifter of brandy. Maggie glanced up into Jon's amused eyes. "Are you sure the actors on *Lost* aren't being stalked by a real-life smoke monster? Or that Zac Efron scored a recording contract only because he knocked up his *High School Musical* costar and they need the money for a gold-plated crib?"

Laughing, Jon plucked the *National Enquirer* from her hands. "I never would've guessed this was your choice for reading materials."

"What did you think I'd read?"

"A computer magazine. Or a book about dance techniques that will give you the edge to win the competition. Then you wouldn't have to be gone all the damn time."

She ignored his snarky comment and inhaled the musky aroma of his body-heat-warmed cologne. "I am multi-dimensional. I also read erotic romance."

He raised an eyebrow. "Is that where you learned the twisty move with your tongue? Because I really love that one." His voice dropped to a sexy growl. "Maybe we oughta sneak back to one of the study rooms. You can drop to your knees and give me another demonstration."

"In your dreams."

He slid next to her on the couch and stole a kiss. "I missed you."

"You must have if you tracked me down at the library."

"I got bored sitting at home. So anything exciting happen today, dancing queen?"

Casually, she said, "I got offered a job."

"With who?"

"A computer security company out of Fort Collins."

Jon gave her a sharp look. "When have you had time to interview with them?"

"Via phone and webcam. They sent me some encryption problems. Basic tech stuff tests."

"And you forgot to tell me?"

Why was he bristling? "Like you've told me about your last sudden and mysterious trip out of town?"

"Even if I would've wanted to talk to you about it, you haven't been around." He closed his eyes and took a deep breath. "Sorry. It's just I can't...never mind. This isn't about me. What did you say to the Fort Collins company?"

"I haven't given them an answer yet because I'm already committed to competing in nationals." She tipped her head back and stared at the yellowed acoustic ceiling tiles. "Accepting their offer should be a no brainer. A job in my field doesn't come along every day, especially not one where I can telecommute from rural South Dakota. But if I took the job I'd have to give up dance. Then I'd be back to the same grind I was happy to leave. Yet, I could lead a somewhat normal life again."

"Is that what makes you want to take the job, Maggie? The chance to lead a normal life?"

Wait a second. Had Jon said that with some disdain? Probably not. Probably she was just imagining things. "That's part of it. The money is excellent. There are great benefits. Computer security is something I'm good at."

"You're good at dance," he countered.

"Obviously that's up in the air at this point. So the question is, do I take a sure thing—a steady job which will allow me to live around my friends and family"—*and you*—"hoping this company will hold the position for me for another month? Or do I chase a dream and remain in the same broke-ass position I'm in now? Which will be the bigger regret? If I don't take a chance? Or if I do?"

No response.

Maggie wasn't really asking for his advice as much as thinking out loud. Yes, she loved dancing, but she'd realized she wouldn't be totally fulfilled making it her career. Now that she had distance and perspective, wasn't that part of the reason she'd stopped dancing all those years ago? She knew she wasn't good enough to make a living doing it? She'd never blamed Billy for crushing her dream. She was stubborn enough that if she believed her brother had been blowing smoke, she wouldn't have fallen in line with his way of thinking. She would've stuck it out if only to prove him wrong.

Since clearing the air after regionals, Billy was the one person she could talk honestly to about her career issues. It'd shocked her when the companies she'd sent resumes to months ago, right after she'd lost her job, were now contacting her. She'd never believed the "we're keeping your resume on file" response, but apparently some companies really did that. A few months later those companies had openings and they were looking to her to fill them.

She glanced over at Jon, engrossed in *The National Enquirer*.

Glad my career crisis isn't as interesting as J-Lo's latest crash diet.

Not that she'd say anything to him—they were both a little testy in recent weeks and he never said anything about his career plans, so she let it slide.

Jon had set the biweekly music magazine *Tempest* on the ottoman and she picked it up, absentmindedly flipping through the pages. Toward the end in the "Deals and Steals" section, she stopped to tear out one of those annoying subscription cards, when she saw Jon's name—or rather, Johnny Feather's name. Included in the article were two pictures of him with the members of some band. She skimmed the paragraph below the photos:

Rumors are flying that Johnny Feather has flown the coop from the critically acclaimed Native American rock band Sapa. The drummer has recently been spotted in Seattle with Push and in L.A. with Darkly

Dreaming, and Nashville with Radioactive Tar. He has reportedly auditioned for all three bands with an eye on touring with one of the groups this fall and is in final contract negotiations. The Whiskey A-Go-Go reportedly has Push scheduled to play next month. When contacted, representatives for the bands and the Indian rocker refused to comment.

So that's what Jon—no, Johnny Feather—had been doing? Maggie had stupidly believed him when he said he'd wanted to slow down and settle down, here, in Spearfish.

But he'd never said he'd be out of the public eye permanently.

Now that she thought about it, Jon had complained the last month about her flying to Salt Lake City every weekend, but he'd been evasive when speaking of his weekend plans. It'd made her feel guilty, thinking about him being home alone, when in actuality he'd been flying across the country auditioning for new bands? The thought he'd lied to her slashed her heartstrings; after three months together, she'd started to believe she was in love with him. Not that they'd made any promises to each other or spoken of a shared future, but Jon had implied it, plenty of times.

Hadn't he?

Or maybe she'd misunderstood.

Or maybe he'd just flat out lied to her.

Only one way to find out.

Maggie tossed the magazine in his lap and stood. "So I'm the last to know?"

Jon frowned. "Know what?"

She tapped on the article. "That you've got three prime drumming gigs dangling in front of you and you'll be on tour soon?"

He read the article before meeting her gaze. "No comment usually means the information is wrong."

"That isn't what I asked you."

"What do you want me to tell you?"

"The truth."

When he remained mum, she tossed out the first wild theory that popped into her head, hoping he'd scoff, deny it, or call her crazy.

"Here's what I think. You used the break from Sapa to tell everyone you wanted to take it easy for a while, when in reality, you were shopping yourself into a higher-profile band. You never had any intention of settling down, did you?"

Jon said nothing; he just leveled that implacable stare on her.

A sick feeling bloomed in the pit of her stomach. "When did you plan to tell me? Before I left for nationals? 'Oh, by the way, Maggie. I can't make it to watch you compete that weekend because I'll be in L.A. playing with Push. Oh, and I won't be here when you get back, I'll be on tour with Darkly Dreaming. Or Radioactive Tar. It's been fun. Have a nice life.'"

His mouth flattened into a thin line. "I wouldn't do that to you."

"Is that why you've encouraged me to keep dancing? Knowing I'd be traveling all the damn time, just like you will be? So you wouldn't have to feel guilty about lying to me?"

"No, I encouraged you to keep dancing because I know how much you love it." Jon stood. "Really, Maggie? You think I lied to you? You're going to throw accusations at me based on some bullshit article in a third-rate music magazine?"

"No. I'm asking you outright. Face to face. Is any of it true?"

"Yes, some of it is. But there are a lot of factors up in the air right now that I can't—"

"Stop. Just...stop." Maggie backed away. Mad. Frustrated. Confused. She looked at him and felt she didn't know him at all.

"Everything I said to you is true," Jon said evenly. "I want something permanent. Something stable. Something we've started to build. But it's not like we can talk about any of this when you're so focused on winning a national championship."

Talk about a smackdown. "You're right. It's all my fault. Even your secrets and your lies." She calmly picked up her satchel. "Good thing I don't have the time or the emotional energy to deal with anything else right now besides winning a national championship," she shot back. "And apparently I've been oblivious to a lot of things going on around me, so I apologize if you felt I was ignoring you and your career decisions. Oh right. You didn't even fucking *mention* it. So good luck with the band thing. I hope you win another fucking Grammy."

"Goddammit, Maggie, knock it off."

She slipped the strap over her shoulder and turned away.

He planted himself in front of her. "What are you doing?"

"Leaving for dance rehearsal."

"Sounds more like you're leaving me."

"I am." *Before you can leave me.*

"Like hell you are."

Don't cry. Stay mad. "Get out of my way."

"No, Maggie. Jesus. Wait. I didn't mean—"

"Leave me alone, Jon."

A librarian entered through the side stacks. "You two need to keep your voices down."

When Jon turned around to snarl at her, Maggie snuck out the back door.

And this time, he didn't bother to chase her down.

Probably for the best.

But she cried all the way to Rapid City anyway. More confused than she'd ever been. Her love life was up in the air. She might be facing two dead careers. She parked outside Seth's studio and stared at the door.

What was she supposed to do?

Her Grandma Ingrid's advice floated to the forefront, prophetic words after Maggie's first disastrous college dance class.

Take it one step at a time, girlie. You'll either find yourself dancing or walking the direction you need to go.

Taking a deep breath, Maggie knew that's all she could do. Take one step at a time. One day at a time.

Feet don't fail me now.

She got out of the car.

Chapter Thirteen

Orlando

Four weeks later...

Jon couldn't believe it'd been a month since he'd seen Maggie. His heart ached even as it'd soared as he watched Maggie take the dance floor on Seth's arm. She looked beautiful, regal and confident—exactly the way he'd remembered her.

His stomach roiled with nervousness when the music started. He'd bought a seat close enough to the action to get a good look at her, but not in a conspicuous place she might see him—because this wasn't about him, or them, but her living her dream.

So it was hard as hell to sit on his hands when the semi-finalists names were called and Maggie and Seth hadn't made it past the first round.

Jon stayed through the semi-finals, lingering in the empty arena after the spectators and the competitors had left, knowing Maggie would eventually wander out. The cleaning crew was done sweeping up popcorn and the set-up crew was preparing for the next event. It took every ounce of patience to wait for her to come to him, instead of tracking her down.

Much had happened in the last month. He'd made a lot of professional decisions and faced a lot of personal demons. Jon just hoped he wasn't too late to explain those changes to Maggie.

He heard the *click click* of her shoes first, echoing to him like a drumbeat. She emerged from the tunnel leading backstage and she looked so damn good his heart nearly stopped. She'd changed out of her sparkly costume and into street clothes. Hair scraped into a ponytail. Her ever-present duffel bag hung over her shoulder. But a sort of sadness surrounded her that he could see from up in the stands.

She strolled around the edges of the arena floor. Tipping her head back to look at the lights, the sound system and the huge TV screens that were now dark.

Was she lamenting it'd just been the luck of the draw that she and Seth had been entered in the same flight as the reigning champions? Probably Maggie would take that as some sort of sign. He'd never known anyone who could be called a romantic pragmatist, but she certainly fit the bill.

No one could say she and Seth hadn't given their all to their performance. They'd danced well. Better than they had at regionals. But the other couples in the competition had been better.

How did that make her feel? Had the competition stirred up her competitive streak? Would she be determined to work harder? Or would she back off and reevaluate whether she wanted to pursue getting to the next level in the world of competitive dancing?

Stop lurking and go find out.

Jon waited until Maggie sat on the player's bench before leaving the shadows. She was so lost in thought she didn't hear his approach until he sat next to her. "Hey."

Maggie gasped softly. "Jon? Oh my God. What are you doing here?"

"I came to watch you compete."

She blinked at him as if he were an apparition. "Why?"

"You know why," he said softly, keeping his gaze locked on hers. "I remembered the night after you won regionals you said you liked walking around a venue after it ended to see if any crowd energy lingered."

"I'm surprised you remembered that."

"I remember a lot of things about you, Maggie. Everything in fact."

She glanced down to where her fingers were twisting the straps of her duffel bag. "So you saw us dance?"

"Yes. You guys were good."

"But not good enough."

Typical Maggie response in that no bitterness laced her tone.

"So are you okay?"

"Yes. No. I don't know." She sighed heavily. "Honestly? It all seems pretty surreal. The hours spent rehearsing. The anticipation of getting to wear a gorgeous costume and dancing in front of thousands of people. The fear of failing in front of thousands of people. What a rush."

"It is a serious rush. But it always wears off."

"You would know."

Jon drummed his fingers on the bench beside him, at a loss for what to say.

"And now that we've exchanged polite small talk...maybe you should tell me why you're really here."

"Because even though things were left at a standstill between us, I knew it was temporary and I gave you the space you needed. But I didn't stop thinking about you. Or caring about you. This competition is a big deal in your life and I wanted to be here to support you."

Maggie looked at him. "Wasn't this the weekend you were supposed to play a live show with Push?"

He shrugged. "I told them I had a prior commitment."

"And they didn't mind you bailing on them?" she asked skeptically.

Don't bristle. He kept his tone light. "Hadn't you heard all musicians are flaky like that?"

"Not you. I'd never lump you in with all musicians, Jon."

"But you did."

She was quiet for a moment. "I guess I did. Why is it hard for me to take a leap of faith and so damn easy to jump to conclusions?"

"Human nature. People make mistakes. I did. I should've told you what was going on."

"So what is going on?"

"Push's management got a little pissy about me changing my mind and I realized I don't wanna work with people like that."

"When did you back out of the gig?"

"Last month."

"But..." Her eyes searched his and she seemed totally bewildered.

He knew the feeling. "Yes, that was before I knew whether we'd work this out. I wasn't ready to walk away from you then and that

218

hasn't changed." Jon forced himself to slow down. "I had no idea the music trade mags were snapping pictures and causing all kinds of trouble."

Maggie lifted a brow.

"Look, I'm not blaming the paparazzi for how you found out. I could give you a bullshit answer like I'd signed a bunch of nondisclosure agreements—which is true—but the truth is I'm so used to dealing with all this business crap myself, I haven't learned to open up to anyone. I should've trusted you and talked to you about it. I didn't. I'm sorry. It'll never happen again, I promise."

"So are you going back on tour?"

"No. I really am taking time off indefinitely. The offers were tempting, hell they were flattering which was probably why I even considered them. But I've honestly never been happier, just working on my own stuff on my own time frame, and learning to have a life. I want a life with you, Maggie." He tapped his fingers on his knees. "Sorry. Here I am babbling on—"

She put her hand over his. "You're doing that drumming thing. Why are you nervous?"

"Because I have so many things I want to say, but I wasn't sure if you'd tell me to shove off before I'd get to tell you a single one."

"Ironically enough, I have a lot of things to say to you too." Then she leaned forward to kiss him. "But I planned on sucking back a few cosmos to get up the courage before I drunk dialed you."

He laughed softly and the fear inside him settled a little. "Do you have any idea how crazy I am about you?"

"I've got a pretty good idea since you're here and since I feel the same way."

"God, I missed you."

"I missed you too."

Jon framed her face in his hands. "I don't want to fuck this up again, Maggie."

"Me either, but you don't get to take all the blame for it, Jon. It was a mutual fuck up. But that means we get to start from scratch." She turned her head and kissed the inside of his wrist. "You game for that, rock star?"

"Absolutely."

They didn't speak for several moments. Then Maggie sighed. "I have a confession to make. I took the job with the security company from Fort Collins."

That surprised him. "When?"

"A month ago."

"But that was before..."

"I competed in nationals? Yep. I knew going into this it would be my one shot at a championship. I'm disappointed we didn't win, but I am excited to start my new job."

He was excited too, if it meant what he thought it did. "This is the telecommuting one, right? You'll be living in Spearfish?"

"Yes. I will have to travel to Fort Collins periodically, but I can deal with that. Can you?"

"Heck yeah, maybe we'll turn it into a road trip." Jon's thumb stroked her cheek. "Because I never want to be away from you for very long."

Maggie kissed him again. "Same here. I'm happy I reconnected with my love of dancing because it led me to you. But I also finally understand dancing will only ever be a hobby for me. I'm good with that. And Seth understands. In fact, he's turned over all the upcoming dance classes at the community center to me."

Jon's eyes lit up. "So does that mean you'll be looking for a new permanent dance partner?"

"Uh-huh, but it ain't gonna be you, because sweetheart, you suck."

He nudged her shoulder. "I'm blaming you for that."

Her nose wrinkled. "Why's that?"

"Because you still owe me a dance lesson."

"You think one dance lesson will bring you up to snuff, rock star?"

"Hell no." He kissed her softly. Thoroughly. With such a burst of happiness, he felt like doing a jig. And wouldn't that make her laugh?

"Your seductive kisses won't change the fact it's gonna take me forever to teach you how to dance. You know that, right?"

"Yep. That's what I'm hoping for. A lifetime of dance lessons."

About the Author

To learn more about Lorelei James, read her Author Notes on this and other titles, and see a *Rough Riders* family tree, please visit www.loreleijames.com. Send an email to lorelei@loreleijames.com or join her Yahoo! group to join in the fun with other readers as well as Lorelei:

http://groups.yahoo.com/group/LoreleiJamesGang

Look for these titles by
Lorelei James

Now Available:

Dirty Deeds
Running With the Devil
Wicked Garden
Babe in the Woods

Wild West Boys
Mistress Christmas
Miss Firecracker

Print Anthologies
Three's Company
Wild Ride
Wild West Boys

Rough Riders
Long Hard Ride
Rode Hard, Put Up Wet
Cowgirl Up and Ride
Tied Up, Tied Down
Rough, Raw and Ready
Branded As Trouble
Strong, Silent Type
Shoulda Been A Cowboy
All Jacked Up
Raising Kane
Cowgirls Don't Cry
Slow Ride
Chasin' Eight
Cowboy Casanova
Kissin' Tell
Gone Country
Redneck Romeo

Where There's Smoke

Jayne Rylon

Dedication

For my mom. Nope, you can't read this one either.

Chapter One

Kyana Brady roamed the perfectly imperfect old house she'd inherited using only the silver light of the full moon to guide her through the familiar second-story hallway. Her cornflower-blue silk and lace nightgown seemed extravagant given that she was all alone, but the luxury helped her survive the night. It reminded her of when she'd had money, power and control over her life, not to mention those of the clients who'd depended on her to solve their problems in high-profile legal battles.

Six months ago, those things had seemed like enough.

Her last circuit of the upstairs hallway and the bedroom she'd inhabited as a teenager had given her a chance to debate whether she should email her partners—*ex*-partners—and concede to their relentless begging that she resume her duties. This go around, she paused to stare into Aunt Rose's room, still exactly as the woman had left it when she'd surrendered to liver cancer a few months earlier.

Time had slipped away without Kyana's usual routines to tick off the passing days with the precision of a metronome. Her existence had gone from an intricate melody of bright, well-timed notes to a long-held, somber chord that carried over from measure to measure. One endless night after another supplied infinite hours to ruminate on the direction of her future without a break even to catch her breath. It was long past due for her to admit she'd gotten stuck in an endless contemplative rut and was no closer to understanding the ideal direction for her future. She might just have to take the plunge, get moving again and see where she ended up.

Crap. Relying on fate had never been her strong suit.

She cringed at an ultra-loud creak that shattered the still air. It came from a plank tucked beneath the Persian runner. Funny how the noisy floorboards had seemed charming when Aunt Rose inhabited the house. Now, they verged on creepy. Maybe she could find someone to fix the loose wood.

Logan, her mind whispered. She promptly ignored the ridiculous excuse to call him, talk to him or, God forbid, see him. If she'd resisted, though barely, his sexy rasp spicing up her voicemail on the day of Aunt Rose's funeral, she certainly wasn't about to cave to silly girlish whims now. Still, it might be time to make this place her own. Or move on.

The prospect of shopping for new furnishings began to perk her up. Hooray for the internet, an insomniac's playground. A mental list coalesced. She ticked off places to browse and what she'd need from each as she headed toward her room, seeking the laptop perched on her side table. The screensaver's abstract shapes transformed into others, glowing with colors that lured her closer like a moth to a retail flame. No reason not to get a jump on things. She had saved a folder of inspirational pictures on one of the home-decorating sites she liked to idle away time on while dreaming about...*someday.*

Tomorrow could be someday.

Well, more like today since midnight had drifted past hours ago.

Enough of this stagnation.

Simply because she didn't need to work to survive given the insurance settlement from her parents' deaths, the generosity of Aunt Rose and the success of her previous career, didn't mean she had to idle all her time away. Committed to progress, even something as small as new curtains, she marched deeper into her sanctuary.

From the quaint lavender room Aunt Rose had tried to get her to abandon for a larger space, a flicker of light across the yard caught her attention. Next door, Rose's lifelong friend still occupied his similar home. Built within a month of each other, the two houses had hosted their owners for damn near fifty years, if not more.

There were times Kyana had to catch herself from thinking of her great-aunt's neighbor as *Uncle* Ben. Maybe he was having trouble sleeping again too. It wouldn't be the first time she'd spied his bedside lamp shining like a beacon at all hours of the night since she'd returned home to care for her ailing relative. Some of her partners couldn't understand what they'd called a major sacrifice, but it had been the least she could do considering how Rose had taken her in all those years ago, after the accident that had stolen her parents from them.

Honestly, she regretted staying away as long as she had.

Kyana had learned to switch her own light off to keep from worrying Benjamin. At his age, he didn't need any more stress. Certainly not over her. She could handle herself—or so she'd always thought.

She squinted at the flicker, surprised to see it coming from the kitchen instead of the upstairs as she'd first assumed. Unsteady, the spark began to writhe and grow. Her eyes bulged as she pressed her nose to the glass. A tendril of gray smoke seeped from the windows Benjamin insisted on cracking open at night despite the air-conditioning he'd had installed decades ago and her concerns about security.

A fire!

Kyana snatched her cell phone off her nightstand and dialed 911 before she made it to the landing halfway down the stairs. The operator remained infuriatingly calm as Kyana shouted the address and crucial information at the well-intentioned woman. "Please, come quickly. Ben's bedroom is right above the kitchen."

"Ma'am, I've dispatched the firemen. Please stand back from the scene. You don't want to interfere. You'll be in their way."

She held the phone away from her face and gave it an oh-*hell*-no glare before disconnecting. In their speck of an upstate New York town, the firemen were all volunteers. They had to be roused from warm beds before driving in from who-knows-where. Not a chance in hell she'd let Benjamin sleep in a burning house. Without his hearing aids in, he might not notice the screeching detectors. Hell, half the time the cantankerous guy yanked the batteries from the devices after scorching his toast and left the housings dangling like open clamshells until she noticed and reassembled them.

Wet grass squished between her toes, soggy from the late spring showers they'd had almost every day for weeks. Sprinting across the lawn that divided Aunt Rose and Benjamin's houses, she hoped the dampness would impede the blaze.

As she neared, flares of light and heat billowed from the kitchen window, causing her to stumble backward with a gasp. Losing her footing, she ruined her favorite chemise. An ass-shaped splotch of mud covered the rear. Pain shot up her tailbone and elbow, which took the brunt of the crash.

Acrid smoke scorched her lungs when she recovered from having the wind knocked out of her. She didn't dare pause to catch her breath. The edge of her nightgown would have to pass as a filter. She yanked it over her mouth and scrambled to her feet. She raced up the porch stairs two at a time, palming the key from above the side entryway in half a second flat. Her hands shook. Metal slipped against slightly warmer than usual metal. At least she didn't drop the damn thing. On the second try, it notched into the lock.

She moved the fabric protecting her face aside to yell, "Ben! Wake up! Fire!"

The next breath she took contained enough smoke to have her choking as she finally crashed through the door. The lovely carved maple hit the entryway wall hard enough to leave a mark, but she didn't pause. No way could she dash through the kitchen without becoming a human shish kebab. Thank God the house had a second, if narrow, set of stairs in the rear.

"Ben!"

Kyana made as much noise as possible. Shouts dwindled in her narrowing windpipe. Fumes thickened as she ascended. They turned her cries scratchy. Coughing replaced most of her calls, so she preserved her oxygen.

She opened Ben's door cautiously, relieved to find the insidious conflagration hadn't yet eaten through the floor. However, her eyes watered beneath the assault of dense smoke. Tears streamed down her cheeks when she caught sight of an unmoving lump beneath the fugly harvest gold and green paisley quilt straight out of the seventies. It seemed too small to contain all the laugher and vitality she associated with Ben.

Please, please, don't be too late.

Shaking him didn't seem to help any more than screaming her brains out had. Something downstairs gave a horrible wail then a pop. Silence was followed by the *whoosh* of rejuvenated flames. Kyana couldn't believe how fast the fire had engulfed the lower level.

Neither she nor Ben had time to waste.

Uncertain of where she found the strength, she ducked down and tried to imitate the fireman's hold she'd seen on TV. Ben toppled to the floor, taking her balance with him. She crashed to the ground, smacking her head and shoulder on the corner of a dresser nearby.

Stars danced in her vision, lulling her, tempting her to close her eyes for just one second.

No! Ben!

Staying low to the ground this time, she crawled over the unconscious man and used the cotton of his T-shirt at his shoulders to drag him toward the stairs. Thank God he'd never covered his precious hardwood floors. The polished surface made him easy to slide as she backed up to the landing. Glancing over her shoulder, she caught claws of fire rending the edges of the wall at the bottom of the stairs. She had no choice but to try and make it past before they blocked the entryway.

Sweat poured down her face, neck and back. Not all of it from the heat. Quivering, her muscles strained to obey her commands.

The door to the outside stood open. In the distance, she thought she heard the faint whine of a siren. So close. If she could just make it a little farther, they'd be okay. Someone would be waiting outside to help. She hoped.

Kyana gave in to the very rare temptation to pray. She begged Aunt Rose to watch over them. To let there be something the experts could do to wake Ben up. Allowing herself to think it might be a corpse she hauled wasn't productive. She refused to believe that was true.

"Gonna be a rough ride. Hang on." She lifted his head and shoulders as high as she could without going ass over tea kettle then scooted down the stairs. If every single lungful hadn't seared her from the inside out, she might have winced at the thud of his heels banging on each riser they passed.

Overexertion, or maybe the knock she'd taken on her skull, stole her coordination. She screeched as she slipped, trying futilely to hang on to Ben as she tumbled down the last four or five steps. Landing in a heap at the bottom, she struggled to sort out their limbs. Until a wash of angry fire licked her side.

Instinct engaged. With one final burst of strength, she latched onto Ben's arm and hauled him across the threshold onto the low deck outside. "Have to get away. Farther from the house."

Kyana didn't realize she chanted the mantra as she repeatedly blinked her eyes to clear the haze and infuse some moisture to the dry, tortured surfaces.

"It's okay, miss." Someone pried her fingers from Ben. "I have you."

"Ben!"

"Your friend's safe. Thanks to you. Come on. We'll get you both sorted out." The world tipped and turned. She couldn't bring herself to care or to decipher the surreal sensation of being carried for the first time she could ever remember. "Christ, you're a brave one. Running into that mess is enough to scare our rookies over there."

"No choice." She let her head rest on the black-and neon-striped surface of the fireman's jacket. Even those two tiny words ripped up her throat.

"Shush." He rocked her as he broke into a jog. "You could have actually listened to the dispatcher and not charged into that fucker yourself. But I would've done exactly the same thing. Get used to being called a hero, honey. The news crew is eating this shit up. By tomorrow morning, you're going to be famous. At least around here."

Flashing red lights intensified until they nearly blinded her, given her already impaired vision. The fireman deposited her gently on a gurney. He squeezed her fingers then disappeared, diving right into the hell she'd been so eager to flee.

Medics swarmed her.

"Ben." The emphatic shout sounded more like a rasp.

"He's breathing," a woman informed her. "A good sign. Let my partners do their jobs. How about not making mine any harder by fighting, huh? Settle down."

Gentle touches accompanied the stern request. A mask fell into place over her mouth. Cool air soothed her throat and lungs.

"Inhale. Slow and deep." The woman's dulcet voice charmed Kyana, forcing her to obey for several long minutes while the shock and terror of what had happened began to really sink in. She subdued the urge to rotate for a glimpse of Ben, afraid of what she might witness.

A growl rumbled through the night. "Let me up. Take that crap off me."

"Ben." Kyana smiled.

"I see the two of you are a matched set." The EMT rolled her eyes. "Your dad is going to be just fine."

"He's not—" She stopped herself. In some ways he kind of had been. For both her and his great-nephew, Logan. A vision of the rogue bad boy next door inspired Kyana's insides to cartwheel just as surely as he had during the summer and final year of high school they'd spent as neighbors and friends.

His dark, unruly hair and bright blue eyes were a potent combination she'd never forget. Not even a decade-long parade of handsome actors, who starred in the romantic comedies she adored, had offered up daydream material half as fine.

Unfortunately, she'd never appealed to Logan in the same way. She refused to think of the time she'd begged him to kiss her, right here beneath the sprawling oak tree in the yard that separated their houses. An instant or ten of heaven followed by several weeks of awkward purgatory that'd ended when he took off a few days before graduation.

She'd never even said goodbye.

"Your eyes will probably be watering for days." The woman patted her shoulder. "That's totally normal considering how much smoke you were exposed to."

If only that were the cause. Much easier to treat than an unrequited yet everlasting crush on your ridiculous first...*only*...love.

"Kyana?" Ben's voice took on a new level of alarm. "She *what*? Where is she?"

Rather than risk him injuring himself further, Kyana waved off her tech and slithered to the ground. She stripped the mask from her face, and ignored the vehement protests of most of her body, including her hip, which was visible through the charred hole in her nightgown.

"Right here," she croaked. So much for reassuring him. "Just fine."

"Oh, girly." Ben slumped in his makeshift bed. "You look like shit."

"Gee, thanks." She grinned.

He opened his arms, and she didn't pause before throwing herself into his still-strong grasp. "You're shaking. It's all right now, Ky. At least until I beat your ass for putting yourself in danger like that."

She tried to stop the tears from falling, but couldn't. "I thought I was too late."

"I'm tougher than you think." He ruffled her hair.

"Ms. Brady! Mr. Patterson!" Kyana lifted her face from Ben's shoulder instinctively. The second she faced the intrusion, bright lights gleamed, shocking her already sore eyes. She squinted, trying to make out the person on the other side of the glare. "This is Channel Four news. How did the fire start? Is there anyone else in the house?"

Kyana stammered some half answer, trying to make it stop. The noise, the light, the endless barrage of questions—it was all too much for her battered senses.

"Enough." A tall man dressed in dark clothing emerged from the shadows to issue the grim command. His upright bearing and the panther-like stalk to his approach clearly identified him as Daryl Thick.

Kyana couldn't recall hearing much more than one-word sentences from the ex-military man in all the time he'd lived down the street. To be honest, he'd kind of freaked her out with his stillness and the intensity of his stare on more than one occasion. Like tonight, he always seemed to be lurking in the shadows.

Watching.

Waiting.

For what, she wasn't sure, but she appreciated the effortless way he squashed the newsman's inquisition tonight. "I've got this, Ben. No more questions folks. Move along."

Ben lifted his hand, but Daryl had already run the reporter behind the police line. His imposing form and the stubborn set of his enormous shoulders brooked no argument.

Kyana's gaze roamed from the clash to the rest of the people huddled on the sidewalk. She couldn't recognize all of their neighbors from this distance, despite the orange glow cast by the flames. At the front of the pack was the young couple, the Gittlesons, who'd moved in less than a year ago. She returned their solemn wave. They looked as miserable as she felt, huddled together, horrified.

She had to look away from the pity in their stares before she allowed herself to consider all that Ben had lost. In a matter of minutes, a lifetime of possessions, photographs and memories had been destroyed.

A sob escaped her chest.

"I'm sorry," she gasped. "There wasn't time to grab anything."

"You hauled my wrinkled old ass out of there, girly." Ben patted her back. "Nothing else matters. I've got all the important stuff up here. And in here."

She smiled softly when he tapped his temple then his chest with a gnarled finger.

"Benjamin!" A wail cut through the din of the fire, which seemed to be lessening beneath the onslaught of water and the firemen crawling over Ben's house like fluorescent ants. Barked directions, the squeal of additional sirens approaching and the rumble of the gathering crowd had nothing on the high-pitched screech that emanated from the tiny elderly woman tottering their way.

"Incoming," Ben muttered.

Kyana couldn't help but laugh. Her aunt and Ben had often resorted to all sorts of hijinks in order to dodge their clingy, busybody neighbor through the years.

Why should Myrtle's overdramatic bent lean a different direction tonight? At least she would have plenty to gossip about for the next few weeks.

"Be nice. Let her fuss over you. It'll make her feel useful." Kyana patted Ben's shoulder.

Nothing beat seeing her seventy-two-year-old neighbor rolling his eyes a moment before Myrtle descended on them with gasps, cries and hugs for Ben. For the first time since she'd spotted the wisp of fire from her bedroom window, Kyana felt like things might be okay.

Eventually.

Chapter Two

Logan crashed onto the beat-up leather recliner in his shitty apartment. Sure, it was barely after dawn, but it wasn't early by his standards. Usually he raced the first rays of sunrise to a construction site. This morning was really the end of a long, long night and a terrible day.

His buzz had faded hours ago, somewhere around the time he'd realized he couldn't get it up with the slightly skanky blonde who'd promised to suck all his woes right out of him in some even sketchier alley. Probably the one behind the bar he'd attempted to drown his sorrows in. What the hell was wrong with him?

It wasn't every day a guy got canned, he supposed.

Not that he hadn't seen that train barreling down on him from a mile away. Still, he'd tried his damnedest to save his spot on the renovation crew by working his ass off. Demonstrating superior skills and reliability hadn't been the Hail Mary he'd hoped. Hell, he'd even skipped out on Rose's funeral so he wouldn't have to call off. What a waste. He'd left a pathetic message on Kyana's voicemail, offering condolences he should have given in person. No wonder she hadn't called his lame ass back.

Not now, nor ten years ago when he'd walked out on her and Ben like the chickenshit eighteen-year-old he'd been.

It was about time he got his priorities in order. As soon as he could believe this had really happened. Grief, fury and shock sweated from his skin along with the vile stench left behind by a 40 of King Cobra—the most buzz he could buy for his last twenty, drinking like a hobo. Might as well have duct-taped the bottle to his palm. At least then he wouldn't have knocked it over, spilling some. He really could have used those last six or seven shots. Maybe they would have granted him oblivion.

Logan tipped his head onto the comfortable cushion, which had dented to perfectly contour his form years ago. He tried not to think of the shit he'd lost in his life, like the gorgeous young lady he'd admired and wanted so desperately. Her delicate Asian features, refined manners, unwavering loyalty to her mongrel best friend, and her all-American sass had practically brought him to his knees. Just another thing he'd never really had a chance at holding on to.

What a loser.

Doubly so because the simple thought of her—and the sultry all-woman voice that had transfixed him on her voicemail—had blood rushing to his dick. If it had been her smooshed up against him in that cesspool tonight, there'd have been no performance issues to stand in the way of a mind-numbing good time. Yeah, right. Kyana would never stoop so low as to join him in a dive like that. He didn't blame her either.

"Son of a bitch!" He thumped his fist on the tattered arm of his chair, refusing to give in to the temptation to take matters into his own hands while visions of the polished, perfect girl next door danced through his mind. He'd grown out of that phase back in high school. Okay, he had occasional relapses, but it hadn't been until Ben told Logan she'd moved home—during one of their twice-weekly calls—that he'd regressed to his former obsession.

Ben would be awake in an hour or so. Maybe Logan would call and see what was going on in the old neighborhood. He'd crash-landed there when his mom hooked up with a new guy and didn't have room or patience to take a rebellious teen along to her new picket-fence life. He didn't really blame her.

Better yet, maybe he should pay his great-uncle a visit. It was about time Logan did something useful. Something decent for someone who deserved his loyalty.

He still couldn't believe he'd been played so bad. A total sucker. How hadn't he realized what was up?

To distract himself for a while, he snatched the remote off the side table, which he'd rescued on junk day and restored, before flipping on the TV. Channel surfing his basic cable didn't yield much of interest.

Infomercial, infomercial, infomercial...

News.

It might do him some good to remember there were entire nations of people out there who had it a hell of a lot worse than he did. Fucked up? Yes. But it did make him feel better about the state of his existence. If he could find an old Jerry Springer rerun he'd really be looking fine.

Flames transfixed him as they wrapped around the edges of a window to grasp at the shutter outside. Wow, it would seriously blow to have your pad burn down. Especially if you had a home instead of merely a place you stayed, which is how he felt lately. The fire hypnotized him as it licked at the walls of an older Victorian that looked not that different than the one he'd spent his adolescent summers in. Ben's house had been home. The real kind. For a while.

Maybe Logan could try for that again.

He leaned forward in his chair as a fireman flew off the deck at the rear of the building with a woman cradled in his arms. Raven hair and pale skin wrapped in something that might once have been pretty blue silk were revealed with each cycle of the flashing emergency lights.

Logan's head tilted as he examined the injured woman. He must have been more fucked up than he realized to imagine the damsel in distress looked a hell of a lot like Kyana. Not that he'd studied her photographs in Ben and Rose's houses on his infrequent visits or anything.

Sure, sure. Keep telling yourself those lies. One day you might believe them, buddy.

Shit, he'd even snapped his own copies with his cell phone. The woman he'd spied posing in designer suits or in endless graduation cap and gowns in photos on Rose's vintage mantel didn't seem like the sort who'd doll herself up in gorgeous yet frivolous finery. He scrubbed his eyes with the bruised and cut knuckles of one hand after he realized he hadn't blinked for a solid thirty seconds.

When he refocused, he saw it—the ugly-ass birdbath he and Kyana had built Ben one sweltering August afternoon as kids when her family had been on a round-the-world tour and his mom had been on the prowl for a step up. The broken flower pots they'd recycled made unlevel, garish yard art better suited to Logan's mom's trailer park than Ben's neat and trim community. Despite that, his great-uncle had refused to get rid of the junk.

No! It can't be. He stabbed the volume button on his remote, disengaging the mute feature.

"The cause of the fire is still unknown but the resident was the only occupant at the time of the blaze. His neighbor spotted the fire, called emergency crews, then rushed inside to haul the elderly man from the flames." In the background, a burly fireman toted Kyana's rag doll form as though she weighed nothing at all. Tall and willowy, she probably didn't. The graininess of the image made it hard to tell much, but the tattered nightgown and soot stains covering her sent ice through Logan's veins.

"Neighbors tell us this isn't the first tragedy to strike Oak Avenue this year. The death of a longtime resident next door just a few months ago has some wondering if bad luck really does come in threes. And, if so, who will suffer it next?" The reporter paused while footage cut away from Kyana being loaded onto a gurney outside an ambulance.

"Go back! Go back!" he shouted at the TV. He had to make sure she was okay. And where was Ben? They'd said Ky had pulled him from the burning house, but was he all right?

Batty as ever, Myrtle Jansen entertained the reporter with old wives' tales and superstitions that portended more dire times to come. Logan shook his head and instead studied the rest of the crowd. He didn't recognize the man and woman huddled together in the background. They must be new to the area. Daryl Thick loomed still and watchful on the fringes of the frame. His assessing stare on Myrtle and the newscaster put Logan on instant alert.

"More on this story as it becomes available. Back to you, Tom..."

"What? That's it?" Logan didn't know when he'd launched to his feet. He paced the kitchen as he dug his cell from the back pocket of his jeans. Snagging his keys out of the bowl by the door, he jogged from his apartment.

Ring after ring grated on his nerves until he realized, of course, there'd be no answer at Ben's place. He used his thumb to search the contact list of his basic, un-smart phone for the number he'd only found the balls to dial once. After Rose's funeral. Kyana.

Instead of infuriating chimes, a beeping busy signal greeted him. "Damn it!"

He punched the steering wheel then jammed a key in the ignition of his pickup truck. At least there wouldn't be traffic at this time of day, and he'd gotten gas just a day or two ago. If he pushed it, he could make the drive in an hour.

It was the longest fifty-three minutes of his life.

Logan skidded to a halt in the driveway of Rose's house. No, Kyana's house. The yellow tape blocking off the entrance to Ben's place was completely unnecessary. Stopping there would have been pointless. Char lingered in the air, making his eyes water and his nose itch. He didn't pause to swipe at his face before tearing from the truck. He hopped the flower beds and retaining wall with a single leap before sprinting up the hill to the back stairs he'd used many times in his youth.

The bottom one creaked louder than he remembered. Maybe he'd never subjected it to such force in the past. Today he leapt them three at a time. He swiped the key from its usual hiding place in the grill, tucked in the corner of the deck, then burst through the screened-in porch. Without bothering to ring the bell, he let himself inside.

Lights blazed in the kitchen, so he headed that way first.

Logan was a little surprised to find his uncle awake after all the commotion, which had probably included a trip to the hospital in the handful of hours between the fire and the airing of the piece on the news. His heart stuttered in his chest when he caught sight of Ben, slumped over the dining room table. For the first time Logan could remember, the man looked...old. White hair slicked back from a recent shower. Neat rows left by a comb in his thinning locks contrasted with a fuzzy gray robe, which Ben clasped tight around him. It had obviously belonged to Rose. If Logan wasn't concentrating so hard on not breaking down, he might have snapped a picture.

"Nice outfit." He tried not to startle his great-uncle. The guy didn't need that kind of shock on top of everything else.

"Even without my hearing aids, I could tell that was you clomping up the stairs. Maybe because you were shaking the whole damn house, you big lug." Ben lifted his head and pasted on a wry smile. "How'd you find out?"

"The goddamned news." He tried not to shout, balling his fists at his sides instead. He didn't bother with inane questions like, "How are you?" when the answer was clearly devastated-yet-mostly-healthy. Besides, they were both more comfortable with confrontation than sentimental shit. "Were you going to call me? Or am I so worthless you didn't think I'd come?"

"Logan, please." Ben shook his head, his eyes shining. "Things have been rough lately, I understand. How many decades did I work two or three jobs to earn my house? When you have a dream, you have to go for it. Things—*important* things—have to be sacrificed. I wasn't about to pile any more pressure on you. We'll handle it."

"You and Wonder Woman, huh? I can't fucking believe she ran into a burning building." His guts roiled again at the thought of what might have happened. The ragdoll flop of her lithe body in the fireman's arms had him brewing some punches. Aimed at whom, he couldn't say. Maybe the dude who had been there to rescue her. Logan wished he could have been her hero.

The nightmare vision distracted him from pursuing Ben's revelation. What had the man sacrificed? Logan would give his great-uncle anything in his power. Another time he would circle around and find out.

"I'm torn on that one. Can't say I'm pleased she put herself at risk. At the same time... I'm sure I wouldn't be sitting here right now if it weren't for that girly." Ben sighed. "She's tough. You know she is. But a person can only take so much. She's been in the shower an awfully long time. I'm starting to think someone needs to make sure she's okay. I should have insisted the doctors examine her too, damn it. You know how she gets, though. Hardheaded."

Ben stared at Logan, unblinking.

"I'm on it." Logan bent down and clapped a hand on Ben's back, surprised to find his palm met with more bone than muscle. He manned up and said what he was really thinking all along. "I'm so glad you're all right."

"Me too, kiddo." Ben coughed when he laughed. "Guess I gotta go to extremes to rate a visit, huh?"

"Not anymore. I swear. Things'll be different. Shit, you might not be able to get rid of me now." Logan never broke promises. For one thing, his landlord was likely to boot him into the skid row gutter a millisecond after the dirt bag found out he'd lost his job. But mostly, being here felt right.

Though his world had turned upside down, something in his soul had settled the moment he'd driven his truck onto Oak Avenue—even if he'd executed the maneuver practically on two wheels.

Ben nodded then shooed Logan with a wave of his hands toward the stairs. "Check on Kyana. I'm going to rest for a while. Is it sleep or a nap if it's already six o'clock? In either case, I'll take Rose's room."

They both winced at the reminder of their absent friend.

Overflowing with terror, loss and regret, Logan bounded up the stairs to the second floor. He strode to the bathroom that adjoined Kyana's old room and banged on the door.

No answer.

She'd have to be deafer than Ben to miss his second round of pounding.

Still not a peep confronted his battery against the hardwood.

Something told him he'd have better luck convincing her to open the door if he didn't start bellowing at her from the other side of the six-paneled maple. If she recognized his voice, he'd certainly be left out in the cold.

Then he imagined her passed out. Unconscious. What if she'd slipped and hit her head?

She had to be exhausted.

Drained.

Scared.

Hurt.

It didn't take much for him to visualize her crumpled in the tile basin, bleeding from a nasty dent in her thick skull. Screw that.

He pivoted on his heel and marched into Rose's room. Ben looked at him with a single raised brow when he rummaged through the supplies near the vanity mirror. He held a bobby pin up to the soft morning light, glowing in the window, to judge the wire's gauge.

"You can't just barge in there. Give her space if she needs it," Ben protested, leaning forward from the edge of the bed. His fingers gripped Logan's arm hard enough to leave marks.

"She's not answering. What if she's messed up?" He paused, respecting the opinion of his great-uncle. During the time in between stays, Logan had merely been surviving, not learning and growing like he had been in the glorious summers or the final year he'd spent on Oak Avenue.

"Shit, you're right." Ben closed his eyes. "No choice. Be ready for her to fight you though. She's a wildcat, our girly."

"I think I can handle one wet, naked woman." He groaned. It took all the fortitude he possessed to halt that line of fantasy right in its tracks. "Damn. I didn't mean it like that..."

Ben laughed. "I didn't raise a dumbass. She's likely to tear your nuts off as it is. Good luck, son."

Logan grimaced and adjusted his package as he made his way to the bathroom door. He tried once more, rapping in a more reasonable tone. One deep breath. Two. Three.

He gritted his teeth and got to work finessing the lock. It took him less than five seconds to disengage it even with the crude bobby pin. Some habits die hard.

Yeah, like lusting after Kyana Brady. Somehow he figured what he was about to do wouldn't simplify that situation.

Logan paused with his shaking fingers on the knob. He sighed then turned the antique glass and porcelain handle. Steam billowed from the crack when he pushed the door open, making him wonder how Kyana had managed to maneuver through the smoke in Ben's house. She must have been terrified, but she hadn't let that stop her from saving his great-uncle's life.

He owed her one. A monstrously huge one.

"Kyana?" he called out as he inched forward, shutting the door gently behind him. "Are you all right?"

Waving his arms in front of him, he advanced through the cloud of lightly scented mist. It smelled of something exotic. Jasmine and green tea, which reminded him of Kyana's half-Japanese heritage. He'd always adored her long, black hair and the gorgeous shape of her unusual hazel eyes.

A tiny hiccup yanked him from the memory of her smile.

"Ky?" He tilted his head to make sense of the jumble of limbs curled into a tight ball on the shower floor. For a moment he thought he'd had it right. She must have slipped and fallen. Who knew how long she'd lain there suffering. "Oh, fuck."

Without hesitation, he tugged open the clear glass enclosure and sank to his knees beside her. The door banged a little as it swung closed. The noise startled Kyana. If he hadn't already reached for her, she might have slammed into the wall in her haste to retreat. Instead, he caged her against his chest, giving no thought to his rapidly dampening clothes.

"Where are you hurt?" Warm spray blasted his back. Nothing could have burned as bright as the woman he held in his arms. Even if she was trying her damnedest to break free.

Logan didn't plan to let her go any time soon.

"*What?* I'm not. I'm fine. What the hell—?" She thrashed for a few seconds more, until his gentle rambling broke through her initial fear.

"It's me. Logan. I've got you. Everything's going to be okay. I'm sorry I frightened you. I tried to knock. You didn't respond. I thought you might need me. I was afraid. It killed me to see you lying there. Let me help. Let me help."

She went limp in his arms. So much so, he might have thought she'd fainted for real except the momentary relaxation didn't last. A shuddering sob ripped through her. All resistance fled. Like a pendulum that'd reached one extreme, she swung the other way. Latching on to him, she crawled so close on his lap he might have thought she'd burrowed inside his jeans if they hadn't stuck to him like a second skin.

"It's really you. You're here." She explored the tops of his arms, ringing as much of his biceps as she could with her long, delicate fingers. Apparently satisfied, she gulped then buried her face in his neck.

Sheltering her gave him a purpose, and made him feel a million feet tall.

He didn't pause to protect her modesty. Bold strokes of his hands were designed to infuse her with warmth and strength. He hugged her to him until she squeaked through her soul-deep cries. Somehow, he suspected this could be the first time she'd let her guard drop completely since Rose's death. Hell, maybe ever.

Rocking them both, he allowed his own tears to fall unnoticed. A couple for his job. More for the fear that had chilled his heart this morning. And a torrent for the amazing woman all three of them had loved and lost. But most for the time he'd wasted. Because holding

Kyana now he realized... This was home. The place he'd always been destined to be happiest.

Maybe not right this second. Still, together they could endure anything. They had in the past and they would again if he had anything to say about it.

Little by little, her crying diminished. Sniffles and plaintive whimpers ripped his insides apart faster than the violent heaving of her sobs had. Goose bumps rose on her skin when the water began to cool. "Come on, Kyana-chan."

A delicate snort interrupted her mourning. "I haven't heard that one in a while."

Logan separated them only enough to peer into her bloodshot-yet-beautiful eyes. "Get used to it. I have a feeling you'll be sick of it before long."

"Never." She bit her lip as if to keep it from trembling. Had she ever looked so vulnerable? He doubted it. The usual armor she buckled around herself had vanished along with her clothes. "I missed you, Logan-kun. I'm glad you're here."

"Same goes."

The silence lingered forever between them. He'd never longed to kiss a woman as badly as he did in that instant. Her tongue darted around to soothe her chapped lips and he almost stroked out. For the first time, he allowed his gaze to wander from her face. But instead of sneaking a peak at her high, firm breasts, he caught sight of several massive bruises.

Arms, ribs, hips—the perfection of her body was marred by ghastly purple splotches.

"You *are* hurt." He rose to his feet, ensuring his grip on her elbows lifted her as well. He ducked his shoulder to press in the handle and shut the water off.

"I don't feel it when I'm with you." She smiled up at him. The resulting riot of butterflies in his chest almost distracted him enough to carry her straight to bed.

"Like hell." He set her carefully on the countertop, subduing her shriek on contact. The cooler marble chilled her still-steaming, extra-fine ass. Inspecting her bruises and cuts, he determined only a few needed bandages. The worst of the damage seemed to be the singed patch on her hip.

"They gave me some ointment for that." She pointed toward a pile of supplies he hadn't noticed in his haste to reach her. "If you hand it to me—"

"Shush." He covered her lips with his fingers. Sure, it kept her quiet. Better yet, it stopped him from doing something foolish. Like closing the gap between them to press his mouth to hers. That wasn't the kind of comfort she would appreciate from him. She deserved way better than an uneducated, unemployed twenty-eight-year-old bum.

Without glancing away from her, he retrieved the tube of cream and the loose gauze paired with it. He concentrated on applying a generous layer to her ultra-soft skin without inflicting any more pain. That was the last thing he aimed to do.

No matter how hard he tried to ignore her svelte curves or the long lines of her torso and legs, it was no use. Even more attractive was her self-confidence. Not once did she try to cross her arms over her breasts or arrange a towel on top of her lap. If she could be adult about her nudity, so could he. Mostly. Probably.

Wet, stifling jeans reduced the likelihood he'd succumb to baser instincts and ravage her on the vanity to about a fifteen percent chance. He figured he couldn't hope for better.

As if she read his mind, Kyana traced the shoulder seam of his saturated T-shirt. "You're still wearing your clothes. They must be cold. And weigh a ton."

"I'm fine," he grumbled as he lightly rubbed the last of the adhesive holding the bandage into place, allowing himself a few extra passes to be really sure it held, and to savor the softness of her skin. She shivered.

"You're sort of making mud puddles." She winced as she spied the bathmat that had been collateral damage in their skirmish.

"Oh, shit." He jerked. Count on him to ruin Kyana's pretty things. He whipped his shirt over his head, unbuckled his belt, stripped his jeans down his thighs and kicked off his boots in less time than it took her to reassure him it was no big deal. Placing his filthy shoes in the shower for cleanup later, he faced her once more.

Her jaw hung open.

"Damn. Sorry." He assessed the damage to the rug. "I think I can get that out. If not, I'll replace it. I promise."

"Huh?" She blinked.

Twice.

A slow, irrepressible smile wiped the dread from his mind when he realized she scoped him just as hard as he'd done to her. Except she was far less skilled in subtle appreciation. For once he was proud of the way his hard work had honed his body. From her, the attention felt like a mighty big compliment.

Kyana's chest rose and fell faster as her gaze swept down his torso, over the ink and his piercings to the pronounced bulge in his drenched briefs. The fabric felt like it'd shrunk in the shower, or maybe the constriction was thanks to the massive hard-on his fantasy girl inspired.

She swallowed hard, then choked.

"Thanks," he murmured as he took the opportunity to scoop her off the counter and lower her to the floor. The glide of their damp skin tortured them equally. "Same goes, by the way. You grew up really well, Ky."

"I— Damn. Sorry. I didn't mean to stare." Her pretty porcelain skin turned pink.

"I did." Logan snagged a plush towel off the rack and wrapped her in its softness. He buffed her arms and legs, making sure not to press any sore spots too hard, then wrapped a smaller cloth around her hair before attending to himself with a handful of swipes.

When he turned to put the towel in the hamper, Kyana plucked his clothes from the floor. She arranged his shirt over the shower door then dug into his jeans, rescuing his faux-leather wallet. He didn't stop her fast enough.

His face heated, glowing as red as an overheated saw blade when she removed his ID and the last three crumpled singles he had left to his name. Instead of laughing at his pathetic life savings, she flattened the trio of bills on the counter and propped the cheap pleather open to allow air to circulate through the barren folds.

She distracted him from his discomfort when she peeked up from beneath long, if not curled, lashes. The raw vulnerability he spied in her eyes made him feel a little more on even footing. "Logan..."

"Yeah?"

"Will you stay with me tonight?"

"I don't have anywhere else to go, Ky."

"You're welcome here for as long as you need." She didn't pry, just nodded, though her shoulders seemed to slump a little. Avoiding looking at him, she scooted past, into her bedroom.

"Hey, wait. That didn't sound right." He scrubbed his hand through his hair, thinking of the countless fuck-ups he'd made when it came to her. All the times he'd said the wrong thing. Or had been too afraid to try to find the perfect thing.

No more of that bullshit. Time to man up.

Crossing the threshold to her sanctuary, he took a gamble. "It wouldn't matter. You know, if I had a hundred homes. This is where I want to be tonight. I'm only sorry I wasn't here earlier. You shouldn't have had to deal with this, all of it, on your own. It's been a long-ass time, but I'm still the same guy who was your friend. I haven't forgotten how you always had my back. Now let me get yours."

From a hand-glazed dresser, she withdrew a gossamer garment intended to drive men insane with lust and admiration. Mission accomplished when it fluttered into place around her ideal form, leaving a surprising string of pink, white and red cherry blossoms exposed on her shoulder. He wouldn't have expected her to go for tattoos, but the artwork suited her. It made his cock ten times harder.

"I've got things under control."

"I don't doubt that." He watched her slip beneath the lush duvet and ridiculously soft-looking sheets. "But you can lean on me tonight. Today. Whatever the hell it is out there. And always. I hope you understand that."

He considered getting in bed with his underwear on but didn't want to risk the cheap black dye staining her fancy linens. With a shrug, he shimmied out of the sticky fabric, tossed it over his shoulder into the bathroom then strode to the bed.

Kyana's laser-beam stare tracked his every movement until he obscured her view with the duvet, staying on top of the sheet she rested under. He wasn't some kind of creeper who'd try to molest her when she was down...no matter how desperately the primal parts of his brain encouraged him to try.

They both lay on their backs, staring at the ceiling for a while. A chasm at least a foot wide separated their tense bodies in her luxurious bed. When he couldn't stand it another second, he slid his hand beneath her shoulders and tugged. "This is stupid. We're adults now. Come here."

Thankfully, she didn't fight. She laid her head on his shoulder and curled up to his side, with only the thin sheet separating them.

Logan decided it was time to go all or nothing. Lying wasn't his style any more these days than it had been in high school. Hiding his feelings then had almost killed him.

"Sweet dreams, Kyana-chan." He tipped up her chin and claimed her mouth in a brief kiss. Brushing his lips against hers, he relished her taste and the complete surrender she offered him. Resisting the urge to plunder, he attempted to illustrate the tumble of emotions rolling around in his guts. Slow, tender and lingering contact seemed to do the trick.

When they parted, they both were breathless.

"Welcome home," she rasped.

Something inside of him stood up and cheered, knowing not all of the huskiness in her voice had to do with the smoke she'd inhaled. He linked their fingers on top of the covers and rubbed his thumb over her speeding pulse.

Despite the different worlds they came from and the string of tragedies that had hammered them lately, they both fell asleep with smiles on their faces.

Chapter Three

Kyana stretched, groaning at the soreness permeating her muscles. Especially the ones around her mouth, which guaranteed she'd grinned like a rapper showing off diamond-studded grills all night long. Logan was home. He'd come on his own. And he'd kissed her like he meant it. At least it'd seemed as though he relished the reunion as much as she had.

Shaking her head, she silently swore she wouldn't mistake his inherent passion as desire aimed specifically at her. Not this time. Suddenly she felt seventeen again—clueless, unsure of herself, and bursting with hope despite the reality check her practical side attempted to administer.

She might have thought being swept off her feet by her lifetime crush was some delusional dream—maybe one caused by the pain medication she'd popped before stumbling into the shower last night— if it weren't for the smell of the man he'd grown into, which lingered on her sheets, or the dark scrap of his abandoned briefs on the cream marble tile of her bathroom floor. He certainly hadn't gotten any neater in his maturity. Though he had plenty of perks to offset that quirk.

Ho-ly crap. His wet, sculpted body had been sexier than every fantasy she'd had about him all rolled into one. Defined muscles, bold artwork and his filled-out form were far superior to the lean yet tough build of the teenager who'd convinced her to go skinny dipping once. And that had been a sight to behold. Still, the compassion in his gaze had trumped even his physical perfection in her esteem. As if he'd realized she needed him desperately, like she had when the wound of her parents' loss had been fresh and ugly, he'd appeared from nowhere, materializing out of the steam.

Then again, he'd disappeared just as stealthily. Both the eve of their high school graduation and today, when he'd tiptoed from her room with the grace of a jungle cat. Kyana hadn't roused herself fast enough from the first totally peaceful sleep she'd managed since Aunt Rose's funeral—probably months before then, really—to stop him.

Maybe he'd ridden an adrenaline high after discovering their near miss. Though she'd wrangled her first choice of companions by some miracle, he could have needed someone, *anyone*, to cling to in an attempt to keep the horror of what might have been at bay. She wouldn't blame him in the least for that. Smiling as she drew on a robe, she hoped she'd conjured half as much solace for him as he'd granted her.

The smell of citrus, and something else she couldn't quite put her finger on, lured her toward the kitchen despite the awkward situation awaiting her at the end of the stairs. Salivation kicked in. Her drooling problem had more to do with the shirtless man cooking as skillfully as Hubert Keller than the salmon filets searing in the copper pan he wielded. He handled it as if he were as familiar with it as his best hammer.

Rose's favorite floral hand towel was tucked in Logan's waistband. Kyana had never envied a scrap of terrycloth before. The slight singe mark on the corner had her shaking her head as she remembered the day Myrtle Jansen had accidentally scorched the fabric while heating up some food Rose didn't have the appetite for. They should have tossed the rag in the garbage after Kyana had discovered it smoking in the oven. No one had. Logan ran his fingers down the fabric as if drawing some of Rose's legendary strength from the scrap.

"Too bad, Ben." He shook his head and continued without turning around. "You can't send me away. I'm not going. Not this time."

"You're always welcome, Logan. Don't make it sound like I'm giving you the boot. But I won't have you risking that job of yours. You love it. In fact, you'd best hit the road soon if you're going to be rested enough for those early morning shifts you pull."

"There's nothing to go back to." He dropped the pan on the cooktop with a final clank. "That's what I'm trying to say. Badly. I'm fucked, Ben. I lost everything. I got fired."

"How?" Kyana burst into the room, hands on hips. "I've seen pictures of your work. You're amazing at what you do. This is bullshit."

"Ky." He whipped around. "Damn. I guess there's no hiding anything around here anyway."

"What happened, son?" Ben motioned for Logan to join him at the table, but their impromptu chef didn't do anything half-assed. He concentrated on situating a divine hunk of salmon on each of the three plates he'd garnished with lemon wedges and something green. Where the hell had he scrounged that stuff from?

"Nicholson cut corners. Used cheap material that wouldn't hold up. The bastard asked me to cover for the company. No fucking way. I fixed a few of the issues on my own, couldn't stand to see the homeowners get screwed like that. But I ran out of money fast. So the next time it happened, I told the inspector about the violations myself." His shoulders slumped as he wiped his hands on a dish towel. "The foreman no longer required my services after that."

"This really is crap." Injustice spurred Kyana to don her lawyer hat for the first time in months. "We can fight this."

"And then what?" He shook his head as he approached with a steaming plate balanced on his sculpted forearm and two more laid out on his palms. "I go back to work for a dickhead who has it out for me? Or I'm owed a boatload of cash he doesn't have unless he rips off more unsuspecting homeowners? It's not worth it."

Ben shook his head. "One thing at a time. Help me fix my house. Those outrageous premiums I've shelled out for an eternity should mean insurance can afford what you deserve to make for the job you'll do. This could be the break you need to get your own business off the ground. A portfolio builder."

"If the payout is short or slow, I'll kick in the supplies as long as you provide the labor." Kyana played with the artful arrangement on the plate Logan handed her without meeting his gaze. She knew how touchy he could be about something that meant nothing to her. Money had always been a sticking point between them, no matter how delicately she tread. "Rose would have loved to help you. Hell, she would have insisted."

"Absolutely not." Logan's objection didn't surprise her. "I'm not taking any handouts."

Ben snorted. "This ain't some kind of charity, kid. No one's offering you something for nothing. Your job isn't going to be easy. I'm a damn picky customer. Especially when it comes to my house."

"Ben needs someone he can trust. You wouldn't leave him in the hands of a scammer like your piece of shit ex-boss would you? And being a partner in a startup could be just the project I've been looking for. I can help you with all the legal and management junk." Kyana rushed to bolster Ben's argument when he peered up at her with wide blue eyes.

"I couldn't—"

"You will. You, me and our girly. It'll be like the good old times. When we were a family. She's right, you know. Rose would insist if she were here. So don't argue with your elders." Ben glared.

"Ky's younger than me." Logan pouted.

How could he manage that and still be so damn sexy?

"By three weeks!" She winged a steamed green bean at his smirk, both annoyed and impressed when he caught it out of mid-air then popped it between his bright white teeth. *Mmm.*

"Fine. You can bicker with her all you like. After we eat." Ben rapped Logan's powerful thigh with the back of his hand. "Give me that dish. Let's dig in before this gets cold."

Logan opened his mouth then closed it again, respecting his uncle's wishes. He set a plate in front of Ben, and sank into one of the ornate chairs Rose had hunted from an antique sale. The stately furniture looked like it belonged in a dollhouse when he graced it.

"Good morning to you too, Ojii-san." Kyana kissed Ben's temple lightly then claimed the chair he and Logan drew out for her simultaneously. Sandwiched between them, she felt safe...and hungry. How long had it been since she'd really had an appetite?

"Same to you." He winked. "More like good evening. Logan was going to bring you dinner in bed. Hurry up and scoot under the covers if you want, I won't tell him you're awake. Maybe he hasn't noticed."

"I sure as hell picked up on that, but it wouldn't stop me from making a special delivery." He licked a daub of cream sauce from his fork. The sensuality he harnessed even in such a small gesture gave her heart palpitations.

She cleared her throat before trying to play it cool. "I'm not about to make him serve me after he already did all the work."

"It would be my pleasure." The heat in his stare scorched her twice over yet somehow it gave her shivers too. "You'd better get used to it. If I'm going to be staying here, I'll be pulling my weight."

"I vote for him as our cook." Ben forked up a huge bite of steaming salmon. "No offense, girly. I've had enough cans of soup to last me the rest of my life."

Just the thought of hearty beef and vegetable had her groaning too. The sound quickly morphed into a sigh when she tasted the heavenly dish Logan had whipped up as if it were nothing. "Not going to complain there. You're hired, Logan-kun."

"Welcome home." Ben smiled then focused on devouring his dinner.

Kyana and Logan exchanged a smile over his head.

"Careful. I know the fire chief cleared this section of the structure. Still, I don't like the way the beams were compromised." Logan bounced on a spot that looked a little suspect. It creaked yet held.

"Then why don't you wait downstairs?" Kyana glanced over at his mammoth frame. "I'm not exactly a bean pole, but I'm a hell of a lot lighter than you."

"Hey." He paused his inspection to pat his six-pack abs. "This is all muscle, babe."

Kyana rolled her eyes. "No shit. You're so damn hard, you make a lousy pillow."

"I didn't hear any complaints last night or the night before or the night before that." His infectious grin made her wish she were close enough to smack him in the shoulder. Their friendship had picked up right where it had left off all those years ago.

Still, she didn't bother to argue. Neither one of them had scrambled very hard to find alternate sleeping arrangements. An afternoon or two could have emptied out the spare room in Rose's house to give them each a private spot. Both of them had clung to every available excuse to keep from going to the effort.

"Hell, last night you crashed before I even finished telling you about how me and Jerry Lu got the cow onto the roof of the school. You pestered me for months about that one back in the day. Ben says you're an insomniac. I think he's nuts. I mean, it's not every day a woman conks out in my bed. Well, your bed. Whatever. You know what I mean." He grinned. "Besides, you're not supposed to *sleep* on the hard parts. There are better uses for those."

She hoped he'd interpret her *harrumph* as feminist indignation rather than the self-annoyance that spawned the sound. Because although she knew his teasing was meant to be harmless fun, she couldn't help but wish he was serious.

"How about you put yourself to better use right now?"

He strode toward her with no hesitation. "Here?"

"Where else?" She tried not to laugh when he neared. "Boost me up so I can grab those wicker baskets off the top shelf of the closet. I'm pretty sure that's where Ben meant he kept the fireproof box with the insurance paperwork. The sooner we get this red tape handled, the sooner we can start on repairs. It kills him not to be here, to know it's not all perfect and shiny. He loves this place."

"Yeah. Of course." Logan grimaced as he adjusted himself not so subtly.

Kyana should probably feel bad for triggering his instincts. She didn't. She enjoyed playing the siren, even if he would have had the same reaction to any available woman. Was waking up next to another warm body having the same effect on him as it was on her? The last time she'd been this horny she'd ended up hooking up with a friend of a friend at a backyard barbeque and making a pact with herself that other lawyers were off limits ever after. Each time she saw the scumbag in court, her bad judgment haunted her and his leer inspired the urge to shower.

Before she could brace herself against the hormonal surge Logan caused every time he touched her, he surrounded her waist with his broad fingers and lifted her several feet off the ground. She squeaked when he adjusted his grip, palming her ass with one hand and steadying her with the other.

"Don't worry. I'm not about to drop you. Ben would kick my ass." He laughed. "What's in there?"

Ignoring the heat of his contact, which seared through her jeans, she reached up and grabbed the tallest crate off the stack. When she tipped it forward, a gray metal box shifted. The heavy object threw off her balance and she wobbled.

"Whoa. Easy up there." Logan held true to his word. He compensated, but began to lower her.

"I think this is it. Put me down." She squirmed a bit, eager to verify the contents.

"Hmmm. I don't know." Logan gripped her tighter. "I kind of like the view from here."

"Oh my God. How old are you?" A half-hearted kick of her heel bounced off his steely ribs.

"Old enough to know what to do with a woman as gorgeous as you." He allowed her to sink a few more feet, inch by tantalizing inch. His hands were everywhere on her and she couldn't honestly say she hoped he'd hurry. "Pamper her, worship her, ravish her. Those are pretty high on my To Do list."

As soon as her sneakers hit the ground, he rotated her in his grip, relieving her of the basket, which he set to the side before crowding her against the closet wall. Instead of claustrophobia, a sense of protection settled over her.

"You're killing me, Ky." He surprised her by burying his nose in her hair and breathing deep. "This smell..."

"Stale smoke turns you on?" Being a smartass was pretty much her only defense at this point. This might be a game to him, but if she lost, she would never recover.

"Your shampoo, I've never forgotten how much I loved it." He grimaced. "I spent a while looking awkward once, sniffing a bunch of different kinds from the grocery store, but didn't find the right one by the time the manager walked past me for the third time so I gave up. They must have thought I was nuts."

"It's a salon brand. My mother used to buy it." She squinted up at him, trying to tell if he was serious. The dim light in the space made it impossible to tell what emotions clouded his deep blue eyes.

"Figures." He shook his head. "You always were too classy for me."

"What the hell is that supposed to mean?" She twined her fingers through the belt loops of his jeans when he would have retreated.

"You know damn well what I'm talking about." He looked away from her, though there wasn't anything else to see in the tight confinement. "I'm a mutt, you're a purebred. You deserve a shit ton better than me."

"Logan!" She clawed him when fury flexed her fingers unwillingly. "You think I'm some kind of snob? What the hell did I ever do to give you that impression?"

"You?" He tilted his head, coming to peer at her again. "Nothing. It's just the facts. Even if you've never seemed to realize it. Why the hell do you think I left? It's water under the bridge, but you had to realize how close you came to tangoing with trash that last summer.

Those last weeks. I wasn't about to let you make that kind of mistake with someone like me."

"Holy shit. You moron." She shook him, though he didn't budge an inch. "All this time... I thought you were awkward with me because I tricked you into kissing me. That you were too kind to say no. And then our friendship was shot to hell when I made you uncomfortable around me. Are you saying—?"

"You *what?*" He dipped down until only a tiny gap separated them.

Kyana couldn't help it. Her body went lax and allowed him to press closer.

"You seriously thought I didn't want you? That *you* took advantage of the situation?" He growled as he settled against her fully. "How could you have mistaken the way I looked at you like I wanted to devour you? I couldn't hide it at all anymore. I left before I did something selfish and trapped you here with me. You were going places. Big places. And I sure as shit wasn't about to be the reason you threw all that potential away. It wasn't right. We were like family, Ben said it himself. But there I was, thinking really impure thoughts. And you were so young."

"We're the same damn age, asshole." She smacked her palms on his chest. He didn't flinch. Instead he leaned inward, trapping her hands between them.

"Maybe technically. But I'd had a shit ton more experience than you back then. You had no idea what the real world was like." He shook his head. "How judgmental and cruel it can be. How unfair."

"Seriously?" She would have slapped him if she could have moved. "My fucking parents were killed, stolen from me before I could even really understand how amazing they were."

"They didn't *choose* to abandon you, Ky." He swallowed hard. "Not like my mom."

"You know how I feel about that. She didn't deserve you anyway. That's beside the point. Don't you think being orphaned was a rude awakening for me, too? Sure, I had Aunt Rose. I loved her. I'm not saying I didn't. But... Really, you don't remember all the times you held me when I cried for them? Did you think that was some kind of act?"

"Shit. Sorry." He tilted his head forward until his forehead rested on hers. "That's not what I meant. Not exactly. See, this is part of the problem. I can never make you understand without setting you off or jacking things up. I only wanted to protect you. Even if that meant from myself."

"You moron." The heat had vanished from her insults. "Don't you realize how bad you hurt me by walking away? Who was there to save me from the pain of losing my best friend? The guy I had my first crush on? No one. I never felt so forsaken in my life. Not even after the accident. I missed you. Every day. And since Rose... Well, it's been horrible again. I hate being alone. I don't want to be on my own anymore. You're the only guy who's ever really understood me. Don't do that to me again."

"What?" He flinched as if she'd kneed him in the nuts.

"I wanted you Logan. You pushed me away. When you didn't stick around...it almost killed me. And Ben. I was embarrassed and guilty as hell for stealing you from him. If I'd just kept from stirring things up, you wouldn't have had to go."

"Fuck," he snarled. "See what I mean? I have the un-Midas touch. Everything I do turns to shit. You make me sound like my freaking mom, cutting and running. What the hell should I have done?"

"Why not keep it simple? Maybe more of this would have helped." She smiled the instant before her lips met his. Unlike the timid girl she'd been, she didn't give him a chance to evade and escape. She balled her fists in his T-shirt and kept him close while she took what she craved and gave all she had pent up.

Logan didn't resist. He hummed, deep in his throat, when she flicked her tongue over the seam of his lips. Then he parted them, letting her have the lead. His control lasted longer than she'd guessed it might. For a solid thirty seconds, he allowed her to play—explore, taste and plunder as she saw fit. His gaze never left hers, though his hands began to wander up her hips, careful to skim her injuries as if he'd memorized every bump and bruise the night he'd had her laid out naked before him.

When she nipped his bottom lip, he broke.

Pinned between the wall and his chest, she had no way to evade the sensual assault he captained. Why the hell would she want to?

She reveled in the advancement of his torso, which imposed on the entire surface of her front. Warmth radiated from him, making her curl into the welcome heat of his embrace. He separated them just enough to allow her to wind her arms around his neck when she wiggled then fused them even more completely, if such a thing were possible.

He fit her just right.

Tall, she'd sometimes had trouble finding a guy who could manage to make her feel dainty and feminine. Logan had no problem there. He towered over her, and consumed her with his presence. She clung to him, her thigh rubbing the outside of his hip as she practically climbed the trunk of his body. Anything to get at the honey and ginger taste of his lips, sweetened by the loose-leaf tea he'd sipped from one of Rose's china cups earlier.

The memory of his huge hands cradling the delicate vessel ratcheted her desire higher. Just like he did for her when he grasped her leg at her knee. His fingers teased the underside, and trapped her against his hip. She hopped, wrapping her other leg high around his waist.

Both of them moaned when he fit himself to the juncture of her thighs, settling into the soft cradle she made for him. There they were entirely opposite, his cock so hard against her mound she wondered if it ached. Writhing against him served several purposes. Like rubbing the diamond tips of her breasts on his firm chest and soothing some of the restlessness pervading her. Mostly though, the action helped her snuggle as tight as possible to him, right where she had dreamt of being for so long that no other guy had lived up to her high expectations, established in one decade-old itty bitty kiss.

He sucked her tongue into his mouth, capturing the sensitive muscle then stroking it with his own. When he retreated, she nearly cried out. But only for a moment. Until he laid open-mouthed kisses at the corner of her lips, across her chin then in a meandering path along the exposed length of her neck as her head dropped back.

With a *thunk* it hit the wall of the closet, startling them both.

"Let's take this somewhere a little more comfy? Somewhere we can stretch out." He didn't wait for her answer. Covering her mouth again in a drugging kiss, he kept her from warning him as he hauled her backward. The basket she'd set on the floor loomed behind him. She struggled, but he misinterpreted the message. He chuckled. "I know, Ky. Me too. Just a second. Promise."

His unexpected sweetness made it twice as hard to bear when he tripped over their bounty. He cursed. With the reflexes of a cat, he twisted, taking the brunt of the impact on his shoulders. Though it had to hurt like hell, he didn't flinch, making sure to shelter her from any residual force. Their heads knocked together. Other than that and their pride, they appeared unscathed.

"Jesus." Logan banded his arms around her and rolled. From her new angle, beneath him, she spied the basket teetering precariously. Sure enough, it toppled. With a crash, the fireproof box tumbled to the floor and papers spilled out everywhere.

"What the fuck just happened here?" The dazed confusion in his bedroom eyes had her feeling a tad bit smug.

"I think we almost made it to second base but got tagged out." She winked.

A strangled laugh fell from his sexy smile. "Right. I got that part. Damn lockbox."

"Very secure too." Kyana wriggled from beneath Logan's heavy, though not uncomfortable, frame. She inspected the case, which had divulged all its contents. "I suppose that's what happens when you leave the key in the damn lock."

"Figures." Logan shook his head. "I'm surprised Ben didn't have the papers stuffed in a shoebox under the bed. That's what I would have done."

"Actually, I'm pretty sure he did." She dredged up a hazy memory. "But Aunt Rose bought him the fireproof box for Christmas one year, then guilted him into using it so it wouldn't go to waste."

"Brilliant. Man, I miss her." He reached for Kyana's hand, interlacing their fingers. "I'm so sorry. I should have been here. For both of you."

"I understand, Logan-kun." She raised his knuckles to her lips and dusted a kiss over them. "Rose did too. She told me to tell you she loves you. And that she's proud of the man you turned out to be."

"She did?" His whole body tensed and his eyes glistened.

"Of course." Kyana tugged him to her and nestled into his open arms. "You were like the son she never had. She bragged about you to anyone who would listen."

"Damn. That's...nice." He cleared his throat.

She granted him a bit of privacy, angling away so she could shuffle through the documents littering the closet floor. The insurance policy was easy to spot. Thick folded papers from Salem Mutual had dog-eared corners and a distinctly yellow cast. After plucking them from the wreckage, the rest of the stationery caught her attention.

Finely written cursive swirled over botanical prints. Dozens of letters had been protected from the blaze along with the deed to Ben's house and the title to his car.

"What are those?" Logan peeked over her shoulder as she ran one fingertip across the fine linens.

"Looks like Rose's handwriting. They must have been pen pals for a while. Maybe when Ben took the third shift as a security guard at the oven factory. He always claimed to be bored silly. I remember my great-aunt saying she hated him being gone so much. They really were close friends." Kyana sighed. "I think she once even offered to pay off Ben's house so he wouldn't have to work so hard."

"Like he'd have gone for that!" Logan looked horrified.

"Some things are more important than money, don't you think?" She tilted her head. "Like relationships? You can't buy them."

"Are you saying...? I mean, do you think Rose and Ben...?" He waved his hands adorably in the space between them as his eyes grew wide.

"Actually, no. I don't." She shook her head slowly. "But I *have* often wondered if they might have been more to each other if given the chance."

The instant denial she'd sort of expected didn't materialize. Logan weighed her opinion before shooting it down. He always did. "You know, I think you might be right. Ben never brought women around, though I know he took lovers from time to time. They would call sometimes. He never really dated them though. Never invited them here. I always thought that was odd, but not if he cared for Rose. It sort of makes sense if he didn't want to rub her face in it."

Kyana concentrated on rewrapping the bundle of letters with the pretty lilac ribbon that'd fallen off them. She didn't look up when she said, "It would have killed her to see him with someone else."

"Not something she should have worried about." Logan wrapped his hand around hers on the package. "Ben would never have hurt her like that."

And somehow Kyana knew his great-nephew wouldn't be so crass either. Thank God. She'd claw out the eyes of any woman he brought to their home.

"Ky, before you finish that bow, I think there's another piece of paper under the lid." He deflected them from the awkward stream of conversation.

She reached in the direction he indicated. Instantly, she felt the difference. This rough stock had nothing in common with Rose's refined parchment. Squinting, she examined the typed document.

If she hadn't been a lawyer, the thing might as well have been penned in Martian. As it was, the age of the contract made the verbiage difficult to discern. Not to mention property law wasn't her specialty. Good thing she had a friend in the business. She was going to need some help.

"What's that frown for?" Logan encroached on her space.

She didn't mind. "Sorry. This is some kind of title addendum stipulating conditional sale clauses."

"Come again?" He scratched his head.

"Unless I was really distracted, we haven't gotten there yet."

"Ha ha. No, seriously. Tell me what it means? In English. Simple terms for a simple guy."

"Quit that. You're plenty smart. It says Ben took a discount on the sale of the house that gave the builder options to buy back certain easement rights. For up to fifty years. I'm not sure I get all the nuances, but something like if the house wasn't standing, they could reclaim the land." A knot of unease lodged in her guts.

"What's the date on that thing?" Logan seemed to jump to the same conclusions.

"Fifty and a half years ago. Give or take a month."

"Wouldn't that mean it was null and void?" He looked to her.

"Probably. Yeah." She shrugged. "But who knows how accurate someone might be if they thought they knew what was in here. It'd be easy to flub something by a few months after all this time, right?"

The both scrambled to their feet.

Logan clutched her wrist even as he looked over their shoulders. Where Kyana had felt entirely secure a moment ago, hairs on her neck rose and goose bumps pimpled her flesh. "We're getting the hell out of here. Hand me the box and stay behind me. Close."

There was no use arguing when he made up his mind. "I know somebody who can help. I'll scan this and email it over to him right away."

"Sounds like a plan." They were breathing hard for an entirely different reason when they emerged into the gray haze of dusk.

Kyana was glad for Logan's strong grip on her hand when she caught movement out of the corner of her eye and skidded to a stop. He halted with her, spinning until he faced the offender that inspired her pulse to speed like a racecar driver heading for the checkered flag.

Daryl Thick.

"Jesus," Logan muttered under his breath as his hackles fell into place and the instant alertness of his body relaxed.

The ex-military man ran a hand through his buzz cut and flashed them a quick salute before jogging toward his house with a few glances thrown over his ripped shoulder. It might have been easy to dismiss his presence as a man out for an evening stroll, if he hadn't popped up from behind Ben's hedge like Rambo's pet gopher.

"What do you think he was doing in there?" she whispered to Logan.

"No fucking clue." He shrugged. "We can discuss it inside. Where it's safe. Let's go."

She leaned against his side when he wrapped his free arm around her shoulders and tugged her impossibly near. "Won't hear me arguing. Besides, I want to know what Ben has to say about this stupid contract."

"You and me both, Kyana-chan."

261

Chapter Four

Kyana, both relieved and oddly disappointed, stared at the email glowing on her screen. It had taken almost a week for her friend to completely vet the option clause on Ben's house. The good news... Logan had gotten it correct. No matter what crazy agreement the man had signed to afford his dream home, it was irrelevant today. The expiration date had passed without the rights being exercised. The house and the land belonged to Logan's great-uncle free and clear.

So why had the fire investigator's report shown hints of arson? Ben swore he never used candles, yet there had been one set unwisely close to the curtains Rose had sewn as a birthday gift for him back in the seventies. The hideous polyester had gone up like a match, destroying one of Ben's prized possessions along with kindling the blaze. He insisted he only kept the pillars on hand for emergencies. So who had known where he stashed them, retrieved one and lit the damn thing? And why?

In addition to all that, Kyana wished she could hash things out with Logan. He'd spent every waking minute working on the house since the release had come through the morning after their close call in the closet. Hell, she'd hardly seen him in days. No wonder her insomnia had returned full force. Without him to cuddle up to, the darkness summoned all sorts of demons to torture her awake. And when he finally stumbled in—exhausted—each night, he barely managed to undress and shower before falling into a near coma.

She'd offered to play his assistant. He'd refused, probably since she'd upheld her end of the stupid bargain by fronting cash and drafting a work agreement. Or maybe because he regretted their momentary lapse of decorum between Ben's flannel shirts.

All she knew for sure was that from her window she had a world-class view of him going to town on his great-uncle's kitchen—sans shirt of course. An unseasonable heat wave had crept up on the heels of their mild winter, spiking the temperature into the lower nineties several days in a row. The hot spell coincided with the demolition phase of the project, providing ample opportunity to showcase Logan's sweaty muscles, which glistened as they flexed beneath the strain of his efforts.

Fancy molding around the window dug into Kyana's hip as she leaned against the casing. With the lights off, she'd moved aside the lace curtains for a clear view of her obsession. How healthy could this be? Next she'd be sharing the hedge with Daryl for a better perspective.

Hopefully Logan would smile instead of cringing when she took them down memory lane. At this point she'd rather know where they stood than hanging around wondering any longer. Making a clean break would be tough the more time she spent near him. This was what she wanted, and she wasn't about to wait for him this go around.

Hoping her initiative went over as well tonight as it had the other day, she grasped the metal cylinder tighter between her shaking fingers. With her thumb, she slid the switch. A dull red glow emanated from the end of the flashlight, mostly covered by her hand.

She grinned despite the stuttering of her heartbeat as she remembered all the nights they'd sent messages across the canyon between their great-aunt and uncle's houses. Kids who texted on cell phones or messaged on iStuff or posted on Facebook wouldn't know what they were missing.

Sure, she could have called Logan, but what fun would that be?

Chuckling, she aimed the flashlight toward Ben's house then removed and replaced her hand.

Short. Long. Short. Short.

Dot. Dash. Dot. Dot.

Morse code for "L".

The signal had always made her think of Gotham City paging Batman. In a lot of ways, Logan had been her superhero. Maybe still was. He'd swooped in and improved her life both back then and again recently. When she'd needed him most, he had her back.

It'd probably take a while to draw his attention from the task at hand—ripping out the toasted bones of the cabinetry. Or at least, she'd thought it would. A gasp escaped when he spun to face her window immediately. She repeated the signal. From that distance she could barely make out his broad smile when he realized what had caused the glint.

He held up his palm, then lunged for his battered toolbox, presenting her with a view of his gorgeous, jeans-clad ass. In less than five seconds, he'd returned.

Dash dash. Dot dot. Dot dot dot. Dot dot dot. Pause. Dash dash. Dot.

"*Miss me?*"

Arrogant prick. And right on the money. Damn him.

Dash dot. Dash dash dash.

"*No.*"

She could have sworn she spied him laughing when he sent his next message.

Dot dash dot dot. Dot dot. Dot dash. Dot dash dot.

"*Liar.*"

No use in denying it.

Dash dot dash dash. Dot. Dot dot dot.

"*Yes.*"

She'd barely finished the last letter when he sent her the invitation she'd been hoping for.

Dash dot dash dot. Dash dash dash. Dash dash. Dot. Pause. Dot dot dot dot. Dot. Dot dash dot. Dot.

"*Come here.*"

Kyana flashed one last note, both agreement and her closing initial, before wrapping her gossamer robe around her and sprinting for the door.

Dash dot dash.

"*K.*"

She shouldn't have been surprised when the beam of his light intersected hers from his spot on Ben's deck. Even back in high school, he hadn't allowed her to make the miniscule voyage solo. Heaven forbid she twist her ankle or cross paths with a startled squirrel. Tonight she appreciated his supervision.

As she neared, she scrambled for something to say. Maybe she should have thought beyond the thrill of sharing some time and space with him. "So... How's it going?"

"You tell me. I'm sure you could monitor my progress from your perch by the window." He winked. "How long were you going to lurk there and peep?"

"How did you spot me?" Mortified, she pressed her fingers to her flaming cheeks.

"I didn't. But I could feel your stare on me." He buffed his arms. "You're distracting me, Ky. I nearly smashed my thumb with that last cabinet."

"Sorry," she stammered.

"I liked it." He tugged her into his grasp. Even perspiring, he smelled clean and manly. She had to stop herself from sinking her teeth into the tight pec in front of her lips. "I need a break anyway. It's hot as hell in there. If I add you to that sauna, the windows will steam up for sure."

"Yeah, right." She glanced away.

"I'm serious, Ky." He nudged her chin up with his thumb and index finger. "You're the sexiest woman I've ever met. At least now I don't have to feel like a perv for thinking so."

"What the hell are you talking about?" She tilted her head, dragging his fingers across her chin.

"When I visited, I liked to imagine Ben and Rose and you were my family." He shrugged then rubbed at the spot he'd touched as though wiping away some imaginary stain. "When I started to have other feelings, I freaked. The first time I had a dirty dream about you, I couldn't talk to you for two days. It seemed wrong to go from thinking of you as a little sister—hanging out with you, keeping you out of trouble and giving you noogies to... Well, you know."

"Not really." She took his hand in hers and started to amble down the private walkway in the direction of the woods behind their houses, tugging him along with her. "I mean, *if* there had been something more between us, don't you think most of our foundation would have stayed the same? We'd still be friends first, right?"

"I guess. But that's a more mature rationale than I was capable of then. I couldn't stop thinking about how I'd kick my ass if I were anyone else trying to put moves on you. Though hell, I never was much good at the keeping-you-trouble-free part. You're just too damn good at finding shit to get into."

"Ha. I don't find it. *It* finds *me* all on its own. Remember that blue T-shirt with the sparkly iron-on Ben bought me after we crashed our toboggan into his shed during winter break? It said so." She liked that their steps synchronized without effort.

"Right." He shook his head and laughed. "You loved that damn thing. But yeah, even all this time later I still want to hang out with you, see movies, grill on nice nights, play board games when it rains and bake you a birthday cake every year. All the crap we did when we were younger. Those were the happiest times of my life, Ky. Maybe this go around I could even spring for a nice dinner when it's in my budget."

His frown spurred her to go for broke. If they didn't iron out some of their wrinkles, they wouldn't have a chance at making it long term. A fling with him didn't interest her. It would only screw up everything else they shared. A friendship she wasn't willing to risk. Not when she'd just found it again.

"Why don't you let *me* take *you* out sometime?" She gnawed on the inside of her cheek, hoping he'd trust her and grow just a little.

"I don't know..." He looked like he was grinding his teeth for a minute before he sighed.

"Money is worthless if I can't enjoy it. Spending time with you, eating fine cuisine and maybe sharing a nice bottle of wine sounds like a perfect evening. Would you keep us both from experiencing it just to salve your pride? Who picks up the tab doesn't mean anything, Logan. Not if we're talking about you and me trying to be an *us*. Is that what we're discussing?"

"Damn, you really did grow a pair. A bigger pair, I guess. You always were bold." He wiggled his eyebrows. "I like this new Kyana. You're turning me on."

"You didn't answer my question." She would have tapped her toe if they had been standing still. If he left her hanging now, all her sudden confidence would melt away.

"Only because you're diverting the blood flow from my brain." He scowled before taking a funny stride to give his junk more room in the confines of his ripped jeans. "Yes. I'm doing my best to charm you into dating me. Is it working?"

"Not like you have to try very hard. Probably never have had to do more than crook your finger to get a woman. But if we're going to have a real shot, we have to fix the things we did wrong last time. We can't rewind but we can redo. I'm trying to be brave here. So don't say no."

"I hate it when you make sense," he grumbled.

"I'm not a kickass lawyer for nothing. Logic is my business, buddy." She poked him in the side. "So it's a date?"

"Hell yeah." He turned to her with a grin. "Things on my new and improved list to try... Number one, let my sugar mama take me out for a juicy porterhouse and get sloshed on fancy-pants booze. Now, about those noogies. Hmm... I haven't done that to a girl in a while."

She yelped and dodged his swipe, shaking her hand free of his.

He humored her by letting her trot ahead down the illuminated path. The solar lights Ben had installed on either side of the river rock would glow softly for hours yet. When her breath came in short pants and her robe fluttered behind her, she slowed. Right on her heels, Logan grabbed her around the waist and tugged her backward into his chest.

"I remember this. Playing. Laughing. Effortless enjoyment. Carefree joy when we were together," he whispered in her ear, not the least bit winded. "I've missed this. You."

Kyana angled her head enough to grant him permission for more. He accepted the offer.

Cupping her cheek in his palm, he guided her to his mouth. Gently, they exchanged a soft kiss before separating with a sigh. It was as if he had the same idea she did. The same destination in mind. If there was anything she wanted a repeat performance of—a chance to rewrite—it was the night they'd done *almost* this. They started down the path together again, allowing a buffer between them to keep them from ripping each other's clothes off where they stood.

After a few seconds, Logan cleared his throat.

"Remember how we used to help Myrtle gather her leaves every fall? We'd pile them so high we could jump off her porch railing into the mess before she'd chase us off and scoop them into the burning barrel." He sighed. "At least you always took the plunge. I was jealous as I got older and watched from the sidelines."

"I wouldn't have judged you for acting like a kid." She hugged him with one arm as they rounded a bend beneath the canopy woven from the green shoots of old trees, which reminded her of the new season of her relationship with Logan. It had been a hard winter for them both.

Fall seemed like a long way off, but soon enough the same plants would be red and gold and crispy. Perfect for frolicking in. A mental note would remind her to force Logan to join her this time.

"I know, you never looked down on me like a lot of the other kids in school when I didn't show up wearing anything that had been fashionable in this century and my lunch got paid for by the state. I guess I just learned to fend for myself with my mom never around and it got harder to let go of the tough-guy act. I was afraid I wouldn't be able to give up the luxury when I had to survive on my own again." He groaned. "I sound like some nutcase on *Dr. Phil.*"

"You don't watch that shit, do you?" She cracked up.

"Hell no, but you get the point."

"I do." She nibbled at the corner of her mouth as a structure coalesced from the shadows. The dock at the edge of the pond. Thank goodness the moon was bright. Or maybe if it had been dimmer she'd have had more nerve.

"Are we really going to do this?" He rubbed the sensitive skin between her thumb and forefinger. "Are you sure you're ready?"

"I never was the kind of person to dip a toe in. If we're going to do this, let's make a splash. Okay?" She squeezed her eyes closed as she waited what seemed like an eternity for his response.

"Shit, yes." He sped up, dragging her along. "Only this time, I want to do more than swim with you, Ky. A hell of a lot more."

"Thank God." She kicked off her sneakers mid-stride as they reached the first weathered planks.

"One thing though..." He stopped mid-stride. "I, uh, don't make a habit of carrying condoms on me. I didn't expect you to step out of my fantasy tonight."

"Oh." She blinked. "Damn. I'm not on the pill or anything. It's sort of been a while for me."

"I'm not going to lie." He smiled. "I like the sound of that. Don't worry, Ky. I can still take care of you. I always will."

Tripping seemed like a very real possibility when Logan flicked open the button on his jeans and spread the fly wide. A trail of fine, dark hair drew her gaze downward.

"If your eyes get any bigger, babe..."

"Bigger? Not in this lifetime." A well-placed smack on his tight abs echoed through the stillness.

Logan grabbed her wrist and used it to draw her near. "Now, that wasn't very nice."

She fought half-heartedly against his grip. "What are you going to do about it?"

"Maybe I'll spank you later." He growled. "But for now I think this will do."

A squeak escaped her parted lips when he shoved the robe from her shoulders then grasped the hem of her silk tank and whipped it over her head in one lightning-fast move. Her matching boyshorts didn't last much longer. And before she could panic, he'd stripped her naked.

"Damn, you're beautiful." He sank to his knees at her feet.

Kyana shifted, awkward in the beam of his attention. It shone brighter than her flashlight had earlier, exposing all her flaws.

"Why don't you believe me?" He grasped her hips, his thumbs stroking maddeningly over the curves of the bones there while he kissed the soft swell of the belly she couldn't erase no matter how often she worked out. Probably because she had a weakness for cupcake-flavored ice cream. How could she resist the veins of icing and sprinkles swirled inside it?

She'd loved it since she'd been a child.

Some things never changed. Like her feelings for the man in front of her, whom she was pretty sure she adored even more than ice cream.

"It's not that I don't feel good about myself." She buried her fingers in his hair to keep upright when his wandering caresses invoked dizziness. "It's just that you're...perfect. You should be dating a supermodel or something."

He laughed so hard the pattern of his touches stuttered.

She punched his shoulder lightly. "I mean it."

"You have a way of making me feel like so much more than I am." He grew still as he peered up at her from his place at her feet. "I love the way you do that. Pump me up. Always have. Thank you."

"I only treat you like you deserve." She rubbed her thumb over his damp lips.

"Let me do the same for you, Ky." He sucked the digit into his mouth, thrilling her with the heat and pressure of his gentle sucking. "I'll give you everything I can. I swear."

"Then how about losing those jeans." She gulped. "Let me see you again."

"I'll let you do a hell of a lot more than that." He rose and shucked the denim before she could brace herself for the impact of his bare-naked glory.

When his cock fell free, thick and heavy against his thigh, she nearly drooled. The unseasonably balmy night had nothing on the way he made her overheat. If she didn't do something to cool off she'd explode. "First you'll have to catch me."

She sprinted for the edge of the platform and dove into the water, relying on muscle memory from the million times she'd executed the maneuver in their past to guide her. Cool, refreshing water sluiced over her body—face, hands and bare breasts. When her lungs began to burn, she surfaced, throwing her head back to clear the wet hair from her eyes.

"Christ, you look like a mermaid," Logan muttered from the dock.

She was a little disappointed he hadn't joined her until he perched on the edge of the structure. Wicked ideas swam into her mind. She tipped onto her back, stroking until she floated by his shins. His skin was tan even in the moonlight.

"Now that's a sight I'll never forget." He muttered oaths and curses into the night.

"Testing the water, Logan?" She teased him for his slower method of entry.

"I'm not sure shocking the boys is the right approach when I'm trying to make a good first impression." He grimaced at the thought of the cool liquid.

She grinned, letting her legs sink until she treaded water between his knees. Then she walked her dripping fingers up his legs, using him to anchor her. He'd always done that for her. When she reached his thighs, he shivered.

"Whatcha doing, Ky?"

"Playing." She peered up at him as she buoyed at the surface, her lips now following the path her fingers had taken. "You won't spoil my fun, will you?"

"Too much of that and you'll ruin it yourself." He groaned.

"You can handle it." She nipped the sinew of his inner thigh. His hands fisted at his side a moment before reaching under her arms to help her stay afloat while she explored. He tasted amazing. Like early summer and salt and man. "Besides, if there are no condoms in your wallet, you might as well let me solve this problem another way or you're likely to hurt yourself walking home."

"Never had my hard-on referred to as a problem before." He scowled adorably.

"Really? Fitting all that inside seems like it would be a delicate operation." She measured him with a slow circuit using the tip of her finger. "I've certainly never been with a guy your size before."

"We'll go slow when the time comes. It'll work just fine, I promise." He lost his breath as she considered the possibilities.

After reaching up to band her arms around his waist and lay her head in his lap, she hesitated. Near her prize, her breath washed over the incredibly long, thick shaft of his cock. From here she could spot a bead of wetness at the tip. She licked her lips.

"You're killing—" His declaration ended in a gurgle when she lapped at the head of his erection with the flat of her tongue, savoring the flavor of him. Slowly and sweetly, she dusted him with kisses before drawing him into her mouth. When she'd taken as much as she could without choking, she began to suck in a series of soft, delicate swallows. The thrill of new and different sensations magnified her natural excitement. This was Logan. And it was really happening.

Not intending to race to the finish, she reveled in his surrender and set herself to granting him as much pleasure as she could. Because if she knew him at all, he wouldn't take for himself very long before returning the favor. A million times over.

Cicadas helped her keep a rhythm. Her head moved delicately over her treat. It amazed her to finally have him in her grasp. And to be thrilling him. Because the noises bubbling from his sexy chest were clear indications he was enjoying himself.

Immensely.

Her hands wandered up and down his furred thighs as she grew more comfortable with his girth, which spread her jaw wide. She kicked her feet lazily to assist her in the natural bobbing motion she required. The cool water and the warm night combined to awaken every nerve-ending in her skin.

At the first flick of her tongue over the sensitive underside of his tip, Logan hauled her upward as though she weighed no more than a legal-sized notepad. He held her suspended, half-submerged, far enough away from him that she had to stop her teasing.

"Maybe I had my strategy all wrong." Husky whispers thrilled her. Could she really have done that to his voice? "I should have realized that with you, I'm going to need all the help I can get to restrain myself from ending this party before it starts."

"Don't hold back." She wriggled until her belly brushed his erection, encouraging his surrender. "I want to make you crazy."

"You can check that box. Fucking great." He scooted closer to the edge and lowered her until she could feed more of his shaft between her lips when she descended again. Still she couldn't take the whole thing. Instead she wrapped her hand around the base of his cock and massaged in time with the ministrations of her mouth. "This is going to be embarrassingly easy for you."

"Mmm." She hummed against his shaft, loving the flex that followed the vibrations.

"Damn. Yes." He twined his fingers in her hair, guiding her in the rhythm he preferred. "Just like that, Ky. Better than I imagined."

Tracing each vein with her tongue, she studied his topography. Therefore, she caught the difference right away when he grew impossibly harder and the ridges became more pronounced.

"I'm going to…"

She added a twist of her head as she rose off his throbbing cock before plunging down once more. Faster and harder, she suckled him as jets of come blasted from his plum-shaped tip. Water splashed as his legs kicked, his feet breaking the surface when his hips began an involuntary thrusting. His whole body moved sinuously, making her sure she wanted to experience his release from beneath that amazing frame someday. Soon.

His muscles flexed, then trembled. He slumped, breathing as hard as if he'd just carried ten loads of supplies from his truck to a job site on the fifth floor of an apartment building with no elevator.

Petting his flank, she rested against him, smiling while he recovered.

"You look awfully proud of yourself." If she were a cat, she would have purred when he petted her hair then traced her lips, swiping the last bit of fluid from them.

"Shouldn't I be?" She peeked up at him from behind her lashes.

"Hell yeah." He reached for her, drawing her out of the water completely this time.

Droplets rained from her skin, dripping onto him. He seemed to relish the relief from the heat, and tugged her closer until he nearly singed her with his torso. His arms wrapped around her, holding her tight to him as he leaned in to claim her mouth.

Kyana had never been kissed like this—tender yet rough, gentle yet insistent, carnal yet sweet. She could have kept going forever. All the while, his hands roamed her back from shoulders to ass, spiraling her need higher until a whimper escaped her.

"You're pretty when you beg, Ky," he murmured against her neck before nipping her there just hard enough to have her arching in his hold. Her breasts rubbed against his chest, stimulating her diamond-hard nipples.

"I did no such thing." She tried to deny it. No use.

"Your body is speaking for you." He smiled, long and slow. "Don't worry, I'm listening."

She sighed when he separated them enough to turn, setting her on the dock with one last deep kiss. Then he entered the pond without a splash. The power and grace of his well-muscled shoulders and ass left her in awe. With him beneath the silvery surface, which glinted in the moonlight, she thought maybe she'd imagined the entire interlude.

Until he rose from the depths like a mythical creature designed to lure her into temptation. A male siren. She'd willingly fall into his trap. Any price would be worth the paradise he promised with a sweltering stare and the curve of his sexy smile as he swam back.

"Come closer." He tugged on her ankle until she perched with her ass on the edge of the dock. "Lay back."

Without argument, she did as he instructed. He might as well have charmed her like a snake in a basket for all she wished to disobey.

"That's right. Stay on your elbows so you can watch me. I want you to see how much I enjoy pleasuring you." He lifted one of her feet from the silky water.

Logan tagged a kiss to her arch before beginning a slow press and release of his fingers that quickly turned into a full-on massage. Her toes curled when he rubbed her just right. Having mastered that part of her anatomy, he proceeded to climb to her ankles.

"Will you wear heels for me when we go on our date?" He licked the skin there. "I'm picturing you in a power suit and killer stilettos. Your hair back, no nonsense. I can't explain how hot your lawyer pictures made me when I spotted them in Rose's house. Tell me you have some shoes tucked away with all that naughty lingerie you hoard."

"I might have a pair." She scooted at least three inches closer when he nibbled on her calf.

"Or twenty, I bet." He hummed against the inside of her knee, driving her mad.

"Who's counting?" The question barely snuck past the constriction of her throat and a similar squeeze on her heart. Could he really be here, delighting her?

To reassure herself, she petted his silky hair. So soft, even wet.

"Yeah, I'm not going anywhere." He read her mind. Then he blew it with a few well-placed swirls of his thumb over the apex of her slit. Not once did she consider closing her legs despite his intimate position, which would have unnerved her with any other man. Good thing awkwardness never entered the picture since he'd blocked the possibility of hiding by inserting his torso fully between her thighs. "I'm dying to taste you, Ky."

"Do it." She let her hands slide palms down on the wood behind her. On straight-locked arms, she leaned back. "Please."

Droplets ran down his chest when he hoisted himself up a few inches higher, enough to seal his mouth over the lips of her pussy, which shimmered in the moonlight, more from his influence than the refreshing liquid of the pond.

Kyana gasped.

His tongue insinuated itself between her lips and teased her swollen clit. A flutter, to preview his skill before he warmed her up with long laps and kisses on the ridges and valleys of her folds. Sure, guys had gone down on her before. None of them had performed with as much gusto as Logan. Never had a man made her feel like he enjoyed the act as much as she did.

Logan devoured her like the starving kid he'd been.

Not some sort of repayment for her blowjob, though she had to admit she'd done her best for him. Hell, he seemed satisfied to drive her wild if his hums of appreciation and approval were any indication.

The drumming of her heels on his shoulders forced him tighter to her core. He took the opportunity to prod her opening with the tip of one finger, pressing inward until he breached the tight rings of muscle at her entrance.

"Oh, fuck me." She blushed when she realized she'd shouted into the night.

"Next time, sweetheart." He nuzzled her softness, burrowing deeper with simultaneous oral and manual assaults. "I promise. I'll be the first guy in line at the pharmacy tomorrow."

Her giggle turned into a moan when he added a second finger then scissored them while he started that flicky thing with his tongue again. After that, she couldn't think about anything other than the bliss he instilled in her and the magic of the moment. Holy shit, why hadn't they done this right the first time? They'd wasted a decade apart.

"Where'd you go, Ky?" Logan whispered against her mound before returning his attention to her—twice as fast, twice as intense.

"We lost so much time." She felt herself unraveling as he lifted her higher. Euphoria laced with regret made the triumph that much sweeter.

"We'll make up for it." He didn't pause longer than it took to utter the pledge.

Shudders began deep inside her, an early warning sign of the explosion brewing. When he looked up at her to gauge her reaction—or maybe to command her surrender—she got lost in his gorgeous blue eyes. The connection, so strong, pushed her over the edge.

She called out his name as wave after wave of ecstasy flooded her heart and soul along with her corporeal form. Endless pulses of pleasure transmitted ecstasy through her muscles until she'd wrung every last drop of delight from the experience.

And when she had mostly stopped seizing, she realized he'd withdrawn gently from her body and levered himself onto their stage. He collapsed on his back and drew her to his side, where she curled up as if she'd done it a million times before. Sleeping with him the past week or so had ranked high on her list of lifetime achievements. Now his protective hold and his familiar warmth seemed even more welcoming.

"Feel better?" His husky voice proclaimed he knew he'd satisfied her.

"A little bit." She laughed when he tickled her. "Okay, yeah. A ton."

"Me too, Ky. Open your eyes. Check out all the fireflies." He drew her attention, encouraging her to blink open extra-heavy lids.

The view was worth it. Dozens of tiny stars winged around them, flickering on and off in a mating call she could certainly relate to. Hell, she half expected to see her skin glowing when she glanced down.

Navy blue sky peeked through the shadow of the trees and warm yellow sparks dotted the landscape, highlighting the natural beauty all around them.

"I could stay like this forever." She hugged him, welcoming his echoing squeeze.

"I wish we could. Sorry, Ky. You're shivering." He kissed her forehead then sat up, hauling her with him. "Time for bed."

As if on cue, she yawned.

"Here, lift up." He slid her camisole over her arms then helped her step into her silk shorts and bundled her into the thin robe before collecting his pants. He shimmied into them with an adorable wiggle of his damp ass.

The contorted face he made when he spun around had her laughing out loud.

"Ugh. Everything's stuck together. Let's get home before this causes permanent damage." He stalked to her side. "Maybe we should take a shower together..."

She grabbed his hand and tugged as she slipped on her no-lace sneakers. "I'm pretty sure that's a good idea."

"Not sold?" He pinched her ass. "I must not have done this right, then."

"Oh, you did just fine." She winked. "But I think I need to try it again to be certain I like it."

"You're on." He lunged for her, swinging her into his arms as he took off, loping down the path back to the house.

When he jerked to a stop about halfway there, she squeaked.

"Shh." Easy joy drained from his body, replaced by tension. "I thought I saw something."

"There are a bunch of deer that roam around this part of the property." She couldn't think of any other explanation. "Or maybe it's Bigfoot."

"Not funny." He never once took his eyes from the general area he'd been scouting. He set her down and stepped in between her and the direction he'd peered. This time he raised his voice. "Who's out there?"

Kyana gripped his hand hard enough she feared she might break a bone or two. A heartbeat passed and then another before a cracking twig had them both jumping.

"It's just me, Logan." Daryl Thick stepped from the shadows. "You've got a good eye. I always told you to try the military."

"I still say I wasn't made to take orders. But I would like to know what the hell you're doing sneaking around all the time." His shoulders spread and his chest puffed up as he confronted the retired veteran.

Kyana was about to jump to the man's defense when he shocked the hell out of her.

"I was watching you two lovebirds."

Fists immediately formed at Logan's sides. "You did what?"

"Jesus, man." Daryl waved his hands in front of his chest. "Not like that. I just meant I saw you head out to the dock. Was making sure no one surprised you."

"No one other than yourself, right?" Some of the fight leeched from Logan. He stepped back from the confrontation while keeping Kyana behind him. When he reached his hand out, she grasped his fingers and didn't plan to let go.

"Whatever. I have the internet. I don't need any more porn. Though next time you might want to pay attention, or be a little more discreet. Not that I minded listening." Daryl shrugged. "Going home now. Have a nice night. Tell Ben I said hi."

"You asshole," Logan growled. "Keep the hell away from us. Next time I catch you creeping through the shadows I won't be so friendly, *neighbor*."

Daryl waved without turning. He vanished around a bend in the path. How did he do that?

"Come on." Though the night hadn't cooled off any, Kyana chafed one of her arms with her free hand. "Let's get inside."

"Good idea." Logan scanned the darkness in every direction as they practically jogged back to the house with their fingers still woven tightly together.

Chapter Five

"Ben?" Logan joined his great-uncle on the porch.

"Yeah, kid." The older man leaned his elbows on the cedar railing while overlooking the expanse of green that united his house with Rose and Kyana's.

"Don't worry, I'll have you home as soon as possible. Everything just as you left it. You'll never know anything happened at all." He slapped Ben on the shoulder.

"Actually, I've been thinking maybe it's time to update a few bits. I saw what you've done so far. You're making great progress on the demolition and it's sort of a blank slate. We should take advantage. Maybe tonight we can sit down and work out a design. Give me your input. Help me invest in some shit that'll up the resale value."

"You're thinking of moving?" Nothing could have shocked Logan more.

"Hell, no. This neighborhood is where I belong. I'm too old for new places at this stage. But you're working on your inheritance kid. Gotta do what's best. Make it your own."

"Jesus. Don't talk like that." Logan scrubbed his face with his knuckles.

"It's just practical." Before they could argue, Ben continued, "So, what'd you come out here for? Need something? Or should I say some*one*?"

Logan cleared his throat. "Sort of. Where's Ky?"

He'd worked like crazy all morning to hit his milestones and free up the afternoon. Being his own boss kind of rocked. He'd planned to use the opportunity so they could hustle somewhere private to put the stash of condoms, which she'd deposited on top of the duffle he'd been living out of since the day after the fire, to good use. Soon he'd have to make a final—more thorough—run to his apartment to salvage what he could before his landlord evicted him. Not much was worth the effort and the gas gauge in his truck had sunk perilously low so he'd put it off. He mentally added a modest hourly pay rate to the list of topics to discuss with Ben later.

After he found Kyana.

Stolen kisses and some ultra-quiet, beneath-the-covers fooling around hadn't come close to satisfying him since she'd blown his mind on the dock two nights ago.

It'd taken him a solid couple hours swinging a sledgehammer after the discovery of the goodies to wrap his mind around the fact that his girlfriend had to buy protection for them because he couldn't afford it. At least she must have realized what the holdup had been without him having to spell out his inadequacy. She'd always been sharp.

Thirty-seven hours had never gone by so slowly.

And now that he'd worked up to approaching her, she was nowhere to be found. Figured.

"Girly headed to Town Hall to search for some records from the holding company Rose and I bought these lots from. I told Ky not to bother. Her friend even said it. Those old papers don't mean jack. Plus that whole office burned down back in the seventies. There's no other information to be uncovered. No funny business with the mortgage. Nothing to do with the Gittlesons and their petition either."

"Rewind a second." Logan tilted his head, thinking of the young couple he'd spotted huddled at the edge of the sidewalk during the fire footage on the news. "I think I missed something. What petition?"

"About a year ago, Laura and Dean made a push to run a ramp to the highway through our backyards. It didn't get very far. Most of the other residents voted it down. But there's no bad blood. They followed the process and agreed with the majority. I'm telling you. This whole thing is just bad luck." He sighed. "The world is going crazy. Rose, my house, you kids acting all weird around me. What the hell is going on, Logan?"

"I don't know, but we'll get through it." Uncommon melancholy from his great-uncle concerned Logan. He and Kyana had agreed not to pile on another worry by telling Ben they were fooling around with their friendship. After his complicated relationship with Rose, they were afraid he'd be upset. Or object. Neither of them could stand to have their bubble burst when things were bright and new and promising. Although their joint occupancy of her bed had to be raising some questions. The guy was no dummy.

Logan's train of thought reminded him of something Ben had said recently...

"Hey, I've been wondering. What'd you mean the other day when you mentioned sacrificing for your dreams?" He shuffled his boot along a seam in the porch. One board lifted higher than the rest. He'd level it out later.

"It's hard to say anymore what might have been."

"I don't understand." Logan lifted his head, observing Ben's faraway stare.

"I regret a lot of things in my life." He rubbed a gnarled hand over his chest. "Not the least of which is you."

"Shit." Logan reeled at the revelation, something like rejection tearing through his guts. He thought he'd armored himself against disappointment years ago. Apparently not. "I know I was a pain in the ass. I ate a ton and you spent a shitload of money on my clothes and school supplies before you sent me back to my mom each year—"

"If you say one more damn word, I'll show you I'm not too decrepit to put you over my knee or shove my boot up your ass." Ben scowled. "Though you're proving my point nicely. I love my niece, but she didn't do right by you. I could see the damage her selfishness caused and I didn't step up to the plate. Not soon enough. By the time you came to me to stay for that last year, it was too late to fix it all."

"What are you talking about?" Logan scratched his chin.

"You're a damn fine man. The stuff of you has never changed. I could see it in you as a kid. You had a kind heart, you worked hard, and you were loyal to a fault. I should never have let your mom take you away from here at the end of the summers. But I knew I worked too much to be any kind of father figure. Too stubborn. For all of our goods."

"Who do you mean?" Logan squinted, trying to make sense of the rambling self-deprecation oozing from his great-uncle.

"Me. You. Rose. Kyana." He sighed. "There could have been something there. All my life, I knew Rose was special. She was the one for me. The only woman I could have loved. I thought she deserved better. I wouldn't accept her help. Some of her enormous inheritance. Hell, I didn't even take her up on the date she asked me on once. I

281

regret every single day that I live on after she's gone, never knowing what *might* have been if only I'd looked past my pride. We could have been a family, Logan. It's my fault you didn't have that. Because of me, you're unsure of the facts I see plain as day. You're a decent person. And you're head over heels for Kyana Brady. Have been since you were old enough to sneak nudie magazines from my shed by the garden."

"Uh... You knew about those?" He scrubbed his face with his hand. "I don't know what to say to that, Ben. That's a lot of shit to carry around."

"For us all. I hurt her. Rose. No matter how much I thought I was doing the right thing. I could see it more as the years went on, but I assumed it was too late to change. So much time had gone by. How stupid. That's only true when you're dead, Logan."

"You sound like a Hallmark card." Logan squeezed Ben's shoulder, hanging on a little longer than man-to-man interaction deemed appropriate. "Don't you fucking worry about me. Not for a second. The time I spent here saved me. You showed me the kind of person I wanted to be. And... Ky and I are sort of working on things. You know, between us."

"You are?" Ben's whole bearing changed. He perked right up and a smile erased his frown.

"Yup. She actually asked me out. I guess she's more like Rose than I realized. We have a date tomorrow night. Reservations at Fleur." He hoped like hell he wasn't blushing.

"Thank God you're smarter than me, kid." Ben grinned. "Want me to stay out late? I think Myrtle is having a bridge game I could join in."

Logan started to deny it, but then thought better of it. "If you don't mind..."

"In fact, I might tie one on and end up spending the night. Yep, that sounds like a damn fine idea. She's offered her couch plenty of times. It looks comfy, too. And I think you might even fit in my suit jacket. It's too big for me anymore. One good thing 'bout not being trendy, you shouldn't be hideously out of fashion."

"Thanks." A million ideas flashed through Logan's mind.

"You got it."

"Hey, Ben. One more thing..." Logan hopped the railing, but paused to look over his shoulder on the way to his truck. "I'm pretty glad right now that I didn't grow up with Kyana as some kind of sister."

Ben doubled over laughing. "That might have been hard to explain to people, huh?"

"Yeah." He cleared his throat. "Still, some bonds are simply understood. You might never have said a thing about it. And maybe you never acted on it. But Rose knew you were connected, every bit as much as you did. There's no way she doubted you loved her. I'd bet our new business on it because I always knew you did. Even before I understood what the words really meant."

"I hope you're right, Logan." Ben sank into the glider on the porch. He seemed smaller than ever, huddled beneath the last golden rays of the afternoon. "But I'll never know for sure. Go to Ky. Make sure she understands."

"I will." He nodded as he climbed into his truck. "I promise."

A bell tinkled when Kyana pushed open the heavy door to the brick building that housed their village's records and the lone policeman's office. She stepped into the stuffy building, peeking around the corners. "Hello? Is anyone here?"

"Good afternoon." A woman spoke from behind her.

Kyana slapped her palm to her chest, over her racing heart. She hadn't heard anyone emerge from behind the receptionist's desk. "Oh, Laura. Nice to see you again."

"You too." The young Mrs. Gittleson smiled sadly. "How's Ben holding up?"

"Eh. He never complains, but I can tell he hates seeing his house in disrepair. I think it helps to be staying in Rose's space though. It's probably comforting, having her things around."

"He's spent enough time there over the years. It's more like an extension of his own place." Laura nodded. "But I'm sure you didn't come in just to chat. Can I help you with something?"

"Would you mind if I asked you some questions?" Kyana took a deep breath. "About the petition you raised."

"Ah, yes. I was surprised you hadn't mentioned it before." Laura wrinkled her nose. "We were new to the neighborhood and didn't really understand what Oak Street was all about. Dean and I are thrilled we lucked into such a tight-knit community. It makes up for the longer commute he has to make, going around town to the other side of the lake."

It was hard to imagine her large, toothy grin as anything other than genuine.

"Who else supported the proposal?"

"Why?" Laura hesitated. "Do you think that has anything to do with the fire? The easement right clause on Ben's mortgage expired several months ago. Didn't it?"

"Yes." Kyana nodded. "But I'm wondering if someone didn't realize that. Or maybe they were just bitter?"

"Wow." Laura perched on the edge of her desk then flipped her hair over her shoulder. "I can't imagine anyone going to those lengths. The only other people who signed the petition were new to the neighborhood, I think. I stuck a copy in record storage in the basement. You're welcome to have a look if you want. Fair warning though, it's not very neat down there. Filing isn't my strong suit."

Refusing to ask what other possible job requirements there could be besides answering the phone, Kyana shrugged. "Sure, that sounds good."

"If you don't mind, I actually was planning to leave early today. It's Dean's birthday and I'm making his favorite, duck l'orange, for dinner. Would you lock up behind you when you leave?" She dug an enormous key ring, complete with at least ten dangly bits boasting a variety of cheesy vacation destinations, from her purse and held it out to Kyana.

"Uh, no problem." She jangled the keys. "Don't worry, it's impossible to lose these. I'll swing by and drop them off when I'm finished."

"Maybe just leave them in the mailbox." Laura winked.

Kyana couldn't help herself. She laughed. After charging down here prepared to dislike the Gittlesons, she admitted Ben had been right. They were a little slow to catch on, but nice people. Maybe she'd invite Laura and Dean over to cook out sometime soon. Logan would enjoy having a conversation about something other than bad knees and the best denture cream on the market. Though she had to admit he looked pretty cute hanging out and drinking a beer with all the elderly guys on the block after quitting time.

"You got it. Thanks."

Laura showed her to the basement. The heavy door creaked when she tugged it open. Kyana batted a few cobwebs out of her way then started down the old wooden stairs. "Now you see why I'm not too keen on spending quality time with the records."

"I'm getting a clearer picture by the minute." Kyana flipped on the yellow overhead lights when she reached the cement floor. "I'll make this quick then."

"Okay, I'm out of here. Hope you find something that helps." Laura shut the door with a wave. Her heels clicked on the linoleum above until the front door opened, bell tinkling again, then shut hard enough to dislodge a sprinkle of dust. It rained down on Kyana.

She swiped her hands over her bare arms, imagining the number of spiders per square inch to be similar to the amount of germs in a gas station bathroom. *Blech.*

Either Laura had turned off the air-conditioning or the luxury wasn't a line item in the tiny town's budget. The basement grew stuffier by the minute as Kyana rummaged through stacks of paper, dismissing them out of hand since the top sheets were no more recent than last decade.

Fanning herself, she sidled over to one of the rectangular windows. After standing on a chair and worming her hands around the bars on them, she gave up on cracking the thing open. About nine million coats of paint, probably lead-filled, had sealed it shut.

"Great. Just look faster. Let's move this along." Kyana flew from box to box, trying to gauge which had the thinnest layer of grime on top. One looked a bit newer than the rest. She flipped the top off and grabbed a paper at random. It had a date of last spring.

Bingo.

Leafing through the documents, she came closer and closer to the general time Ben had guesstimated the petition had surfaced. A bead of sweat rolled off her forehead and dripped onto the records, smudging the ink. "Okay, this is nuts," she muttered to herself.

While she was talking, a noise caught her attention. It almost sounded like the bell on the door. Maybe Laura had forgotten something. She decided to haul the likely box upstairs and do more investigating where she could catch her breath, never mind seeing clearly.

The damn thing weighed a ton, but she hoisted it to her hip and began to climb the open-backed staircase. A thump startled her when she was a few treads from the top. "Hello?"

No friendly voice answered this time.

"Who's there?" She continued to ascend, her arms starting to tingle from holding the files. With the box balanced on her thigh, she reached out a hand to turn the knob.

It didn't budge.

"What the hell?" Had the sheriff come in and locked the damn thing as part of his standard end-of-day routine? Had the ancient hardware broken?

Kyana pounded on the paneling, almost losing her balance in the process. "Someone help. I'm stuck in here. Are you there?"

As she strained for any answer at all, she heard it again. The suddenly not-so-sunny ringing of the bell on the door. No way could anyone have been upstairs yet not heard the racket she was making. The hair on the nape of her neck stood up straight and her instincts went on red alert.

And that's when she saw it.

A wisp of smoke snaked through the gap beneath the door and rose in beautiful yet deadly formations.

"Oh my God." She almost tumbled backward. Forcing herself to stay calm, she scurried down the stairs, dropped the box at her feet and hauled her cell from her pocket. Only to see the glaring red X of her no-signal symbol. "Shit. Shit. Shit."

A dull roar above her turned into a pop then a *whoosh*. Dry, old timbers of the floor overhead were clearly visible from her position. They would do a hell of a lot poorer job than the asbestos ceiling tiles Ben's house had contained to prevent the fire from eating through to her hideout.

She raced to the other window, hoping for something different than she'd found earlier. No such luck. Scanning the room, she latched on to the pile of decorations for the front lawn. She dismissed the Christmas tree and the bunny costume but landed on the pitchfork next to the cornucopia and inflatable turkey. That could work.

Kyana grabbed the tool and lunged toward the window. She didn't hesitate to jab the rusted metal at the tiny pane of glass. It surprised her when her first blow glanced off the surface. Exertion combined with thickening smoke to induce a coughing fit. She ignored it.

The next swing cracked the glass and a third busted out several large chunks. A few more had fresh air pouring in. Thank God. Still she couldn't see a way to get past the bars. Who had thought that was a good idea? She supposed Town Hall had made their own personal fire code. Probably to keep bored kids at bay in their ho-hum town. Petty mischief, like putting the town's Christmas lights up in March, was common when there wasn't much other entertainment to keep teenagers occupied.

She yanked her tank top upward to cover her mouth. Hell, she was practically an expert at this now. Abandoning her war with the grate, she crossed to the other window and smashed it to smithereens too. Climbing on top of the chair, she stretched her neck, placing her face as close as she could to the outside without risking cutting herself on the wreckage.

"Help!" She screamed as loud as she could manage, over and over, until her throat was raw. The building sat far away from the street and the small shops that lined the block near the town's only stoplight. In the distance, she could see the glowing sign of the pizza parlor and, ironically, the back of the firehouse. No one was around.

The temperature had risen substantially. Sweat began to pour down her back. She glanced over her shoulder just in time to see flames eat a hole in the rafters. Embers plummeted to the floor of the basement and ignited a box of files.

"No!" She dashed toward the blaze, stomping out what she could. For every spark she squashed, another three lit up the dimness with angry red spots.

Fury washed over her. She'd just found Logan again and she hadn't even gotten to fully enjoy the man. She was not about to let some asshole steal the experience of a lifetime from her. No way was she going down without a fight.

Smashing the pitchfork into the grate only cracked the wooden handle, and left her arms vibrating from the impact. She jumped up and grabbed on to the metal, letting her whole body hang from the bars. They creaked. Bouncing up and down, she cheered when one bolt stripped out of the concrete around it.

By placing both her feet on the wall, she gained some leverage. A yank seemed to loosen another corner. Not enough to give her much hope. The fire crept closer, faster than she could ever have imagined, fed by the boxes of old, dried paper.

"Help!" She knew it was pointless, but she screamed again when the heat began to feel intense enough to blister her skin. It wouldn't be long now. Maybe she should breathe in the smoke after all. Passing out would save her from experiencing the horror of burning alive.

A tear rolled down her cheek and she dropped from the bars.

"Kyana?"

It was then she knew she was doomed. She was hallucinating. Dreaming of being rescued by the one man who really mattered. "Logan?"

"What the hell is going on? Where are you? In the basement?"

Her eyes snapped wide open. Just in time to see scuffed work boots come to rest outside her prison. "Yes! Yes! Down here. Fire. Stuck. Can't get out. Bars."

"Holy shit." He didn't waste any time. "Step back."

There wasn't much room to move as the flames crept closer, so she ducked. He must have kicked the metal. It rang with the reverberation of his impact. Still, when she peeked up, there were at least three bolts hanging on. Crumbling gray mortar got in her eyes. She blamed that for the moisture dripping from her chin.

The crackle of blossoming flames grew so loud she wasn't sure he could hear her as he hammered the bars again and again with diminishing success.

"Logan. None of this was your fault. You did your best. I'm glad you're here with me now."

"Stop. Talking." A loud bang punctuated each word of his command. "I'm getting you out of here. It's loosening. I can feel it."

"Not enough time." She didn't want him to wonder ever about how she'd felt. "Logan. I love you. I've loved you since we were kids. No one has ever replaced you in my heart. No one has ever lived up to the standard you set. I'm glad we had this time together again at the end."

"No!" His roar would have terrified her if it'd been aimed at her. The next clang seemed ten times as loud. Especially when the bars dislodged and crashed to the floor.

She popped up and stared into his wide-open eyes. Level with her, he'd flattened himself on the lawn.

"I love you too." He swore as he extended his hand and reached toward her.

"Wait. This first." She swung the box of files into his grasp. Before he could argue she shoved. He pulled, tearing some things and spilling others when the box distorted to squeeze through the window. Barely. She figured it served another purpose as shards of glass rained from the opening.

And not at all too soon, Logan's strong hand was back. This time she took it. And held on tight. His other arm reached in and she grasped that one too, locking their fingers around each other's wrists. She didn't have time to warn him about the jagged surface before he hauled her out.

Even if she had, the heat and smoke wouldn't have allowed them to take their time.

A low, keening wail ripped from her throat when a remnant of the window sliced her shoulder on one side. She cringed, but no more pain followed. She writhed, helping Logan thread her through the small egress.

"Almost there, Ky. Hang on. I've got you."

In the distance, men shouted. Several dashed up the hill from the firehouse while others ran back for the truck, equipped with all their gear.

Her feet cleared the window and Logan hauled her the rest of the way up into his arms. She couldn't tell if it was her or him trembling. The world around her jittered as he ran away from the building, onto the lawn. When they'd gone far enough to ensure their safety, he dropped to his knees, cradling her against his chest.

"Are you okay?" He rocked them both, back and forth, until the motion took the edge off her terror. His smell and closeness helped more than she could say.

"I think so." She nuzzled her face into his neck so he wouldn't see the tears she couldn't stop. "Because of you."

"Thank God." His fingers buried in her hair, holding her tight against him. He rained kisses over her head, neck and the side of her face. "What the fuck happened?"

"I don't know." She tried to explain. "Someone locked the door to the basement. Laura Gittleson went home earlier. I was searching for the petition."

"Who the fuck did this to you?" Logan had rarely resorted to anger.

Before she could reassure him, a familiar man approached. The fireman who'd carried her across Ben's yard stood to their side, arms crossed over his chest. "We have to stop meeting like this. If you want my number, all you have to do is ask. I'd be glad to share."

Logan growled. "I don't think so, buddy. Don't you have a fucking fire to fight?"

"So it's like that is it? I see, I see." The fireman laughed, his palms held outward as he retreated a few steps.

"Could you do me a favor?" Kayna asked.

Logan stiffened until she clarified. "Please grab that box of files by the window before it gets soaked, or catches on fire or everything blows away."

"You got it." He'd jogged over, claimed the records and delivered them to her before she could help Logan come down from his adrenaline high. "Glad to see you're mostly unharmed again. See ya. Duty calls."

Kyana raised a hand when her new friend paired up with another fireman then dashed into the burning building.

"What the hell did he mean by that?" Logan glared at her.

"He was just teasing, Logan. You know, it's not every day I tell a man I love him. *I* wasn't kidding. And it wasn't something I blurted just because I thought I wasn't going to make it."

"Yeah." He swallowed hard. "Same goes. But I was talking about the '*mostly* unharmed' part. Where are you hurt?"

She peered down at herself, taking stock of the various aches and pains the glow in her heart had masked.

At the same time, Logan ran his hands over her. He paused when he touched her shoulder. She squeaked at the stabbing pain that raced down her arm. When he pulled his hand away, it was red. "Shit. You're bleeding. A lot."

He separated their torsos long enough to strip his shirt off. She was glad for the visual anesthetic when he wrapped the cotton around her. Tight. As more and more people joined the crowd, drawn to the black smoke rising—thick and dark—into the evening sky, Logan waved his hand and shouted.

None other than Daryl Thick answered his call.

"You!" Logan glared. "What are you doing here?"

"I passed Myrtle Jansen coming back from the post office. She told me there was a fire. So I came to see if I could help." He lifted a small plastic kit. "I'm trained in first aid from the Army, you know?"

"Fine." Logan didn't make her wait for someone else's assistance. He wanted to get the hell out of there before the news crew showed up and questions started. "Could you take a look at Ky's arm? She must have sliced it on the window. Sorry baby, I didn't realize when I pulled you out..."

"There wasn't time, Logan." She kissed his frown until it melted away. "You rescued me. If you hadn't shown up—"

They both shuddered.

"I saved myself too," he murmured despite Daryl's presence. "You're everything to me."

They shared another kiss. This one slower and gentler than the last. Kyana nestled deeper into his arms.

"Okay, kids. Enough canoodling until I get her patched up." Daryl flipped open the lid of his case, snapped on a glove and unwound Logan's ruined shirt. "Damn, you might need a couple stitches. You want to go to the hospital, or should I sew you up here?"

Kyana peered at Logan. "I'd rather stay with you. Do you mind? Will it gross you out?"

"Hardly." He laid his forehead on hers. "I'm not going anywhere, Ky. Not now. Not ever."

"Me either." She beamed up at him.

Daryl's quick administration of local anesthetic and his deft handiwork didn't seem so awful. Especially with Logan to distract her. Before she knew it, the tough stuff was over, reports were logged, the arson investigators took their information for later and they were heading home.

Together.

Chapter Six

Kyana nibbled the corner of her lip as she stared into her glass. She swirled the remnants of her dessert wine around the bottom of the vessel, entranced by the pattern as she thought back to earlier in the night.

She'd been sitting at Rose's dining room table, the box of files spread out before her, when Ben came into the room. He'd whistled then said, "You look great, girly. Extra girly. You're gonna give my kid a heart attack. Now enough of this nonsense. Go out and have a good time tonight."

He'd waved his hands at the documents she tried to show him, uncaring that she'd finally found the petition. How could he brush off the only clue they might have to the fires?

"I know I'm probably not supposed to talk about the johns at any dinner table, and especially one as fancy as this—" Logan returned from the bathroom, sliding into their corner booth on the same side as her. "But damn. There were a lot of high-quality materials in there. Marble everywhere, a fancy vessel sink and I think the faucet and hardware were even gold-plated. You might want to check it out. Maybe someday I'll get Nowak Construction to the level where I get jobs like those."

"I know you will." She took his hand and smiled at his enthusiasm, but he was getting to know her pretty damn well. Better than the couple guys she'd dated for close to a year.

"What's wrong, Ky? Am I fucking this up?" His brows drew together. "I'm sure I used the wrong fork, but I didn't think you'd care. That rack of lamb was the best thing I've ever eaten. Well, until dessert anyway. My stomach is full enough to bust. At least it'll go happy."

She couldn't resist leaning over to kiss the last dot of chocolate from the corner of his lips. "Sorry, I didn't mean to spoil your fun. It's nothing you did. I guess I'm just having a hard time pretending like everything is fine when someone tried to kill Ben. And me. I just don't understand what's going on. And…"

"Yeah?" He stroked her hair out of her face and tucked it behind her ear. "Don't stop now. I'm listening."

"I didn't want to ruin our dinner, so I didn't tell you that I found the petition this afternoon."

"You did?" He sat up straighter. "That's great. What'd it tell you? Who was on it?"

"That's the thing." She slumped against his side when he slung his arm around her shoulder. The comfort he infused her with was welcome. "It was pointless. All of that was for nothing. The names were mostly the new people to the neighborhood. You know about the Gittlesons, and a bunch of the other couples that commute to the city. Myrtle Jansen and Daryl Thick and a couple of the crankier residents. Still, nothing that surprised me."

"Were you hoping the bad guy's name would be written in invisible ink on the paper like in a movie?" He knew just what to say to cheer her up.

She laughed, then socked him in the side. "Shut up."

"Ugh. That's not a good idea. I'm already trying to digest faster if I'm going to have my dessert."

"Logan-kun, you already ate yours plus half of mine." She grinned. Watching him scarf the confection had lightened her heart.

"That's not the kind of treat I'm talking about." He leaned in close and nibbled the lobe of her ear before whispering, "We have the house to ourselves tonight. Ben's staying at game night."

"What?" She whipped around to look at him so fast they almost bumped noses. "He is?"

Logan nodded. "Yup. Myrtle said she'd take care of him. Hell, she seemed pretty excited about it. Maybe he'll get lucky too."

Kyana's hand shot up as a waiter neared their table. "Check please."

Logan's laughter, and the squeeze of his fingers on her thigh, had her forgetting all about her worries. With him, she was safe. And she'd let things she couldn't control any more than gravity keep her from enjoying herself for too long.

Logan reminded himself for the five thousandth time that he wanted to take things slow. And yet he found himself making out with Ky in his truck in the driveway like they were still adolescents. He'd hauled her across the bench seat and pressed her to his side as they drove. The instant he'd parked, they'd fused together as completely as his fingers had the time he'd gotten epoxy on them as an apprentice. Only this was a hell of a lot more enjoyable.

He searched for any long-lost scrap of propriety he might have in his genetic makeup. Nothing meant more to him than ensuring their first time was special. This was the girl of his dreams. The woman of his future...if his luck held. And he wanted to do this right.

With a groan, he retracted his tongue from her mouth, which tasted pleasantly of the wine they'd shared. She didn't make it any easier on him when she chased him with licks and kisses of her own.

The dazed stare she leveled at him had him sure he was making the right decision. They had to take this party inside before they ended up half-dressed, mashed against the steering wheel. The last thing they needed was the neighborhood watch bearing down on them when someone's elbow tooted the truck's horn by accident.

"I know where there's a nice comfy bed inside. No rotten old boards or the cab of my truck tonight. Fancy sheets and puffy pillows all the way." He held his hand out to her when he stepped down. She allowed him to lift her and set her beside him. The pleated skirt of her filmy layered dress floated into place around her knees. "Only the best for someone as amazing as you. I wish I could have taken you to a swanky hotel or someplace crazy like Paris."

"Been there, done that. I like where I am right now better. As long as we're together, that's where I want to be." She raised their joined hands to her lips and kissed his knuckles. "Though the thought of getting horizontal somewhere soft and warm sounds pretty fine right about now."

She shrieked when he scooped her into his arms and loped up the hill. He let them in through the back door off the deck then took the stairs two at a time. "That I can do."

They laughed as he spun her around a few times before depositing her on their bed. He couldn't do more than stare when she rose onto her knees. Gazing into his eyes, she hoisted her hem a little bit at a time. Along the way she revealed classic black, lace-top thigh highs held in place by some strappy contraption he couldn't wait to reverse engineer.

An expanse of pale, creamy skin stretched over her belly to the matching bra that cupped her to perfection. And before he could share how absolutely gorgeous he thought she was, she'd abandoned her dress and crawled toward him, her onyx hair cascading off her shoulders onto the bed beside her as she stalked closer.

Powerful, graceful and alluring, she stole his capacity to do anything but react on a basic level.

When she neared, he tipped up her face with two fingers under her chin.

Her smile brightened his world.

"I can't believe that just a few weeks ago, I thought I'd lost everything. And now I have all I've ever dreamed of. Family, home, the start of a business, passion and...you."

"They say things happen for a reason, Logan-kun."

"You're my reason." He didn't need to say more.

She nodded, her eyes shimmering. "Same goes. And you know what else they say?"

"What's that?" Trying to stop her from unbuttoning his slacks or drawing down the zipper would have been ridiculous.

"Where there's smoke...there's fire." She hiked his dress shirt up and nipped the ridge that led from his hip bone, arrowing toward his cock.

The silk of his tie unraveled in a hurry. He couldn't risk her destroying his restraint with the clever fingers that dropped his pants, shoved his briefs to his ankles and cupped his balls in the blink of an eye.

"Damn." He choked when she weighed his sac in her palm.

"That's what I'm saying." She ran the tip of one finger along his entire length. "You seem even bigger tonight, now that I can really see you."

"That fancy petting you're doing certainly isn't making it any smaller." He grunted when she squeezed. "Unless you do it too much. Enough of that."

She gasped when he kicked his feet free of the tangle of fabric pooled around them, then whipped his tie off and twined it around her wrists before she realized what he intended. "Logan?"

The note of uncertainty in her cry had him pausing. "Do you like to be bound, Ky?"

"I don't know. I've never tried it." She flushed, every inch of her turning a pretty salmon color. "I haven't felt comfortable enough to ask guys to experiment."

"That should have been clue number one they were all wrong for you." He nuzzled her jaw, taking the sting out of his rebuke. "But you've thought about it?"

"Yes." She closed her eyes. "A lot. Giving up control isn't easy for me."

"I know." He kissed her eyelids, cheeks and lips gently. "Thank you for trusting me. You're one of the only people who ever believed in me. All the way. I won't let you down."

With no hesitation, she echoed him. "I know."

"Hell, I'll even let you keep your power pumps this time."

"Logan, you like these shoes even more than I do. And that's saying a lot." She smiled before he kissed her.

He stretched her out until she lay completely on her back, restrained hands above her head. The full weight of his body bore down on her.

Kyana didn't squirm. She didn't attempt to escape. Instead she reveled in the heat of their connection, and spread her legs until he sank into the V of her thighs. The moist tip of his cock glided across her thigh, reminding him of practical matters.

One hand shot out to the drawer in the side table and removed a condom from the pile he'd deposited there. After sheathing himself, he went to work on ridding Kyana of the last obstacles to their joining. He'd waited forever for this moment.

If the desperate whimpers emanating from her were any indication, so had she.

It took him a few seconds to figure out how to remove her panties while leaving her garter intact. Though it tempted him, he didn't take the easy way out and rip the packaging off her present. No, he wanted to enjoy the sexy trappings for many sessions to come. Destruction wasn't his thing.

Carefully, he divested her of the scrap of lace, exposing her bare mound to his elevated breathing. She arched upward, presenting him with the perfect opportunity. He couldn't resist tasting her again. The flavor of Kyana had been burning through his palate since their interlude on the dock.

More delicious than their meal earlier, she encouraged him to devour her, preparing to accept him as best she could. While he laved her pussy, his hands snuck upward. They flicked over the front fastener of her bra, making quick work of the clasp. Unwilling to free her from the web they wove together, he yanked the material up, reinforcing the bond made by his tie while leaving her breasts exposed.

No one could fault him for pausing to admire the full yet modest swells and the dark tips that had puckered in the evening air, or for detouring to taste first one then the other. The instant he felt her fingers in his hair, nudging him, he froze.

"Did I tell you to move those hands, Ky?" A love bite on her breast captured her attention.

"N-no." She lifted her arms, placing them near the headboard once more.

"Nice." He kissed her long and sweet.

"What are you doing to me?" She practically panted.

"Loving you." His hips rocked, guiding his full erection along the furrow of her pussy.

"Please. I need you." Kyana tried to align herself to encourage penetration.

He nudged her, but refrained from entering the damp tissue kissing his shaft. Gritting his teeth, he committed himself to enhancing her experience then reached between them. The tip of his cock grazed her saturated pussy.

They both drew a sharp lungful of air.

"Keep breathing." He rubbed his thumb over her lips until she sucked it into her mouth. "Let me inside."

A series of moans and cries encouraged him as he advanced, pressing himself deeper with rocks of his hips until she'd managed to envelop him in her sweetness. Nothing had ever felt so right. He whispered, his face pressed to Ky's neck, "You know, I've never done this before either."

"Hmm?" She sounded as coherent as he felt.

"I've never *made love* to a woman before." He pulled back just enough to stare into her eyes. "Sex never mattered so much."

"Don't worry, I'll be gentle." She craned her neck to kiss the tip of his nose. "At least at first."

Laughter interrupted more kissing as he seated himself to the hilt. When he bottomed out, she rotated her hips, pressing her clit against the plane of muscle at the base of his cock. They locked tight together, perfect counterparts.

At first, he was content to stay there, grinding with her and enjoying the steady pulses that clamped her rings of muscle around him in the most erotic massage of his life. After a while, her kisses grew sloppy and she writhed beneath him with enough vigor he worried she might aggravate her injuries. At least the tie kept her arm out of danger's way as he'd intended.

"Tell me what you need." It wasn't that he didn't know. More that he had to hear it. Had waited a lifetime to live this dream.

"Fuck me, Logan." Decorum fled in the face of their raw, primal lust.

He delivered, fulfilling every dirty encouragement she shouted at him. Thank God they'd waited until they were home alone to unleash their desire.

"I want you to come for me, Ky." He grunted as he picked up the pace, adding a swivel to each thrust, designed to drive her wild.

"No."

Her refusal caused a hitch in his stride. Then a redoubling of his effort. "What did you say?"

"No." She grinned up at him. "Not without you."

"That's not going to be a problem." Electric shocks had been stirring in the base of his cock for a good long while. Hell, she was lucky he hadn't gone off the moment they touched.

He didn't realize it, but he'd modified his strokes. Dots and dashes of an entirely different nature spelled out the way he felt, even if he wasn't quite brave enough to say it and put the best night of his life in jeopardy. Someday soon he'd verbalize the sentiment his cock impressed on her in long and short lunges.

"It's okay to let go, Ky." He stroked a sweaty lock of hair from her brow. "I'm here. I've got you. I won't ever let you down."

"Yes!" She screamed it louder and louder until the clamp of her pussy synched with the cries. The orgasm that washed over her had her milking every last drop of his release from the very tips of his toes. Or at least that's how it seemed.

Endless euphoria crashed over them. Each flex of her channel hugged him, eliciting another blast of come. He worried he might overflow the condom for about ten seconds, until he realized he might not care if he did.

And when the violent storming had passed, he collapsed onto the bed beside her, unfettering her hands so they could bask in the afterglow as if it really were a lazy, rainy weekend.

Logan smiled as an aftershock jolted Kyana. He rolled to his back and held her tight, rubbing the tension from her ass, sure that they would have plenty of chances to practice their techniques in slow, gentle sessions. Right after they did this a few dozen more times to take the edge off a decade of yearning.

Chapter Seven

Logan threw one arm over his head. He watched Kyana stretch then push up on her elbows. She swung a leg out of bed. "Where do you think you're going? I kind of liked you where you were."

Understatement of the century.

"I have to pee if you don't mind. I didn't realize this was going to be a sexathon." He hadn't thought it possible, but she was even cuter when she blushed.

Logan rolled over and smacked her on the ass as she sauntered away. "Hurry back."

"I promise." She smiled. "I haven't had my fill of snuggles just yet."

"No problem. I have lots more where those came from." He winked. "And some other tricks up my sleeves too."

"It's big but I doubt it fits up your sleeve."

He choked.

"I like you speechless." She giggled, and he adored the carefree sound from his too-serious lover.

"I have a feeling you'll do that to me plenty. You know, like when I bury myself inside you again…" He pushed out of bed as if to chase her.

"Give me a minute. Then I'm all yours." Her radiant smile brightened his heart an instant before she closed the bathroom door.

Since he was already up, and didn't dare risk falling asleep without her or before round five, he wandered to the window and pushed back the curtains. Not on the side of the room facing Ben's house, but on the opposite wall, near his side of their bed.

Damn, he liked the way that sounded. *Their bed.*

Rubbing the scratches Kyana had left on his chest with those sharp little nails of hers, he peered toward Myrtle Jansen's place, wondering if Ben was really comfortable or if he should go bring his great-uncle home. An orange cast to the living room window caught his attention. Was Ben still up at this late hour?

No way had the games gone on this long. Hell, some days the old timers didn't last through the four-thirty episode of *Judge Judy*, their idol. If someone was still awake, it meant they couldn't sleep. Crap. Kyana would understand if they cut their fun short, wouldn't she? There'd be plenty of time later to play. Every night for the rest of their lives, he hoped.

As he debated, he monitored that uneven glow.

And that's when he saw it.

A shadow crossed between Logan's perch and Myrtle's living room.

The bulky silhouette could belong to none other than Daryl Thick based on its size and the fluid way its owner stalked across the lawn.

"Motherfucker." He spun around, nearly plowing over Kyana.

"What's wrong?" The fear that drew lines in her pretty face made him itch to toss some punches. Daryl was older than him by a solid twenty years, but the dude had clearly been trained. This wasn't going to go down easy.

"Nothing. Stay here for a minute. I need to grab something out of my truck." He hated lying to her, but wouldn't risk her getting hurt.

"Like what? A tire iron?" She tipped her head. "There's nothing you could have forgotten and your eye ticked. Tell me the truth. If we're going to be partners—"

"Shit. Fine." He couldn't chance stepping wrong now. "Daryl is slinking around Myrtle's house. It's no coincidence that's where Ben is tonight. I'm putting a stop to this bullshit once and for all."

"Let me call the police." She reached for his hand.

He glanced over his shoulder, monitoring Daryl's progress. The asshole had already crept up to the window and was taking something from a bag Logan hadn't noticed at first. "Go ahead. Notify them, then wait here for me. I think he's up to something. I'm going to stop him before it's too late."

"Be careful, Logan." Somehow she knew better than to tell him not to go.

He dragged on his jeans, shoved his feet into his boots, then kissed her quick and hard. "I'll be right back. Then we'll see about that snuggling, okay?"

"'Kay."

"Love you." The unfamiliar phrase flew off his tongue without hesitation.

"Love you, too." She kissed her fingers then blew the smooch toward him.

Ridiculous or not, he caught it before clomping down the stairs. Doubly pissed off at Daryl, for causing trouble and for interrupting his time with Kyana, Logan channeled all of his anger into sneaking up on the wily bastard. He'd had some experience with this—during those bad judgment years—since his mother had left him to his own devices, sometimes for days or weeks at a time.

When he'd crept as close as he dared in stealth, he launched himself at the dirt bag's legs, tackling him into the juniper bushes.

"*Mufphh.*" Daryl tried to rant. It made no sense with branches in his face.

Logan hauled him backward and gave him a nice, solid shake. "What did I tell you about skulking around? Was it you who set those fires? Why? Why are you doing this?"

"Quit your yammering. They'll hear us." Daryl ignored the inquisition.

"Good. Kyana called the cops too. I want everyone to know about all your snooping." Logan curled his fingers in Daryl's black shirt to keep him still.

"I can see. She still has her phone to her ear." Daryl might have been lying, but Logan looked anyway. Sure enough, Ky stood not ten feet behind him with her cell and a fireplace poker, watching his back.

"What are you—?"

Daryl seized the opportunity granted by Logan's momentary distraction. The man relied on his skills to evade Logan's hold. The ease with which he broke free made it clear he'd only allowed the illusion of capture to keep from entering a real fight. "Listen to me, lovebirds. I'm not the guy you need to be getting your panties in a bunch over."

"Oh yeah, then who else is out here causing problems?" Logan glared at their nosy neighbor.

"Myrtle." He sighed. "She's batshit crazy. I've known that for years."

"Hell, everyone knows that." Kyana agreed with Daryl, obviously trying to calm him down.

"Yeah, but what I didn't realize was that she's getting more unstable as she gets older. Completely off her rocker and dangerous too. She's the one who's been setting your fires. I've been trying to gather some concrete evidence, but she slipped away from me the day of the Town Hall incident." He shook his head. "I have no idea how. She's wily."

"Are you fucking kidding me?" Logan shook his head. "You expect me to believe we're in danger from an eighty-five-year-old, retired... What the hell did she do anyway?"

Kyana gasped. "She used to work at the Town Hall. Until it burned down the first time. And she won some kind of worker's comp settlement. Rose used to joke that our taxes were hard at work supporting her."

"Seriously?" Logan took his eyes off Daryl for the first time.

"Yeah." The man grunted. "She's always torching shit in that barrel of hers too, no matter how many times Sherriff Collins tells her to knock it off."

"Uh-oh," Kyana added.

"What, *uh-oh*?" Logan raised his brows.

"One day when I ran out to get Rose's prescriptions filled, Myrtle stopped by. She said she'd watch my aunt while I was gone. When I got back...there was a small fire in the oven." She covered her mouth with one hand. "I didn't think anything of it. Myrtle said she'd tried to heat up something for Rose to eat but there was only a dishtowel in there when I looked. I thought she was getting senile and I didn't want to embarrass her."

Daryl nodded. "It's okay, hon. It took me a long time to figure it out, and I was looking. I didn't expect the little old lady to be a fucking pyromaniac."

"So what do we do now?" Kyana's eyes glistened in the light of her phone.

"Let's wait for the police and let them handle it." Logan now agreed with her.

"I wish we could." Daryl eased along the edge of the bushes, speaking very softly. "But I'm afraid that glow is getting stronger. And it doesn't look like any kind of lamp to me."

"Son of a bitch!" Logan had assumed his eyes were adjusting to the night. No such luck. Daryl was right. The unsteady flickering was growing by the second.

"Ben," Kyana cried out.

"Shh..." Logan reached for her, hugging her tight to his side. "Let's not give away our advantage. We'll get him out of there, don't worry."

"In all the time I've been watching, I've never seen her with a weapon. Just the silver lighter she carries. I'm willing to risk it." Daryl marched over to the front door, which opened into the living room, where the light seemed strongest.

"No, don't." Logan tried to stop him. With Kyana under one arm, he didn't make it in time.

"Wish me luck." Daryl stepped back and kicked down the door with a smooth move that impressed Logan even as he cringed. "Stop! This is a citizen's arrest."

Logan shoved Kyana behind him, ignoring her protest, and dashed over to assist. When he reached the threshold, his stomach dropped to his feet. Ben stared at him with bugged-out eyes. He thrashed on the couch, trussed up like a calf at a rodeo.

Myrtle hovered above him, humming. She was dressed in a wedding gown that looked almost as old as she was. Had she had it all this time?

A shiver ran down Logan's spine when he realized she was singing the wedding march as she poured gasoline on the floor. Candles of all shapes and sizes ringed the room. It was only a matter of time until the fumes ignited and the whole thing went up in smoke.

Ben grunted and gurgled, no doubt telling them to get the fuck out of there. Pronto.

Unfortunately, he drew Myrtle's attention to them.

"Have you come for the ceremony? I didn't think anyone had gotten the invitations." The toothy grin—complete with several black gaps—she leveled at them froze Logan's heart. "So glad you could join us. Come in, come in."

"Oh, Myrtle." Kyana's sigh was laced with enough pity to tug at Logan's chest.

"You!" Instead of welcoming her, Myrtle became enraged. Logan wouldn't have been surprised if she started foaming at the mouth. "You're not welcome here, Rose. You home wrecker. Trying to steal my man. You've always kept him from me. He's never seen anyone but you. Now that you're gone, he's mine. All mine. Get out! Get *out!*"

As she screamed, she waved her hands, sloshing more gasoline. Logan cringed, hoping the heavy fumes stayed low to the ground long enough for them to escape. Otherwise this place was going to go up like a firework on the Fourth of July.

Lacy doilies, curtains and piles of junk to rival an episode of *Hoarders* made perfect fuel. They had to get Ben and go. Surely they could fend off one little old lady, even if she was totally loony.

Daryl looked over at him. "You grab Ben, I'll get Myrtle."

Logan nodded. "Three, two, *one.*"

They rushed forward in unison. Daryl leaped the couch in an impressive imitation of an Olympic hurdler. Logan snagged Ben and threw the bound man over his shoulder. When he turned, the horror in Kyana's face caught his attention. Before her scream left her lungs, he felt himself being thrown forward toward the door.

The impact left him shaking his head, trying to put things to right.

Fortunately, it seemed like Kyana and Ben had made it out of the danger zone and onto the soft mulch of the perfectly tended flower beds. They were huddled together as Ky worked the knots free on Ben's ropes then helped him up.

Logan struggled to his feet, spinning to look for Daryl. The man hovered outside a flaming heart, which encapsulated the sofa Ben had been held captive on. Inside the horrifying shape, Myrtle danced. The train of her yellowed dress dragged perilously close to the fire.

Daryl tried to reach her. She spun out of his grasp. A flare-up prevented him from jumping across the boundary between them. Instead, he retreated several steps.

"Get out of there!" Logan shouted at their resident hero.

Daryl looked as if he might object until Myrtle lifted the can of gas over her head, drenched herself and gave one final curtsey that turned her into a living fireball. She cackled as she charged Daryl, trying to take him with her to her own personal hell.

"Fuck this." He sprinted for the door, and Logan didn't hesitate to follow.

They left the thick oak standing open.

Myrtle never emerged.

Hours later, Ben huddled together with Kyana and Logan around the table in the bright, cheery kitchen of Rose's house. "This is getting to be a habit. Not that I don't love spending time with you kids, but...we've got to quit doing this."

Kyana took his hand in hers and squeezed. Logan did the same for her.

She smiled up at him, hoping they were about to call it a night. Again.

As if he could sense their restlessness, Ben rose. He shuffled toward the stairs and said, "It's a shame about that couch. Myrtle was right. It was pretty comfy."

Kyana just stared at him with her jaw hanging open while Logan cracked up.

"If you don't laugh, you'll cry." Ben shook his finger at her. "And I'm not wasting any tears over that woman. Rose is the only lady who deserved those from us. Have a good night. And for the record, I'm taking my hearing aids out."

Logan looked to Kyana. He wiggled his eyebrows.

She climbed into his lap right there at the table and kissed the shit out of him. When they were both breathless, she whispered, "I'd like to cash in my rain check for snuggles now."

"Whatever you like, ma'am." He carried her upstairs to their bed.

Epilogue

Six months later

Logan had never been so sure of something, and yet so nervous about it, in his entire life. He paced the sparkling kitchen of Ben's house and snapped the box in his hand open then closed for about the gazillionth time. Inside, a simple antique band nestled among dark maroon velvet. It hadn't broken the bank—which was shored up by the three jobs Nowak Construction had won after people had gotten sight of his craftsmanship—but something about the delicate scrollwork on the side had reminded him of Kyana.

He stood in the dark for a minute straight, breathing deep and slow. Then he took the flashlight from the countertop in front of him, flipped it on and covered it with his palm.

Dash dot dash.

"K."

He only had to flash the sign three times before the high-powered beam reflecting off her bright-white ceiling roused her. Just like the old days.

Dash dot dash dash. Dot. Dot dot dot.

"Yes?"

A smile crossed his face despite the sweat making his thumb slick on the on/off switch. Now or never.

Dash dash. Dot Dash. Dot dash dot. Dot dash dot. Dash dot dash dash. Pause. Dash dash. Dot.

"Marry me?"

No light answered his question. His heart tripped in his chest as seconds turned into a minute. He tried again.

Dash dot dash.

"K?"

Still nothing. Had he read her wrong this whole summer? Had he rushed her? It seemed like forever to him but maybe because he'd known what he really wanted from the time he was sixteen. If he screwed it up now, he'd never recover.

He set down the flashlight carefully on the freshly installed granite countertop, switched on the new pendant fixtures over the island, then sighed.

Right before the door burst open and Kyana raced in. She leapt into his arms from several feet away. The force of her advance didn't matter. He caught her easily. Never would he drop her.

"Yes!" She took his face between her palms and kissed him over and over. Between each smack of her lips she said it again. "Yes, yes, yes, yes, yes, yes, yes."

"Mmm." He nipped her lip then set her down. "Let me do this right."

"What?"

"This." He got to one knee on the new hardwood floors and popped open the ring box. "Kyana Brady, you are the only love of my life. Please stay with me. Let's build something special. We've worked on this remodel together, just as we've revamped our relationship into something amazing. I thought it was only right that I ask you to be my wife, here in this house."

"Yes. And yes again." She practically jumped up and down, making him laugh as always.

It made it harder, though not impossible, for him to slide his ring onto her finger.

"It's gorgeous, Logan." She got misty-eyed as she inspected the band.

"I figured you could pick out a diamond. Or maybe something of Rose's to wear with it." It didn't bother him anymore to think of her deep bank accounts. They shared everything. She'd made him see cash was just another example. Not the most important one by a stretch.

"I know just the piece." She nodded. "I can't believe this is real. It feels like a dream."

"Stay awake a little bit longer." He led her toward the counter, where an envelope rested.

"This is for you. Us. From Ben. An early wedding present," he said. Logan waved at the paper, still unable to believe what was inside.

"What?" Kyana peered up at him as she unfolded the deed to Ben's house. "Why?"

"He says we picked everything, it should be ours. And he wondered if you'd let him stay in Rose's house. Well, he asked to rent it. I already rolled my eyes at him for you."

"It's where he truly belonged, all this time." Kyana sniffled. "Of course, Logan. Rose would love that."

"And so will I." Ben spoke softly from the doorway. "I'm so happy for you both. I feel like this is what I worked all those years for. To have you here. Like this—together. It was worth it. Every minute, every sacrifice."

Logan and Kyana opened their arms and drew him into their circle.

The documents shook in Ky's hand. Something fell to the floor.

"What's that?" Ben stooped to claim it. When he saw what it was he froze. "Where did this come from? I put those papers in there myself this morning. The deed was the only thing in the envelope."

Kyana and Logan peered over his shoulder at the bright red rose petal he held clasped in his fingers. They looked to each other and shrugged.

Ben smiled.

About the Author

Jayne Rylon is a *New York Times* and *USA TODAY* bestselling author. She received the 2011 Romantic Times Reviewer Choice Award for Best Indie Erotic Romance. Her stories usually begin as a daydream in an endless business meeting. Writing acts as a creative counterpoint to her straight-laced corporate existence. She lives in Ohio with two cats and her husband, who both inspires her fantasies and supports her careers. When she can escape her office, she loves to travel the world, avoid speeding tickets in her beloved Sky and, of course, read.

You can visit Jayne on the web at www.jaynerylon.com and she loves hearing from fans at contact@jaynerylon.com.

Look for these titles by
Jayne Rylon

Now Available:

Nice and Naughty

Men In Blue
Night is Darkest
Razor's Edge
Mistress's Master
Spread Your Wings

Powertools
Kate's Crew
Morgan's Surprise
Kayla's Gift
Devon's Pair
Nailed to the Wall
Hammer It Home

Hot Rods
King Cobra
Mustang Sally

Play Doctor
Dream Machine
Healing Touch

Compass Brothers
(Written with Mari Carr)
Northern Exposure
Southern Comfort
Eastern Ambitions
Western Ties

Compass Girls
(Written with Mari Carr)
Winter's Thaw
Hope Springs

Print Anthologies
Three's Company
Love's Compass
Powertools
Love Under Construction

It's all about the story...

Romance

HORROR

www.samhainpublishing.com

CPSIA information can be obtained at www.ICGtesting.com
Printed in the USA
BVOW07s1654070813

328106BV00001B/1/P